The Might Have Been

The Might Have Been

A NOVEL

Joseph M. Schuster

BALLANTINE BOOKS

NEW YORK

The Might Have Been is a work of fiction. Names, characters, places, and incidents are the products of the author's imagination or are used fictitiously. Any resemblance to actual events, locales, or persons, living or dead, is entirely coincidental.

Published in the United States by Ballantine Books, an imprint of The Random House Publishing Group, a division of Random House, Inc., New York.

BALLANTINE and colophon are registered trademarks of Random House, Inc.

Library of Congress Cataloging-in-Publication Data
Schuster, Joseph M.
The might have been : a novel / Joseph M. Schuster.
p. cm.
ISBN 978-0-345-53026-4
eBook ISBN 978-0-345-53246-6
I. Title.
PS3619.C48324M54 2012
813'.6—dc23   2011040473

Printed in the United States of America on acid-free paper

www.ballantinebooks.com

9 8 7 6 5 4 3 2 1

First Edition

Book design by Caroline Cunningham

For Kathleen and my children—Joe, Dan, Veronica, Liz, and Bob . . . and for Joe V.

The truth is, we are reminded each day of what we can't do.

—Todd Jones, major league pitcher,
The Sporting News, June 30, 2008

Author's Note

For purposes of the narrative, I have taken some liberties with the facts of minor league baseball history and organization. In some places, I have created fictional towns; in others, I have used present or past minor league towns but changed their major league affiliations. Where I have used names of actual baseball players, I have done so for their iconic value and in no way intend these depictions to suggest events in their careers.

Part I

1976

Chapter One

A long while later—after the accident that would shape his life in ways he wouldn't understand for decades—Edward Everett Yates would feel sorry for the naïve young man he was then, the one who mistook that summer as the reward for so many years of faith and perseverance.

He turned twenty-seven and was lean and fast, in his tenth year of professional ball, playing left field for the Cardinals' triple-A team in Springfield, Illinois—well past the age of many of his teammates, who were not much more than boys, twenty, twenty-one, with acne on their chin, two years removed from borrowing their daddy's car for the prom. One—a nineteen-year-old, rail-thin left-hander with a wicked slider—still had a voice that broke an octave higher when he talked.

Nearly everyone he had begun with a decade earlier had moved on, up and out of the minors or out of the game itself. His roommate from rookie ball, Danny Matthias—a weak-hitting catcher—was in his fourth year with the Milwaukee Brewers, despite averages near .200. But catchers who had the confidence of a pitching staff were rare; singles-hitting outfielders like Edward Everett were not. The previous December, when Danny and his wife sent him a Christmas card, Danny had enclosed one of his baseball cards and written, "The best-looking backup catcher in America." He'd meant it as a joke, but Edward Everett was envious nonetheless, imagining boys throughout America opening a pack of Topps and finding Danny's glossy face dusted with sugar from the gum, along with Reggie Jackson and Hank Aaron.

The others—those who had lost patience and faith—had been back in the World for years, selling real estate or tires, finishing college, starting families. One enlisted after his brother died in Vietnam and came back minus a leg, long-haired and strident, on the evening news in his wheelchair, burning a flag.

He woke up that season, found some capacity he hadn't in previous years when he'd played well enough to stick but not enough to push past the wall that separated the minor leagues from the majors. In the first game, he had four hits in five at-bats against Tuscaloosa, two doubles, a triple and a bunt single in the ninth, when he noticed the third baseman playing back on the outfield grass. From then on, he played what the sports columnist in the *State Journal Register* termed "inspired ball," with a sureness that surprised him, settling in to what they all called a "zone" at the plate, *see the ball, hit the ball,* seeing nuances in a pitcher's motion he hadn't noticed before, often having a sense of exactly where a pitch would go and how it would move—up, in, down, out—seeming to see it even before the pitcher released it as surely as if he were living a fifth of a second ahead of everyone else on the field.

He was dating a girl named Julie, a twenty-year-old sophomore at Springfield College, who talked to him about auras, ideas he listened to because he knew if he seemed to pay attention he'd get her into bed. But as the season progressed, he wondered if he'd been wrong to dismiss her notions, because once in a while, standing at the plate, digging his spikes into the Midwestern soil and settling into his stance, he felt that in some way the entire ballpark was an extension of himself.

By the end of June, he was batting .409, forty-five points higher than the next best average, and on the third of July, after a five–four victory in Omaha, in which he caught the final out by leaping against the fence and extending his glove a good foot above the top of the wall to bring back what would have been a three-run home run, his manager called him into his office.

Three decades into his future, after he came to understand the full meaning of that moment, Edward Everett would remember it with rare clarity. And why not? He had imagined it ever since he was a boy, imagined it before falling asleep while he listened to Bob Prince and Jim Woods calling Pirates games on his transistor radio, imagined it as he knelt at Mass when he should have concentrated on the sufferings of Christ on the cross, even imagined it once while he was making out with a girl at a bonfire the October he was sixteen: noticing the shedding poplars silhouetted by the fire, he remembered that the Dodgers were playing the Twins in the Series that night, and wondered, as the girl nuzzled his neck, what the score was, and then saw himself in another October not too far off, in the on-deck circle, in the still point before coming to the plate, while around him the crowd flickered in an anxious and hopeful roar. He had imagined his being called up so often that his imagining seemed more a memory than a desire.

On that day more than half his life ago, Edward Everett sat in his manager's office—it was Pete Hoppel then—waiting while Hoppel finished a tired conversation with his wife on the phone. He had a practice, Hoppel did, of stripping off his uniform and leaving it crumpled on the floor for the equipment man to pick up and then sitting, his ankles crossed on his desktop, wearing nothing but a red Cardinals logo towel around his waist. Because he was a large man, the towel did not adequately cover him and so, sitting across from him, Edward Everett tried not to notice that his genitals were exposed, but this was difficult since he kept hefting himself in his chair to scratch his hip. In that state, he seemed to Edward Everett, for the first time, shockingly old: the giddy man who had sailed his ball cap into the crowd after Edward Everett's catch to end the game—that man was in his fifties, Edward Everett realized. In his uniform, Hoppel seemed substantial but, naked, he just looked fat, with folds of flesh cutting across his hairy chest and belly. His legs seemed like kindling that shouldn't be able to support his bulk and he picked at scaly patches of hard yellowed skin on the balls of his feet while he talked to his wife about whether they could afford a mason to repair their patio. Thirty years earlier, he had been as lithe as Edward Everett was in that moment. On the wall behind his desk hung a picture from when he was with Boston for two seasons, Hoppel's long arm draped over Ted Williams' shoulder, two skinny young men in dusty jerseys grinning for the photographer after they each stole home on successive pitches in a game against the Yankees.

"Babe, I gotta go," he said finally, giving Edward Everett a wink and hanging up the phone. He took his feet off the desk and pushed himself until he was sitting upright, letting out a groan from the effort. "Don't never get old, Double E."

"Yes, sir," Edward Everett said, not certain it was the right answer.

"Look," Hoppel said, "you done good. Last year, I would've said you was going nowhere. You got the body, but your brains was for shit. This year . . ." Hoppel shrugged. "Long story short. You're going to St. Louis."

Edward Everett felt his heart leap in his chest. "I . . ." he started to say but couldn't think of any words. Today he had been playing a road game in Omaha, sleeping four to a room at the Travelodge, and tomorrow he'd be in St. Louis, where Musial, Hornsby and Gibson had played and where he'd step onto a field with Lou Brock as his teammate. "Called up"—the words seemed in some way holy.

"It's maybe just for a month," Hoppel said. "Perry tore up his ankle going into the stands for a pop fly. But here's a word of advice. Don't fuck up. Make it tough for them to send you back. Do what you been doing here, and you got a chance to stick. Now get the fuck out of here."

"I won't—" Edward Everett said, but Hoppel picked up the phone and waved him out of the office. "Hey, Benny," he said, without even saying hello. "You still have that concrete connection? That guy, what's-his-name—he played at Altoona that one year?"

By the time Edward Everett got to the ballpark in St. Louis for the one p.m. holiday afternoon game against Pittsburgh the next day, the team had already finished batting practice and was in the dugout. From down a long concrete corridor that led to the field, he could hear the stadium announcer introducing a woman who would sing the national anthem. The clubhouse was nearly empty. Beside the door, a guard sat on a folding chair, a short and thin man who tugged on his sideburns as he worked a crossword puzzle. A clubhouse assistant laid folded towels on a shelf in each of the lockers, while another set bottles of soft drinks into a cooler in a back corner. A player hobbled out of the training room, his thigh wrapped in an ice pack.

"You Yates?" asked the equipment man distributing towels. "That's you." He pointed at the back corner to a locker nearly blocked by a stack of cases of Coke. A white home jersey hung there, his name sewn across the yoke in all capitals; number 66. Edward Everett felt suddenly dizzy and sat down hard on a bench in the middle of the room to keep from passing out.

"A fainter," the equipment man said, laughing. "You're not the first."

Dressed, he rushed down the tunnel to the dugout but hesitated at the entrance. Beyond, the stadium blazed with color—the patriotic bunting draped against the blue outfield walls, the green of the artificial turf, the red and white shirts of the fans rustling in their seats. On the field, the Cardinals worked through their pre-inning warm-ups, outfielders throwing high arcing balls that spun against a nearly cloudless sky, infielders taking ground balls.

"No tourists," snapped a player on the bench, someone Edward Everett recognized as a relief pitcher, a squat man tightening an ace bandage around his left knee. Edward Everett was going to say he belonged, but the pitcher laughed. "Hey, Skip," he called. "New blood."

The manager glanced briefly at him and mumbled something he couldn't make out but which he took to mean that it wasn't the time for formal introductions to a rookie.

Not certain of the etiquette, Edward Everett sat at the edge of the bench beside the water cooler and bat rack, trying to form his face into a mask that didn't reveal his absolute awe at finally being here, his sense that someone was, at any moment, going to tell him it was all an elaborate joke; but once the game began, he might as well have been invisible. Time after time, not paying attention, the other players—*my teammates*, he thought—tromped on his spikes as they fetched a bat for their turns at the plate. Once, getting something to drink, one of them, distracted by another player whistling and pointing to a blond woman leaning over the railing of the box seats to peer into the dugout, fell over Edward Everett's feet, landing half in his lap. "Mother fuck," the player snapped, "watch out," as if Edward Everett had been the one tripping and falling and not sitting as he was on the bench, squeezed into the corner, trying to take up as little room as possible, his feet trod upon, players not paying attention when they tossed aside their paper drink cups, flinging them at his shoulder, his lap and once his face instead of the trash can.

The game, as some did, became contagiously static, neither team hitting much at all, through three innings, four, five, easy ground balls, shallow flies, players on the bench seeming to sag as the innings passed, eight, nine, ten, fans growing bored, the crowd shrinking, inning by inning, fourteen, fifteen, sixteen, fans pushing their way out of the ballpark for their barbecues, family dinners, horseshoes and backyard sparklers. In the top of the seventeenth, however, the Pirates threatened to score, putting two runners on with only one out. The next hitter stroked a line drive to deep left field, where Lou Brock was playing. He dashed across the turf and, just as the drive seemed destined to fall in, leaped for it, his body parallel to the earth, snagging the ball in the webbing of the glove, and then slammed to the hard ground, bouncing slightly but holding on. So quickly that Edward Everett didn't see him get up, he was on his feet and throwing a strike to the second baseman standing on the bag, doubling off the runner who'd left too soon.

When Brock reached the dugout, his teammates clapped him on the shoulder but he was hurt—his slide on the turf had ripped his uniform pants at the left knee, raising a strawberry that oozed blood, and he limped to the bench, grimacing.

"You, Whosis," the manager said, pointing to Edward Everett. "You're hitting for Lou. Get out on deck."

He didn't move at first, unsure the manager meant him, but the player beside him elbowed him. "I wanna get home before my boy starts shaving. And he just turned one."

Edward Everett realized he'd left his bats in Omaha and searched the rack for one to hit with. He found one engraved "Dan Vandiveer," a catcher Edward Everett had played with at Grand Rapids five years earlier and who'd spent ten days with the Cardinals the previous season, someone who was out of baseball already, thirty-four and doing God only knew what. When he stepped onto the field, the heat assaulted him. In the shade of the dugout, he hadn't realized how warm the day was, but in the open, under the late afternoon sun on a cloudless day, the temperature attacked him with a force that made him gasp. That evening, watching the news in his hotel room, he saw that it had been 99 degrees during the day; by the time he went to the plate, it was still near 90, but the radiant effect of the Astroturf and the concrete beneath it must have added another twenty degrees.

The stadium came into his consciousness slowly: bending to pick up the weighted donut for his bat, he became aware of the washed-out green of the turf; on television, it appeared a seamless piece but, bending there, he noticed the warp and woof of the thick fabric. He saw, too, the scaling white paint that described the on-deck circle and noticed his red cleats, which, although they had been freshly polished when the equipment man had given them to him, were scuffed and gouged from being stepped on.

He had no time to warm up. As soon as he dropped the donut onto his bat, Ron Fairly, leading off, laced a drive just inside the first base line, a ball that skipped to the right field wall, Fairly on with a leadoff double, the potential winning run in scoring position.

Edward Everett walked to the plate, suddenly aware of an incredible amount of activity around him. In the stands, the fans began a rhythmic clapping, some stomping on the concrete decking, a thunderous sound that it seemed could bring down the stadium around them. In the third row behind first base, a small girl wearing a too-large red T-shirt snatched a handful of cotton candy off a stick her mother held. A row behind her, a fat man in a gray suit and blue-and-silver striped tie yelled through a popcorn megaphone, "Let's go, Birds!"

The stadium announcer said, "Now batting for Lou Brock, Ed-dee Yates," although no one had called him Eddie since the second grade. He could feel the crowd's enthusiasm sag as their clapping and stomping quieted. It was not the reception he expected but if he were among them, expecting an All-Star and getting instead a player he'd never heard of, he would have been disappointed as well. A sudden vision came to him: his redemption in their eyes. Not a home run—that was something for the movies—but his slicing a base hit into an outfield gap to score Fairly, the fans jubilant, his new teammates leaping up the steps from the dugout onto the field, surrounding him at first base after Fairly was in with the win.

Edward Everett stepped into the batter's box, trying to shut it all out, his imagined heroics, the movement of the crowd like a field of red and white grain stirred by the wind, the noise that was starting to build again, the organ playing a cadence, *bum bum bum bum bum bum*, Fairly at second base, taking a cautious lead, one, two, three steps.

Down the third base line, the coach was going through the signals, swiping his shirt, tugging the brim of his cap, tapping his thigh. Edward Everett realized no one had taught him what the signals meant.

"Time," he said, stepping out of the batter's box when the umpire gave him the time-out and trotting down the line to meet the coach halfway.

"What you need?" the coach said, standing close to him. His breath smelled of cigarettes and something else that was sour.

"Signals," Edward Everett said. "I don't know what you want. No one—"

The coach laughed. "You're the only guy in the fucking area code who don't know. Pop quiz. Runner on second, none out, bottom of the seventeenth, no score. What would you do?"

"Bunt," Edward Everett said, deflated. "Bunt."

He went back to the plate, trying not to show his disappointment.

True enough, even the Pirates knew what he was going to do. The entire infield edged closer, the first baseman and third baseman playing well in front of the bases, the second baseman edging toward first, the shortstop playing behind Fairly to hold him close. For a moment, Edward Everett thought about changing them all up, swinging away, lining a hit to right field, the crowd erupting in joy. But he knew he wouldn't do that; he would sacrifice.

At the plate, he took his stance and looked out at the pitcher, who was rubbing the ball between his palms. He was a rookie himself, younger than Edward Everett, maybe only twenty, a stocky, round-faced kid who seemed more like a fast-food fry cook than a professional athlete. The thought pushed into Edward Everett's head: five or six years ago, the pitcher might have been in junior high. Edward Everett saw him as a boy in a white oxford shirt and blue slacks, sitting in a . . . but he shoved the thought aside. The past meant nothing. There was only this moment: the pitcher nodding to the catcher's signal, holding his stretch for a scant second, as Edward Everett slid his right hand along the barrel of the bat, noticing and then dismissing a rough spot in the wood, cradling the bat partway over the plate.

The pitch came in on the outside corner, and Edward Everett caught it with the meat of the bat, dropping a slow ground ball that trickled toward first base. *Stay fair,* he thought, dashing down the baseline for the bag, wanting to make it more than a sacrifice, thinking, if this were grass instead of artificial turf, it would die in the grass and he could beat it out, but this was not grass but turf. He willed himself to go faster, leaping for the base, urging his body to take off, hearing the *ssszzz* of the first baseman's throw from behind him, hearing the slap of the ball into leather at perhaps the instant his foot met the bag, just a touch off-stride, making him stumble slightly as he took his turn into foul ground, thinking he was on with a single, but the umpire was throwing his right fist into the air, and grunting, "Out."

Edward Everett waited for the coach to argue but he just clapped his hands and shouted, "Good sac, good sac." And indeed, Fairly stood on third. Edward Everett had done his job.

He jogged off the field. In the stands, fans gave him polite applause before resuming their roaring and stomping as the announcer introduced the next hitter.

Then it was over. With the infielders drawn in for a play at home on a ground ball, the hitter punched a flare over the second baseman's head that fell just at the edge of the outfield grass, and Fairly was in, the game won.

Later, in the hotel room the team had rented for him across the street from the stadium, Edward Everett stood in the dark, looking eight stories below at the ballpark. The game had been over for hours by then, and the infield was covered by a blue tarp that glinted under the stadium lights. In the bleachers, workers moved through the aisles, bending to pick up trash. From some blocks away, where the city was staging a fireworks show on the riverfront, Edward Everett could hear the muted explosions celebrating the holiday. Every once in a while, a red or blue trail streaked across the sky within his field of vision. He stood there until the finale lit the sky in brilliant yellows, oranges and greens, and as the last flares faded, as the lights went out in Busch Stadium below him and all he could make out was the great dark gaping bowl of it, he thought about calling someone.

His mother would be at his aunt's house for the barbecue she had every year. If he called there to tell her about what he'd done, she would pass the telephone around, to uncles, aunts, cousins, and he would have to repeat his story over and over for everyone. His mother would say, *Oh, if only your father were still alive to see this,* and then she'd cry and he didn't want that, not tonight, not when he'd finally made it this far, the beginning of what he knew would be his years in the major leagues. He thought of the girl he had been seeing in Springfield, Julie, but whom he had stopped calling for no reason he could think of, just made a decision one day when he got back from a road trip that he didn't want to see her again. For the first time since then, he regretted it, because she was someone he could call to tell, but now he couldn't.

Stepping away from the window, he caught his dim mirrored image in it, and he actually seemed to be outside, hovering in an incomplete, ghostlike room. There was the reflection of a bedside lamp, a slash of the bed, the table where he'd laid his suitcase. He pressed his face against the window again. Below, knots of people leaving the fireworks show moved up the street toward their cars and, he knew, eventually home. He felt suddenly the fact of his being a stranger in a city of two million people where he knew no one.

He turned from the window and switched on the television, flipping channels until he found a sportscast. The announcer was talking about the game and Edward Everett sat on the edge of the king-sized bed, wondering if he'd be mentioned.

The account of the final inning showed Brock's catch and throw for the double play, twice—once at full speed, and once in slow motion. Then it cut to Fairly's double to start the home half of the inning, but then it jumped ahead, and Fairly was taking his lead off third.

"Then with one out," the sportscaster said, "and Fairly on third, Hernandez singles over the drawn-in infield and the Cards get the win."

It was, Edward Everett thought, like a baseball miracle—there is Fairly on second and then abruptly on third, through no human agency. *Poof.* In a way, he might never have even been there. Indeed, he knew what his line would be in the box score the next day, all zeros—no at-bats, no hits, no runs, no RBI, just "Yates PH 0000"— a miracle of nothing.

Still, he thought, he was here. There was a uniform in a locker across the street with his name on it and only six hundred men out of how many tens of millions of men in America could say that. Tomorrow was another game and the day after another still. He would have his chance and he would do something with it.

Chapter Two

The end of Edward Everett's season came with such abruptness that, even years later, it could nearly take away his breath to think about it: in the latter part of July, three weeks after he was called up. The Cardinals were in Montreal for a three-game weekend series and on Saturday, he came to the park and found he was in the starting lineup. It surprised him: since his sacrifice bunt on Independence Day, he had ridden the bench—game after game in St. Louis, then Cincinnati, Pittsburgh, Philadelphia—suppressing a dread that his single plate appearance would be the sum of his major league career. Perry would heal and Edward Everett would go back to Springfield to resume a sad march toward thirty, when even he would have to realize that his faith had been pointless, that he had crossed the line between hope and delusion, and would have no choice but to return to the World.

Day after day, he arrived at the ballpark and chased down fly balls during batting practice until it was his turn in the cage, where he took his cuts, ten swings and out for someone else, then back to the outfield to chase down more flies until game time, when he sat at the end of the bench, waiting and waiting, ashamed that, after the last out, as he filed into the locker room with his teammates, his uniform was pristine save for the powder from the husks of the sunflower seeds he ate compulsively, while theirs were stained with dirt and grass, knees torn, where he took a shower he didn't need and then went outside where the kids pestered them all for autographs—the stars, the regulars, even Edward Everett, who had done nothing that would make anyone want him to scrawl his name on a scorecard or a baseball. And so when he signed, he did it quickly, not meeting any of the kids in the eye, his mark a kind of lie, the kids asking him because they had no idea who most of them were, just that they were coming out of the right door, their hair damp, pushing through the swarming flock of children toward the team bus.

Then, in Montreal, he got his opportunity.

There had been problems getting into the city from Philadelphia late Thursday night; the Olympics were going on, and the airport was chaotic, long lines at the customs desk and confusion at the baggage claim. One of Edward Everett's teammates had made a derogatory remark about French-Canadian efficiency and the already irritated official had made them all open their carry-on bags so that he could inspect them, counting, in a deliberate way, cigarette packs and confiscating pill bottles from one of Edward Everett's teammates, who argued, honestly but in vain, that they were natural dietary supplements.

They didn't check into their hotel until after four in the morning and, as a result, were out of sync by game time. They dropped pop flies in the infield, botched coverage on stolen base attempts, only winning because Montreal was even more inept than they.

On Saturday then, a twelve-fifteen game, the Skipper decided to give half the regular starting lineup the day off and started Edward Everett in right field, leading off.

It was a miserable day, windy, raining throughout the morning. The teams couldn't take fielding practice because the grounds crew kept the field covered, and Edward Everett feared they would cancel the game, that his chance would come and go, and his entire career would add up to nothing: a single sacrifice bunt that didn't count as an at-bat, a batting average that wouldn't rate expression in numbers, because even to have an average of .000, he had to have at least one unsuccessful official time at-bat. But no, there was a benign God, because at a few minutes to one according to the scoreboard clock in right field, he stepped to the plate to begin the game.

The atmosphere in the park was entirely different from that in St. Louis for his first plate appearance. The Expos were a bad ball club and, with the poor weather and the Olympics in the same city, the crowd was sparse, perhaps fewer than a thousand people scattered throughout the stands, many huddled under blankets and plastic rain gear against the unseasonably cool weather.

"You going to hit or watch the people?" the umpire snapped. Edward Everett realized he'd been lost in the moment and stepped to the plate. On the mound, the pitcher bent from his waist and looked in for his sign from the catcher. He was in his forties, a left-hander with a round belly and a plump face. As Edward Everett set himself, he remembered that he'd had the pitcher's baseball card when he himself was a grade school boy. The pitcher had been with the Braves then, something of a stud with a fastball that sometimes hit 100 miles an hour. He'd once had what Edward Everett's mother would call "matinee idol looks," but now, a bloated, almost fuzzy version of his younger self, he was in the game only because a poor team needed bodies to fill out the roster.

Edward Everett took the first pitch, a good one on the inside that he could have driven hard, but the third base coach had given him the "take" sign—one pitch to get used to the idea of being there; one pitch to remind himself that he shouldn't be thinking about who was on the mound and who he once was; one pitch to remind himself to *breathe*, see the ball, hit the ball.

The second pitch came in even better than the first. Behind him, Edward Everett could hear the catcher groan, his gear clicking as if he were adjusting for a pitch not going where he expected it, a break- ing ball that hung on the outside, fat and inviting, and he swung and hit it not quite perfectly but well enough, a line drive that hooked down the right field line and skipped on the wet grass to the fence.

Edward Everett flung his bat aside and made the dash to first, where the coach was windmilling his arms, yelling, "Go go go go," and he made the turn to second base, just a bit too wide, he thought. As he approached the base, he glanced toward the third base coach, who was signaling, "Come to me, come to me," and Edward Everett did, coming in standing up, a triple. In the stands a handful of fans applauded, Cardinals fans, and the coach gave him a smack on the butt. Then the coach was yelling to the pitcher, "First hit, first hit," and the pitcher obligingly tossed the ball toward the dugout, where it rolled in: his first trophy.

The next hitter grounded out to second, but he'd done his job, hit to the right side of the infield, solid team play, scoring Edward Everett, and when he came into the dugout, some of his teammates clapped him on the back until someone said, "It's just one, for Christ's sake," and he sat down, breathing hard, not from the exertion, but from the excitement, thinking so many things he couldn't sort them out: there he was in Hoppel's office at Springfield, listening to the all-but-naked manager tell him he was going up; there he was back at home the next winter telling stories about the season that lay ahead of him now, bright with promise; there he was a dignified old man at the podium at Cooperstown, tearing up as he reminisced about his first hit on a cold and wet July day in Montreal . . . then someone was tossing a glove at him, saying, "Nap time's over," and he realized he'd missed the rest of the inning, when they sent eight men to the plate and scored five runs, the last on a two-run home run by the second baseman.

From then on, the entire team seemed to have come out of its somnolence of the night before. In the second inning, after the pitcher struck out, Edward Everett started things with a single, and he batted again in the fourth, when he doubled. When he came to the plate in the top of the fifth, St. Louis was already up eight–nothing, and there were men on second and third, with two outs. It was raining then as he dug his spikes into the ground, a slow rain at first, large drops plopping like random pebbles kicking up tufts of dirt around the plate, and then, abruptly, more steadily. The crowd had thinned and most of those who remained—were there even five hundred left?—began unfolding umbrellas or dashing up the aisles for cover.

It was yet a different pitcher this time, the third he had faced in his four times at the plate, another refugee from athletic old age hanging on for the money and the camaraderie that ordinary men didn't have going to the office and mowing their lawns in the suburbs. This one was Laurel to the first pitcher's Hardy, tall and skinny. Unlike the first pitcher, who had come up relying on velocity, this one had survived through guile, picking at the edges of the plate, changing speeds. As Edward Everett waited in the box for the first pitch, he was beginning to feel as if he were playing some kind of game underwater. Rain dripped from the brim of his helmet; his jersey was soaked through, the fabric prickling his wet skin; his bat was slick in his hands. Before the pitcher could throw, Edward Everett held his hand up to the umpire—*time*—and the umpire gave it. He stepped out, clamped the handle under his arm, between his sleeve and the body of his jersey, and drew it out again: still damp, but at least not too wet to grip.

"It's no skin off my ass," the catcher said, "but the day you're having? I'd want to make sure the game got through five."

Edward Everett glanced at the scoreboard: it was the top of the fifth inning, not yet an official game. For it to be official, they would have to finish five full innings, four more outs. He stepped back in, thinking for an instant about making an out intentionally, to move the game just one more step toward counting, but he flicked the idea away as if it were a gnat and set himself, aware that mud was clumped on the bottom of his spikes, that they felt like they weighed another twenty pounds, thinking he ought to knock some of it out so he wasn't slowed down if he hit the ball, but put that thought aside as well.

The third pitch came in on the outside of the plate, and he hit it, not quite squarely, a high fly ball down the right field line, and he flipped his bat away in disgust, lighting out for first base, thinking maybe the fielder would misplay it in the wind and the rain, thinking if he did, he might be able to get two out of it, but the mud on his cleats made him feel earthbound, a tired man slogging through sludge. He watched the ball arcing through the rain, although he knew he was breaking a rule, let the coach worry about where the ball went, just run, and then improbably, just as the fielder seemed to settle under the ball a few steps in front of the 340-foot sign that hung on the chain-link fence bordering the field, a gust of wind seemed to push the ball, and it was over the fence, and the first base umpire, who had jogged into the outfield to make the call on the play, was jogging back in, tracing circles with his right hand in the air, signaling a home run. When Edward Everett was back in the dugout, some of his teammates gave him a gruff check, their shoulder to his, knocking him about, and he sat, dripping and incredulous, until someone threw him a towel and he dried off his face and hair, kicking his spikes at the concrete step beneath the bench, knocking out clods of mud.

In the bottom of the fifth, although Montreal tried to stall, the hitters insisting on stepping out after every pitch, to dry their own bats, to call over to the batboy to bring them a rosined rag, and then taking their time to wipe their bat handles, the St. Louis pitcher retired the first two with remarkable efficiency, one on a slow roller back to the mound, the second on a weak line drive to second. In right field, Edward Everett found himself praying, *One more out, one more out*, and then they would call the game, and it would be in the books, eleven–nothing, Edward Everett four-for-four, a cycle, it came to him for the first time: single double triple home run.

The third batter was left-handed, someone who didn't hit for much average but had some power, seventeen home runs already, and Edward Everett drifted back slightly. The rain was falling harder; from two hundred feet behind the infielders, he felt separated from them by a liquid silver curtain that shifted in the wind. At the plate, the hitter stepped out, and even from where he was, Edward Everett could tell he was making some remark to the umpire about the lunacy of playing in such weather, but the umpire gestured him to step back in, and he did.

Because of the wind and the rain and the distance, Edward Everett could see him swing at the one-ball, two-strike pitch, but the sound of the bat striking the ball got swallowed up and came muffled a moment later, and he had no idea how to judge it; he saw a flash of beige arcing toward him and he wondered, *Come in or drop back?* He hesitated, unable to figure its trajectory, watching it push through the rain—was it climbing or falling, climbing or falling?—and then he picked it up, descending, and he started to run in to catch it, before realizing he had misjudged it. He backpedaled, tripping momentarily over his own feet but keeping his balance, his eye on the ball, until he felt the change in the ground beneath him, grass no more, but clay and cinders, the warning track, and then his back was pressed against the eight-foot-high chain-link fence and he knew if he jumped, he could catch it for what he knew would be the end of the game, five full innings in the books, his cycle safe, not erased by the rain.

He locked his fingers into the chain link to give himself balance for his leap and then he jumped, reaching for the ball, knowing he had gauged the flight of it impeccably, but then he was twisting, falling away from it, one of his spikes caught in the fence, and he was flailing, still reaching for the ball, although he knew it was beyond him, out of the park, and he was falling to the ground, his cleat still caught in the fence, his right knee twisting in a direction he never thought it could go, and still the fence held him, dangling, his shoulder on the wet track, gravity pulling him against his own body, until the fence finally let him go, and he lay there, pain slicing his knee.

Then he was two people: the body lying there, pelted with rain and something else, hail the size of peas, and the self saying to the body, *All right, get up now,* and the body saying *No.* He was laughing, he realized, the body of him was laughing, and the other self was thinking, *You're in shock, you're in shock,* and the pain rolled in waves up his leg, into his hip, and then rose higher on his body, seeming to swallow him for the briefest of moments. He blacked out.

Chapter Three

Years later, he thought of that moment when he was caught in the chain-link fence in another country as a kind of border defining the geography of his life. There was his self on the far side of the line, the major league ballplayer, and his life on the other side, where he was an exile from the country where he wanted to be.

"You brood about it too much," his second wife said to him on one of the days when he was more taciturn than usual, a day not long before he came home from a trip and found she'd moved out. "I'm not thinking about what you think I'm thinking about," he protested, although he was.

He didn't want to be one of those men whose lives were all about missed opportunities and regret, men like his father, for example, who stayed in the same high school coaching job for more than twenty years but who was haunted by what he saw as his moment of failure, when Woody Hayes invited him to be one of his assistants when he left high school football to coach a bad Denison University team; his father had turned him down because it was too risky: what if he went to Denison and they failed there? He remembered too well the Depression, his own father sullen and unemployed for three and a half years, his family renting out their house to a family who

did have a husband and father with a job, and moving into the basement; his own father sitting in a basement corner staring angrily at
the ceiling, grimacing every time the other family made a noise upstairs in what should have been his home, their feet clomping on *his*
floors, their scraping a chair across *his* dining room. Worse yet were
the days on which the family upstairs had a party: the door opening
and closing and opening and closing as they admitted their friends;
the explosion of laughter or the high chatter of children. Edward
Everett's father remembered that all too well and didn't want to become his father, an exile in his own home, and so he said no to Woody
Hayes. The first year, when Hayes' team went two and six, it seemed
a shrewd decision, but then Hayes became a coaching god at Ohio
State. And so Edward Everett's father did become his own father,
unhappy in his life, waking up on a Saturday morning after yet another loss by his own poor high school football team, sitting in the
living room, not wanting to tune in the Ohio State game on the radio
but doing so, and then turning it off and then on again, thinking
about the country that could have been his life, instead of the one
that was: the coach of a mediocre high school team. Until he hung
himself from a ceiling joist in his office just off the locker room in
the high school.

"It's not the same," Edward Everett's wife told him that day
shortly before she left. "It wasn't as if you walked away from the
major leagues."

"No, I was carried off the field away from them," he said, and she
shook her head in what he thought was a gesture of mock frustration
but which, in the end, was real.

In the hospital, he had his own room that looked out across the street
to a church he later learned was called Oratoire Saint-Joseph du
Mont-Royal. From his bed, all he could see was part of its green
bronze dome rising above a thick stand of trees and the cross at its
apex, but all through Sunday morning he listened to its resonant bell
clanging the call to Mass. He wasn't much of a churchgoer anymore;
the idea of getting up early on a Sunday to go to Mass when he was

with the team embarrassed him. On his first Sunday when he was in rookie ball, eighteen and full of self-consciousness, he was awakened at dawn by the sound of one of the three teammates who shared his room moving around—the *click* of his suitcase latch, the *huff* when he opened it, the *clang* of his belt hitting the bureau. Edward Everett was lying on the carpet where he'd slept the night before. The room had two double beds, but no one shared them: first two men in the room took the beds, the other two earned the floor. He realized it was Sunday, and thought, *I ought to go to Mass.* But before he could get up, another of his teammates snapped, "Jesus Christ, Turner, keep it down." Turner apologized and left; as the door closed, the player who'd complained spat out, "God damn holy roller." Edward Everett debated for less than a second, thought about the damnable offense it was not to go, and then got off the floor and fell into the bed Turner had left, plumped the pillow, thinking *Mattress!* and went back to sleep.

But in the hospital in, he realized, a foreign country, with his right leg in a cast from above the knee to the middle of his shin, he longed for the comfort of the ritual and surprised himself by beginning to weep. It was the injury, he knew, as well as the effect of the painkillers and the fact that, despite the drugs, he'd slept not at all. At the same time he realized that he nonetheless felt like a child and told himself to stop what his mother called a "pity party": *Break out the hats and favors,* she'd exclaim when he sulked as a boy. *Pity party; can I come, too?*

Sunday was the longest day he could remember. Through the window, he could see that the poor weather of the previous two days had passed and the sky was a deep blue. When the nurse had come in with his breakfast at seven o'clock, she'd pulled up the blinds and cranked open the casement window, saying something in French he couldn't understand but which he took to mean "fresh air." The breeze that came in was warm and every once in a while a gust pushed into the room, the blinds clanking against the window frame. All he could do was lie there, listening to the sounds of the life outside: the cathedral bell, the traffic, muted singing during one of the Masses and then, when the service was over, the rise and fall of human conversation from the street, the occasional shriek of a child.

Around noon, a nurse came in with his lunch on a tray, a different nurse this time, a slip of a girl, sixteen or seventeen. Maybe she wasn't even a nurse, but a Canadian version of a candy striper. Setting the tray on his bedside cart and removing the plastic cover, she gave him a shy smile. Thinking noise would mute the evidence of outside life, he asked for the TV remote, but she gave him a look that made him wonder if she spoke English, and so he gestured toward the TV, repeating, "The remote, the remote," as if she were a pet who would learn commands through repetition. She flushed but gave him the remote, holding it toward him in a way that their hands would not meet even accidentally, and fled the room.

He turned on the television and clicked through the channels; there were only two that came in with any clarity, one that showed a program that appeared to be about gardening, a white-haired woman standing behind a rosebush, shears in her hand. It was in French, and he could understand none of it. The other program, also in French, had four well-dressed men in a studio, arguing animatedly.

He turned off the television and, after deciding he didn't want to eat, pushed the bedside cart away and tried to sleep, but he couldn't because of the sunlight and the noise pouring in through the open window. He wondered if anyone from the team would come to see him. It was twelve-thirty, half an hour before the game, and so they would all be at Jarry Park, in the clubhouse, changing from their batting practice jerseys into their powder blue road game jerseys, going through their before-the-game rituals, he knew, after living side by side with them for only three weeks, close enough that they were living in one another's jocks, as the joke went: checking the rawhide knots in the fingers of their gloves, some of them shaving, some taping weak ankles.

At one point, a priest came to his door and tapped on the frame. He might have been eighty or more, skinny and slightly hunched, almost entirely bald, save for thin wisps of hair over his ears and on the back of his head. He carried a small ragged black zippered leather case and Edward Everett wondered if he was also a doctor.

"May I enter?" he said in accented English, wheezing slightly. When Edward Everett told him he could, the priest pulled the room's one armchair up to the bedside, then consulted a piece of paper he unfolded after removing it from his pants pocket. The tips of his index and middle fingers were stained yellow and he reeked of stale tobacco.

"Monsieur Yates," he said, glancing up from the paper.

"Yes," Edward Everett said.

"You have indicated Roman Catholic. Do you wish to receive the Eucharist?"

It had been since early February that he had set foot into a church, still playing the dutiful son when he visited his mother before the season started, but he said yes. The priest nodded and unzipped the case and took out a wrinkled white stole, kissed the cross embroidered near one end of it and draped it around his neck.

"You are in a state of grace?" the priest asked. From down the hall, a child let out a gleeful laugh, and a woman shushed him. Edward Everett thought of telling the truth, that he wasn't in a state of grace, but then he might leave and Edward Everett didn't want to be alone. The priest nodded at his assent, snapped open a small pewter case, extracted a thin host and held it in his hand a moment, inviting Edward Everett to recite the Our Father with him, before extending the host for him to take onto his tongue. The priest groaned slightly from the exertion as he leaned closer to Edward Everett to give him Communion. As he took it on his tongue, he tasted nicotine from the priest's fingers and considered for a moment the sin he might be committing, but thought, *You're not a boy any longer.*

While the priest sat beside him with his head bowed in a moment of reflection, a nurse came to the door and said, in a grave tone, that she had to close it for a moment, and did. He wondered why she'd had to do that. As if the priest could read his thoughts, the old man said, in a disturbingly matter-of-fact tone, as if he were commenting on the weather, "Someone died. They close the doors because they don't want the patients to see them removing the departed." Indeed, in the hall, beyond his closed door, a gurney rattled past, a wheel squeaking. The priest began murmuring something in French in a low voice: a prayer, Edward Everett realized, the Hail Mary, perhaps. When he finished, he looked up at Edward Everett and coughed slightly.

"They will open it when they are finished," he said. "How did you . . ." He nodded toward Edward Everett's leg that was in a cast.

"Playing baseball," Edward Everett said.

"Ah." The priest nodded. "For your college?"

"No, for the Cardinals."

"The Cardinals?" the priest said, cocking his head in a quizzical manner.

"The St. Louis Cardinals."

The priest chuckled. "Naturally, I was thinking the College of Cardinals."

Naturally, Edward Everett thought.

"I imagined you performing on a field of play before the Princes of the Church, entertaining them with your athletic skill."

The picture came to Edward Everett out of the man's assumption and his stiff manner of speaking: himself doing leaps and somersaults in the middle of a wide meadow while a cluster of older men in crimson vestments sat in bleachers, applauding politely.

Then they were in an uncomfortable silence for a while longer, until Edward Everett blurted out, "I lied before." He hadn't meant to say it and was surprised as the words welled up in his throat on their own, as if the priest were some sort of magician, finding coins behind Edward Everett's ears and producing Ping-Pong balls from his mouth, coins and balls and admissions he hadn't known were there.

The old priest closed his eyes and nodded. "Would you like to make a confession?"

Edward Everett considered the question. It had been how long since his last confession? Since before he had gone off to play ball. The previous December, when he'd gone home for Christmas, his mother asked him about receiving the Sacrament of Penance, and Edward Everett had left the house on a Saturday afternoon, telling her he was going, and drove off toward the church, but instead went to Memorial Park, where he parked overlooking a frozen lake where a teenage girl was teaching a half-dozen small children how to ice-skate. He sat in his car, watching the children stutter-step and fall on the ice, drinking coffee he'd bought at a gas station, as snow swirled like dust across the frozen water. After an hour, he went home. Was there a statute of limitations on forgiveness, a point at which he had accumulated too many sins and it had been too long since his last confession?

But he began, "Bless me, Father. My last confession was eight years ago," and then paused to see if the priest would blanch, would say, yes, any hope he had of absolution had expired. But the priest merely nodded, and Edward Everett began telling him of his life, beginning with the lies he had told his mother about going to confession; about the times he had gone to Communion although he was not in a state of grace; about how he had slept with so many women whose names he could no longer remember, had taken amphetamines to wake himself up for a game after long and uncomfortable bus rides, had not kept the Sabbath—the sins tumbling out in no particular order, as if he were some sort of spiritual bag of marbles that had gotten torn and the aggies and cat's eyes were bouncing madly around the room; he had been envious of teammates who had been called up before him, had once slept with a teammate's girlfriend after the teammate had been promoted ahead of him, from single-A to double-A. He had done it, he knew even at the time, while the girl undressed in the dark room, less for the sex and more for the anger he felt at being passed over. She, of course, had done it out of her own anger, knowing her boyfriend would not come back for her. But still it was a violation: one did not sleep with a teammate's girlfriend.

When Edward Everett finished his litany, he realized he was weeping quietly, and the priest was handing him a tissue from the box on the bedside table. As he wiped his cheeks, and said his Act of

Contrition, the priest traced the sign of the cross through the air and told him to say three Our Fathers and three Hail Marys as his penance before giving him the final admonishment: "Go and sin no more."

Not long after the priest left, what turned out to be the last Mass of the day let out across the street, and the chatter of the faithful floated through his window. He imagined them going home to mow lawns or off to restaurants for pleasant Sunday brunches. He thought, *I am one of them again, a good and true Catholic,* and fell asleep.

When he woke, it was evening and a soft rain fell. Cars shushed by in the wet street and in a breeze the limbs of the maple outside his window shook, showering the screen with spatters. He felt a kind of gratitude. Perhaps this was why he hurt his leg, so that he could find grace again, he thought. He would miss the rest of the season, the doctor had told him. In six weeks, in September, he could begin physical therapy. If he worked at conditioning over the winter—running, regular stints in the batting cage at his old high school, playing catch in the gym—he could be ready for spring training in February. Maybe the injury would turn out to be a blessing: he would show up in Florida in the best shape of his life.

Maybe the Cardinals would keep him on the big league roster. He had shown them something in the three weeks he had been there; he had hustled in warm-ups, had raced after fly balls when he patrolled the outfield during batting practice. While other players had been nonchalant about it, had caught the ball if it came within a few paces of where they stood, joking with one another, he set out after balls as if it were crucial that he catch them, leaping and sprawling out on the turf. "They don't do highlight films of BP, kid," one had said to him, but it didn't dissuade him and when he came back into the dugout, to drop his glove and grab his bat when it was his turn to take his cuts, he looked at the manager out of the corner of his eye, to see if he would say something to him: *I like your hustle,* but he never gave him a sign. In his first game, when they asked him to sacrifice, he'd done it, and when they had put him into the lineup, he had responded then as well: four hits in four times to the plate, a cycle.

Except, he thought, it hadn't counted. It would go into the books as nothing, or would never go into the books at all.

After he went down in right field and lay on the ground waiting for the gurney to wheel him into the clubhouse, the hail had stung his face and torso. On the gurney, bouncing across the field, the bumps sent shooting pains up and down his leg. By the time he was under cover, in the tunnel from the dugout to the clubhouse, the umpires and players rushing in filled the tunnel with the dense scent of wet polyester and perspiration. They waited for two hours, he learned from the newspaper, before the umpires finally called the game, one out shy of being official.

He tried not to think about it, lying in his hospital bed, tried to concentrate on the good that would come later, his chances for next season, but the optimism faded. He was like Moses, the story he remembered from religion class, about sinning so that God did not allow him to enter the Promised Land, only led him up a hill so that he could gaze down upon it before he died. Was that going to be his experience in the major leagues, the only thing he had ever wanted? To spend years bouncing around blacktop roads in an old bus, playing in bandbox parks sometimes in front of a few hundred people, most of whom had probably come for the bonus entertainment: the toddlers' race around the bases between innings, the old man who called himself a "baseball clown" and who imitated the umpires, his rubber limbs flapping, the giveaways of Frisbees or a dozen donuts?

He wondered again if any of his team would come to see him. He knew none of them well. Hell, most called him by what he had on the back of his shirt—his name if he was wearing a game jersey, his number if he was wearing the practice one. "Hey, sixty-six," someone would call if it was his turn to hit in the cage. He had a roommate, a left-handed pitcher who had been with the team for two weeks longer than Edward Everett, someone who had come from the Philadelphia minor leagues in a trade in the middle of June. But the pitcher and he shared little more than the same room on the road; he was from Boston, from what Edward Everett's mother would call

"Real Money," and he and Edward Everett didn't socialize. No, the pitcher wouldn't come to see him, would probably not even notice when Edward Everett wasn't in the room, would look over at the other empty double bed and mutter, "Huh. Something's different."

Except, Edward Everett realized, the bed wouldn't be empty, might not even be empty as soon as tonight, when the team went to Chicago for a series with the Cubs. The Cardinals would have already called up someone else from Springfield, probably Cook, a big kid from Arizona who didn't run well but who was moving up through the system because he could hit for power.

He thought of Cook in the bed in the Chicago Palmer House that should have been his, saw the clubhouse attendant putting a swatch of masking tape inscribed "Cook" in bold marker over the locker that should have been his, saw the powder blue road jersey with "Cook" spelled out across the yoke hanging where his jersey should have been, saw Cook coming in to pinch-hit in Wrigley Field, which, because of the winds, they called "the friendly confines"; they wouldn't ask him to lay down a bunt but let him swing away, and he'd jack one out of the park onto Waveland Avenue, where joyous boys would chase the ball as it bounded away from them: a home run that rain wouldn't wash away.

Cook would be a success, Edward Everett thought, and when February came, it would be Cook the team would keep on the big league roster, not Edward Everett. He would go back to Springfield, and that would be where he would stay. He felt suddenly foolish for the optimism he had let wash over him: the feeling of grace was nothing but another side effect of the painkillers.

There was a radio on the bedside table, and he switched it on, turning the knob to scan the frequencies, to see if he could find the ball game although, at the same time, he didn't want to hear it. They were playing a doubleheader, to make up for the game that had been washed out the day before, and it should be the middle of the second game by then. He picked up the familiar ambient sounds of a game, the slight background thrum of a small crowd, a vendor near the broadcast booth calling out "Labatt," but the call was in French, and so he scanned further until he found an English language play-by-play. It was the seventh inning of the second game and he could tell by the announcer's voice that the Cardinals were winning. He was indifferent as he called the balls and strikes, as if the Expos were so far down they could never come back. Indeed it was so: as the home half of the inning ended, the score was eight–one, and the Cardinals were going for the sweep, having won the first, two–nothing.

He turned it off, depressed by their success. He would not be missed, not at all. On the flight to Chicago, the team would be loud and brash, as they were after a good series. They still would be behind the division-leading Phillies but in the hunt. They would be thinking, Win two of three in Chicago, and two of three from here until the first weekend of October, and they would have a chance. It would stand before them, a done deal. They would do it without him and he wouldn't even be a tickle in their brains, just the man who had never been there.

Until that moment, he hadn't wanted to call anyone, certainly hadn't wanted to call his mother; she would want to come to Montreal to see him, and he hadn't wanted to see her look when she saw his leg in the plaster, or hear her *Oh, honey* making him feel five again: *Come kiss my boo-boo, Mommy.* But he didn't know whom else to call, so he reached over to pick up the phone, snagging its cord with his right hand and pulling it to him clumsily, first the receiver and then dragging the base behind it. He dialed the number and as it rang, he thought of his mother. It would be near dinnertime; she would be in the kitchen, peeling potatoes: roast beef, mashed potatoes and corn every Sunday he could remember. But, no, the picture was false, he realized: his mother wouldn't cook such an elaborate dinner for one. He hung up after the third ring.

From outside his room he could hear that visiting hours had begun. Across the hall, an excited voice exclaimed, "Oh, my goodness, Johnny," and that was followed by other animated voices giving greetings.

If he hadn't broken up with Julie, he thought, she might be someone who would exclaim in delight when she saw him, someone who could comfort him for his injury and not have it be a boy-thing but a man-thing, a man tended to by his woman. Telling himself she wouldn't want to hear from him and would have no sympathy for him, he nonetheless dialed her number.

Chapter Four

He had met her the previous summer, after her freshman year at Springfield College, a tall redhead from an even smaller town in Illinois than he came from in Ohio.

She had gone to a ball game with her roommate, Audrey, and Audrey had flirted with him from the bleachers as he warmed up between innings. But Edward Everett had been more struck by Julie, who seemed embarrassed by Audrey's aggressiveness, keeping her head down, her hands folded in the lap of the brown jumper she wore over a yellow blouse. It reminded Edward Everett of the uniforms the girls at his grade school wore and when Audrey asked to meet him after the game, he agreed. "Hell," he said, "why don't you both come along?" The three of them went to a pizza restaurant not far from the park, but up close, Audrey became more shy the longer they sat there and Julie said little, while around them the restaurant buzzed with conversations and the jukebox blared Tony Bennett and Frank Sinatra. Finally, when a lone slice of pepperoni pizza lay on the serving plate in the middle of the table, Julie said quietly something that Edward Everett couldn't hear, except for the end of her sentence, "convention of Carmelites."

"What?" he asked.

She blushed. "I said, 'I feel like I am at a convention of Carmelites.' " Edward Everett laughed, partly out of relief that someone had broken the silence.

Audrey said, "I don't get it."

"It's," Julie said, "an order of nuns who take a vow——"

"Of silence," Edward Everett said.

Julie looked at him with interest for the first time.

"You thought I wouldn't know what they were," Edward Everett said. "My mother, she's pretty into the whole Catholic thing."

That was the end of the conversation. Ten minutes later, they were outside the restaurant, buffeted by other parties coming in and going out. Edward Everett wondered if he should just leave them there, but the manners his mother had bred in him wouldn't allow that, and so he offered to walk them to their car.

"We didn't drive," Julie said. "We only live a few blocks away."

"Home, then," he said. They set off to the apartment building where Julie and Audrey lived. It was past midnight. Off the main drag, the city was quiet, most of the homes dark. In a few yards, gas lamps burned dimly. Edward Everett tried to conjure something to say, but all he managed was "Carmelites," giving an embarrassed laugh.

When they reached the apartment building, he stood at the curb until the women went inside, waving to him just before the door closed behind them. Two nights later, restless after a game, he went impulsively to their building again, and stood in the lobby studying the mailboxes. None said "Julie," but one had two names embossed by a label maker, "J. Aylesworth, A. Humphrey," and he went up the stairs looking for the number that corresponded with the names. As he knocked, he realized it was past ten-thirty; he had no idea whether Julie would be home, or whether it would be Audrey he'd find there, but Julie answered, opening the door as far as the chain lock would allow, and peered into the hall.

"Audrey's not——" she said.

"Actually, I came to see you," he said.

"Oh," she replied, blushing.

"It's late," he said, but, after hesitating for a moment, she slipped off the chain.

"I can't keep you in the hall," she said. "But I have work tomorrow, so you can come in for just a minute."

He asked for her phone number so he could invite her on a proper date and they began seeing each other whenever he was in town; in the off-season, when he went to Grand Rapids to work installing flooring for a company a teammate's father owned, they talked long-distance twice a week and picked back up when the new season began. After games, she waited outside the ballpark with the other players' wives and girlfriends and he would take her to a late dinner; on off-days, he waited outside her classroom building, sitting on a concrete bench the college had put there in memory of someone named Bartholomew Wesley, holding a book open in his lap so that people might mistake him for a student. Neither owned a car, and so they walked everywhere: to Abraham Lincoln's house, to a small botanical garden, to a café called Oscar's where the waitress came to recognize them and sometimes brought them plates of broken muffins the shop couldn't sell. They could not go to Edward Everett's place: he lived in a rooming house owned by an elderly woman whose husband had pitched a season with Springfield in the 1930s, when it was a Brooklyn farm club, and who made money after baseball as a paper wholesaler. The house had at one time been a splendid three-story Victorian in which the widow and her late husband had intended to raise, in her words, "a passel of kids," but they'd never had any and after he died she started renting to ballplayers. She was strict, forbidding women in the players' rooms, and the one time Edward Everett brought Julie over on a rainy Sunday, to visit in the living room, she hovered: straightening books on the shelves, plumping cushions and watering plants until finally Edward Everett took Julie home.

Because of Audrey, neither could they have privacy at Julie's apartment: if Audrey came home and found Edward Everett there, she would give an embarrassed apology and go to her room and shut the door, but Edward Everett could hear her shuffling papers, sometimes typing, listening to some sad girl singer on her stereo, going into a sneezing fit because of her allergies.

They talked about spending the night together often before they finally did, on a Friday in April when Audrey went home for her mother's fiftieth birthday party. Until then, Julie had been shy about sex. "It's not that I don't want to," she said, "it's just that the nuns get in your head, you know?" Before then, they had advanced to the point at which she would take off her blouse and bra, but even when they were like that, on the couch, bare torso to bare torso, she would worry Audrey would come home early. It was frustrating but she was sweetly apologetic, promising him, "One of these days, look out, mister."

On the Friday, Edward Everett came over after the game, self-consciously carrying a small overnight case holding a change of clothes and his razor and toothbrush. Julie opened the door, gave him a quick peck on the cheek, and looked past him into the hall—to see if any of her neighbors were observing them, he knew. Inside, she took his case into the bedroom and they had dinner, baked chicken and brown rice with a salad and wine. She had set the table formally—or as formally as she could on her undergraduate's budget—with a green tablecloth and two white tapers in candleholders that didn't match, one clear cut glass, the other a miniature yellow porcelain lady's slipper. He talked about the game he'd played, one in which he hadn't had a hit but had reached base on an error by the shortstop. Julie told him about a paper she was writing for Sociology, an observation of the relationships between the cooks and waitresses at the Big Boy restaurant where she once worked.

After a second glass of wine, he felt warm in a satisfied way and regarded her across the table from him. She was a pretty girl, he thought: it wasn't that he hadn't appreciated it before but he saw her afresh, this attractive woman with whom he was having a relationship. She had, he realized, very fine eyebrows, which made him wonder if they were naturally so or if she plucked them; her nose was dusted with freckles and her chin came to a point that he found charming.

"What?" she asked, coloring slightly.

"I was just looking at you," he said, and she covered her face with her hand in a manner that caused some pleasant feeling he couldn't name, and he wondered if he was in love with her. He hadn't told anyone that since he was sixteen and, racked with confusing adolescent passions, had said it to the girl he took to the junior prom, a sophomore cheerleader with nearly waist-long black hair that her mother had set in ringlets. They were dancing to something slow, revolving in tidy circles, his arms locked around her waist and hers around his neck. He was thinking about how she would be naked later, their first time, and was wondering what her breasts would look like and how her skin would smell, and had said quietly, without really thinking about it, that he loved her, and she had purred in a throaty voice that she loved him back. They broke up four weeks later, after he behaved badly when she told him—not accurately, thank God—that she might be pregnant and he saw his hopes of baseball replaced by a job as a stock boy at Connor's grocery until he was old enough to go down into the mines. After that, he was careful about, as his friends put it, "mistaking his dick for his heart," and promised no one anything.

Watching Julie blush from his attention at dinner, he thought it must be the true thing: he was an adult now, settling into what would be his career, baseball, and maybe it was time and she was the one. So many of his teammates were married already; one had four children with a wife he'd married when he was seventeen. He saw himself living forever across the dinner table from her, talking about his games, her talking about whatever she did as a career, and so the words fell out as if he'd been holding them in his mouth so long they needed to spill out if he was going to be able to take in a breath.

They, too, broke up weeks later when he came back from a trip through Kansas and Iowa, during which he had met a woman in Wichita with whom he hadn't slept but had wanted to because she was funny in a brassy way, and his teammate with the four children got a call from his wife saying she had to borrow money from her uncle because doctors had found a hole in their second child's heart and another teammate got a Dear John letter from his fiancée, who had fallen in love with her dentist.

In the hospital in Montreal, as his teammates were scoring another three runs in the eighth inning, during which Cook (already!) didn't hit a home run but did double in two runs in his first major league plate appearance—in the hospital, then, he knew it had been a mistake to stop seeing Julie because of a momentary flirtation and a bout of fear.

Before he could tell himself not to, he dialed her number, thinking he should hang up, wondering if she had found a new boyfriend since he had stopped calling her, wondering if perhaps they were in bed right now, Julie and the imaginary boyfriend, someone smarter than he, more well read, wittier.

She answered on the fifth ring.

"Hello," he said.

"Ed?"

Then he wasn't sure what to say to her; how foolish it was to call her. What did he expect, that she would give him sympathy after the way he had treated her?

"Ed? Are you all right?"

"I'm great," he said. "No, that's not true. I actually got hurt."

"I thought—I thought I'd never hear from you again," she said, as if he hadn't told her about being hurt. "I wrote to you and . . ."

He had forgotten about the letter she'd sent, but now he remembered seeing the pale blue envelope on the mail table in his rooming house, and her neat handwriting that made clear she had paid attention to her Palmer penmanship classes as a girl. "I don't know why you stopped calling me. I can live with not seeing you, but I need to know why." He had thought about responding, but the team left town the next day, and by the time he got back a week later, he had put the letter out of his mind.

"I'm in Montreal," he said.

"It's been almost two months."

"I know. I just—"

"Montreal? What are you doing in Montreal?"

"Baseball, playing baseball."

"You got there," she said, but he couldn't tell if her tone carried congratulations or indifference.

"Yes. Three weeks . . ."

"That's good for you," she said, and then a silence hung between them, filled with the small clicks and static of the long-distance connection. "You hurt me," she said. "I wasn't going to say anything about it, but you did. First you tell me you love me and then you're the Invisible Man."

"I was a jerk," he said.

"More than a jerk."

He wondered if she had been a virgin before that Friday night at her apartment and felt more ashamed: he was a cad who deflowered women and left them in the lurch.

"Yes," he said. "An asshole."

"Even more than that," she said.

He told her about the road trip he had taken before he stopped calling her—not all of it; he left out the details about the brassy woman he'd met in the Burger Chef in Kansas, but told her about the players with the medical bills and the Dear John letter.

"Don't you think I got afraid, too?"

It hadn't occurred to him, he said.

"I wasn't some girl who came to college for an MRS degree, for Christ's sake."

Then silence hung between them again; in the background of their connection, he could hear the vague metallic chirp of other voices. He tried to picture her in her apartment, sitting as she did when she read, in a corner of her sofa, her legs curled up.

Someone knocked at his door and pushed it open almost immediately: a candy striper with his dinner. "Excuse me," she said when she saw he was on the phone. He nodded in response.

"Is someone there?" Julie asked.

"Hang on a sec." He laid the receiver in his lap while the candy striper set the covered plate onto his bedside table. "Thank you," he said. When she left, he picked up the phone again. "Sorry," he said, and let out a bitter laugh. "I'm actually . . ."

"What?"

"In the hospital here. That was the nurse leaving me my dinner."

"In the hospital? Are you sick?"

He told her about the game . . . the *non*-game, as he was calling it. Leave it to him to get injured during a game that didn't exist officially. Another miracle of nothing.

"This will make Audrey feel guilty," she said. "She said I should light a candle, praying you'd get hurt or die. I said, 'It's not voodoo,' and she said, 'What good is it?' "

"At least I've succeeded in making someone happy," he said, and realized it was a joke: a small one, but a joke nonetheless.

She came to Montreal on Thursday, the day after the hospital discharged him. They talked by phone each day, her calling him when she got home from work because she didn't want him to worry about the long-distance charges the hospital would add to the bill he already had no idea how he would pay. As it turned out, he didn't have to pay it; health insurance he hadn't known he earned as a major league ballplayer paid most of it, and the team took care of the rest . . . and they hadn't forgotten him, either, at least the organization hadn't, even if none of his teammates ever visited him. The traveling secretary called him in the middle of the week, apologizing for not contacting him sooner. "The flight to Chicago was a nightmare, almost as bad as the one into Montreal," he said. Because the Olympics had the entire city in a tangle, the baggage handlers mislaid half of the team's equipment and it hadn't even gotten to Chicago until halfway through Monday's game. "We started out playing in souvenir jerseys until the fifth inning, when our stuff showed up."

The traveling secretary asked Edward Everett what he wanted to do for the time being; if he wanted to stay in Montreal until he was more comfortable, the team would put him in a hotel, pay him his per diem and send his payroll check wherever he directed.

As it turned out, because he was injured, the team had to carry him on the disabled list for the balance of the season, which meant he would earn major league pay until the end of September, more money in the last two months of the season than he would earn for an entire year at triple-A.

He and Julie lived lavishly, at least by their own modest Midwestern standards. The hotel the traveling secretary found was at the edge of downtown, overlooking a wide boulevard and a lush park. From their window on the eleventh floor, they could watch the electric city as long as the Olympics were going on. Lines of pedestrians seemed endless, continuing to cross intersections even when the traffic lights were against them. Cars crept from block to block so slowly it seemed they seldom moved at all.

They ordered room service and ate far beyond his per diem: lobster and salmon and oysters served on a chilled plate floating in a crystal bowl of crushed ice. He was earning five hundred dollars a week for breathing in and out, he said, and in a fit of giddiness tried to calculate how much each breath was worth, but the sum, which he thought would be grand, was disappointing: eighteen breaths a minute times sixty times twenty-four times seven, around a penny for every four breaths.

"I guess I'm just not worth as much alive as I thought," he said.

Sex was awkward because of his cast, so they made love only three times in the week, once on the day she arrived, the second time early in the morning a few days later, when they both woke before the sun rose, and the third time not long before Julie left. The second time was especially difficult because he moved suddenly with her above him and she twisted in a way that made him wrench his right leg, causing him to cry out.

He worried that he had damaged his leg even more and became glum. Finally, on the day after the Olympics ended, Julie suggested they were coming down with cabin fever. She ordered a wheelchair from the concierge and pushed him through the streets. The city, still littered from the crush of people who had attended the Olympics, was not as pretty as it had seemed from their hotel window. Crumpled food wrappers blew along the gutter and, here and there, Julie had to steer the wheelchair around broken bottles and, once, an overnight case that someone had abandoned, spilling its contents across the sidewalk: the slacks and blouses and underwear of some large woman. It had been, it appeared, one big party that no one wanted to clean up after.

They ended up at a church, Mary Queen of the World, which, with what Julie called "neo-Gothic architecture," seemed out of place among the office buildings where workers in suits, carrying briefcases, went in and out of revolving doors. As they stopped at the entrance, Edward Everett realized that Julie was panting from the effort of pushing him and so they went inside so that she could rest before they set off back for the hotel.

The church was cool and dim, and their movements echoed beneath its great dome: the squeal of the wheelchair's hard rubber tires on the stone floor, the squeak of Julie's canvas deck shoes. Scattered through the pews, a few people knelt in prayer; others stood in the main aisle, gawking up at the ceiling mosaics that glittered back at them. A small boy let out a "Yap" that resounded and his mother reached down quickly to cover his mouth with her hand.

Julie genuflected beside the last pew and slid into it, sighing. "You are one heavy load," she whispered, but loud enough that it came back to them as a hiss.

He shut his eyes. Things had turned out better than he thought they would on the darkest day, the Sunday after his injury when he had felt so abandoned in the hospital. In a day, Julie had to go back to Springfield for work. "I'm not important enough that I earn a paycheck for just being alive," she said. The thought of her leaving brought him up short: he hadn't thought about how there was life outside their bubble. He would miss her, he realized, had gotten used to being with her every minute; even the times she went to the lobby for a newspaper seemed like long stretches, when he waited in their room for the old and slow elevator to take its time delivering her downstairs and back.

"You've been very sweet," he whispered.

"I'm a sweet girl," she said in a faraway voice. He realized she was drowsing.

"I made a mistake back in the spring," he said. "I shouldn't have gotten afraid."

"It's all right," she said. "You were who you were."

A heavy door along the side of the church opened, letting in a flood of sunlight momentarily before banging closed with a sharp report. "Shhhh," someone hissed.

"Do you think we ought to get married?" he said.

"Is that a hypothetical," she asked: " 'Is the state of matrimony a good thing?' Or is it a proposal?"

"I don't know . . ."

She turned to look at him and then took his right hand in hers. "Are you asking me to marry you, mister?"

She really was a pretty girl, he thought again. He saw them doing the vague things husbands and wives did together: pushing a cart through the aisles at a grocery, washing dishes side by side. Her in the stands with the other players' wives, red-cheeked on a cool fall day late in the season, exhorting him when he batted.

"I guess I am," he said.

"That's sweet," she said. "You're a great guy and you'll probably be hugely rich if you ever walk again and play ball, and I like being with you, but let's just see. Two weeks ago, we weren't even in each other's lives at all."

"I just don't want to make the same mistake again," he said.

"Ask me again in six months," she said. "If we still like each other, then, probably, yes. But for now, let's go back to the hotel, because if there's one thing that makes a girl horny, it's someone asking her to marry him."

Two days later, she kissed him sweetly, got into a cab for the airport, leaving him balanced on his crutches on the curb, watching her red-and-black taxi until it turned a corner, and he went upstairs and sat in the quiet room for some time, thinking of her pushing through the throng at the airport, thinking of her sitting in a window seat watching the Canadian landscape fall away until the plane was too far up to see land, and then opening a book. Finally, he became aware that he was in what had become a dark room and he turned on the television. And within two weeks he had stopped returning her calls.

Chapter Five

He went home: what choice did he have? Four and a half weeks after Julie left, the team's traveling secretary phoned him.

"This is embarrassing," he said, "but we sort of lost track of you."

"I haven't gone anywhere," Edward Everett said.

"Yes, and that's the problem. We hadn't meant for you to stay there this long but we hadn't realized you were still there until the bill came across my desk this morning. We need to get you out of there, sport. Pronto. You've been burning up the room service."

"I thought the per diem—"

"That's only for when the team is out of town. They got back from that trip weeks ago."

Could that be possible? Edward Everett wondered. Had he so lost track of time? For a week after Julie left, he was a virtual recluse in his room, leaving it only when the maid came to clean and he waited in the lobby until she finished, settled on an ornate couch, watching the guests come and go. It was a fine, old-fashioned place that seemed, although he'd never been off the North American continent, European. The clientele appeared wealthy and sophisticated, and the lobby echoed with voices in languages Edward Everett could not identify, much less understand. Men and women swept in trailed by bellhops pushing carts laden with luggage and all seemed to possess the same regal impatience if they had to wait in line to register or if a clerk fumbled for a room key.

Beyond those periods in the lobby—what were they, half an hour?—he stayed in his room, telling himself it was because he didn't want to miss Julie if she phoned, which she did every evening after she got home from work. She told him about her job answering phones and typing for a podiatrist, describing the people who limped painfully into the office, telling him about the bags of trimmed corns and toenails she carried to the dumpster. For his part, he had little to say: *I noticed the plaster walls aren't square but actually rounded at the corners. I noticed that the paint is flaking outside the window.* Gradually, their conversations began waning sooner and sooner each time.

When he wasn't talking to her, he watched television. He avoided the American programs: they made him homesick. He wasn't certain what he wanted to feel, but not that—not at a time when he wondered what his life would become, when he wondered if he would ever be able to play ball again or if that life was entirely behind him. What was he if not a ballplayer?

He preferred programs that had nothing to do with his life across the border—soap operas in French, newscasts about places he couldn't even, if pressed, find on a map. Watching a story about a tornado in Manitoba that had killed a retired cobbler and his wife, he glanced out his window to the park eleven floors below where a plump man and woman lay in the grass, kissing. On the television, the reporter interviewed the dead couple's daughter, who became so overcome with grief, she covered her face, but where he was, it was a beautiful day.

At night, he had trouble sleeping. It was difficult to get comfortable because of his cast and, outside his room, the hotel always seemed alive with noise:

Children dashed in the hall, shrieking, a mother scolding: "Now, now."

On the other side of him, a couple made love and, afterward, the woman wept while a man's voice buzzed with what Edward Everett assumed was consolation.

The elevator *ding*ed.

He gave up, turned on the television. A preacher standing on a stage, framed by two vases of palm fronds, saying, "God has a plan for your life." On another channel, a test pattern. He turned off the television, tried to sleep again.

Outside, footsteps scuffled by in the carpeted hall.

He eventually began appreciating the hotel's amenities. In the morning, he had breakfast in the less formal of the two restaurants while he read the newspaper, something he had seldom done in the past, aside from the sports pages. So much turmoil in the world: riots in Rhodesia; three hundred Americans evacuated from Lebanon in the face of civil war; Argentina's police killing two revolutionary leaders. He read the paper and glanced around the restaurant, feeling fortunate to be part of the privilege of the place: the deference of the waitress and busboy silently appearing to refill his water goblet and coffee cup. Around him, businessmen made notes on legal pads as they ate their eggs and bacon; tables of women with careful hair declined the pastry cart; obvious newlyweds on their honeymoon regarded each other sleepy-eyed across the table.

He began venturing beyond the hotel, going into nearby shops. One day, he spent two hours browsing belts in a leather shop; another day, he drank coffee in a café across the street from his hotel, counting the number of men and women who went inside. That day, he got back to his room after Julie had called and found a message slip under his door. He sat down in his chair by the window, picked up the phone but the thought struck him that he had nothing new to say, and turned on the television, to *Casablanca*, but dubbed in French, and spent the time until it was too late to call her trying to translate the dialogue back into English. Two days went by with her leaving him messages and his not calling her back, then three. Then a day came when there was no message from her, and a second day on which she didn't call, and a third and a fourth and then he lost count.

The evening the traveling secretary called him, he was dozing in his room, dreaming: riding with his father in a Studebaker he had owned before Edward Everett was in kindergarten; although it was just his father and himself, Edward Everett sat in the backseat. His father was smoking, although Edward Everett had never seen him do so in life, but when he tried to open the window, the crank was missing. They were on a dirt road, racing past a line of barbed-wire fencing that seemed to serve no purpose, as the land bordering the road was overgrown with tall weeds that whipped the car's windows as they sped past. Edward Everett was trying to say *Slow down, slow down* but, for some reason, couldn't speak, and they hurtled onward.

After he got off the phone with the traveling secretary, he went into the bathroom. At first, he thought he would splash water on his face to wake himself a bit more but, standing at the sink, he realized he needed to shower, that he hadn't shaved for days and his hair was unkempt, much longer than he usually kept it. *A beatnik*, his mother would say. He wondered if the team would be angry he had charged so many hamburgers and grapefruit to the room. With chagrin, he remembered that one day he had signed for a ten-dollar tip on a three-dollar check for a waitress who told him he was her last table before she moved back to Manitoba to care for her ill mother. He wondered if they would punish him for it. The owner was wealthy; would he even miss the money? But he didn't get wealthy letting his injured, marginal players live extravagantly.

The plane ticket the traveling secretary couriered to the hotel was for a flight to St. Louis at ten the next morning; from there, he would have to make his own arrangements. It occurred to him he had no place to go. He had given up his room in Springfield, had no home in St. Louis; he had no idea what his future was going to be. He would have to go back to the town where he'd been raised, where he hadn't been in years save for brief visits in the off-seasons. He phoned the front desk, asked for long-distance and gave the operator his mother's number. He wasn't sure what she'd make of his calling her, telling her that he would need someone to pick him up at the Columbus airport—a hundred miles away—but the phone just rang and rang at her house until he hung up.

He thought again of calling Julie, but what would he say? What a shit he was for not calling her, he thought. Not long ago telling her—in a Catholic church, of all places—that he wanted to spend the rest of his life with her, but now, sitting on the edge of the bed they'd shared, he had a hard time conjuring her face. He remembered her eyes were blue, but what he recalled was the fact of it, a detail she might list on her driver's license, not an image of her eyes themselves. Her hair was, what? She was how tall?

Outside, the sky was darkening, perhaps rain moving in. Indeed, after a moment, sporadic drops were splashing against his windows and then a full-blown storm was lashing the glass. Lightning brightened the sky and seconds later thunder cracked. He stripped off his clothes, turned on the shower and, after he finished, dressed and went downstairs for his last dinner in another country.

Chapter Six

T he lobby swarmed with men in dark suits and women in
formal dresses: a wedding party crowding into the hotel,
drenched from the rain, shaking out umbrellas that sprayed everyone, their shoes leaving dark spots on the carpet. The men and
women were giddy: the storm would become a story the bride and
groom would tell for long thereafter. Twenty years from then, with
the way stories grew, maybe they would describe their reception as a
party in the midst of God's fury.

On his crutches, Edward Everett had difficulty navigating through
the mass of people. A stocky middle-aged man in a brown tuxedo too
snug for his girth shoved past him, nearly bowling him over. A tiny
woman in a silver floor-length gown trailing him, her hand gripping
the crook of his elbow, apologized, cringing. A small girl wearing a
white pinafore and white patent-leather shoes banged into his left
crutch, causing him to stumble; she fell into a heap on the carpet,
crying. A woman swooped in behind her and, gripping her by the
wrist, yanked her to her feet. The girl wailed, "I don't wanna."

"Oh, yes, you wanna," the woman said through clenched teeth.
They swept off with the rest of the wedding party toward one of the
ballrooms down a long corridor.

There were two restaurants off the lobby: the coffee shop where he'd eaten his breakfast on so many mornings and a more formal one. It was this latter one where he wanted to have his last meal in Canada, a place the guidebook Julie had picked up at the airport on her arrival said featured one of the best steaks in the city. The dining room was far fancier than anyplace he'd ever eaten in his life. The lighting was subdued and the room seemed darker still because the walls were a deep mahogany paneling. Patrons filled roughly half the tables, speaking in quiet tones. Even their gestures were reverential—the way they picked up a silver knife to butter a roll or laid salad forks onto the plate. He stood at the entrance for a moment, separated from the dining room by a burgundy velvet rope. At a podium on the other side of the rope, a tuxedoed maitre d' spoke into a phone, his brow furrowed, flipping through the pages of a register. "Impossible, impossible," he was saying in a quiet yet firm tone. When he glanced up, Edward Everett gave him a look that he hoped the man would perceive as understanding: clearly the person on the other end of the call was being difficult. Instead of giving him some sign he appreciated the support, he frowned and resumed leafing through the book. When he hung up, he approached Edward Everett.

"*Oui?*"

"I'd like a table."

"A table?"

"Yes. For dinner."

"I'm sorry. There is nothing," the man said, gesturing to the dining room behind him. In a far corner, a man who had been eating a solitary dinner while reading *The Wall Street Journal* folded it neatly into thirds, stood, pushed his chair snug against the table and left.

"But . . ."

"I'm sorry, monsieur. We are booked."

"There are empty—"

"I assure you, sir. Our reservations are full. Besides . . ." He held out his right hand toward Edward Everett. "Your attire."

Edward Everett glanced at his clothing: khaki slacks and a paisley long-sleeved shirt.

"I'm sorry, sir," the maitre d' said. His focus shifted from Edward

Everett as if he had dismissed him from his consciousness. "Yes, sir?" he said.

"Ellison, four," a man behind Edward Everett said.

"Oh, yes, Mr. Ellison. Good to see you again, sir," the maitre d' said, and the party of four swept past Edward Everett as the maitre d' unhooked the velvet rope: three men in their fifties and a dainty, elderly woman; the men in suits and ties, the woman in a lilac dress with a lace collar that rose high on her neck. They followed the maitre d' to a table. He was an entirely different man with Ellison, party of four; he seemed to shrink a bit in his deference.

"Money," a woman said from behind him.

Edward Everett turned. "Excuse me?"

"Money," she said. "It makes me sick." She was somewhere in her forties, he guessed, nearly as tall as he was, wearing a silver floor-length dress. Her red hair was in tight curls, a white orchid tucked behind her left ear. He noticed she was in stocking feet. A pair of slender-strapped silver high heels dangled from her right hand, rain-water dripping onto the burgundy carpet.

"Ever wear heels?" she said, holding her shoes out to him.

"No," he said.

"Avoid it."

"I'll check it off my list," he said.

"I'm a refugee," she said.

"From what?"

"Wedded bliss. My little sister's, not my own."

Edward Everett realized she had been drinking; her breath carried the smell of some slightly sweet alcoholic beverage.

"May I help madam?" the maitre d' said from behind Edward Everett.

"Technically, it's mademoiselle," the woman said. "Much to my mother's horror."

"Does mademoiselle have a reservation?"

"I have many reservations," she said.

"Pardon?"

"Reservations about the wisdom of white after Labor Day. Reservations about supporting either presidential candidate. In my country, not yours. You don't have a president. You have that man with the weak chin who has the wife everyone says is so beautiful although I don't see it. Tell me, Mr. Crutches, don't you think I'm more beautiful than what's-her-name?" She struck a pose, tilting her chin up, laying her left hand on the back of her head, and smiled, showing teeth that were nearly perfect save for her right upper canine, which had a small chip in it.

Edward Everett had no idea what she was talking about. "I'm sorry, but—"

"Perhaps madam and sir—"

"*Mademoiselle,*" the woman said with a surprising fierceness.

"Mademoiselle," the maitre d' said, giving a clearly obsequious smile. "Perhaps you would be more comfortable in our less formal dining room. I can have someone escort you there." He lifted a finger and almost immediately a bellhop stood beside the woman. "I am afraid we cannot accommodate mademoiselle and monsieur," the maitre d' said. "Perhaps you can show them to the Salon de Jardin."

"Certainly," the bellhop said. He was a squat man with what Edward Everett's mother called a "drinker's nose," the cartilage thick, the skin red and pockmarked.

"We're not—" Edward Everett tried to say.

"Are you throwing us out?" the woman said.

"Please, madam."

"Moiselle. Mademoiselle," she said.

The maitre d' gave her another obsequious grin. Edward Everett wondered if he was deliberately taunting her.

"I have never—" she said.

Behind her, a half-dozen people waited for the maitre d': a mother and father and two well-dressed sets of twins, the boys in navy blazers with gold buttons decorated with ships' anchors, blond hair in crew cuts that matched their father's; the girls in black-and-white polka-dotted dresses, their hair held back in identical polka-dotted ribbons.

"Maybe we'd . . . ." Edward Everett said, nodding toward the bellhop.

"Yes, sir?" the maitre d' said to the family behind them, Edward Everett and the woman in the silver dress already in his own personal past tense, his hand on the clip securing the velvet rope to its stanchion in anticipation of another acceptable party.

"Dr. Whitson and family," the man said, stepping forward and around Edward Everett and the woman.

"Yes, Dr. Whitson," the maitre d' said.

"Sir?" the bellhop said to Edward Everett, one eyebrow raised in invitation.

He followed the bellhop to the smaller dining room, although he knew where it was. "Two for dinner," the bellhop said to the hostess seated behind the desk at the entrance, reading a paperback romance novel.

She sighed, closed the book after folding down a corner of the page she was reading, slid off her stool, plucked two menus from the desk and walked off into the dining room, not even waiting for any sort of acknowledgment from either Edward Everett or the woman who was, inexplicably, following him and the hostess toward a table in a far corner. She seated herself in one of the chairs while Edward Everett maneuvered himself into the other, laying his crutches on the floor and nudging them under the table.

"War wound?" the woman said, shoving the stainless ware off the napkin folded on the table in front of her and laying the napkin on her lap.

"I'm sorry," Edward Everett said, "but—"

"Look," she said. "You were going to eat alone. I was going to eat alone, and ..." She gave a little shrug, closing her eyes. Edward Everett couldn't tell, but it seemed she was trying to suppress tears. She took in a deep breath and opened her eyes. "We don't have to talk. Hell, look at most of the rest of the couples here: they're not talking."

Edward Everett glanced around the dining room. At one table, a man made notes in a pocket notebook while the woman with him sorted through her purse as if she was looking for something, laying keys and wadded tissue on the tabletop. At another table, the woman looked up from her plate expectantly toward the man, giving him a small smile. In return, he briefly glanced at her and then looked down at his lap.

"It's fine," Edward Everett said, and opened the menu. He felt uncomfortable sitting with the woman; she was older than he was by clearly more than a decade and, although he told himself he would never see any of the people in the restaurant again and would, at this time the next day, be back in Ohio, he hoped they didn't think he and the woman were a couple: perhaps mother and son, or older sister and younger brother, but not together.

"What is it with men?" The woman closed her menu, slapping it onto the table with enough force that it jangled the flatware.

"What are you talking about?" Edward Everett said quietly. At the next table, two elderly women paused in their own conversation and were studying the two of them.

"I'm not hideous," she said.

"No," Edward Everett said carefully.

"You're thinking, 'I hope they don't think she's with me.' "

"No," he said.

"It's coming off you like an odor. 'She's old.' "

"I don't even know you," he said. "I just came downstairs to have dinner on my last night here. You followed me."

The woman held up her hand. "Please."

"Just don't—"

"Make any more scenes?"

"Yes," he said.

She raised her right hand in a scout salute: thumb and pinky circled, her other three fingers up. "I swear."

Hoping it was as good as the steak for which the restaurant on the other side of the lobby was famous, he ordered a sirloin, medium, and a baked potato. The woman surprised him by ordering the same, except medium-rare, and asked for an extra portion of sour cream for the potato. "And a carafe of your house red," she said. "Wine?" she asked Edward Everett.

"Sure," he said.

"Two glasses, then," she said.

They sat in silence, waiting for their meals. Edward Everett stole a look at the woman, who seemed lost in her thoughts. She stared vacantly at a far corner of the room, tapping a tooth with a long fingernail that was polished a deep red. When she was younger, she was probably beautiful, he thought. Her features were surprisingly delicate; her nose was thin, as were her lips; her makeup was careful in a way that made it appear natural, but as he studied her, he could see it covered wrinkles at the corners of her eyes and creases on her forehead.

"So," she said, startling him. "A six or a seven? At least a five."

"What?"

"You've been staring at me for two minutes. You're trying to decide whether I'm pretty enough. I know I don't rate a nine and certainly not a ten—even when I was your age—but come on, you have to give me a five."

Edward Everett blushed. "I wasn't—" he stammered.

"Okay," she said.

The waitress brought their wine and salads and the woman began shoving the tomato wedges to the edge of her plate. "What's your name?" she asked, lifting a bite of lettuce to her mouth.

"Edward Everett," he said.

"Well, Mr. Everett, I'm Estelle Herron. Two 'r's,' not one like the bird."

He considered telling her that "Edward Everett" was his first and middle name but for the first time in his life it struck him that it was odd he was "Edward Everett" and not "Edward" or even "Ed." She would ask how he got the name and he would have to tell her about his mother's affection for Edward Everett Horton, admitting that he'd been named for a Hollywood second banana few remembered anymore. He let it go: what did it matter? Once the meal was over, he'd be back upstairs in his room, away from a woman he still doubted was entirely sane.

"What brings you to Montreal?" she said, giving the city's name a pronunciation that sounded expertly French.

"I was playing ball," he said.

"Like that?" she said, indicating his cast with her fork, Russian dressing dripping from its tines onto the tablecloth.

"No," he said. "I got hurt a few weeks ago and the team moved on while I was in the hospital. My season's over." *Maybe my career,* he thought.

"Left behind," she said. "That makes two of us." She set down her fork, picked up the carafe of wine, poured them each a glass, lifted hers, tilting its rim toward him, an offer of a toast. He picked up his glass and touched it to hers, then took a sip. He was never a wine drinker—not dinner wines, at least. Whenever he drank wine, it was what he and his friends called "alcoholic Kool-Aid": highly sweet apple and strawberry flavors. This was bitter and he suppressed a cough, not wanting to show her he lacked sophistication.

"So, what school do you play for, Mr. Everett?"

"Not a school," he said. "The Cardinals."

"Really?" she said. "You wouldn't try to fool a girl, would you?"

"No."

"I don't remember any Everett playing for them."

"I've been with the team since July," he said. "I got called up— I was in Springfield." *Could it really have been that long ago: the month before last?*

"Not an auspicious start," she said, and then went on almost immediately. "I'm sorry. I apologize. I have a tendency to—a lot of smarts, my father used to say, but not a lick of social sense. May he rest in peace." She picked up her wine and raised it slightly upwards. "How did you get hurt?"

He told her about the game weeks earlier, about the play that hurt him, but not about his performance at the plate, partly because he heard the account through her perception: to someone else, it would seem a baseball version of "the one that got away." *It didn't count, but the game was thiiiiiiiiiis big.*

"My father was a Cardinals fan." She took another forkful of her salad but paused with the bite partway between her plate and her mouth, as if she was remembering someone. "I'm not from here," she said, taking the bite finally. "We're from Indiana. Hoosiers, rah!" She raised a fist in a way that made him think of cheerleaders, and for a moment he could see her at sixteen, red-cheeked, giving a jump on the sidelines of a football game in November, bouncy with youthful excitement. He tried to calculate when that would have been.

"By rights, we should have been Cincinnati fans, but for some reason . . ." She gave a shrug. "When I was a little girl, my father and I—but you don't want to hear this. We said silence." She held up the scout salute again.

"It's all right," he said. "You and your father . . ."

"You don't have to," she said, taking another forkful of lettuce and then inspecting it as if it were something distasteful, pulling a small brown and wilted leaf from the fork and laying it delicately on the edge of her plate before eating the rest of the forkful.

"You and your father," he said again.

"We would sit up listening to Cardinals games on the Philco. The reception wasn't always clear. We'd get overlap, you know, from other stations. My mother would say, 'Howard, the girl has to get her sleep.' 'There's plenty of time for sleep after October,' he'd say. He was my hero for that."

The waitress brought their dinners but got the orders mixed up: when Edward Everett cut into his steak, a thin trail of blood pooled around the edges of his sirloin.

"Not very ladylike," Estelle said, switching their plates. "To order meat so near to still being alive." She went on with her story. "Even after he died, I kept on with it. It was my way to stay connected to him. I remember when I was just out of college, my mother wanted to take me to Paris. It was what women of a certain sort did after college. She'd done it with her mother and so she and I were going to damn well do it. We were not close, but one did not say 'no' to one's mother. Not then."

She got lost again for a moment in some thought but came back after a second. "I didn't want to go. The Cardinals were still in the thick of things and I didn't want to miss it. They had a chance to go to the Series for the first time since 1946 and I was damn well not going to miss it. She didn't understand. It wasn't the baseball, it was—"

"Your father."

"Exactly. *You* understand that. She couldn't. So we went; they were in first place the day we left and they weren't anymore when we got back six weeks later." She laughed. "It will sound stupid, but I blamed myself. *If I'd been there, listening to the games, they'd've won.* Silly, and maybe you can't understand that. One afternoon, we were going to the Louvre and on the way we passed a newsstand where they had the *International Herald Tribune;* I bought one and, while we were waiting in line to get into the room to see the *Mona Lisa,* I read the sports page. It wasn't much—just a paragraph about a game they had with someone, I don't know: Cincinnati or New York. My mother snatched the paper out of my hands in front of all those people—a rare lapse in decorum for her—and snapped at me. 'For God's sake, Esty. We're in the Louvre.' She stepped out of line and marched the newspaper to a trash can and came back. I could tell the newsprint all over her hands bothered her. It made me think of Lady Macbeth—'Out, damn spot'—the way she kept wiping one hand against the other to try to get them clean. The Cardinals ruined her trip to the Louvre."

"When was this?" he asked.

"No. I won't tell you. You just want to know so you can figure out my age. You're . . ." She closed her left eye and regarded him with her right, calculating. "You were alive by then. I'm certain of it."

"I'm twenty-six," he said, for some reason shaving a year off his own age.

"Twenty-six," she said, laughing. "I'm still not trading you my secrets. Okay, Mr. Twenty-six. What's your story?"

He shrugged. "I don't know. I play ball. I've always played ball. That's it. Not much of a story." He picked up a roll and broke it in two, buttering half and laying the other half on the bread plate between them and then took it back and put it on his own plate, aware of his gaffe: they were strangers. She wouldn't want to eat half a roll he'd touched. "Were you part of that wedding I saw earlier?" he asked her.

"My baby sister's," she said, and then brightened. "She's twenty-five. Younger than you, so there you go. That answers one of your questions."

"Questions?"

" 'Is she old enough to be my mother or just an older sister?' "

"My mother is—"

"Oh, God, here we go."

"She's fifty-nine." Or had she turned sixty by then?

"That's a relief. I'm nowhere near fifty-nine."

She had me late, he thought, but did not say. His mother was thirty-two when he was born, a Catholic woman who by then despaired of ever having children, until he came along: her one and only miracle.

"My sister wanted to be married in Paris," the woman said, cutting a bite from her sirloin and eating it.

"Wow," Edward Everett said. "Paris. Your family goes there quite a bit."

"You see, that's just it. I went. She didn't. The fortunes, well, have fallen since my father . . ." She finished her sentence by waving her fork in the air in a gesture that suggested she was dispersing smoke. "The Herron family, well, had its wings clipped. Financially. This was a compromise. Faux Paris. Here we are in the Salon de Jardin." She gave a short laugh. "*Garden Room,*" she said in an exaggerated Midwestern accent, prolonging the "a" in "garden" and the "o" in "room." She shook her head. "Pretentious—my sister has no idea what this is costing my mother. She took on a mortgage. I only hope to God she can pay it."

"Isn't the wedding still going on?"

"I'm confident it is."

"But you're—"

"Not there. Correct."

"Shouldn't you be?"

"Oh, it most definitely is unseemly that I'm not. The maid of honor has left the building. Not literally, of course. I'm still in the building, but . . . you know what I mean."

"Why?" he asked.

"No. I haven't had enough wine to tell you that particular secret. But maybe soon." She winked at him, picked up the carafe and poured more wine into her glass, although it was only half-empty, filling the glass until the wine rose nearly to the brim. She started to set down the carafe but then, as an afterthought, filled his glass to the rim as well. "Cheers, Mr. Everett. Cheers." She lifted her glass in a toast and when they touched glasses, wine lapped from hers onto the tablecloth. "I am not a good customer today, am I?"

They fell into a silence then, eating their steaks and potatoes, while the restaurant around them began to fill up. Before they finished their meals, every table in the place had a party at it and there were patrons two and three deep at the entrance, some standing on tiptoe, craning their necks to gauge their prospects of being seated. The woman had ordered a second carafe of wine without asking if he wanted any and, between the two of them, the second was nearly empty: perhaps half a glass remained in it. Edward Everett had drunk three or four glasses, Estelle twice as much. Her eyes seemed unfocused and as she cut her meat, her movements lacked the precision they had when they began. He finished the wine in his glass and drained the carafe into it to prevent her from drinking any more. Not that another half glass would matter, he thought.

"Shall we—more?" she said.

"Probably not," he said.

She nodded. "One of us is wise," she said. Inexplicably, she began crying. Not in a way that someone at another table would notice, but silently, her eyes closed, tears welling at their edges, streaking her cheeks with mascara. "I've made a royal botch."

"How so?"

"Have you been paying attention?" she said, fiercely. "Hello? Maid of honor? Fancy dress? Fifty-dollar hairdo? Orchid?" She plucked the flower from behind her ear, regarded it a moment and then crumpled it, letting the petals fall onto her plate, where they darkened as they absorbed the blood and juices from her steak.

"I . . ." he began, although he had no idea what to say. He had never been good with women who cried. His mother. The girls he dated. He had always felt helpless in the face of them, even when he was the cause of their grief: girls he no longer wanted to see, girls who misinterpreted his attentions at parties, when they saw the prospect of a capital "R" relationship after only an hour together and all he was seeing was sex.

"I'm sorry," she said, wiping her eyes with the back of her wrist. "You've landed one crazy, crazy broad here."

A busboy came by to collect their plates and the waitress wheeled a dessert cart to their table: a half-dozen cakes and some sort of torte.

"What's the worst thing you have on the cart?" the woman said.

"Worst?" the waitress asked.

"Most wicked. Dessert that most says 'I am off this diet I've been on for three months to fit into this dress.' That sort of thing."

"I like the triple chocolate cheesecake," the waitress said, holding up a plate that bore a thick slice of the dessert, a chocolate cake with some kind of chocolate crumb crust, chocolate syrup dribbled across it in a pattern of overlapping arcs.

"Done," Estelle said.

"Nothing for me," Edward Everett said.

The waitress wheeled the cart off. Estelle picked up her wineglass although it was essentially empty and drained the last few drops by tilting it above her open mouth and letting them fall onto her tongue. "I don't think they're serving triple chocolate cheesecake at the wedding. I think I won this round."

The waitress brought the cake to the table and set it in front of Estelle, who took up the dessert fork, cut a small bite from the edge of the cake and put it into her mouth, closing her eyes and giving a look that suggested ecstasy. "That is so much better," she said when she had swallowed the bite. "You should have some."

"No, really."

"I insist." She cut a slightly larger bite from the cake and held it across the table toward him, cupping one hand beneath the fork. Tentatively, he took it. The sweetness filled his head.

"Ooh," he said.

"Yes, ooh," she said. She removed the butter patens from a small dish of them, stacking the slivers neatly on the table, cut a piece of the cake, laid it into the dish and slid it toward him.

"Estelle," someone said from across the restaurant. "Estelle."

"Jesus," she said. "Jesus Jesus Jesus Mary and Joseph."

A tall, bony older woman in a blue sequined dress was pushing her way through the crowd of patrons waiting at the entrance.

"Madam, you'll—" the hostess said.

"My daughter," the woman said, pointing toward Edward Everett and Estelle.

The hostess let her pass. Like Estelle, the older woman had an orchid nestled behind one ear. Her floor-length dress wrapped her so tightly that she could take only small steps. Partway across the dining room, she gathered some of the fabric in her hands and pulled the dress until it extended to just slightly below her knees, allowing her to walk more quickly.

"Estelle," she said again when she reached the table, whispering through clenched teeth. "This is unacceptable."

"It's not one of our better days, is it, Mother?" Estelle said. She took a forkful of the cake and made a show of moving it toward her mouth slowly. "This really is quite good," she said. "You should try some, Mother. Miss," she called to the waitress who was pouring coffee at the next table. "Would you bring another of these for my mother?"

"Yes, madam," the waitress said.

"Technically, it's mademoiselle," Estelle said.

"Oh, Estelle," her mother said. "Now is not the time."

"It never is."

"What about your sister?" her mother asked.

"My sister will be fine. She's all well and married. Mrs. John Ogden. He's an attorney," Estelle said in Edward Everett's direction. "She married quite well. Vanderbilt. Law review. Order of the Coif. He's an associate right now, but his father is senior partner and so it's in the cards for him."

"Estelle, I don't understand why you're doing this to us."

"Mother, just go back to the reception. Enjoy yourself. Just say, 'She's Estelle.' That's always been enough of an explanation."

Edward Everett became aware that the diners at the nearby tables had stopped their conversations and were listening intently to the two women. He wondered if he should get up and leave Estelle and her mother in what passed for privacy in such a public place.

"Estelle, please."

"No, Mother. I am going to finish my very nice meal here with Mr. Everett and then—and then, I don't know where the evening might take me." She gave Edward Everett another wink.

"I'm sorry," her mother said. "I don't know—Mr. Everest?"

"Ever-ET," Estelle said. "Not like the mountain. Like the city in Washington."

"Mr. Everett, I don't know what pull you have with my daughter, but, could you?"

"Leave him out of this, Mother."

"Maybe I should go," Edward Everett said, extending his good leg to snare his crutches so he could draw them out from under the table.

"And leave me with the check?" Estelle said. "I see your plan."

"No. I can just sign . . ." Edward Everett lifted his hand to signal the waitress.

"I was being funny," Estelle said, touching his raised arm, and he lowered it. "Please stay."

"Who—" Estelle's mother said.

"Mr. Everett is a serial murderer," Estelle said.

"Mr. Everett, I don't know anything about you, but my daughter—"

"She didn't believe me," Estelle said. "Tell her."

"I'm not a serial—" he started to say.

"Estelle," her mother said sharply. "This has to stop now."

"No," Estelle said. "The only thing that has to stop is the scene you're making. We were perfectly enjoying ourselves until you came in. Please go. Please give Alicia my love. Tell her that I hope she and Jack will have many happy years."

Her mother gave a sigh, shook her head. "The Ogdens will wonder what sort of family they have married into."

"It's not like they can wrap her up and take her back to the store. It's a no-deposit, no-return deal."

"I can't go back and face those people."

"Yes, you can, Mother. Courage under fire. That's the motto. *Courage sous le feu.* Remember? *Sous le feu.*"

"This is just making Frank's decision——"

"Leave him out." Estelle banged her palm on the table, rattling the dishes and toppling Edward Everett's wineglass. Only his quick reflexes kept it from tumbling onto the floor and shattering.

"Is there a problem?" the hostess said, approaching the table.

"Estelle, one last time." Her mother's tone was pleading now. She began wringing her hands in a gesture that he imagined might have been the same one she used in Estelle's story about the *International Herald Tribune* and the Louvre.

"The last time?" Estelle said. "Good. Then we're finished."

Her mother opened her mouth as if to say something but instead sagged as if she had been staggered by an actual physical blow, turned and left, a little unsteady on her feet. After a moment, the silence that had descended on the restaurant during the scene broke: flatware clinked against plates, conversations began again, no doubt people rehearsing the stories they would tell when they went home. *You will not believe what happened in the restaurant tonight.*

"I am sorry, Edward," Estelle said. "So so *so* sorry. I didn't mean to drag you——"

"It's fine," he said. Still, how he had ended up across a table from her, part of an argument with her mother, was vague to him.

"Who is Frank?" he asked her.

"He was someone I was with and now I'm not anymore. That's all."

Their waitress approached their table and set the slender leather portfolio containing the bill onto it. "Will there be anything else?"

"I don't think so," Edward Everett said, opening the portfolio. The sum staggered him. Fifty-seven ninety-six. If he added a fifteen percent tip, it would approach seventy dollars. He had never seen a restaurant check for so much, at least not one that he was paying. He studied it—two steaks, potatoes, salads, two carafes of wine, two chocolate cheesecakes, one of which they'd never received— waiting for Estelle to offer to pay half but she did not. He took the pen the waitress had slid into the portfolio, glanced at Estelle, noted a tip of ten dollars, and scrawled his name on the line at the bottom of it.

"The restaurant should just hang on to the check," Estelle said. "That might be worth something someday, what with your autograph."

"That's not likely." He realized he had gone more than half an hour without thinking of his injury, without the thought that next year at this time, he might be stamping prices on grapefruit and bananas in a supermarket instead of playing ball.

"Oh, come on, now. As my mother always said, *Courage*." She gave the word a French pronunciation, rhyming it with "garage."

"Well," Edward Everett said. "It's been——"

"Are you going?" she said.

"I have to pack. I have to phone——" he stopped short of saying "my mother," as that would make him sound like a boy, and went on, "——to make arrangements for someone to meet me at the airport. I'm sure you will want to get to the reception after all."

"No," she said. "I don't know what I'll do." She gave him a look, one he understood to mean, "Don't leave." Did she want to sleep with him or just not be alone? He doubted it would be the former: there were so many years' difference between them.

"I should go," he said.

"Okay." She sounded disappointed. "I'll walk out with you, though, if that's okay."

"Sure."

Getting up, he realized for the first time that he was slightly drunk. Over the past weeks, he had become adept at maneuvering on crutches but as he left the restaurant, he had trouble getting his arms in sync as he hefted himself across the dining room, weaving through spaces that were more tight now than when he had gotten there, because of how crowded it was. At one table, where four obese men incongruously ate four identical cottage cheese salads, he had to reverse course because he could not slip between their table and the one beside it, where a pregnant woman nearly reclined in her chair

rather than sitting up in it. By the time they reached the lobby, pushing through the dense crowd of people waiting for a table, he was
exhausted, as if he had just run several miles.

The lobby, too, was crowded. Outside, the rain—which he couldn't
hear when he was in the windowless restaurant—continued to pour
and a throng was gathered just inside the doors to the hotel, peering
out at the street. He turned to say good-bye to Estelle, but for some
reason she was shrinking back into the restaurant.

"What is it?" he asked.

"It's Frank," she said, pointing to the lobby beyond them. Edward
Everett looked in the direction she was pointing but could not tell
whom she meant: a heavyset man in plaid shorts with a Mickey
Mouse T-shirt that was too tight for his belly was talking earnestly to
a plump woman in a matching Minnie Mouse T-shirt, clutching a
shopping bag from the Museum of Fine Arts. An athletic, bespecta-
cled, ponytailed, white-haired man in a blue suit stood chatting with
a young blond woman in a gold dress that barely reached mid-thigh.
Three middle-aged men, in nearly identical brown suits, stood at the
concierge desk, listening while she gave directions to somewhere,
tracing a line on a map one of the men held out for her.

"I don't know—" Edward Everett said. Estelle shifted her position so that Edward Everett was between her and the lobby, as if she
needed him to buffet a strong wind.

"Can we wait here for a minute? Then you can have your life
back. I promise."

Edward Everett maneuvered so that he was facing her, nearly losing his balance when he set one of his crutch tips onto a slightly
uneven spot on the floor.

"Esty?" a man said. "Esty?"

"Shit, shit, shit, shit," Estelle said.

Edward Everett turned his head. The ponytailed man in the blue
suit was making his way toward them, the young woman trailing
behind with her hand laced through the crook of his arm as if she
were being escorted onto a dance floor.

"Esty, your mother has been going crazy looking for you," the
man said.

Estelle stepped around Edward Everett. "She found me, but she's probably still going crazy."

Up close, the man seemed perhaps as old as sixty, the woman with him nearer to Edward Everett's age. He could tell that her hair was not naturally blond; where she had parted it, not quite at the center of her scalp, the roots showed through as auburn.

"You really should go back, Estelle," the man said.

She let out a bitter laugh. "I think you gave up any right to tell me what to do, oh, I don't know, seven or eight weeks ago. Isn't that what it's been, Barbara?"

The girl gave the man a tentative look, biting her lower lip in clear discomfort.

"This really isn't a good time for this," the man said.

"I'm sorry to inconvenience you, Francis," she said, drawing out the "s" of his name in a prolonged hiss. "Edward, this is Francis Mattingly and his 'plus one.' Francis and plus one, this is Mr. Everett."

"Estelle," Frank said, touching her forearm. She flinched as if he had burned her.

"Don't put your hand on me. Ever again."

"Mr. Everest, maybe you can convince her—it's her sister's wedding."

"Leave him out of this."

"Look," Frank said. "We're leaving. We're leaving and you can go in. That's—"

"I don't think I told you this part of the story," Estelle said to Edward Everett.

"Really," Frank said, dropping his voice to a near whisper, "you needn't."

"Need, no. Want, yes. I think I neglected to tell you that I was engaged up until seven or eight weeks ago. What was it, Barbara? Seven or eight?"

"I don't—" Barbara said.

"How could you come to this wedding?" Estelle said.

"Jack is my—" Frank started to say.

"I know who the fuck he is. I just didn't think you would have the—" She let out a guttural scream, balled up her fist and struck

Frank on his left shoulder. Then, suddenly, she was swinging wildly at him. One of her blows knocked the glasses off his nose and they flew across the lobby, landing several feet away, where a bellhop wheeling a luggage cart toward the registration desk ran over them, crushing them.

"My God," Frank said, his right hand flying to his face, feeling for the glasses that weren't there any longer. "You're crazy. I knew you were crazy." At the registration desk, the hotel manager was squinting in their direction, reaching for a telephone.

"Maybe we should . . ." Edward Everett said, certain the manager was calling the police. Estelle was weeping audibly now, standing in the middle of the lobby, her face buried in her hands, rocking back and forth where she stood. He should just walk away; she was no one to him, just a crazy woman who had attached herself to him an hour or so ago, someone whose last name he couldn't even remember—some sort of bird, she'd said.

Frank was hunched over his glasses, picking up the pieces, the bent and snapped frame, the larger shards of glass, putting them gingerly into the breast pocket of his suit jacket as if they were something he could mend if he was careful enough.

The manager was crossing the lobby toward them, followed by a man in uniform.

"Estelle, you should really go," Edward Everett said.

Estelle lowered her hands. Her face was blotchy from tears, her cheeks darkened with mascara. He should just leave her. He wasn't part of their story. He didn't even know what their story was. But he said, regretting it as he did, "Come on, Estelle."

He began making his way unsteadily toward the elevators, Estelle following him.

"Damn it, Estelle," Frank was saying. "What am I supposed to do?"

"Fuck you, Frank," Estelle said. "Fuck you."

Incredibly, they made it to the elevators with no one stopping them. As they reached them, the nearest opened, the bell *ding*ing, the green "up" signal lighting. They pushed their way amid the crowd of people waiting, just barely fitting into the car. As the doors closed, someone on the other side of the doors called out, "Hey!" One of Edward Everett's crutches was caught in the doors and they began to slide open. He pulled it toward himself, losing his balance and stumbling back against the obese man in the Mickey Mouse T-shirt.

"Watch it, man," he said, giving Edward Everett a shove forward with his belly. But the doors shut. As they did, Edward Everett caught sight of the manager and a man in uniform. "Madam, madam," the manager was saying.

"Mademoiselle," Estelle said quietly, but they were safe, on their way up to the eleventh floor, while in the lobby, no doubt, Frank was telling whoever would listen about how he had been assaulted and giving a description of Estelle and Edward Everett. It struck him that Frank had no idea what his last name was. *Everest*, he can hear Frank saying, *Something like that, like the mountain.* That was not him; it was someone else.

Upstairs, he led Estelle to his room, where she went into the bathroom, closed and locked the door. Edward Everett, exhausted from the physical effort, slightly tipsy from the wine, dropped his crutches and fell back onto the bed. In the bathroom, Estelle had the sink faucet on all the way, the water splashing loudly into the basin. Despite that, he could hear her weeping.

This is crazy, he thought. How had he ended up with a sobbing stranger in his bathroom? An even better question was, how would he get rid of her?

He pushed himself from the bed and made his way to the closet, dragged out his suitcase and dropped it open onto the floor in front of the bureau in the room. He began packing. When he had moved into the hotel, he had tipped a bellboy to bring his bag up to his room, and he lived out of it until Julie arrived. "Tch," she said when she saw that even his clean clothing was a mess, as he had kept it all in his suitcase, pulling it out when he needed it. She had unpacked it, phoned the main desk to ask for an iron and an ironing board. He'd had no idea he could do that: call and it would appear with a knock on the door. She carried his dirty clothing downstairs, where there was a Laundromat, then brought it back upstairs and ironed everything, hanging his shirts in the closet, folding his underwear and jeans and slacks and laying them neatly into the drawers of the bureau, and then balled up his socks by pairs. Telling him he needed more clothing, she had read the labels in his jeans and shirts, taken money he'd given her and gone to a department store, coming back with bags of shirts and slacks.

But now he had to do it all himself and it was cumbersome. Finally, he supported himself on one crutch, pulled everything out of the closet and the bureau drawer and dumped it onto the floor beside the bed, hefted the suitcase onto the mattress and sat on the bed, stowing it all as best he could. When the suitcase was full, he had three pairs of slacks and four shirts that didn't fit. He considered what to do: Repack? Leave them for the maid?

The bathroom door clicked open and Estelle emerged. She had brushed her hair, washed her face, reapplied her makeup. She seemed composed, yet when he looked at her, she averted her eyes, as if she was embarrassed he was watching her.

She sat in the overstuffed chair where he'd spent so many of his hours in the room during his pity parties—watching television or staring out the window.

"Are you better?" he asked.

"Yes," she said in a quiet voice. "Much."

He waited for her to offer some explanation or bit of gratitude for what he'd done—kept her company, rescued her from Frank—but she said nothing. She stared out the window, although it was full-on night now and she couldn't possibly see much, save for pieces of buildings illuminated by streetlamps or the lights of the hotel on the far side of the park. The rain had stopped and the sky was clearing, the fat nearly full moon framed almost squarely by his window.

"I should finish my packing," he said.

"Don't mind me," she said.

He reopened his suitcase, pulled out half of the clothing he'd stuffed into it and began folding each piece as neatly as possible and laying it into the suitcase.

"Frank was my teacher," Estelle said, squinting out the window as if she were trying to make out an object in the distance. "I went back to school when I was twenty-six. I wanted a—well, it doesn't make any difference. I didn't finish what I was studying. I met Frank.

He was my professor in a seminar I took on Old English literature in my second term. I was—now he just seems like a pretentious shit. I mean, a ponytail? Since when? It's to impress that little tart." She took in a breath and let it out slowly. "He was electric in the classroom. Do you know anything about literature?"

"Not really," he said; the last book he'd read was a Perry Mason mystery.

"Well, this won't mean anything to you—I don't mean to offend you. I mean, it's okay that you . . ." She laughed. "You've been so nice to me and here I am sounding like . . . What was it Agnew said? I'm an 'effete intellectual snob.' "

"It's okay," he said.

"I remember sitting in class one day while he was giving a lecture on the Junius manuscript. It meant nothing to most of the people in the room. I mean, who reads Old English? No one was paying attention to him. One girl was knitting, another was addressing invitations to her wedding, but in front of the room, Frank was alive, talking about—but who the fuck cares? I was a silly girl. Hardly a girl. That was—how the fuck could I have been engaged to him for eleven years? Who is engaged for eleven years?"

He realized she wasn't really talking to him; he was just another human being who happened to be in the room as she rambled.

"Do you want to fuck?" she said abruptly.

"What?" he asked.

She stood up from the chair beside the window and crossed the room toward the bed where he was sitting.

"Fuck," she said. She sat beside him and, after hesitating a moment, laid a hand on his shoulder. "You're not married or anything, are you?"

"No," he said. Was his proposal that hung in the air between himself and Julie an "or anything"? He hadn't talked to her in weeks. He imagined her in her apartment, reading, glancing expectantly at the telephone on the table beside her couch, a yellow princess phone that had a small chip in the receiver from a time Audrey had slammed it into its cradle when a boy she liked told her he didn't want to see her anymore.

Estelle slid closer to him on the bed until her hip rested against his. "I'm forty-one," she said. "It seems old, I know. A girl in my high school got pregnant our freshman year and the baby she had would be your age now. You could be my son; I'm that old." She began tracing an index finger lightly along the inside of his thigh. "But forty-one isn't that old. You'll find that out."

"You're just angry," he said. "That's all. You don't really want to do this."

"Maybe angry, yes," she said. "But I want to do this." She cupped her hand over his groin. "You do, too. We both need this."

Chapter Seven

In the morning when he woke, she was snoring loudly, lying on her back, tangled in the top sheet, her right breast exposed, her left foot poking out from the bottom of the blanket. The light outside the window suggested it was perhaps six. He studied her. She was not an unattractive woman, despite the fact that she was a good deal older than he was. Her hair was disheveled and he could see now there were gray hairs among the red. On the underside of her bare breast was a dark mole the size of a pencil eraser. He gingerly pulled the sheet up so that it covered her and she startled but stayed asleep.

Moving slowly, as much because of his cast as from a desire not to wake her, he got out of bed and dressed without showering. He was leaving at seven-thirty. If she was still asleep, he would write a note saying she could stay until checkout time. He wondered what she would do. Could she face her family after the scene last night? Was forty-one old enough that maybe how your mother and sister regarded you didn't matter?

He wondered what kind of life she had, where she lived. She had said something about Indiana, but that was where she lived when she was younger. He realized it had been two years or more since he'd slept with a woman he didn't know well. When he was a younger ballplayer, and certain of his power, in life and over women, he often slept with girls whose names he didn't know. They waited outside the ballparks, in the shadows away from the lamps that arced over the parking lots surrounding it, stepping into the light when the players began filing out of the locker room. He thought of them as a kind of sexual smorgasbord: tonight, maybe someone tall and thin; tomorrow, maybe a plump brunette. He never understood the attraction the women felt for him and his teammates, why baseball was such an aphrodisiac. At the level they were at when they rolled into Ottumwa, Zanesville, Parkersburg, they had no money to speak of. The boyfriends the girls forsook earned more fixing cars or running a separator at the dairy than Edward Everett and his teammates did; they were better prospects, more stable.

Last night, they had knocked his suitcase and clothing off the bed, scattering it on the floor. He eased himself up, hopped to a wooden chair pushed up against the desk and pulled it out. Awkwardly, he moved it until it was beside the bed, sat down, opened the suitcase and began picking up his clothing, folding it as neatly as he could, pressing it into the suitcase. What didn't fit, he would leave behind. It didn't matter anymore.

Someone knocked on the door. It was too early for the maid, wasn't it? Maybe the manager had figured out who he was even though Frank had the wrong name.

He pushed himself from the chair and, bracing himself on the wall, hopped to the door. The knock came again, five muffled ticks against the wood. "Coming," he said in a voice he hoped was loud enough that whoever it was could hear but that wouldn't wake Estelle. He glanced at her just as he reached the door to see if she was still sleeping. She was, muttering something he couldn't make out. "Coming," he said again.

When he reached the door, he flicked the dead bolt and turned the knob, hopping backwards two or three steps to allow the door to swing inward.

It was Julie. She stood in the hall, holding a small overnight case and a makeup kit. "I shouldn't have come," she said. "I called you so many times and you didn't—and I swore I wouldn't come, wouldn't call anymore, but—"

"Ed?" Estelle said, her voice groggy. "Is someone . . ."

Julie peered into the room. Estelle was sitting up in bed, uncovered, both her breasts bare now. "Oh, my God," Julie said, stumbling back as if someone had struck her.

"Is everything all right?" Estelle asked, gathering the top sheet, covering herself. Julie snatched up her cases and fled down the hall.

"Julie," Edward Everett said. He hobbled after her, bracing his hand against the wall for support, regretting he hadn't gone back into the room for his crutches. At one point, his hand slipped on the wall and he came down hard on his bad leg. The pain was excruciating and he nearly crumpled to the floor from it, his eyes filling with tears, but he kept his balance and continued after her.

She stood in the hall, waiting for an elevator, jabbing at the "down" button repeatedly, muttering "Come on, come on, come on."

"Julie?" he said when he reached her.

"Don't," she said, not looking at him.

"I can explain," he said, although he had no clear notion of what had gone on. He laid a hand on her shoulder and she whirled around, swinging her makeup case at him, catching him on his cast and this time he did fall, landing hard on his healthy knee, crying out, reaching for a small decorative table that sat across from the elevators, holding a house telephone and a stack of *See Montreal Now!* brochures. The table gave under his weight, one of its legs cracking, the telephone clanging as it hit the floor, the brochures scattering.

The "down" arrow lit and the signal *ding*ed. Julie stepped toward the door, waiting for it to open.

"Julie," he said, pushing himself to stand.

"Leave me alone." The doors slid open. The elevator was crowded. A family of seven stood waiting, a mother, father and five young children, all holding suitcases. They squeezed together to allow Julie room to step onto the elevator. "I'm pregnant," she said as the doors started to close. "I wasn't going to tell you but—"

The doors closed, swallowing her words. Through the crack between them, he watched the light in the shaft change as the car descended. After a moment, he heard a muffled *ding*, signaling that the elevator was stopping at the floor below. He punched the "down" button, certain he would reach the lobby too late: she'd be gone by the time he got there. His knee throbbed and he could feel his pulse thrumming in his ears. That she could be pregnant had never occurred to him. She was on the pill, he was certain. Once while she was in Montreal, she'd taken the plastic disk of them out of her purse while they were in a restaurant, snapped it open, plucked one from its slot, popped it into her mouth and taken a swallow of water. "Baby-proofing," she said, giving him a wink and then slipping them back into her purse, blushing, just as the waitress brought their plates of waffles and sausage.

The other elevator arrived and he staggered onto it. A bellhop with a luggage cart nudged it toward the back of the elevator and the only other passenger, a withered woman who supported herself with a cane topped by a silver lion's head, inched her way deeper into the car as well. When the doors slid closed and the elevator began to fall, she wobbled and put a bony hand onto his elbow to steady herself, giving him a small smile of gratitude.

When he reached the lobby, he looked for Julie. A line of guests stood at the desk, keys and credit cards in hand. At the head of the queue, Estelle's Frank leaned against the desk, holding his bill close to his face, squinting at it. Through the glass doors leading to the street, Edward Everett spotted Julie at the curb, beside a taxi, waiting while a tall man in a lime green leisure suit counted bills into the cabdriver's hand. Edward Everett limped toward the doors, wincing with every step. He knew what he was doing might set his recovery back by weeks, but he was determined to catch her before the cab pulled away. Just as he reached the doors, the cabdriver took Julie's luggage from her and laid it into the trunk as she got into the backseat.

"Julie," he called, pushing against the revolving door, struggling to find the strength to move it. She glanced back at him, pulled the cab door closed and settled into the seat. He hobbled outside. Walking was even more difficult now, as he was able to do little more than take a step with his left foot and then drag his right, weighted by the cast, after it. "Julie," he said again. Getting into the driver's seat, the cabdriver glanced back at him. He saw himself through the man's eyes: he must seem mad, unshaven, in jeans and a sleeveless T-shirt, barefoot, his hair as wild as if he hadn't combed it in weeks. "Wait a minute," he said to the driver. The man looked uncertain and glanced at Julie; she didn't move but he could hear her say, quietly, "Just go." The driver gave Edward Everett a shrug and ducked his head, climbing into the car. Edward Everett had reached the cab by then. He bent, knocking on the window beside Julie. "Please," he said to her.

The driver shifted the cab into gear and began to edge away from the curb, but Julie said, "Wait," and he stopped. She rolled down her window.

"I'm—" he said, trying to figure out how to explain the crazy woman he had encountered, her sad, sad story and how he had felt sorry for her. It was nearly true—or was a kernel in a much more complicated truth. But she cut him off.

"I am going to say this and then I want you to never call me again." She raised her hands, palms up as if she were pushing something away from herself. "I have been through hell ever since I found out. I wasn't going to call. I wasn't going to call. Then I called. And called. And you never called back. Not fucking once. I was just going to decide on my own. End it? Keep it?

"My dad. I will never forget telling him. Waiting in our living room for him to come home, knowing what I had to tell him. I was his little girl and I was going to disappoint him." She paused. Edward Everett realized the cab's meter was running. Through the open window, he could hear it ticking off the fare. He glanced at it. Eighty-five cents, ninety-five. "He said you had a right to know before I—" She shrugged. "I was going to send you a letter but I thought, I had no idea when you would get it. My dad gave me plane fare. He—" She shook her head, fighting tears. " 'It's okay,' you were going to say. All the way here, that's what I heard you say. 'It will be okay.' " She shook her head. "I'm going to leave now and I don't want you to call me or try to see me."

"What are you—"

"Going to do?"

He nodded.

"I don't know yet."

"Can't you at least tell me when——"

"No," she said. "You don't get to know. Not anymore." She tapped the headrest of the seat in front of her and made a gesture to the driver: *Go on*.

"Wait," Edward Everett said, but there was an opening in the flow of traffic and the cab pulled away from the curb.

He became aware that people had been watching: the family of seven, the woman with the lion's-head cane, the attendant at the valet parking podium. He hobbled back toward the hotel, where a bellhop held the door for him, giving him a curt nod.

Upstairs, the door to his room was locked and he realized that he had left the key on the dresser. He knocked. "Estelle?" he called, but there was no answer. "Estelle," he said louder, but she still didn't answer. He hobbled to the hall where the elevators were. Someone had propped the broken table against the wall, where it leaned unsteadily on its three remaining legs. The courtesy phone sat on the floor beside it. He picked up the receiver and dialed "0" and asked the person who answered to please send someone up to his room. He'd locked himself out.

When the bellhop let him in and then left, he could see that Estelle was gone. She had made up the bed and his suitcase sat beside it, snapped closed, none of his clothing in evidence. On the table beside the bed, he found a piece of hotel stationery with the single word scrawled on it: "Sorry."

He sat on the bed for a moment, trying to think what to do. When he got to the airport, he had intended to buy a ticket to fly on to Columbus. He thought: *I should fly to Springfield instead, find Julie, tell her the entire story of sad sad sad Estelle. Bring her flowers. Every day. Court her.* He remembered the afternoon they'd sat in the church when Julie had pushed him through the throngs just after the Olympics left town. She'd done so much for him, both when she came to Montreal and when they were seeing each other in Springfield. Once, as he was about to leave on a road trip, he'd told her that he hated the long bus rides and she'd brought him a gift at the ballpark just before the team shoved off. It was four-fifteen in the morning and he had been surprised to see her standing beside the team bus, holding a grocery sack. The rest of the team had chided him. "No broads on the bus," someone said. "Are you going to share?" someone else said. Julie had blushed and handed him the bag. He gave her a quick kiss and didn't open the bag until the bus was under way. In it, he found a paperback murder mystery, a box of snack crackers and a package of salted peanuts. Sitting in his hotel in Montreal, he realized he had forgotten to acknowledge the gift. And now she was pregnant. With his son or daughter. He picked up the phone, dialed the desk and asked for a bellhop to come to his room to help him with his bag.

When he stood to limp across the room to retrieve his crutches, his right leg went out from under him. He had used up whatever strength he had in it chasing after Julie. He sat on the floor until the bellhop knocked.

"You'll need to unlock it," he shouted, not sure the bellhop could hear him through the door. "You'll have to——" But the bellhop had heard and opened the door.

"Can you . . ." Edward Everett said, nodding toward his crutches leaning in the corner near the door.

At the airport, when the taxi let him out, he asked a baggage checker at the curb for a wheelchair. He couldn't go to Springfield like this, he knew. How could he? He couldn't even get around on his own; he needed physical therapy. He took his ticket out of his breast pocket and consulted it. "Gate 22-B," he said to the baggage checker.

He'd go home, get healthy. Spring training was nearly half a year off—time to heal, to learn to walk again, to run without pain, to get in shape. He would heal and then he would go to Springfield, find Julie—right after Christmas, he promised himself. Soon after the first of the year at the latest. She would be large with the baby then.

If she kept it, he realized. If she kept it.

Part II

1977

Chapter Eight

The next June, he drove to an Indians tryout camp in Cleveland, booking a room in a Holiday Inn a few blocks from the stadium. It was an extravagance. He had less than six hundred dollars to his name and the three days and two nights in the city would consume a third of it. But he knew the less expensive places would be near the highway and the constant thrum of traffic would keep him awake. He saw this as a last chance: if they gave him a contract, it wouldn't be for the majors, but no worse than double-A, six hundred a month and within shouting distance of the big club if he played well and found some luck—an injury up the line, a trade, a manager who wanted to shake things up.

He had hoped his room would have a view of the stadium but it didn't; it was on the second floor, overlooking the littered roof of the parking garage. A convention of optometrists was in town and nearly every room within a mile radius of the city center was booked; he was able to get the one he did only because the hotel had a cancellation. "It's a sad story," the clerk said, taking his reservation two days earlier. "They were coming for their sixtieth anniversary but the gentleman was hospitalized."

"For what?" Edward Everett asked.

"I'm not certain," the clerk said. "Is that Y-E-A-T-S?"

Although the anniversary couple had canceled their reservation, guest services clearly hadn't gotten the word. When Edward Everett checked in, three vases holding five dozen roses sat on the bureau, a card stuck among the flowers: *To my Gloria, all my love, Jasper.* Beside them, a bottle of 1961 Grand Dom champagne chilled in an ice bucket. He considered calling the clerk, letting her know it was there, but didn't. If he got a contract, he could take it home, celebrate. It struck him: if he didn't get a contract, he might just drink it to toast the end of his days in baseball.

He left a six a.m. call. The tryouts began at nine but he wanted to get to the stadium early; show them that he was willing to do whatever it took to get back into the game. When the desk clerk phoned to wake him, he ordered a bagel and grapefruit and gave the bellhop who brought it a five-dollar tip on a two-and-a-half-dollar expense. He was not much more than a kid: short, skinny, wearing an ill-fitting uniform, the jacket cuffs swallowing half his palms. Edward Everett thought he'd be surprised by the tip, appreciative, but he only glanced at the bill and left without a word. *No matter,* Edward Everett thought. It was about aligning the stars in his favor.

When he arrived at the stadium shortly after eight, already a dozen or fifteen players were running sprints across the right field grass or playing toss. In the right field bullpen, two pitchers warmed up, their throws smacking the catchers' mitts with a sharp *snap.*

In the shade of the home dugout, a stout older man in a Cleveland Indians polo shirt sat in a folding chair behind a card table, and Edward Everett went over to register. As he filled out his form, he glanced at those from the other players, lying loose on the table. So many were younger than he was, he realized with a sinking heart: eighteen, seventeen, twenty-one. He considered shaving five years but didn't. If they signed him, they'd find out his true age soon enough. He handed the form back to the man, who gave it a quick glance, flicking his finger against the box that Edward Everett had checked: "Professional experience."

"Release?" the man said, snapping his fingers and holding out his hand without even bothering to look up. Edward Everett felt color rising in his neck and unzipped his equipment bag where he'd stowed his wallet, fished it out and found the letter he'd folded into it: the notice the Cardinals had sent him saying they were letting him go, that he was no longer their property. It was an absurd document, he thought, as he passed it to the man: less than a quarter of a page, a single-typed sentence:

"The St. Louis Cardinals National Baseball Club hereby grants Edward E. Yates his full and unconditional release."

His name was not even typed, but scrawled in ink above a blank line in the text, in handwriting that appeared to be that of someone in a hurry, his first name rendered as a capital "E," a lowercase "d," and then a squiggled line. The signature of whoever sent the letter was not even an actual signature but rubber-stamped and smeared.

The man gave just a twitch of his eyes in the direction of the paper, as if he had seen hundreds of them, and then thrust it back toward Edward Everett and mumbled something that took Edward Everett a moment to decipher: "Guwuhma." *Go warm up.*

"Yes, sir," Edward Everett said, and stepped out of the dugout onto the field in search of someone to play catch with.

The release had come in the mail on the day after Christmas. He was carrying out the holiday garbage—a trash can overflowing with torn wrapping paper and the carcass of the turkey his mother had cooked for dinner the day before—when the postal truck pulled to the curb. The mail carrier gave him a honk and a wave out the window and then held the mail aloft for Edward Everett. "I think you're gonna wanna see this one," he said, waving a business envelope in the air. They had been classmates, Edward Everett and the carrier, Geoff Symons. "It's from the Cardinals," Symons said, opening the door. He was vastly overweight and thrust himself out of the truck only with a great effort, then waddled to the curb with the mail in his hand, the letter from the Cardinals on top. "What're they offerin' this year? A hundert grand, I'm guessin'."

Edward Everett felt his head go light when he saw the envelope. Contracts came in thick manila envelopes, but only one thing came from the team in a thin business envelope. He took the mail from Symons dumbly and walked back inside.

"Ain't you gonna open it?" he was aware of Symons calling after him, but went on into the house. "Man, you're going to have one great-ass season."

"What on earth are you doing?" his mother asked. She was re-hanging the ornaments the cat had knocked off the tree and he only then became aware that he was still holding the trash can, canted at an angle so that daubs of dressing and cranberry sauce oozed onto the carpet. He set the trash can down and stared at the mess he'd made.

"Oh, my God," his mother said. "Someone died. Who died?"

"I did," he said.

By then, he was nearly fully healthy, walking without pain. When he ran, he was still conscious of the fragility of his joint, though: doing laps at the high school track, his knee was often stiff and he could hear disconcerting pops. He had yet to test it completely, running full-out, but he knew he would have to get past his fear if he was to play again: speed had been his greatest asset, compensating for his shortfalls—it added points to his average because it gave him eight or ten more hits in a season than someone slower might have, and that was the difference between batting .300-something and .280-something; without power, .280 didn't get you noticed, but .300 did.

He called Hoppel, certain someone in a rush had copied a wrong name onto the letter. It would turn out to be something they laughed about. *Frame it, kid,* Hoppel would say. *The letter will be as famous as "Dewey Defeats Truman" someday.*

Hoppel's wife answered the phone. He couldn't remember her name: "M" something. Madeline. Martha. She was large-boned and lacked what Edward Everett's mother would call "polish": her voice was gruff and her movements awkward. On the one occasion Hoppel brought her to the clubhouse, he seemed to show her off as if she were a great prize of a woman. Some of the team was undressed, coming out of the shower, wet towels draped over their shoulders, but she gave them no mind. "Hell," she snapped as one of them—

a young black kid who played second base—darted back into the shower when he saw her, "ain't nothin' I ain't seen before."

"Yeah?" she said into the phone now, as if challenging whoever called. When Edward Everett asked to talk to Hoppel, she shouted, without taking the receiver away from her mouth. "Hop? Hop?"

"What is it?" Hoppel said when he picked up. In the background, Edward Everett could hear voices: loud laughter and the squeal of a baby.

"It's—" Edward Everett started to say, but Hoppel interrupted him.

"Hang on." To someone in the background, he yelled, "I ain't done with that plate yet. Leave it."

It was obvious that Edward Everett had interrupted a family meal, Hoppel and his children and grandchildren.

"Sorry to bother you, Skip," Edward Everett said.

"Who is this?"

"Yates," he said.

"Yates?" Hoppel said as if he were trying to place him.

"Double E," he said, hating the nickname as he said it, as if he were a pair of shoes for some large man.

"What's goin' on?"

"I got this letter—" he began.

"Those fuckers," Hoppel said.

"Yeah, I thought it was a mistake," he said, thinking that Hoppel was going to say the letter was meant for someone else or at least curse the team for cutting him loose, but Hoppel went on: "Christmas. They send those things out at Christmas. Christ."

Edward Everett felt a stone in his stomach. "It's not—"

"Look, here's my advice. Go sell straw or whatever the fuck it is guys sell in whatever neck of the woods you're from. Indiana, right?"

"Ohio."

"Ohio, Indiana, whatever. Go sell straw or whatever. Tell guys stories. Civilians eat that shit up. If you can't think of a story, make one up. You'll sell a lot of straw."

"Straw?" Edward Everett said dumbly.

"Straw. Tractors. Pitchforks. It don't matter a crap."

"Are you saying—"

"Hey," Hoppel shouted. "Leave my fucking plate alone." He hung up and Edward Everett looked at the phone in his hand for a moment before he replaced it in the cradle. He'd expected Hoppel at least to say that the team had made a mistake; that Edward Everett would surely hook up with another organization. It was as if, now that he was dead to the team, he was dead to Hoppel as well.

Chapter Nine

He didn't sell straw, or tractors or pitchforks, but he did sell flour. His father's brother, Stan, repped for a mill in Steubenville and Edward Everett went to work for him shortly after the start of the new year. At first, his job consisted primarily of getting into his uncle's Cadillac at five-fifteen every morning, Monday through Friday, and riding with him as he made his rounds of the restaurants, groceries and bakeries in the valley.

His uncle was a beefy man, less than five-foot-six, and so big-bellied that, after he yanked himself behind the steering wheel, he could barely reach the accelerator. When he drove, he was frantic, constantly moving, scratching his cheek, picking his nose with his right pinkie, drumming his fingers on the steering wheel, smoking. In the car, at least, he rarely finished the sentences he began:

"John Roberts is the purchasing . . ." "Christ, I . . ." "Can you reach . . . ?"

Despite that, Edward Everett was soon able to pick up on what he meant: John Roberts is the purchasing *agent at the supermarket in Oriole.* Christ, I *hate this song* (stabbing an angry finger at the selector button to change the station). Can you reach *back and grab a fresh pack of cigarettes from the carton on the backseat?*

His uncle smoked constantly, often lighting one cigarette from another, flicking the spent butt out his window. More than once, it bounced back into the car, landing in his lap, and his uncle would bat frantically at it to knock it to the floor, taking his eyes off the road, the car weaving madly from the shoulder to across the center line. Edward Everett was certain he would be dead by March.

In the offices of supermarket purchasing agents or the owners of mom-and-pop bakeries, his uncle was a different man, however. He kept a metal file card box perched on the backseat and, before going in for a meeting, he flipped through the cards until he found the one that corresponded with the person they were meeting. On each, in surprisingly delicate handwriting, his uncle had made careful notes about the names of wives, the health of parents, the school activities of children, along with symbols that reminded him of changes he needed to make in his attire: tie, no tie; jacket, no jacket; pinkie ring, no pinkie ring. He'd glance at the card, spritz Binaca onto his tongue, yank himself out of the Cadillac and toddle inside for the appointment. There, in offices or industrial-sized kitchens, he was friendly and solicitous, flirty with the women, no matter how old, how attractive. To some of the men, he would relate a dirty joke but, outside in the car, he would say, "Christ, if Margaret," shaking his head. Christ, if Margaret *knew I told jokes like that, she'd have me going to confession seven days a week.*

Edward Everett hovered in the background, watching his uncle work. If someone glanced in his direction, he would give a smile and say, "I'm just here to learn from the pro." His uncle had told him to say that. "Jokes," he said, shrugging. Jokes *break the ice.* Jokes *make people like you.* Jokes *make the sale.*

In his second week, at a family-run bakery in Otto, overlooking the Ohio River, his uncle drew him into the conversation for the first time. It was a sale that was not going well. The owner—a thin young man with a face pockmarked by acne scars, who wore his pants high on his waist, secured by bright yellow suspenders—countered every claim Edward Everett's uncle made with one of his own: *Our current supplier gives a larger discount. Our current supplier can respond to special orders within forty-eight hours.* It was past one in the afternoon and Edward Everett was hungry, leaning against a stainless steel counter, where the man had been wrapping loaves of fresh-baked pumpernickel, and the scent of the bread made his stomach gurgle. Through the door to the sales floor, he was watching the owner's sister chat with customers, pluck sugar cookies and banana nut muffins from the display case and drop them into white bags. She was pretty—how such a person could be related to someone as unappealing as the owner was beyond his understanding. She was twenty-one or twenty-two and reminded him slightly of Julie: redheaded, wearing a sweater with a V-neck that showed the curve of her breasts disappearing into her robin's egg blue bra whenever she bent to fetch a sheet of baker's tissue from the shelves behind the register. He was wondering how he could manage to talk to her rather than her unpleasant brother, when he realized his uncle was talking about him.

"Ed would know," he was saying.

"What?" he said.

"How the Pirates are going to do this year."

He had no idea; he hadn't paid attention to the game since the letter from the Cardinals arrived. Every week, *The Sporting News* showed up in the mail (a gift from his mother) but he had not opened a single issue. In one, he knew, in an agate type column listing player transactions, was his name, followed by the single word: "Released." The rest of the paper would be optimistic projections for the season: the promising rookies, the feel-good stories about veterans making gallant comebacks, articles about players he knew. He could tolerate none of it.

"If their pitching holds up, they have a shot," he said, cringing because he sounded like the TV sportscasters he despised: jovial and slick-haired, spouting clichés that he and his teammates laughed about in the clubhouse. *You have to score if you're going to win in this game. You play them one at a time.*

"Ed here played for the Cardinals," his uncle said.

"That so?" the baker said, dubious.

"Yes," Edward Everett said. In the shop, the baker's sister was leaning across the glass counter toward a man wearing a weathered leather cowboy hat over stringy blond hair. "Yes," Edward Everett repeated in a tone that held more defiance than he intended.

"Ed got hurt last year in a game . . . where was it?" his uncle asked.

"Montreal," Edward Everett said. In the shop, the baker's sister playfully tugged on the cowboy's hair. The cowboy grabbed her hand and she laughed, snatching it away.

"Really?" the baker said. "I played in high school. But that was—man, the Cardinals. Brad Gibson. Lou Brock."

Bob Gibson, Edward Everett wanted to correct him, but a look from his uncle prevented him from doing so.

"Yeah, Gibson, Brock. All those guys," Edward Everett's uncle said, reaching up to squeeze the back of Edward Everett's neck in an affectionate manner. "Maybe you guys could compare notes sometime."

"Sure," the baker said.

His baseball career became as much a means of closing deals as were the bits of information on the cards in his uncle's file box or the jokes he told. At first, Edward Everett felt uneasy, both because his ambition had become a kind of currency to exchange for contracts for a half ton or a ton of flour a month and because of the false impressions he left with people, talking about Brock and Gibson as if he knew them, although he had never spoken more than a word to Brock and had not actually played with Gibson, who had retired the season before his one-and-only in the major leagues. He had, in fact, only been in the room with him once, at a dinner the organization held for Gibson the spring the pitcher announced he was retiring. It was in the St. Petersburg Hilton, in a banquet hall decorated with a life-sized cardboard image of Gibson delivering a pitch, heaving it as he did with the entirety of his being, a wonderment of balance, able to stay upright at the same time he was flinging not merely the ball but his *self* toward the hitter. As a minor league player, Edward Everett had been at a table near the kitchen, and several times a server carrying out trays of steak dinners banged into his chair. He and the other minor leaguers had been in awe at the dinner, speaking among themselves in quiet voices as if they were in a church, while Gibson's former teammates at tables near the dais told loud stories and every once in a while erupted in raucous laughter. They were men used to deference and privilege and Edward Everett watched them, wondering if he ever would belong among them. At one point, a stranger opened the door and peeked in: a gaunt man with his greasy black hair in an obvious comb-over. He gave a slow blink and Edward Everett caught his eye. He realized that, to the man with the comb-over, he was no different than the men at the loud tables, part of the fraternity. He leaned into the player beside him and made a comment about the waitress who'd just brushed against him laying a roll onto his plate. The player laughed and Edward Everett glanced again at the man with the comb-over, who blushed, shutting the door.

The bakers and grocers in his uncle's territory were, in their own ways, that man with bad hair. They drove Cadillacs or Lincolns; they spent January in Florida or Arizona; they earned ten times what Edward Everett ever had but, in his presence, they became again their boyish selves who had dreamed of playing ball, asking, *What's it like up there?* as if he had been to a country their passports would not allow them to enter.

He told them stories—some true, some embellished, some patently false.

"Never disappoint," his uncle told him, and he didn't. If they asked about Gibson, he gave them the Gibson he thought they wanted. If they wanted a Gibson who was a fierce competitor, he described a Gibson who knocked down a hitter with a high-and-tight pitch; if they wanted a friendly Gibson, he invented a story about Gibson fronting a rookie meal money, telling him to forget about paying it back.

In the first week of February, his uncle took him to lunch at a country club he belonged to in St. Martinsville. It was past the noon rush and the tables were mostly empty, white-coated busboys gathering tablecloths and replacing them with fresh linens. They knew his uncle there; the hostess chatted with him in an easy way as she led them to a table beside a large window that looked out onto the golf course. The temperature was in the twenties but the course was free of snow and outside a foursome trailed up a slight rise in the tenth fairway, pulling wheeled golf carts behind them.

"Gotta admire the passion," his uncle said, nodding toward the golfers and taking a pack of cigarettes out of his shirt pocket, extracting one and lighting it with a silver lighter engraved with his initials and the logo of the flour company.

A waitress brought a tumbler of scotch and water on the rocks and set it in front of his uncle although Edward Everett had not heard him order a drink.

"Thanks, dear," his uncle said, giving her a slight pat on her hip.

"Would you . . ." she said, nodding to Edward Everett.

"Yes, he would," his uncle said, and the waitress left them there.

"I don't really—" Edward Everett said.

"Today you do," his uncle said, reaching into the inside breast pocket of his jacket and pulling out a cream-colored business envelope with the word "Ed" typed where an address would be. His uncle held it out for him and gestured with a slight nod that he should take it. "Go ahead and open it," he said. Inside was a payroll check for January from the mill: one thousand thirty-seven dollars and eleven cents, along with a check stub enumerating deductions for Social Security, state and federal taxes. Aside from his signing bonus ten years earlier he had never held a single check for so much money.

"In two more months, you can get the health insurance," his uncle said. "You can also sign up for payroll deductions for the stock plan."

The waitress came back with a drink for him and his uncle picked up his own glass and clinked it against Edward Everett's. "*L'chaim*," he said, taking a swallow. Edward Everett took a drink himself. He had expected it to burn but it didn't. Instead, it filled his entire body with a sense of warmth.

"Your mom asked if I would take you under my wing. She's had a hard time. Even before your dad—may he rest in peace." His uncle traced a perfunctory sign of the cross. "I thought, *Hell, I'll do it for a month, tell her we gave it our best shot, but . . .*" His uncle shrugged. "You're raw but you have more of a gift than you know."

"What do you mean?"

"What do you do when we go to see someone?"

"I pretty much listen—" Edward Everett was going to say, *to you,* but his uncle interrupted with enthusiasm.

"Exactamundo. You *listen*. But the other thing you do is, those stories are great."

Edward Everett blushed. *I make them up,* he wanted to confess.

"I know they're bullshit," his uncle said. "I know something about who played when. Roger Maris quit, what? Ten years ago? And Gibson: the guy would have to be schizophrenic as hell if he was all the people you described." His uncle gave a laugh that shook his entire body. "People don't buy flour. Flour's flour. Our flour. Their flour. This other guy's flour. They buy *you.* Well, mostly I like to think they buy *me,* but . . ." He laughed. "I just had one of the best months I've had in, shit, I don't know when."

Edward Everett wondered how much his uncle earned if the mill was paying him more than twelve hundred dollars gross for trailing him like a lost puppy. He had always thought of his uncle as a fat, ridiculous man, especially compared with his own father, who had done all the calisthenics he'd asked his football players to do up until the day he hung himself when Edward Everett was twelve. At family parties or Fourth of July picnics, whenever the two stood side by side in the requisite photos, they seemed like random strangers caught in the frame of the camera's lens, not men who had shared the same bed until the older one, Edward Everett's father, turned ten. Yet, for all of Edward Everett's father's fame in the town—for all of the photos of him in the back pages of the weekly newspaper where it ran the sports articles, for all of the backslapping by the men of the town whenever Edward Everett went out with him—it was, he realized, his uncle who was successful, the silly man with the belly people joked about (*How long are you going to carry that child, Stan?*) rather than his father, whom people compared to Gary Cooper. So many of his parents' conversations suddenly made sense: when they needed a new transmission for their nine-year-old Buick, when the water heater went out the day before a Thanksgiving when his parents were hosting seventeen people for dinner. *Let's ask Stan. Let's ask Stan.* As a boy, Edward Everett had thought his uncle some sort of savant to whom his parents went when they were stumped and needed guidance. *Why, I think I'd take it to a mechanic. Why, I think it would be a good idea to call a plumber.* Sitting with him in the country club, as the waitress set identical plates of filet mignon, roasted red potatoes and asparagus in front of them, he realized for the first time that it wasn't his uncle's wisdom his parents were after, but his generosity: the First National Bank of Stanley Yates.

"You didn't have to do this," Edward Everett said, cutting into his steak.

His uncle glanced up, steak sauce speckling his chin and cheeks. "Family's family," he said, picking up an asparagus spear with his fingers and folding it whole into his mouth.

Chapter Ten

His uncle began letting him take the lead on some sales calls, although he botched many at first. While his uncle knew unit prices and shipping lead times, Edward Everett had to page slowly through tabbed sections of the catalog binder his uncle had given him and calculate quantity breaks by doing math on a scratch pad tucked into the binder. Often, in his haste to quote a price, he made an error and it was only after he had told it to the customer that he would realize he had forgotten to carry a digit from one column to the next or had forgotten that two thousand pounds made a ton, not one thousand. Still, his uncle was patient and explained his awkwardness using baseball references, calling him "Rookie," joking about giving him a tryout. His income continued to rise. By March, his check was for nearly fifteen hundred dollars.

They went to a men's clothing store in Braverton, where his uncle helped him pick out three suits: a charcoal pinstripe, a navy blue and a tan. A tiny man who may have been in his eighties measured Edward Everett, standing on tiptoe to stretch the tape from shoulder to shoulder. His touch was so delicate and he moved the measuring tape from shoulder to arm and around his neck so quickly,

Edward Everett wondered if he was merely making a show of it, but when he picked up the suits they fit him better than anything else he had ever owned. It came to more than five hundred dollars but when he flinched at the bill, his uncle said, "It's not an expense; it's an investment."

He moved out of his mother's house, renting an apartment upstairs from the weekly paper; every Tuesday morning at three, the roar and vibration of the press shook him from his sleep. He bought a car, a four-year-old Ford Maverick. "Buy American," his uncle advised. "A lot of these guys fought in the big one and wouldn't like to see you pull up in a piece of Jap crap." Despite his car, his uncle still picked him up in the morning because it made little sense for them to drive separately, since they were going to the same bakers and grocers and purchasing agents' offices.

On the first Monday in April, his uncle brought Edward Everett to his house so he could begin teaching him the bookkeeping part of their work. Edward Everett had never been to his uncle's house—not this one anyway. When his father was alive, his uncle had lived not far from them, in a modest three-bedroom place on a tree-filled lot. Some years before Edward Everett began working with him, however, he had bought ten acres that had been part of a prosperous dairy farm that once belonged to the district's congressman, who had to sell it to pay legal bills when he got into trouble for skimming campaign contributions for a D.C. townhouse for his mistress. Edward Everett's uncle and aunt had built a sprawling ranch house on the property: three bedrooms, three full baths, a large dining room with a vaulted ceiling. His uncle's office was at the back of the house, where a large picture window looked out onto a pond the congressman had stocked with trout.

It was after seven in the evening and the sun was setting on the other side of a windbreak of maples on the far edge of the pond. Three ducks settled onto the water and paddled lazily. Edward Everett could hear his aunt in the kitchen, making dinner: the creak of the hinges on the broiler as she opened it to turn the steaks they were going to eat, and then the juices of the steaks sizzling. As she worked, she sang a song quietly but still loud enough that Edward Everett could make out that she didn't know many of the words: "The moment I dada before I dada dadada, I say a little prayer for you." At his desk, Edward Everett's uncle leafed through a thick red-and-black ledger, each page a neat line of names and columns of quantities, dollars and dates. His uncle invited him to sit in his leather chair to enter the day's orders and gave him a fountain pen, a gold-and-tortoise Visconti that weighed more than any pen Edward Everett had ever held. He took his time, as if he had never written a letter or a figure before, making each stroke deliberately, nervous about ruining the precision of the other lines on the page. The totals staggered him: he knew they had been selling what he considered a lot of flour but, adding the figures, he saw that their sales over the two and a half weeks recorded on that page approached fifty thousand dollars.

"Hon, I'm making a Manhattan for myself," his aunt called from the kitchen. "Can I make one for you and Ed?"

"Sure," his uncle said, not waiting for Edward Everett to answer.

Edward Everett's aunt brought the drinks to the office and they sipped them, his aunt and uncle side by side on a leather couch, Edward Everett in a matching upholstered wing chair. His aunt and uncle chatted but Edward Everett didn't really listen, catching only snatches of their conversation: a banquet at which his uncle was going to receive some sort of award from the diocese for fund-raising, a friend who'd had quadruple bypass surgery and who, three days out of the hospital, was already smoking a pack a day. His aunt, who was heavy with a round face, was not what he would think of as an attractive woman, but it was obvious his uncle loved her by the way he touched one of her plump knees to make a point or when he laughed at a story she told him about a misunderstanding at the butcher's.

The drink relaxed Edward Everett and he watched the evening soften and darken. He thought, *If I stick this out, take over my uncle's territory when he retires, I could have my own house overlooking a pond, where my own wife would bring me a Manhattan just as I finished recording the evidence of our good fortune.*

That month, as his uncle suggested, he began buying stock in the company. Many evenings, he went home to his apartment, showered, changed into Levi's and a T-shirt, and walked down the block to a diner, stopping at a newspaper box just outside to buy a copy of *The Wheeling Intelligencer*. He sat in a booth beside the front window and, after ordering, turned first to the stock pages and, running his finger down the column of agate type, found the symbol for the mill, GnFlr, to check the closing price for the day before. It rarely varied more than a quarter point, but was up three of every five days. It gave him satisfaction: partly it was watching his investment growing, but also partly because he had a sense that he was participating in something larger than himself, something he couldn't understand fully, owning pieces of the American economy. Within two years, he estimated, the value of his stock would reach several thousand dollars, nearly as much as he earned for some seasons in the minor leagues: so much money for doing nothing, checking a box on a form that sat in a file drawer in an office somewhere he'd never been. In five or six years, he could cash it in and buy a house—a small one, yes, but a house nonetheless. It struck him that he had been foolish to give so many of his years to a game that gave so little back, realizing that, only half a year removed from it, he was already thinking of his life in terms of investment and return. If he'd gone to work for his uncle six or seven years ago, he'd have that house now.

As he ate his dinner—generally fried chicken and mashed potatoes but sometimes a chopped steak and fries—he went through the newspaper, reading nearly every page: the national and international news, the local news, the features, the comic strips, but avoiding the sports section. Merely glancing at an article about baseball was something painful, even as he thought he'd moved beyond it, like seeing the published engagement announcement of a girl he once dated. It was enough to remind him that, for the first time since he'd been eighteen, he wasn't part of the baseball machinery in some way. In the past, he had a sense of the game as a giant Rube Goldberg mechanism, with every player, himself included, a cog: a third baseman in

Atlanta tears a hamstring trying to beat out a ground ball and goes down for six weeks; the Braves trade with the White Sox for a third baseman and a shortstop from Richmond. In the Sox system, a pitcher and a middle infielder get their release to make room for the players the Sox acquired. And on and on, gears turning, levers pulling, the machinery grinding, hello, good-bye, hello, good-bye, hello, good-bye.

Chapter Eleven

In the middle of April, he began dating a woman he had grown up with, Connie Heidrich, after he saw her when he and his uncle made a call at the high school where she taught English. It was near the end of the school day when they got there, a stormy afternoon. Edward Everett's uncle was edgy, in a foul mood; he'd been trying, unsuccessfully, to sell flour to the school's food service director for more than a decade, he said, and at their previous stop, the baker had complained that his last shipment of flour had weevils in it. "Look at this," he'd said, opening a plastic vat, revealing pale insects burrowing into the flour, scurrying up the sides. It was evident to Edward Everett that the fault probably lay with the baker; his kitchen was filthy. Stainless steel bowls sat unwashed in the large sink and the floor was so covered in grease that Edward Everett's uncle had slipped coming in, only keeping his balance by steadying himself with a hand on the doorframe. Despite this, Edward Everett's uncle said only that he would pass on the baker's concern to the mill. Back in the car, however, he said, "I should have. Shit. Shit."

Then, on the way to the school, they ran into the foul weather. One moment they were cruising at eighty miles an hour on the interstate, under a partly cloudy sky, and the next, as they crested a rise and started descending into a valley, the sky was black, rain and hail banging against the roof of the car and washing across the windshield. Edward Everett's uncle refused to slow down, plowing on past more timid drivers until the Cadillac came upon a cattle truck lumbering in the lane ahead of them. Edward Everett's uncle stepped hard on the brake and they started fishtailing, Edward Everett certain they'd slam into the back of the truck. A half-dozen Holsteins turned to look at them but seemed unconcerned. Somehow, his uncle slipped into a space in the right-hand lane just in front of a Rambler, then skidded onto the grassy berm before he regained control and stopped.

"Don't tell your," his uncle said. "Jesus, I."

They sat on the shoulder while passing traffic sprayed their car with rainwater. When he found a break in the flow, Edward Everett's uncle merged and went on to the school, taking his time. There, in the lot, they made a dash for the building. By the time they reached it, Edward Everett was soaked, his shoes oozing rainwater.

The food service manager's office was just off the cafeteria, a small, windowless room that stank of onions and fryer grease. The office was cluttered, the desk a jumble of file folders partly spilling onto the floor. Balanced on one precarious pile was a cafeteria tray holding the remnants of a half-eaten sloppy joe and a mound of baked beans. There were only two chairs in the office, the swivel chair behind the desk where the food service manager sat and a molded Plexiglas chair stacked with magazines and newspapers. The food service manager—a grossly overweight man whose bulk was squeezed between the arms of his desk chair—did not offer the second chair to either Edward Everett or his uncle and they stood there, Edward Everett thought, like two boys who had been summoned to the principal's office for not doing their homework.

"We've been over this," the food service manager said, not quite looking at them but instead watching a chewed-up pencil he rolled between his palms. "We're pretty locked in . . ."

"We've got a new pricing structure," Edward Everett's uncle said, opening his briefcase by balancing it against his thighs, snapping the brass latches, and then reaching inside to pluck out a sheet of paper filled with columns of numbers. "I think you'll find—"

"We're really . . ." The food service manager finished his sentence by waving the pencil as if he were a conductor signaling an orchestra to stop playing. "Savvy?"

"Look," Edward Everett's uncle said. "I don't know why you have to be——"

The food service manager let out a laugh. "You go talk to Dick Thornberg and ask him why I have to be."

"Dick Thornberg," his uncle said.

"That's right," the food service manager said, giving his uncle an odd smile.

"I see," his uncle said, returning the pricing sheet to his briefcase and snapping it shut with an exaggerated flourish. "I'll sure give old Dick a call."

Edward Everett felt as if his uncle and the food service manager were speaking a language he did not understand and he cocked his head quizzically toward his uncle, but if his uncle noticed, he gave him no sign and they left the office.

Upstairs in the main hall, most of the students were gone. From the band room came a discordant version of "Do You Know the Way to San Jose," one of the tubas letting out a *blatt* a beat behind the others in his section.

"Not one of our red-letter days," his uncle said. "We'll get them tomorrow."

Outside, the rain was still falling but its vehemence had abated. In the distance, beyond the neighborhoods that marched up the hillside away from the school, pale patches of sky appeared amid the clouds. A car pulled to the curb, a battered gray Rambler missing its left front quarter panel. The driver, a woman, pushed open the door in a way that suggested the hinges were worn, hopped out, leaving the engine running, and dashed for the entrance, holding a newspaper over her head as a makeshift umbrella.

"Whew," she said, ducking into the door that Edward Everett held open for her. "That's one wet afternoon out there." She rolled the newspaper and then twisted it, squeezing out the water; it ran black along her forearm. "That was not the smar——" she caught herself in mid-word and cocked her head. "Ed?" she asked, narrowing her eyes as if squinting would bring him into clearer focus.

"I'm sorry," he began but then realized he did recognize her. "Connie?"

"Oh, crap," she said, covering her face with her hand. When she removed it, newsprint smudged her cheeks and forehead. "I look like, well, not at the height of my pulchritude. I thought you were off ..." She held the newspaper as if it were a bat and swung it, clucking her tongue against the roof of her mouth in imitation of a ball hitting the bat, darkened drops of rainwater spattering Edward Everett and his uncle.

"I was," he said. "I got hurt and—this is my uncle, Stan. I'm working with him."

"We were just calling on your Mr. Osgood," his uncle said.

She laughed. "He's hardly *my* Mr. Osgood."

"He's a tough nut to crack," Edward Everett's uncle said.

"With 'nut' being the operative word," Connie said. "I'd better— I left a stack of term papers on my desk that if I don't grade this weekend, my American Lit students are going to revolt on Monday."

"You're teaching here?" Edward Everett asked.

"My second year," she said.

"I'm sorry, but Margaret and I ..." his uncle said. "George Jones is at the Jamboree tonight and I need to get on home. I don't mean to break up the reunion."

"I need to skedaddle myself," Connie said. "Paper grading! Friday night fun!" She turned to go but stopped. "I'd love to catch up, Ed."

"Sure," he said.

"Do you have a piece of paper? I'll give you my number."

Edward Everett fished out the small spiral notebook he carried in his shirt pocket and took out a pen, handing both to her. She took them, scribbled her name and number into the notebook and started to give them back to him but then snatched the pen away. "This I'll keep as a hostage until you do call me. That way, it takes all the pressure off. We're not making a date. You'll just be retrieving your pen."

Within a week and a half, they were seeing each other. On a Sunday morning, he was waking in her house for the first time and he realized that, without ever planning it, he had been with her nearly every day since he first ran into her. He was alone in her house; she had gone for a jog at sunrise, giving him a quiet kiss on the forehead that he dimly remembered as he lay in her bed, contemplating getting up. From down the hall, he could smell a pot of coffee simmering. She'd been divorced for seven years by then—a Polaroid marriage, she called it, wed at eighteen, divorced a few days after she turned twenty, not even old enough to celebrate the end of her marriage with a legal glass of champagne—and her bedroom was decorated as if she had tried fiercely to eliminate any trace of masculinity: the bed was canopied with a scalloped lily-print fabric, posters of Degas dancers hung on the walls and a crystal bowl on the bureau held potpourri so pungent he wondered if she had bought it anticipating he would, indeed, spend the night. They'd actually slept together the first time they'd gone out, the previous Sunday. He'd picked her up to have lunch. She hadn't wanted him to come to the door because she had a son, a nine-year-old who had bad eyesight, asthma and a horrible father. She'd enumerated the conditions as if they were of the same magnitude of affliction. "It's too soon for him to meet you," she'd said, and then rushed to add, blushing, "Not that he ever needs to meet you. It's just lunch, nothing more." He sat in his Maverick at the curb, the engine idling, listening to WPOP out of Wheeling, an upbeat tune about a boy and girl who share an umbrella at a bus stop and end up marrying.

At Connie's house, a small hand drew back the curtain over a window but then snatched itself away as if he'd been burned, no doubt because someone had scolded him for spying on Edward Everett. A moment later, Connie came down the walk to his car. As a girl, she had taken dance lessons since she was three and, for as long as he could remember, her movements all possessed a certain fluid quality, no matter how ordinary: taking a pen out of her purse, opening a math text, scratching her calf while listening to one of their teachers. They were paired as partners for a chemistry experiment once. It was early fall in their senior year and Connie had worn a sleeveless blouse. As she used a pipette to measure drops of sodium hydroxide into a beaker holding a copper wire, Edward Everett could see the slight curve of her breast and an edge of lace from her bra. He had no idea what the scent was that she gave off (her shampoo, some perfume) but he was certain that he would pass out from inhaling it. They'd almost gone out not long after, when he'd learned that she and her boyfriend, Lloyd, who played linebacker for the school with a vicious aggression, had broken up. The day he found out that they were no longer a couple—it was a Tuesday, he remembered—he'd gone to her locker to wait for her and while she stowed her books, they'd agreed to go see *Fantastic Voyage*. On Thursday, however, she told him she'd discovered she was pregnant and would be marrying Lloyd and before graduation she'd changed her place in the line of students, from somewhere in the middle as an "H" to the front, as an "Adams," directly in front of her husband as they marched into the football stadium, Lloyd clowning, pointing at Connie, making a gesture above his own belly describing an arc in the air, and then giving a thumbs-up.

Walking toward Edward Everett's car, Connie still had her girlish grace, absently taking a strand of her hair that blew across her face and tucking it behind her right ear, giving him a shy smile as she opened the car door and got in.

They'd had lunch at a tearoom in a hundred-year-old brick house that was a Victorian museum, not the sort of restaurant he would have chosen ordinarily, with its delicate sandwiches and meager salads, a restaurant that catered to women like his mother, who saw it as a bastion of finery in a town that otherwise offered taverns and corner diners. He had suggested it because he thought it was the sort of place Connie would prefer, but while they ate he realized they were, by twenty years, the youngest people in the place and that, aside from a rotund ruddy-faced man in a blue serge suit and a polka-dotted bow tie, he was the only male. Their conversation went in fits and starts, as if they could never land on a subject either had much to say about: her taking six and a half years to finish college because of her son, Billy; her ex-husband's mocking her when she told him she wanted to become a teacher; Edward Everett's expurgated stories of playing ball in towns not much larger than their own.

After they finished and were walking back to his car, he felt as if he'd been holding his breath for the entire hour they'd been there. He was unsure whether it was the restaurant or that, after almost ten years, he and Connie had nothing to talk about. He would take her home, make a polite comment about how they should do this again, and then not call her, but on their way back to her house, they'd passed the building where his apartment was and she'd said, "Don't you live upstairs there?" He'd been surprised she'd known that. "I'd like to see it," she said. Upstairs, he regretted inviting her in. He was not the best of housekeepers. The suit he'd worn the day before lay crumpled on the couch in the living room, and the can of Pabst he'd drunk while he was watching *The Rockford Files* was on its side on the floor beside his chair, still dripping beer. But she'd said, "This is actually charming." Not long after that, he was kissing her.

Twice since then, she'd come to his apartment in the early evening, while her mother visited with Billy, and they'd made love. With the windows open and the sound of voices passing beneath his apartment, he felt as if they were having sex in a public place and wondered if the people whose conversations he caught pieces of could also hear the noises they made: his headboard banging against the wall, Connie's whimpers when she had an orgasm, his groan when he had his own. ". . . the prices . . ." a woman's voice said once. ". . . your schoolwork . . ." said another. ". . . liver and onions . . ." said still another.

The weekend after they had their first lunch, Connie's son went off with his father. "He's taking him turkey hunting," Connie told Edward Everett, wrinkling her nose and shaking her head. " 'I'm going to make a man out of him,' " she said, imitating her ex-husband's laconic way of speaking. She invited Edward Everett for dinner on Saturday night, telling him she would make him a home-cooked meal. When he arrived, bringing a bottle of wine, the house was redolent of meatloaf and boiling potatoes. She greeted him at the door wearing an off-white canvas apron that had "Mom's Kitchen" spelled out in awkward, childish letters that he guessed her son had finger-painted. She gave him a peck on the cheek and rushed back to the kitchen because a timer *ding*ed. In the kitchen, she had set the table with china and crystal goblets, two at each place—a red-wine glass and a water glass—and silver. "I never have adult company," she said quickly when she saw him looking at the table. "It's an indulgence, I know. There's a corkscrew in the drawer here." She gave the top drawer next to the stove a shove with her hip as she turned off the gas flame under the boiling potatoes and then poured them into a colander in the sink. He opened the drawer, which was a jumble of miscellaneous junk: transistor radio batteries, half-used rolls of Scotch tape, a coil of picture wire, a coffee-stained instruction manual for a dishwasher. It was, it struck him—as someone who had not lived in the same city for long over the last decade—the junk drawer of someone who had stayed put. He found the corkscrew and opened the wine, pouring out two glasses. He set one on the counter beside the stove for Connie and leaned against the sink drinking his. "Are you trying to get me drunk?" she asked, winking, then poured the boiled potatoes into a mixing bowl and took a break to sip her wine.

During dinner, Connie talked about people they'd gone to school with—Derek Colombo, who'd died when his fishing boat sank the year before; Felix Chase, who'd gone off to be a priest but who had met a woman while he was in the seminary, forsaken the priesthood, married her and had five children already, crammed into a tiny ranch house on the western edge of town, "Poor as church mice but happy as a lark," she'd said. They were all merged into adulthood—lawyers, teachers, coal miners, a veterinarian; owners of hardware stores, service stations—so many with children and mortgages and revolving credit accounts at Sears that they used to furnish those houses, and here he had been, in some sort of limbo, waiting for his life to start, as if he were forever in a train depot, always on his way elsewhere, wherever the club that owned his contract told him to go, living in places that always had the feel of temporariness: boarding in houses owned by widows who needed the rent to pay the mortgage, living in houses owned by former ballplayers who sometimes let the rent slide in exchange for some nineteen-year-old kid listening, for the fifteenth time, to a story about the day their landlord hit a home run off Dizzy Dean in a spring training game back in 1935; living four players to a one-bedroom apartment, sleeping on a cheap couch someone found in an alley next to a dumpster; because none of it mattered, none of the addresses were where you'd end up, all of them just stops on a journey toward the major leagues.

As they cleared the table after they finished eating, it occurred to him that this was the sort of life he could have if he wanted it: domestic, living in the same house for years on end. It was, it struck him, not a bad life. All he had to do was get off the train once and for all: sell flour; hunker down with a woman he'd make his wife; raise up some kids.

One day, he realized he was part of a family. *Poof;* just like that, not anything he had set out to acquire but something he just found he had. It was four weeks after their lunch in the tearoom. They were in line at a crowded grocery on a Saturday afternoon in mid-May, waiting among customers with carts piled as high as if they'd just received a bulletin that the store was closing forever, and they would never be able to buy another ounce of food: hams and beef roasts, cellophane packages of hot dogs, bags of potato chips, cases of Pepsi. He was standing behind Connie, affectionately resting his chin on the top of her head as she flipped through a *Ladies' Home Journal,* stopping at a two-page spread on gardens for small yards. "What do you think?" she asked. "We could do a variation of this in the back." The photograph showed a yard in Wisconsin where the owners had replaced most of the back lawn with an English-style garden, a white rose vine climbing an arbor, two Adirondack chairs in the shade of a flowering dogwood, a folded newspaper resting in the seat of one of them as if the occupant had just gone into the house for a glass of tea.

More than the photograph, however, what struck Edward Everett was Connie's use of the word "we," as if he already had moved into her home and had enough ownership to say, "I'd prefer pink roses over white," one of the Adirondack chairs *his* chair, where he'd sit on Sundays, reading the financial pages. With his increasing income on top of her modest one as a schoolteacher, it struck him, they could renovate the house. Standing with her in the grocery line, waiting to pay for their ground beef and cold cuts and macaroni salad, her house transformed in his head as if he were watching a time-lapse movie like those he'd seen in high school, showing a caterpillar's evolution to butterfly: the stained living room carpeting replaced with hardwood; the cracked linoleum in the kitchen replaced with tile like his uncle had; the mildewed asbestos shingles replaced with vinyl siding.

They began spending even more time together, doing what they called "everyday life" instead of merely dating. He kept his small apartment over the newspaper but, aside from going there to pick up his mail and fresh clothing, he was, for all intents and purposes, living with Connie and her son. In the evenings, as she washed dishes and quizzed her son on spelling words and state capitals, he spread his purchase orders across the kitchen table and made entries into his account ledger. After they finished their work, they watched television, Edward Everett and Connie on the couch, Billy sprawled on the floor, head propped on two cushions, laughing at shows he thought he should have found inane but, in their company, enjoyed: *Happy Days* and *Welcome Back, Kotter*, before Connie sent Billy to bed.

At first, they made love every night—quietly because Connie didn't want Billy to hear them. But within a week and a half, her period came and their abstinence for those days brought them to what she said was, ironically, a new sort of intimacy: the comfort of a man and woman sleeping in the same bed because it was where they slept and not because they were just there to have sex. At first, he found it odd to be beside her without making love—he'd never been in bed with a woman unless they were going to have sex. Then he, too, saw it as she did: they were becoming comfortable living side by side, sleeping side by side.

One Sunday, after a rainstorm when her gutters had overflowed, he climbed an extension ladder and hefted himself onto the roof so he could clean the gutters, scooping out foul-smelling handfuls of leaves and maple seeds, filling half a dozen lawn-and-leaf bags with the detritus. As he cleaned them, he saw that the gutters themselves were in sorry condition: bent where tree limbs had fallen onto them, riddled with holes where they had rusted. The entire roof, in fact, was in poor shape. At one point, as he shifted his weight to move so he could reach the next length of gutter, a piece of a shingle broke off, slid down the roof and sailed into the yard, where Connie was collecting branches.

"Hey," she called, picking up the fragment. "You destroying my roof up there?"

"Just seeing if you're paying attention," he said.

The next week, he called a former high school teammate, Ralph Sellers, who ran a roofing company with his father, and bought Connie a new roof without telling her: eleven hundred twelve dollars and eighteen cents. A year ago, the sum would have seemed insurmountable but he had it in the bank—his account was by then close to four thousand dollars, as he had few expenses—and it stunned him how easy life was with money in the bank. A year earlier, late in the month, before payday, he and his teammates scouted for all-you-could-eat breakfasts at church halls and went four at a time to a Red Lobster, split one dinner and filled up on bread-and-butter refills a waitress brought them. Standing in line at the bank to pick up the cashier's check to pay Ralph, while a customer in front of him argued about an overdraft, Edward Everett realized he had more in the bank now than he had earned for the entire season five years earlier in double-A ball.

Three mornings later, just after Connie turned the corner from the house, driving first Billy and then herself to school, Edward Everett met Ralph at her house and handed him the bank envelope holding the cashier's check. As he signed the paperwork for the job, a massive dump truck backed into Connie's drive and two workmen scampered up to the roof, where they began scraping the shingles off more quickly than Edward Everett could have imagined, pushing entire sections of shingles into the truck's bed.

He left them there, the workers trotting across the roof with as much certainty as he had jogging on flat ground, and went off to make his calls for the day. He'd scheduled appointments only until two that afternoon because he wanted to be at the house before Connie arrived; when he got there, the workers were using an electric nail gun to attach the ridge cap. Ralph was sitting in his pickup, smoking. "Wanna take a look?" he asked, and led Edward Everett up the ladder to survey the roof. It was beautiful, the tar at the seams glistening. Ralph stepped out onto the shingles, the ceramic grit crunching under his work boots. He crouched and ran a hand appreciatively over the work while Edward Everett stood on the ladder, reluctant to step out onto the roof in his good suit. "You and Con getting married?" Ralph asked.

"I don't know," Edward Everett said.

Above them, one of the workers was coiling the extension cord for the nail gun while the other swept nails and cut shingle fragments toward the roof edge.

"You gotta be a helluva lot better for her than Lloyd." Ralph turned to his workers. "We got time to get to the Chestnut job. It's small and the daylight will hold."

Then they were gone, the driveway and roof cleaner than when they had come. An hour and a half later, when Connie returned with Billy, they were both in a sour mood. Edward Everett was cleaning the house, vacuuming the living room carpet, when he saw Connie's Rambler pull into the drive and went outside to meet them.

"Ed? Is something wrong?" Connie said from the driver's seat.

"Everything's fine," he said, opening her door. Behind her, Billy stared glumly out the window for a moment, then unbuckled his seatbelt and went inside without a word.

"I was worried when I saw you here already."

"Nothing wrong," he said. "What..." He nodded toward the front door, which had just closed behind Billy.

"The fucking father from hell strikes again," Connie said, picking up her briefcase from the passenger seat and getting out. She gave Edward Everett a distracted kiss, all but missing his mouth. "It was Father's Day. They do it in May because the actual Father's Day... anyway, they have a lunch and a music program and an art exhibit. 'Drawings of My Dad.' Except the asshole..." She let out a muted scream.

Edward Everett glanced at the roof, wondering if he should call it to her attention now or wait until later, when she had vented her rage toward her ex-husband.

"He worked so hard on his drawing. He even had his grandpa bring him teensy pieces of coal so he could glue them to the paper so—" Then she peered past him, her glance upward. "What? Something looks—" She took a step toward the house, then took several steps backward, until she was standing in the street, her eyes narrowed.

"I got you a new roof," he said.

"A new—"

"The old one—Ralph said it's a wonder you didn't have leaks."

"But I can't afford to pay you back for this."

"It's a gift," he said.

"You shouldn't have done that," she said, shaking her head, her voice serious.

"I had the money."

"It's not right," she said.

"What if we were engaged?" he asked, surprised as the words came out of his mouth. He hadn't even considered the notion seriously to that point; at times, when they were all at a McDonald's, Billy blowing a straw wrapper toward his mother after he tore it off to drink his Coke; when they were standing shoulder to shoulder, watching drain cleaner pour into the kitchen sink to clear a clog—at times like that, a vision came to him of being a family, but he had never put the words together into a coherent sentence: engaged, married, father. Even as he said it, the thought nudged him: *it's too soon.*

But she said, "Engaged? Most men would just give a girl a ring; you gave me an engagement roof. The last of the red-hot romantics." Then they were standing at the edge of the street, kissing, while a Volkswagen Beetle swung out to the middle of the street so as to avoid them, giving them a feeble bleat of its horn.

The next evening, he took her to Pence's Jewelers in St. Martinsville to pick out a proper ring—a two-thirds-carat diamond in a shape the jeweler called a "marquise," seven hundred fifteen dollars, and, after he went back to pick it up after it had been sized, she cried when he slipped it onto her finger.

"Billy! Billy!" she called to her son, who was in his room, writing an essay about the Blessed Virgin. When he came out, she showed him the ring, clapping her hands in delight. "You're getting a new dad," she said, hugging him hard. As she let him go, Billy regarded Edward Everett shyly. "It's okay," she said. "You can go back and do your homework." After he was gone, Connie said, "He gets quiet when he gets excited. He will love you. He'll finally have a dad who isn't an A-number-one jerk-of-the-century."

Then she dashed out to the kitchen and began making phone calls. "You'll never guess what," she began each of them.

Two days later, when he went by his apartment to pick up his mail and begin packing to move permanently into Connie's house—what would be his house—he found an envelope addressed to him at his mother's and forwarded to his apartment. There was no return address, and a Chicago, Illinois, postmark. When he opened it, he found a blank sheet of typing paper folded around a Polaroid snapshot.

It was of a hospital nursery, shot through what was obviously the glass window in the hall that allowed visitors to view the newborn children. At the center of the picture was a crib that held one of the infants. Edward Everett couldn't make out many of the features: the baby wore a sky blue sleeper, his hands mittened, his head covered in a blue bonnet. Whoever had taken the picture had not thought about the effect the glass would have on the image because of the flash: in the upper left corner of the snapshot, a bright circle of light washed out part of the frame. The glass also captured a reflected ghost of the person taking the photo, a woman in a robe and nightgown, her face almost entirely obscured by the camera she held up to take the picture: Julie. There was no note save for, on the back of the photograph, the smeared word, "Boy," and the date, April 22, 1977.

It shocked him to realize that he hadn't thought of Julie in months. When he'd first gotten home from Montreal and was convalescing at his mother's house, he tried vainly to call her but the number he knew was not in service. One day, he dialed it four times, punching the buttons slowly, wondering if perhaps his fingers had pressed an incorrect number, but all he got was a series of tones and a recorded voice: "The number you have dialed is not a working number. If you feel you have reached this number in error . . ."

He tried to remember the name of the small town her parents lived in and got out a road atlas, turned to the state of Illinois and ran his eye down the list of cities and towns. Several times, his eye caught a name that he thought was correct, only to spot farther down the column another town he was equally certain was the one she'd told him she was from: Alton. No, Benton; something "-ton." No, maybe it wasn't "-ton," but "-ham": Chatham.

He thought he recalled she was from the southern half of the state, so he began running his eye across the map itself, but the disorganized array of names dotted along the interstates and county roads only made him all the more confused. He was no longer certain it had two syllables: Carlinville? Effingham? Carbondale?

Holding the photograph in his hand, he tried once more the number that had been hers, knowing it would not abruptly turn into her number once again. In the moment before he heard the series of tones and the recorded voice, he realized he was holding his breath: if it rang and she answered, his life would suddenly become very different than he expected, than he hoped. But it did not ring; he heard the tones, the recorded message.

He hung up and regarded the photograph again. He could not make out any feature of the baby with any clarity: it was someone who belonged to the category "baby" and he realized he should think in some profound way: *My son. I have a son,* but if there was a connection between him and the infant, maybe the geographic distance between them stretched their bond too thin to have any palpable effect on him. He slipped the photo into his wallet, then took it out again: how would he explain it to Connie the next time they were out and he went to pay for a restaurant check and she saw it:

What's that?

I have something I need to tell you.

Briefly, he thought about tearing it up or burning it, but it was a picture of his son after all, even though it appeared he might never see the boy or perhaps hear of him again. He slipped it into his pocket and, when he got out to the car, put it into the glove compartment, beneath the highway maps and the folder with the receipts from his oil changes and tire rotations, and drove to Connie's, where they were going to meet someone he planned to hire to replace the guttering. Slowly, he was rebuilding her house: next week, carpeting; the week after, a carpenter to replace the rotted boards in the porch. His bank account was dwindling but it did not concern him. Beginning in August, his uncle had told him, he was going to be dividing his territory, giving part to Edward Everett. He would earn close to three thousand a month, his uncle said, adding, "I've been wanting to slow down. In a few years, the entire thing will be yours."

When he reached Connie's house and she greeted him at the door, he thought for a moment of telling her about the baby. She saw the hesitation on his face.

"What?" she said. "Do you have some other surprise you're going to spring on me, beyond a new roof and an engagement out of the blue?"

A long while later—the first time he confessed to another soul that he had a son—he would remember that opportunity on her porch as an invitation to one kind of life he might have had, but instead became the moment in which a lie began weaving itself into his life. *I'll tell her sometime,* he thought, *just not now.*

"I'm just crazy about you, is all," he said.

Chapter Twelve

On the last Sunday of May, Edward Everett, Connie, Billy and Connie's father, Walter, drove to Pittsburgh to see the Pirates play the San Diego Padres. It was Billy's tenth birthday and he had never seen Major League Baseball before. First pitch was one-fifteen and the drive was an hour and a half but they left at eight-thirty because Billy was so anxious.

The morning was beautiful: the sky clear. In the thin strip of the West Virginia panhandle they had to cross between Ohio and Pennsylvania, they saw a half-dozen hot-air balloons drifting over the hills; one, decorated like a round American flag, was so low that they could make out the three people in its gondola, a woman and two men; the men wore tuxedos and top hats and the woman a dress that reminded Edward Everett of *Gone with the Wind.* Almost at the moment their car was alongside the balloon, a gust of wind caught one of the men's hats and it went sailing, end over end, skittering on the air currents, passing directly over them. Billy rolled down his window and unsnapped his seatbelt. "Hey," Connie said, thrusting an arm across the seat toward him. He poked his head out of the rear window and waved furiously at the people in the gondola, but they weren't looking at him and, when the car rounded a bend, the balloons were lost to their sight, save for the uppermost arc of one painted to promote an insurance agency.

"They were waving back," Billy said nonetheless, his face flushed as he refastened his seatbelt.

Connie gave Edward Everett a smile and squeezed his knee. "That's very nice, dear," she said.

When they reached Pittsburgh, the city was more alive than Edward Everett would have expected for a Sunday morning. Driving across the Monongahela River Bridge to the tip of Point State Park, they saw swarms of people throughout the grounds. Some sort of fair was going on: colorful booths, their fabric awnings flapping in the breeze; red, green and yellow pennants snapping. A Tilt-A-Whirl and a Ferris wheel, lit with blue and green fluorescent tubes, were already full of passengers, lines waiting at the turnstile entrance to each ride.

"This is all for your birthday," Walter said. "I think I see a banner saying, 'Happy Birthday, Billy Adams.' "

"Where?" Billy said. "Oh, you're kidding."

"We have time before the game, don't we?" Connie asked.

"Oh, only about three hours," Edward Everett said.

He got off the highway at the exit for the park and they snaked their way through heavy traffic, avoiding streams of pedestrians walking across the streets as if they had no concern about being hit, until they came to a parking lot where a fat teenage boy waved an orange flag indifferently, directing them into the lot.

"Three bucks," he said in a bored tone. Edward Everett gave him a five-dollar bill and then drove on without waiting for his change.

"Hey," the boy called, holding up the bill.

"Keep it," Edward Everett said, although he was certain the boy couldn't hear him.

"You're feeling particularly flush these days, aren't you?" Connie said.

"Maybe he needs new gutters," Edward Everett said.

When they parked, Billy wanted to run on ahead to the fairgrounds but Connie restrained him. "We're not going to drive a hundred miles just to lose you," she said, taking a firm grip on his hand. Still, he pulled her along, straining to get to the rides and booths. "If he yanks my arm out of the socket . . ." she said.

"You've got a spare," Walter said.

When they reached the fairgrounds, they learned that the festival was for Memorial Day. At a booth marked with a sign reading, "Ride and Refreshment Tickets," Edward Everett gave ten dollars to a girl for a long strip of cardboard tickets. Milling throughout the crowd, men in garrison caps and khaki vests decorated with badges and military medals were collecting donations for wounded veterans. Walter stopped to talk to one of them, a fifty-something redheaded man missing his left arm, the sleeve of his shirt pinned to his shoulder. When Walter finished his conversation, he took out his wallet, pulled a twenty-dollar bill from it, stuffed it into the can the man was using to collect donations and walked away, sunk in his thoughts.

"What is it, Dad?" Connie asked, linking her free arm with his, but he merely shook his head, and the three of them walked on a step or two ahead of Edward Everett, daughter and father, mother and son, until Billy caught sight of a waffle stand, and again yanked on his mother's hand, saying, "I'm hungry."

"You should have eaten breakfast," she said. "That's not exactly healthy."

"Ah, it's his birthday," Edward Everett said, leading them all up to the stand and buying Billy a waffle, which the vendor set onto a paper plate and coated with a cloud of powdered sugar. Billy wolfed it down as they walked on through the crowd toward the rides, his cheeks and chin coated with the sugar.

"Don't get sick," Connie warned.

As they reached the gate for the Tilt-A-Whirl, the carny was just closing the latch, ready to start the ride, but when he saw them he called, "Room for two more."

"Come on, Mom," Billy said.

"Do you mind us going without you?" Connie asked Edward Everett. When he shook his head, Connie collected two tickets from him, handed them over to the carny, and they boarded the ride. As the carny secured the safety bar across their laps, Billy bounced in his seat. Then the ride started, the motor rumbling and clanking as if it were about to throw a gear, black exhaust drifting out across the crowd. Edward Everett and Walter stepped back to be free of it and for a moment he lost sight of Connie and Billy, but then he found them, moving in a slow arc as the ride gathered speed, their car spinning on its pivot.

"You've been real good to Connie and the boy," Walter said to him.

"Connie's . . ." Edward Everett began but didn't know what to say.

"At first, I worried you was taking things too fast. She's been—well, Lloyd . . ." his voice trailed off and he shrugged. "You knew Lloyd back in school, didn't you?"

"I did," Edward Everett said.

"Lloyd ain't never going to grow up. Billy was—well, none of us expected it when Connie told her mother and me. But he's been, well, good can come from bad, my dad always used to say, and Billy's a lot of good."

They stood watching the ride spin for a while. Edward Everett wondered if Walter was waiting for him to compliment his daughter, praise his grandson, but before he could say anything, Walter went on. "That fellow I was talking to before, with one arm gone, said he lost it in Ardennes. That could've been me. Or worse. But I got strep throat just before the offensive and was laid up in a field hospital, an IV stuck in me." He laughed. "I guess that was my war wound. A little needle stick. Life's about chance and accident. That, and what you do with it."

"That makes sense," Edward Everett said. He thought of Montreal, his trying to catch the fly ball, his spikes caught in the fence. Then it occurred to him: Julie showing up while Estelle was in bed in his hotel room, the pill failing to stop whatever it was supposed to stop and, voilà, there was a baby in a hospital crib, photographed through glass.

"I guess it would, to you," Walter said. Connie and Billy were spinning past them now, their heads thrown back in laughter.

"How do you mean?"

"Your knee. A year ago, bet you never thought you'd be standing next to an old man talking nonsense the day before Memorial Day."

The ride was beginning to slow. Billy pushed hard against the side of the car he shared with his mother, trying to make it continue to spin, but he was not strong enough.

"You been good to them. I thought: engaged? How long you been going out?"

"Six—" Edward Everett was going to say *six weeks*. Could it have been so short?

"It don't matter. I haven't seen her so happy since before the day she came to tell us she was pregnant. The louse sat in the car at the curb, waiting to see if I'd shoot him. Which I mighta." Walter laughed and was still laughing when Connie and Billy came through the gate, stumbling and weaving from dizziness in the wake of the ride.

"What's funny?" Connie said, laying her hand on Edward Everett's arm for balance.

"You are," Walter said.

They wandered the fair for a while longer. Billy seemed determined to eat every variety of food they came across: a corn dog, an Eskimo Pie, cotton candy, and Edward Everett gladly paid for it all.

"You're staying awake with him tonight when he's throwing up the entire state of Pennsylvania," Connie said.

"Oh, he'll be fine," Edward Everett said.

"Little you know."

When it was nearly time to go back to their car to cross the Allegheny River for the ballpark, they came to a booth that featured a ball toss game: throw three baseballs at a pyramid of six milk bottles, knock them down and win a stuffed bear. Although Edward Everett was certain Billy considered himself too old for such a toy, the boy asked him to see if he could win one for him.

A lanky teenage boy was throwing at the bottles when they got to the booth, while a thin girl in pink eyeglasses and braces stood beside him, clasping her hands in hope. The boy's first throw sailed wide of the pyramid and smacked into the canvas draped behind the bottles. His second nicked the topmost bottle, which spun, tottered and then fell, leaving the other five bottles standing. His girlfriend gave his arm a squeeze. The boy took a breath, held the ball in front of his face, sighting toward the pyramid, and heaved it but it, too, was wide of the mark. The boy's shoulders slumped. "It's okay. It's okay," his girlfriend said, kissing his cheek. "I can't believe you tried. No one ever tried for me before."

The boy and girl turned to go but the carny called after them, "You got a prize here." He held up a shallow cardboard box filled with inexpensive plastic trinkets, shaking it. The boy nodded to the girl, who began fishing in it until she found a green plastic spider ring, which she slipped onto the fourth finger of her left hand and held it up for the boy to admire, as if it were a diamond instead of some silly toy.

When they left, Edward Everett stepped to the front and handed the carny two tickets, the cost for three balls, and the carny pointed toward a cardboard box of baseballs. It was a motley collection: the seams of some of the balls split, showing the wound cord beneath the horsehide cover. Edward Everett picked one up. Faded red letters promised it was a "Professional League Baseball," but the manufacturer had scrimped on the cover and the split in the seams showed clearly. He took a step back and hurled it toward the pyramid but he was no more accurate than the teenage boy before him: it hit the canvas backdrop a good three feet above the pyramid.

"Two mo'; two mo'," the carny said.

Edward Everett reached into the box and plucked out another ball but its condition was too poor, a flap of the cover loose, and so he dropped it and selected another one, a ball whose surface was so worn any words that might have been stamped on its face were long gone. He realized it had been months since he'd held a baseball, whereas his entire life to that point had centered on it. The ball seemed foreign, as if he had never seen anything like it before. He could feel the imperfections in it: the frayed threads of the seams, a gouge where it rested in the V of his index and middle finger. He took in a breath and let it fly. His aim was better and he hit almost precisely between the two bottles on the second row of the pyramid, but only the one on the right fell, along with the topmost bottle. The left bottle on the second row teetered but held. He threw another ball, catching the left bottle on the bottom row, sending it spinning away, but three bottles stood. He realized that they were weighted in such a way that even hitting them directly wouldn't mean that all six would fall.

The carny brought out the tray of trinkets. Edward Everett ignored it and handed him two more tickets. The trick, he realized, lay not so much in strength—not throwing the balls as hard as you could directly at the pyramid—but hitting them when they were unstable. He plucked three balls from the box, took one in his right hand and held two in the palm of his left, stepped back and, echoing a drill he'd learned when the team considered briefly turning him into an infielder, a drill in which he threw as many balls as he could through the center of a tire in thirty seconds, took a breath and then snapped the ball in his right hand toward the pyramid with a quick release, like a second baseman flicking the ball to first to catch a quick runner coming down the line, then fed the second ball to his right hand, snapped it almost instantly after releasing the first toward the pyramid, not waiting to see if he was successful at dislodging the bottles and then, almost instantly, flicked the third ball toward the pyramid. By the time it hit the bottles, four were down, only the center and left bottle on the bottom row standing, but they were wobbling when he threw at them, and so when the ball hit them dead-on, the center bottle toppled almost immediately, while the left tipped to the right, hesitated, and then clattered off the shelf.

"You play ball in high school or something?" the carny said.

"Actually," Walter started to say, but Edward Everett cut him off: "Yeah. In high school," he said.

The stuffed bear that Billy picked out was nearly as tall as he was but he insisted on carrying it to the car, nearly stumbling two or three times because he couldn't see the ground in front of him. Connie walked hand in hand with Edward Everett, giving his hand a squeeze. "It's not even noon yet," she said, "and it's his best birthday ever."

At the car, Edward Everett opened the trunk so Billy could lay the bear into it, but he wouldn't.

"He can't breathe in there," Billy said.

Edward Everett, Connie and Walter laughed but the bear rode in the backseat, between Billy and Walter, strapped into a seatbelt of his own.

Even stopping for the fair, they arrived at the ballpark before the gates opened, while the parking lot still had far more open spaces than cars. Billy worried that if he left his bear behind someone would steal it but Connie convinced him that the bear, whom he had already started calling Mr. B, would be safe on his own—although Billy rolled the rear windows down a fraction of an inch each so that Mr. B wouldn't suffocate.

All around the perimeter of the stadium, vendors sold boxes of popcorn, Cracker Jack, peanuts, as well as pennants, T-shirts and caps. Billy wanted everything: even on top of the ice cream, corn dog and sugar waffle he'd had, he wanted roasted peanuts and a large box of Cracker Jack, as well as a T-shirt and a pennant. Connie told him he could choose one souvenir and that they'd buy him a hot dog in the third inning, if he was hungry then. In the end, he settled on a St. Louis Cardinals T-shirt. "Because Ed played there," he said. Connie gave Edward Everett's hand an affectionate squeeze.

Their seats were good: in the third row behind the San Diego dugout, courtesy of Edward Everett's uncle. As they kept descending the steps, passing row after row, drawing nearer to the playing field, Billy repeated, "Wow. Wow. Wow."

Even before they reached their seats, however, Edward Everett knew it had been a mistake to come. Perhaps it was how near they were to the field or perhaps he would have felt the same if they were in the nosebleed section, which is where he had sat the only other time he came into a major league ballpark as a spectator. That had been almost twenty years earlier, when his father had taken him to a game in Cleveland to celebrate Edward Everett's birthday. Then, their seats were high in the upper deck down the left field line, part of their view blocked by an iron post, a third of left field obscured because their angle of vision didn't allow them to see the near corner; when someone hit a ball there, Edward Everett had no idea whether the fielder caught it or it fell in for a hit, except for the crowd's response.

Now, near enough to the field that he could see the acne scars on the cheek of one of the Padres' reserve catchers, near enough that he could hear the clatter of bats as players pulled them from the rack, the full effect of what had happened to him became clear. It was one thing when he settled into this life: putting on his tie, driving through the hills of southeastern Ohio, nodding sympathetically with bakery owners and restaurant GMs about the price of wheat and fuel, telling them about his ballplaying days. Then, the years he'd spent in the game had begun to seem like stories about an interesting person he once met, rather than a life he'd lived. In the new life, he'd never been a ballplayer: his life had always been flour and Connie and Billy and thinking about carpenters' bids and bathroom fixtures; had always been the chart of sales in the company newsletter and where he and his uncle stood: neck and neck with Jerry Remmer for salesman of the year.

Less than a year ago, however, when he'd been the age he still was, he'd been running in this very outfield, taking his hacks in BP in this very batting cage. Perhaps, he thought, he should have waited fifteen years before going to a game, when he would be old enough that he would have no chance of getting back in, a middle-aged man whose life by then truly would have swallowed up the years he had spent in the game so sufficiently that it would be as if his ballplaying self were his own ancestor.

Out on the field, one of the Padres' hitters taking batting practice sent a long fly ball to right. Standing halfway between the infield and the wall, a player who was so new that his number wasn't even in the scorecard Edward Everett had purchased dashed toward the warning track, seemingly almost before the hitter made contact. Lined above the wall, a cluster of fans extended gloves and held baseball caps upside down like small woolen baskets, eager for the souvenir. As he reached the warning track, the fielder slowed, stretching out his bare hand, feeling for the wall. Finding it, pushing his fingers into the vinyl-covered padding, he paused, crouched and leaped, snaring the ball just at the yellow line at the top of the wall and then tumbling to the ground. The fans there let out a selfish, disappointed groan but as the fielder scrambled to his feet, he—not looking—flipped the ball over his shoulder into the crowd, where it caught everyone off-guard and tipped off fingers and hands and seat backs, bounding away from all of them.

Edward Everett realized he was on his feet, that he had gotten to them at the moment he saw the fielder sprinting across the great grassy expanse after a ball that meant nothing except that the hitter was finding his stroke for the day, while the other fielders loitered in the outfield, joking among themselves, ignoring their teammate going back for the ball, as the fans finding their places in the boxes near Edward Everett were scanning the ballpark for beer vendors and peanut vendors, and women were wiping suntan lotion across their shoulders and arms, the air redolent of coconut, and boys were craning for autographs and souvenir baseballs, not caring who they were beseeching, *Hey, pitch, hey, pitch, throw me the ball, pitch*, and Connie was saying something in a low voice to Billy while her father was exclaiming, "You could touch them from here, we're that close," as the fielder dashed toward the wall (For what? Nothing in the world would live or die if he caught the ball or didn't catch it), his head turned to track the flight of the ball across a sky so bright it was difficult for Edward Everett to see the ball, although in his memory he knew what it would look like, the way the gray horsehide and the red seams would be spinning in a tight spiral as it descended on its way toward the end of its meaningless flight, caught by a player who, it would turn out, wouldn't even get into the game but would be up and down and up and down on the bench all day, crashing his palms together when one of his teammates hit a single or snatched a ground ball before it could skip into the outfield for a hit.

Two weeks later, without telling anyone, Edward Everett went to the tryout camp.

Chapter Thirteen

By nine in the morning, the field for the tryout was cluttered with players tossing baseballs back and forth, well
more than a hundred balls arcing across the blue sky. Edward Everett
was playing catch with a kid who appeared to be seventeen or eighteen, a skinny blond-haired boy who wore a cheap souvenir Cleveland Indians batting helmet perched on his head. He had little
ability: his throws sometimes sailed over Edward Everett's head,
sometimes bounced three-quarters of the way to him. One caught
another player on the ankle, sending him to the turf in pain. "Sorry;
sorry," the kid said. Once, chasing another errant throw, Edward
Everett noticed two of the scouts—a short, burly man in his sixties
with a crew cut, and a trim younger man with curly hair—pointing
in his direction, the younger man making a note on a clipboard.

Everywhere was a mix of the talented and the inept. Perhaps
twenty yards from Edward Everett and the blond-headed kid, two
players in Ohio University jerseys played catch and even in the cacophony of balls smacking leather, Edward Everett could hear the
sizzle of their throws. Near them, two stocky men who might have
been in their thirties made lollipop tosses, dropping more balls than
they caught.

Finally, the burly coach called for the players to stop warming, directing them to line up against the outfield wall. Edward Everett tried to move away from the blond boy but he stuck to him like a lost puppy, following him so closely that several times he kicked the heels of Edward Everett's cleats.

"You been to one of these before?" he asked when they reached the outfield wall and were waiting for whatever came next.

"No," Edward Everett said, not really wanting to talk to the kid. He had bad breath, smelling of cigarettes and garlic, and was missing his left upper canine.

What he said was not precisely true. When he was the kid's age, he'd been invited to a scouting combine workout at Crosley Field in Cincinnati: Edward Everett and seventy-five other ballplayers throwing, fielding and hitting while scouts from a dozen teams clicked stopwatches and made notes on index cards in advance of the professional draft. They were all talented, all of them all-state, all-American, all-everything and they were all going to be drafted—the only question was by whom and how high.

Edward Everett had done well. At one point, he was in the cage, taking his ten swings. When he finished—everything off his bat a line drive—one of the scouts asked him if he'd stay in for another twenty pitches. "It's no fair," the next hitter complained. He was a squat catcher from Nebraska who couldn't hit much—his defense and arm were his strengths—but Edward Everett got back into the cage. The scout waved off the bullpen coach who'd been doing the pitching and replaced him with a right-hander from the Reds who had just come off the disabled list and had been doing some throwing on the side; he'd gone after Edward Everett as if he were in a crucial spot in a game. The first pitch came up and in at Edward Everett, who ducked back to keep from getting hit. The second was down and away, but Edward Everett was expecting it: up-and-in followed by down-and-away was part of the baseball dance men had been doing for a century, and he stepped into it and drove it to center field. Sliders, curveballs, changeups, tailing fastballs: Edward Everett hit nearly all of them; the next to last, a curve that held up in the strike zone, he sent over the screen above the left field wall.

When he finished, he was drenched in sweat, his arms shaking from so many consecutive swings. He looked to the scout, who just went back to making tiny symbols on his clipboard. "Asshole," the catcher from Nebraska said, stepping into the box.

It was enough to get the Cardinals to take him in the fourth round, whereas before he might have gone later in the draft; enough that he got a three-thousand-dollar bonus just to sign the contract— enough that he drove to his high school graduation in a new Thunderbird two-door hardtop in Green Fire.

"I told my mom I'd buy her a house if I got signed," the kid in the souvenir helmet said. Edward Everett looked closely at him to see if he was serious. He really was a boy, Edward Everett realized and felt sorry for him: to be so clueless as to think he had a chance for a contract.

"What we gonna do next?" another player asked. He was short, his belly hung over his belt and he hadn't shaved in two or three days.

"We run and then do fielding drills," one of the players in an Ohio University jersey said. Close-up, Edward Everett could see that he and the other player from Ohio University were identical twins; the only marked difference was that one had a scar that ran from his chin up toward the left corner of his mouth. "We were at Riverfront day before yesterday with the Reds and I think they run these things pretty much alike."

"What about hitting?" asked the unshaven player. He mimed swinging at a pitch, but the motion seemed more like someone chopping weeds than swinging at a baseball.

"They make a first cut after the running and the fielding and then the ones they still want to look at get to hit," said the twin with the scar.

"Oh, man," a player in what was clearly a brand-new Indians souvenir hat said. "I can't field worth crap but I can hit the hell out of a baseball."

"All right, all right," the stocky coach called out, clapping a hand against the back of his clipboard to get their attention. "We're gonna do some running. Everybody but the pitchers. You pitchers head on over to the home bullpen to do some throwing. Everyone else line up by number."

Perhaps a third of the players trooped to the right field bullpen and, as the rest lined up, Edward Everett tried to appraise them. Number thirty-two was a grossly overweight man who might be in his thirties, his Stroh's T-shirt taut across his torso. Number forty was nearly seven feet, with long arms that dangled loosely from his shoulders; he had a nervous tic, his hands constantly in motion, tugging at his hair, scratching his ears. Number twenty-two was, Edward Everett realized with surprise, middle-aged. When he took off his frayed Indians hat to wipe his brow, his curly hair was thin and graying. Putting it back on, he gave Edward Everett a grin.

"I'm forty-six," he said, winking.

"But—"

"They aren't going to sign me," he said, laughing. "But how could I pass up a chance to come out here?" He touched the padded wall beside them tenderly. "I called in sick." He held up his palms alongside each other, imitating a balance scale: Left hand higher: "Sit at my desk, listening to an asshole from Toledo bitch about a broken office chair." Right hand higher. "Come to the ballpark where Bob Lemon and Lou Boudreau played." He dropped his hands. "Easy peasy." He pulled a sheet of paper out of his jeans pocket and unfolded it. It was the same information letter the team had sent to Edward Everett when he called about the tryout; the only difference was the name and address. "I'm going to frame this. Tell my grandkids I had a tryout with the Indians."

Edward Everett understood then that the team had handed out invitations to anyone who asked, the day as much a public relations gimmick as a search for players for the organization, and he wondered how many others had come down as if it were an amusement park. Instead of roller coasters and Ferris wheels, there was a romp in the outfield grass. The customer service clerk. The fat guy in the Stroh's shirt. The kid in the cracked souvenir helmet. It made him angry: so much wasted time for people on a lark.

When it was his turn to run, he lined up beside the customer service clerk.

"You could use a sundial to time me," the clerk shouted to the two scouts at the finish line holding stopwatches. He pounded his chest, coughing. "Two packs a day."

"Ready," said the scout beside them. "Go."

Edward Everett was off at the word. He had babied his knee in his training runs, not so much worrying that it would fail but expecting it, thinking with each step, *Is this the moment? Is this the moment?* As he ran across the outfield grass in Cleveland Stadium, it struck him that he despised his knee. *Fuck you*, he thought. *Go ahead and give way.* Once, when he was eight and his father was hitting ground balls to him at the Little League field, teaching him to play, a ball hit a pebble in front of him and bounced up, driving his lip back against his teeth, drawing blood. Edward Everett fell to the ground, curling up. "Little baby," his father taunted, then hit another ground ball toward him, and it slammed against his stomach. Edward Everett staggered to his feet and his father hit another ground ball toward him; he snagged it and hurled it back at his father in a rage, surprising his father, who threw his hand up, blocking his face, and the ball ticked off the tip of his middle finger, tearing the nail partway off. He thought his father would punish him, but he merely sucked on his finger and gave him a wink, as if Edward Everett had learned something.

That same rage, he felt for his knee. *Fail*, he thought, dashing toward the finish line, his left foot finding a small crease in the ground, his right a clod of dirt, his left a slick spot, his right another crease. *Fail, fail, fail.* From behind him, he could hear the customer service clerk gasping, but on he ran, waiting for the instant when the ligament in his knee would tear, once and for all, but it held, and he raced past the finish line, dimly aware of the scout clicking the stopwatch and muttering something to the scout beside him, making notes on a clipboard.

"Man. You was. Fast," the customer service clerk said, wheezing, doubled over, hands on his knees. "It was like. You was being chased. By a man. With a gun." He let out another wheeze. "If I die. Tell my kids. I love them."

Then there was nothing to do but wait for the other players to finish their runs. He sat in the box seats behind the home bullpen, where the pitchers were throwing, two at a time, side by side. Throughout the box seats, families of some of the players had turned the day into a picnic. They had brought baskets of food, small coolers of Coke and Tab. Not far from where he was, a middle-aged couple sat behind a kid, obviously their son, the mother squeezing his shoulder as he sat with his head bowed, the father with his head turned aside, tapping an index finger alongside his nose in a show of disappointment.

Out on the field, when it came time for the kid in the cracked souvenir helmet, Edward Everett leaned forward to watch. He found himself hoping that the kid was better than he'd seemed. But almost as soon as the scout shouted, "Go," it was evident he had no talent. He slipped on his first step and as he ran seemed to be off balance the entire way, a grim look on his face, his plastic helmet bobbing on the top of his head. He reached up to hold it in place, his free arm pumping jerkily. The player running alongside him—maybe twenty, at the camp in a Youngstown State University jersey—raced past him. As the kid in the cracked helmet finished, he made his way toward Edward Everett and plopped down in a seat in the row in front of him.

"I coulda done better," he said. "I run a lot at home." He fished into the front pocket of his jeans and came up with a crumpled pack of Kool cigarettes, pulling one out.

"I don't know if that's a good idea," Edward Everett said.

The kid gave Edward Everett a cockeyed grin and stuffed the pack back into his jeans. "Not a good impression," he said.

"No," Edward Everett said, and pretended to watch the next pair of runners with keen interest. One of them was the seven-foot player. He was awkward, loping more than running, taking long, heavy strides across the outfield grass.

"I'd give anything to be that tall," the kid said. Although Edward Everett did not prompt him, he went on. "Shrimp. Punk. Tyke." He shook his head.

"I'm going to find something to drink," Edward Everett said. He pushed himself out of his seat and made his way up the aisle toward the concourse at the top of the steps. There, he found quite a few of the players cooling themselves in the shade of the roof, some lounging against the wall, drinking and smoking cigarettes. A couple, including the overweight man in the Stroh's T-shirt, shared a can of beer, passing it back and forth.

"It's warm," the man in the Stroh's shirt said, holding the can up, offering it. "We found it stashed in a stall of the men's." Edward Everett shook his head and moved away, not wanting anyone to associate him with their cavalier attitude: he had risked too much to have the scouts discount him because they thought he was there on a whim. He wandered up the ramp. At an outside wall, he stopped, looking down toward Lake Erie. He had once heard that people called Cleveland Stadium "the mistake by the lake," and from here it was evident why. The stench was nearly overwhelming. What was it? Dying fish? Dying fish mixed with decaying detergents that someone had dumped into the lake?

He walked on, past the doors to the press boxes on the mezzanine level. One was open and, looking around to see if anyone would stop him, he stepped inside. In it, two tables were bolted to the carpeted floor, fiberglass chairs sitting in front of banks of typewriters. Although the Indians had last played at home two or three days ago, the press box was cluttered with trash. In a paper cup of what was now flat Coke, someone had dropped a cigarette, the paper dissolving, tobacco flecks floating on the surface.

He sat in a chair, looking at the stadium below him. In the outfield, players continued to do their sprints. The pair out there now was as mismatched as Edward Everett and the customer service clerk: a rotund player who was more walking than running, his arms oddly stiff at his sides, while fifteen yards ahead, a slender Asian kid dashed toward the finish line.

On the table in front of Edward Everett, a sportswriter had left a piece of yellow second sheet in the typewriter platen, three words typed on it and then abandoned as if he was spirited away mid-sentence: "better suited to." Beside the typewriter lay a mimeographed sheaf of pages from the media relations office, most of it columns of statistics for the Indians and the Detroit Tigers. Edward Everett flipped through it. At the bottom of the statistics for the Tigers was a player with a line that must have looked like his own to sportswriters last summer: a second baseman with whom Edward Everett had once played in A ball at Danville, a baby-faced kid from Oregon who bellowed top-40 hits while he took fielding practice, the kind of player clubhouse attendants sometimes tried to chase off as if he were trying to sneak in to collect autographs. And now he was in the major leagues, his cheerfulness and love for the game condensed to a single typed line, a single at-bat.

Down on the field, the final runner was at the starting line for his dash. Edward Everett could see most of the other players scattered throughout the grandstand, some there on a lark but others there to get a chance to have their own line on a mimeographed sheet in a press box somewhere. Hoppel had said he was one-in-ten for getting as far as he had; most of the men down on the field would say they'd be satisfied with that: a chance to step to the plate just one time in Pittsburgh or Kansas City in a uniform, under the lights, in front of twenty thousand fans. They were wrong, he thought. Nothing would ever be enough. If he played five years, he'd want six. If he made it ten, he'd want fifteen.

He thought about Connie and his uncle and how he had deceived them. He had told them he was going to Cleveland but, to each, he had told a different lie—Connie that he was going to a trade show; his uncle, that he and Connie were taking a short vacation. The previous night, before he had gone to sleep, he had called Connie to say good night.

"I miss you," she had said. "Two months ago, we weren't even in each other's lives and now I'm sitting here on the bed, thinking how it's going to be empty tonight."

He had almost told her the truth then, struck with remorse. Sitting in the press box, he thought of her. It was the last week of school and she would be in her classroom, having a party, cookies and Kool-Aid they'd bought with their own groceries. In part to assuage the guilt he felt because he was withholding from her the information that he was going to the tryout camp, that the life they had discussed might not happen, he'd taken her to a Waldenbooks in Wheeling to buy paperback classic novels that she could pass out to her students to encourage summer reading. "It's too much," she'd said when he wrote the check, nearly a hundred dollars, as a clerk stacked cartons of Dickens, Austen and Hugo onto a hand truck to wheel out to his car.

"I'm just trying to help you encourage your students to be better," he replied. In the press box, he imagined her in her classroom, her students lined up at her desk as she handed each a book when they filed past. She really was a good woman, he thought: most of the students would never open the books, he knew, spending their summers working at the Tastee Freez or the new McDonald's in St. Martinsville, drinking illegal beer, having sex by the reservoir. The notion struck him: he should pack it in, walk away from the tryout camp, drive back, take up the life into which he had only begun to settle, sell flour, become wealthy like his uncle, marry Connie, be a good father to her son. It would be, he thought, a kind of retribution for the fact that his own son, wherever he was, would not have a father; would, at least, not have him as his father.

He stood, stretched, started to walk down to the field. There was a slight hitch in his knee. It didn't hurt, but there was a pop and stiffness. He shouldn't have sat down; he should have kept moving. As he walked along the concourse, looking out over the lake, it struck him that, if he could see to the other side of the water, it was Canada—another country, where he had been eleven months earlier. He saw himself crossing into it that first time, waiting in the long line at customs while the officials methodically searched the team's carry-on bags. He was naïve then, he realized, thinking he was at the start of everything, the road of his life mapped out like one of the AAA TripTiks his mother ordered before a vacation, the path drawn out in dark black arrows pointing in one direction, page after page of the spiral-bound TripTik, leading inevitably to where he planned to end up. He felt a little sorry for the confident self he had been then. That younger him hadn't seen that the TripTik hadn't taken into account the detour that lay ahead.

From out on the field, he could hear one of the scouts speaking in a loud voice. He couldn't make out what he was saying but he knew it was time for everyone to go back down to the field. For another moment, he hesitated. If he left then, he could be at Connie's house by the time she and Billy got home from school.

Oh, I wasn't expecting you so soon.

One day with flour salesmen was enough.

He'd take them out for dinner; there was a new putt-putt golf course to which he had promised he'd take Billy and where he intended to let him win.

Out on the field, the players were warming up again, loosening their arms before the fielding drills. He could hear the slap of so many balls hitting so many gloves, a rapid *pop pop pop*, and he began walking down toward it. He realized the stiffness in his knee was passing. Indeed, it may be gone altogether and what he was feeling was just the memory of it. He went back to where he'd been sitting in the stands, picked up his glove: should he stay or should he go? Slipping the glove on, working his fingers into it, he realized he had forgotten how much he once had the sense that it was an extension of himself; not a piece of leather tied up with cowhide that he wore, but part of himself.

He walked the rest of the way toward the field, passing from the shadow over the grandstand and out into full sun. The sky was blue and opportunity beckoned.

Part III

2009

Chapter Fourteen

On the fourth day of the rain that April, a week after his wife, Renee, left him, Edward Everett discovered water in his basement—a half-dozen rivulets slinking across the concrete from the wall, toward the drain near the water heater. In the ten years he had been in Perabo City, Iowa, he had never had water there before; while his neighbors carried damp boxes of mildewed clothes and books to the curb after heavy spring rains, his basement had stayed dry. That year, however, his luck ran out.

He was waiting for Renee to bring their dog by; although he had given the Pomeranian to her as a gift, she'd said that what she called her "new circumstances" didn't allow her to have a dog. He had no idea what her "new circumstances" were, and when he asked her about them during their phone conversation the day before, she only replied, "I'll have Grizzly there when I get a break at the office." Then she hung up.

He had discovered the water when he'd gotten distracted while cleaning the house for her visit; his mind wandering as he carried stacks of *The Sporting News* and *Baseball America* to the recycling bin in the corner of the sunporch, he found himself trying to remember the name of a left-handed reliever who had pitched for him a dozen years ago, when he was managing at Quincy, and had gone down to the basement to search the boxes where he'd stored his scorebooks and game log cards. There, he made two discoveries. One, the water: soaking a mound of bags into which he'd folded clothing he'd collected from his mother's house when she died; soaking the bags of his father's clothing she had shipped to him years earlier; soaking boxes of canceled checks, photographs; soaking the cardboard boxes in which he kept his handwritten records of every kid who'd ever played for him in the twenty years he'd been managing in the minor leagues.

The second thing he discovered was more disconcerting: the reliever he remembered clearly—a bulldog of a kid from South Dakota who lost two fingers on his right hand fooling around with a lawn mower when he was six—hadn't pitched for him at Quincy. Nor, he found after pulling out game logs from several seasons, had he pitched for Missoula or Limon, but Cumberland—and it hadn't been a dozen years ago, but twenty . . . and when he recognized the name, Gabe Bullard, he realized he had all of his fingers intact. Who'd had the mangled hand? Had anyone?

Looking further into the boxes, he found that his mind had also invented players who apparently hadn't existed. He remembered, for example, an alcoholic, redheaded third baseman named Jamie Fagan who sang with a band in bars after weekend home games, but when he read through every roster he had, there was no Fagan—although he held a clear image of him standing unsteadily on a stage, backed by a guitar and drums, growling out "Born to Run." Besides Fagan, he recalled a player named Al Reinbach, who had (in his memory) hit for the cycle with a broken arm the team doctor found after the game—although there was no one by that name in any of his records. Where had they come from, these players who didn't exist but who were more vivid than the actual players whose index cards were soaking with rainwater?

Although he realized it would ruin the effect he was trying to create for Renee—that he was fine without her and therefore, paradoxically, convince her she had been wrong to leave—he nonetheless brought the boxes upstairs, to see what, if anything, he could salvage of the records that measured out his professional life, and stacked them in the living room and began taking the damp cards out of the more heavily damaged boxes, laying them to dry across his couch and kitchen table. While the rain fell, sometimes turning to hail that banged against his roof, he read the cards: dates, times at bat, hits and errors for players who'd been out of the game for as many as twenty years—some after major league careers much longer than his own; some dead: car accidents, cancer, one of a heart attack while he sat in a school auditorium, watching his six-year-old daughter sing Christmas carols, dressed as an angel.

In the afternoon, when it became apparent there would, for the second day in a row, be no game that evening, his pitching coach, Biggie Vincent, came by to pay him a hundred dollars toward the thousand Edward Everett had loaned him when his girlfriend needed a root canal. During the off-season, Vincent worked in a waterproofing business with his girlfriend's brother and, standing on the porch, not wanting to come in since he would drip all over the floor, he said, "You got a problem here, Skip." He pointed to the front of the house; when Edward Everett poked his head out, he saw a waterfall coursing out of the gutters. "You gotta clean them," Vincent said. "That's bad for the foundation. Water gets in the soil and ends up in the basement. And it ain't pretty what happens."

After Vincent left, Edward Everett went outside as the rain fell, crouching at the foundation, the water rolling out of his gutters soaking his hair and jacket. He poked a finger into the ground as if it would let him measure the water beneath the dirt that he worried was ruining his home. He imagined the walls bowing in, eventually giving way.

When the rain abated, he hauled a stepladder out of the detached garage, climbed to the roof of his sunporch, dragged the ladder up behind him and, from the flat roof of the porch, climbed to the roof over the house. It was foolish, he knew. The ladder was old; the screws that held the spreaders and brackets in place were no longer tight. It wobbled with each step and when he went to pull himself onto the main roof, he had to climb onto the head step, despite the sticker warning him not to, brace himself by gripping the gutter and, trusting that the ladder would not collapse, scramble up.

On the roof, he had a dizzy moment and sat down on the damp shingles to keep from falling, waiting until his head stopped buzzing, wondering what his neighbors would think if they saw him up there: *Crazy coot.* He remembered being on a roof years before—what was it, twenty? No, it had to be more. Thirty, thirty-five? Not his roof—that of a woman he was going to marry but didn't and, in fact, hadn't thought of in so long it took a bit for her name to push to the surface. Connie. *It must be the rain and nothing to do,* he thought, *opening up my memory like this: former players, former loves.*

His head clear, he stood and did what he should have done last year and so many years before that: clean the leaves and debris out of his gutters. As the trees in his yard spattered him with drops, sometimes so frequently it seemed the rain had started up again, he crawled along the edge, digging into the muck and tossing globs of matted leaves and mud onto the lawn. When he pulled his hand out of the gutter, it reeked as if he had plunged it into the sewer. By the time he finished, his khaki work pants were torn, his knees scratched and bleeding, and rain had started again—only a drizzle at first, but enough that when he stepped onto the slick head step of the ladder, his foot slipped. He managed to catch his left foot on the third step down but the near fall caused him to shake so much that when he lowered the ladder to the ground, he accidentally dropped it sideways into an azalea, leaving him stranded.

He considered jumping down but, before he could, a red Prius pulled to the curb and parked. The driver poked an oversized Mid-Iowa Bank golf umbrella out into the increasing rainfall and proceeded up the front walk toward his house. The person stopped at the ladder and tilted the umbrella back, looking up toward the roof. At first he didn't recognize her: a well-dressed woman in a navy pantsuit and a belted, beige raincoat, her loosely curled blond hair falling just short of her collar.

"What are you doing?" she asked. It was, he realized, Renee; Renee with her dark hair dyed, curled and shorter than he had ever seen it; Renee dressed more formally than he could remember, save for when they had gone to a wedding or a funeral; Renee driving a car that cost perhaps half of what he earned in a year.

He tried to think of a joke but none came to him. "The gutters—" he said.

She clucked her tongue. "Ed, you're almost sixty. You're supposed to hire people to do that sort of thing." Trying to keep her umbrella over herself, she attempted to turn the ladder upright but the wind yanked her umbrella out of her grasp, knocking her off balance. She sat down hard in the midst of a puddle. "Drat it," she said in a voice more annoyed than angry. Standing, she fetched her umbrella and set the ladder upright.

"Don't you fall," she said, steadying the ladder as he stepped onto it, the ladder quaking, its rear left leg sinking into the wet ground, tilting the ladder to one side. Renee laid her hand against his lower back to support him as he descended.

"That was not your brightest decision," she said when he was on the ground. He picked up the ladder, yanking it free from the mud but leaving behind one of the swivel feet when a rivet popped. Rather than carrying it all the way to the garage, he folded it and left it leaning against the side of the house, hidden by two yews. With some satisfaction, he looked at the gutters; rain was no longer spilling over the lip. Maybe water would stop running into his basement; maybe the house wouldn't collapse after all.

"Let me go get Grizzly," she said. She went back down the walk, opened the passenger door on the Prius; the dog hopped out and trotted toward the house.

"It's a nice car," Edward Everett said.

"Look, can we just go inside?" she said in a way that made him wonder if his observation embarrassed her. "I'm drenched." Indeed she was; her clearly expensive slacks were soaked, as was her raincoat. Her hair was matted, water dripping down her face.

"I'm sorry." He opened the door and stepped back so she could precede him inside after propping her open umbrella on the porch to dry. Grizzly trotted in before both of them, leaving swatches of mud on the hardwood floor and area rug in the living room.

"Grizzly," Renee snapped as the dog began shaking himself, sending a shower of brown water over everything.

"It doesn't make a difference," he said, regretting letting her inside even given her condition and the weather. Despite his hours of cleaning, the boxes of player records made the house seem even more cluttered than when she had moved out; the cards he'd foolishly spread across the couch had left a dark stain. He scooped up some as an invitation to sit, disappointed that she would never know the effort he had made to get ready for her.

She laughed at his invitation. "I can't sit. Not like this." She turned, lifting the hem of her coat so that he could see the wet seat of her slacks.

"It wouldn't matter," he said, nodding toward the ruined couch.

"Oh, that poor thing." Renee shook her head. "It's not even six months old."

"I'm sure we could get it cleaned," he said.

Renee winced, narrowing her eyes, her meaning clear: *There is no we.* "I didn't expect you to be here when I came," she said. "I thought I'd just stick Grizzly in the kitchen, leave a note, and you'd find him when you got home."

"There's no game today," he said.

"Rain never stopped you from going to the ballpark before. 'Neither rain nor snow nor' something something something 'will keep this manager from his appointed rounds.' Or however that little joke used to go."

"I stayed home on some rain days," he said, attempting to not let his defensiveness show in his voice.

She sighed. "This is why I wanted to come when you weren't here. I want this to be as easy as possible."

Easy for whom? he thought.

"For both of us," she said, as though she knew what he'd been thinking. "Please, can we just not get into anything?"

From the kitchen, he could hear Grizzly shoving his plastic dog bowl around, his signal that he was hungry.

"You'd better feed him before he tears the house down," Renee said, snapping open her purse and taking out an envelope. "Here," she said, holding it out to him. When he didn't take it immediately, she gestured that he should.

"Doesn't the sheriff usually serve these?" he asked, still not taking the envelope.

"Serve?"

"Divorce papers."

She let out a small laugh. "These aren't the divorce papers." She pushed the envelope toward him. When he opened it, he saw it contained a photocopy of a signed, notarized quitclaim, removing her name from the deed to the house, dated two or three days before he had left on a ten-day swing through Wisconsin and Illinois, the road trip from which he returned to find her gone—dated, he realized, while they were still living in the same house; already filed while she was making his favorite dinner the day before he departed for the road trip, her mother's ziti recipe. Already filed when, in bed later, he had stroked her hip, for years a signal that he wanted to make love, and she had said quietly, "I think the dinner upset my stomach," before turning over and going to sleep.

"The house was yours before we got married," she said. "It was generous for you to put my name on it but now it's yours again."

"Where are you staying?" He refolded the form and slipped it into the envelope.

She narrowed her eyes, suggesting he had crossed a line he hadn't known was there, then said, "If you look at our savings, you'll see I withdrew what I figure I put in. If you think I'm off, let me know and I'll take another look. If I made a mistake, I'll reimburse you." She laced her forearm through the strap on her purse and pointed to the living room. "You were cleaning the house, weren't you?"

"How can you tell?"

She pointed to the floor beside the overstuffed chair. "The ten years or whatever of *The Sporting News* and whatnot. They're gone."

He flushed. "I was trying—" he said, intending to explain about the water in the basement and his wanting to salvage the records of his former players.

"That was sweet," she said. "But I'm not coming back. It's not like last time."

"I still have no idea why you left," he said.

She sighed. "Looking in the rearview mirror makes it difficult to see the road before us," she said. It sounded like something she had read in one of her self-help books. He saw her taking out the yellow marker she sometimes used, drawing a decisive line through the passage. She turned the doorknob to let herself out but then paused. "My dad—please don't bring him into this," she said. When he didn't respond, she said, "Please?"

"All right," he said.

Then she was out the door, raising her umbrella, and down the walk toward her car. He watched her through the window to see if she turned back, showed a glimmer of regret. She didn't; she went to the car, opened the door, closed her umbrella and got in. After waiting a moment to let a passing FedEx van go by, she pulled from the curb and was off, down the street.

In the kitchen, Grizzly was licking the food bowl, although it was totally clean.

"Mom's gone," Edward Everett said, immediately realizing how pathetic he sounded. "Come on, boy." He scratched the dog behind his ear as a gentle means of distracting his attention from the bowl. He had once made the mistake of plucking it off the floor when the dog was licking it and Grizzly snapped at him. Now, when the dog lifted his head from the bowl, Edward Everett picked it up, set it onto the counter and opened the cupboard, looking for the bag of dog food. He located it, squashed under two cans of chili without beans. There was less than a quarter of a cup left, much of it only powder. He poured it into the bowl and set it back on the floor before filling the water dish.

Edward Everett had bought the dog for Renee when they'd been married for four months, just before his first road trip after their wedding. In the days before he was supposed to leave, she became increasingly quiet and he knew it was because she dreaded his being gone, didn't want to come home to an empty house after working at the bank all day. "Your folks are next door," he said.

"Oh, so I should be the little girl running home to Mommy and Daddy because I get lonely?" she snapped.

On the morning he was supposed to leave, he woke her early although she didn't need to get up for work for another two and a half hours. "I thought you could make me some coffee," he said, nudging her shoulder with his empty thermos.

"You want me to get out of bed at"—she squinted at the clock on her bedside table—"three fifty-eight? To make you coffee?"

"Is that unreasonable?" he'd asked.

She'd sat up, pushed the blankets to the foot of the bed, plucked her glasses off the bedside table and gone out to the kitchen. When he heard her banging cupboard doors, he'd gone to the garage to get the puppy he'd bought the night before and left there, a quaking ball of fur no bigger than his fist, bedded down on two towels he'd laid in a cardboard box. He hadn't counted on the towels being soaked with urine, three tiny turds the size of little smokie sausages scattered in the box, or that there'd be feces stuck to the dog's fur. By the time he got the dog cleaned up and wrapped in yet another towel, Renee was already back in bed, the coffeemaker hissing. He'd taken the dog and sat on the side of the bed but she lay there with her back to him, clearly fuming.

"Renee," he said.

"Maybe by the time you get back, I'll be speaking to you again."

He laid the dog against her neck, where it tried to nestle against her for the body heat. Renee swatted at it.

"No. Just go."

The dog whimpered and Renee turned over. Edward Everett snatched it away so she wouldn't roll over onto it.

"Don't kill it," he said. "It's not the dog's fault that your husband is a jerk who asks you to make coffee at three fifty-eight."

"What dog?" she said, sitting up. He held it out to her. "You bought me a dog?" she said, taking it and pressing her nose against the dog's.

For some reason, however, the dog didn't understand that he was Renee's, or that Edward Everett, in fact, didn't like dogs. When Edward Everett was home, Grizzly followed him from room to room. When he sat at the kitchen table, writing up the reports he sent to the big club, the dog lay at his feet. At night, he wanted to sleep at the foot of the bed on Edward Everett's side. When he and Renee made love, they had to close the dog in the kitchen with a baby gate because, in the same room with them, he pawed furiously at the box spring. In the kitchen, he would whine and bark the entire time. "I swear he's your father's agent," Edward Everett once said when they sat in the kitchen, having eggs at midnight. "It's not enough that your father is next door, thinking, 'What's he doing to my little girl?' He has to have the dog spy on me, too."

Cracking an egg into a bowl, she'd laughed. "Daddy's girl is past forty, been married once before and lived in sin twice. He doesn't give us a thought."

Now the dog finished his meager dinner quickly and began pushing the dish across the floor, lapping at it furiously, obviously still hungry. "Sorry," Edward Everett said. "I guess I'm a lousy husband and a lousy dog owner." Grizzly looked up at him, his face seeming to express a canine disappointment that mirrored, in a way, Renee's, cocking his head to one side and blinking at him slowly.

Later that evening, Edward Everett went out to the grocery store to buy dog food, a dozen roses wrapped in cellophane and a card he addressed to Renee, writing inside it simply ☹. The previous time she left him, not long after last Thanksgiving, he had courted her to win her back, tucking flowers under her windshield wiper at work, bringing chocolate to her office, emailing articles he found online that he thought she would find interesting. A few days before Christmas, she agreed to meet him for dinner. "But only dinner," she had said. "We'll take it slow." Dinner had ended with them in bed. "You laid successful siege at the gates to my heart," she said in a drowsy voice just before she fell to sleep. Perhaps that was what she needed again: his attention, when he hadn't been giving it to her, preoccupied as he became in-season.

He waited until the Duboises' house next door was dark, then carried the roses between the two backyards, creeping up the steps to the deck, and leaned the bouquet against their door. As he placed it, the wrapper crinkled and he froze, wondering if anyone had heard. A possum rustled leaves in one of Renee's mother's flower beds. In the distance, a car with a broken muffler accelerated. But nothing in the house stirred.

Chapter Fifteen

The next morning, Edward Everett as usual got to the ball-park before anyone else, seven-forty, long before his two coaches or the trainer or clubhouse assistant would appear.

As he let himself in and entered the code to disarm the security system, he nearly stumbled over a pallet of unopened boxes marked "Programs." They had been delivered since the last time he'd been there and were already out of date, he knew, more than four weeks late, one of the consequences of the team owner Bob Collier's budget-cutting—acting as his own general manager after the previous GM had taken a job with the Marlins organization, using a college intern in the public relations staff at his meat company to do the team's publicity. A nearly anorexic blonde, she had confessed to Edward Everett in a voice that squeaked that, while she had played soccer in high school, she knew little about baseball and would he mind terribly reading the bios of the players she had tried to write before the yearbook went to press? Three of the players in the yearbook were already gone, one traded to the St. Louis organization, one promoted to double-A and one out of baseball—Tom Packer, an infielder who had left in the second week of the season to join a church group volunteering in Kenya. Sitting in Edward Everett's office to tell him, Packer wouldn't meet his eye. "My girlfriend showed me this documentary on YouTube," he said in explanation, his neck coloring as if he were admitting to some great wrong rather than a decision to help the poor. "I feel real bad, letting you guys down like this. I hope you can forgive me, Skip." His team was, in fact, still a man short on the roster as, while the big club had replaced the first two players, it had yet to replace Packer. Wryly, Edward Everett thought of it as punishment for Packer's skewed priorities, at least in the eye of the organization, feeding the hungry and tending the sick instead of working to improve his pivot on double plays and his sense of the strike zone.

In his office, Edward Everett switched on his computer and, while it booted up, took the coffeepot to a sink in the shower room and filled it with water. By the time he got back to his office, put in a new filter, spooned out coffee and poured the water into the reservoir, the box on the computer screen was asking for his log-in and password. The big club had sent him an email not long ago, reminding him that he was supposed to change his password every month, but he had a hard enough time remembering any of his passwords. His entire life was a password: his debit card PIN number, the password for his bank account online, his log-in for baseballamerica.com, and so he hadn't changed it in four years. It was still Renee's birthday, 112363.

While the computer went through its start-up sequence, and water began dripping through the filter, he opened the scorebook from the last game they had gotten in before the rains shut everything down so he could enter the stats onto his game log cards; it was a five–four win in the ninth inning, his kind of ball when he was a player; David Martinez, his leadoff hitter, bunting down the third base line with the fielder playing back, a stolen base, a wild throw into center field by the catcher, trying to nab him at second, sending him to third and then scoring on a ground ball to first. Transcribing his players' cards was tedious, senseless work—at least according to the big club. Last fall, not long after they hired a new director of player development—a thirty-something-year-old who seemed proud that he had never played a day of professional ball and who signed his emails "Marc Johansen, MS, MBA"—the team had sent

him to a ten-week course at the junior college to learn a suite of statistical computer programs. "You've got a lot of what I call 'Old
World' knowledge," Marc Johansen, MS, MBA, said when he told
Edward Everett he was asking him to learn the programs. "Just think
of how valuable you'll be if you can marry that 'Old World' to the
twenty-first century." Although Marc Johansen, MS, MBA, had
phrased it as a request, Edward Everett knew he had no choice:
shortly after Marc Johansen, MS, MBA, took his job, he'd sent an
email to the organization. "I know that when changes occur at the
top, everyone gets nervous. I want to assure you that we won't make
any personnel moves for at least sixty days." The subtext was clear:
starting on the sixty-first day, no one had a guaranteed job.

So, grudgingly, every Tuesday night from early October to just
before Christmas, Edward Everett sat in a computer lab with kids less
than a third his age and hunted-and-pecked his way through the
exercises the instructor gave, making spreadsheets of fictitious daily
sales of fictitious products of a fictitious company. He was slow, and
so, after the instructor explained an assignment and the other students were attacking it with verve—keyboards clattering away—he
would sit beside Edward Everett and go over and over the exercises,
reaching over his shoulder and hitting computer keys and clicking
the mouse, often so quickly that Edward Everett couldn't follow what
he was doing.

"Here," the instructor would say. *Click:* a mathematical function
occurred on the screen, a sum appearing at the end of a column.
"See?" he would ask. Edward Everett didn't see but nodded like a
dumb mule anyway, thinking he just had to get through the class,
because Marc Johansen, MS, MBA, said he had to, wanting the instructor just to leave him on his own, because he knew the special
attention reinforced the notion that the other students had, that he
belonged to a sub-class of human beings: people too old to live.

In time, Edward Everett did learn to use the programs well
enough that he could finish the reports he needed to upload every
day so that Mark Johansen, MS, MBA, could do what he called "mas-
saging the data." Nonetheless, he could not stop first doing it the way
he had done it for twenty years—it was easier for him to slide a ruler

from row to row on a card to see how much more patient Martinez was at the plate, or how his catcher Sean Vila was hitting against left-handers or how deep into a game his starter Pete Sandford went before he started giving up hits and walks to batters who had no business getting on base against him.

On some mornings, he was late uploading his spreadsheets. Then, he would get a scolding phone call from the assistant in the PD department, Mike Renz, his voice high-pitched and nasal: "We can't do much with numbers we don't have." Edward Everett had met him at last year's annual meeting for the organization's managers and coaches. Marc Johansen, MS, MBA, was in Lucerne for his honeymoon and bad weather delayed his return flight so Renz stood in for him. He was a skinny kid, his hair spiked with gel that glistened under the lights, and he droned on for an hour with a lecture he titled, "The Future Was Yesterday," in which he outlined an alphabet soup of statistical tools: VORP, DIPS, WHIP, and what he called a "proprietary metric," which allowed the team to predict how a minor league player might perform in the major leagues. "Of course," he said when he clicked on the projector for his PowerPoint, "I don't expect you to understand any of this."

By eleven-thirty, when Edward Everett took a break to make himself a sandwich from the cold cuts he kept in the small refrigerator in his office, he had uploaded his stats and was ready for that night's game: his lineup card, his notes about the order in which he would use his bullpen staff when Sandford faltered. The big club wanted him to begin stretching Sandford out, having him get into the seventh inning, although he hadn't been much more than a five-inning pitcher. Off the mound, Sandford seemed a comic exaggeration of a human being: six-foot-six and not much more than bone thin, with a gaunt face and ears that protruded so much that opposing teams taunted him with "Dumbo." When Edward Everett talked to him, he blinked so slowly that Edward Everett wondered if his mind was able to process anything he was told. Despite all that, until he hit the inevitable barrier after five innings, he had such control that he seemed capable of threading a needle with a baseball. Beyond that, his speed was deceptive. His arm motion was fluid, seemingly effortless, but his fastball came in at more than 95 miles an hour, according to the radar gun Biggie Vincent aimed at him from a seat behind the plate in the stands. Several times a game, the gun registered triple digits. A month earlier, after one of Sandford's starts, Edward Everett and Vincent had gone for a beer and Vincent slipped the pitching chart across the table to him, the notations of the pitches that had hit 100 or more circled in red. Vincent had had four or five beers by then and as he passed the card across the table, he was teary-eyed. "Don't get the idea I'm turning faggot, but I love this boy." Sandford's curve, which he threw with the same motion as his fastball, hit 83 and his change had come in as slow as 71. Routinely, even going but five innings, he tallied seven or eight strikeouts, often with only a single walk. Then, when he reached his Achilles' heel sixth inning, he pitched as if he had never held a baseball in his life to that point.

Edward Everett wasn't sure what would help him become the pitcher that Marc Johansen, MS, MBA, wanted, but he needed to figure it out. The grace period Marc Johansen, MS, MBA, had promised everyone had expired months before. While he hadn't yet, eventually he would begin firing people and there wasn't much room in baseball for minor league managers who were approaching sixty.

Chapter Sixteen

An hour and a half before game time, there was a crisis. Brett Webber, his shortstop, was missing. Webber was a moody kid from a small town in Ohio near where Edward Everett was raised; Edward Everett had sometimes gone to high school dances there after he and his friends decided that it would be easier to get girls who didn't know them than the ones who did. Three years earlier, when Webber was a high school senior, Baltimore took him in the first round of the draft but then let him go in a trade after his second year, even though the team had given him a two-million-dollar bonus just to sign his contract and Webber had led the Florida State League in hitting. With his talent, he should be at least in double-A ball by now but it was clear that unless he matured, he would never get beyond single-A. He had been undependable all season: he was a week late for training camp and then had missed two games when he went to Chicago for a concert. When Edward Everett benched him as punishment, Webber had said, "It was The National, dude. So worth it." Edward Everett told the big club it should just cut him loose, but Marc Johansen, MS, MBA, talked about his superlative zone rating, his similarity scores—arcane statistics that Marc Johansen, MS, MBA, derived when he massaged the spreadsheets that Edward Everett sent him—and wrote, "Talent carries a price. Have confidence you can smooth out rough edges in BW."

Today, irrespective of his dislike of Webber, Edward Everett needed him to show up because they were short yet another player: Jim Rausch, his remaining backup middle infielder, had gone back to Alabama three days earlier to bury his father and to figure out what to do with his fifteen-year-old brother. Their mother had died four years earlier and they were, in Rausch's own words, "orphan boys now."

Edward Everett felt bad for him: nineteen and a surrogate father to a boy who, Edward Everett knew, had responded to his father's illness by drinking a six-pack of Pabst Blue Ribbon one night and cracking up the pickup truck Rausch had bought their father with his bonus money. Still, it was tough running a team with twenty-three players, especially when only four of them were natural infielders. With Packer's spot empty and without Rausch and Webber, it would mean moving Minnie Rojas from second base to short and bringing in either Ross Nelson or Josh Singer from the outfield to play second, and that wouldn't be pretty, especially since, when he wasn't striking hitters out, Sandford tended to induce ground balls. At least until the sixth inning, when the other team started banging hits off the wall.

An hour before game time, Edward Everett was on the field, hitting fungos to Nelson at second base—ground ball after ground ball, starting him off easy to let him begin to gain confidence. Through the stands, some of the high school boys and girls that Bob Collier hired for next to nothing—team T-shirts and a chance for one of the thousand-dollar college scholarships Collier awarded to the kids who worked for him—were moving among the seats, swiping at them with towels that were clearly soaked. As they worked, Edward Everett could see the spray of water their towels flung up. For them, the point seemed not to dry the seats but to get one another wet. Their laughter echoed amid the other pre-game sounds: Edward Everett hitting ground balls to Nelson, the splash of the footfalls of his outfielders running in the wet grass, the happy tunes of Phantom Frank

Fitzgerald on the organ, old Broadway songs, mostly, something from soundtracks of thirty-year-old movies: *Star Wars, Rocky, Butch Cassidy and the Sundance Kid.* Phantom Frank thought of them as new—he was beyond eighty, his eyesight so bad he couldn't read music anymore, could only play by feel and memory, and sometimes his fingers started out on the wrong spot on the keyboard and until he found his place again, what he played seemed as if it were a song Edward Everett felt certain he knew but couldn't quite name and then, when Phantom Frank stopped, found his place and continued, Edward Everett would realize it was "Raindrops Keep Falling on My Head," but three notes off. But he had played the organ in P. City for forty-two years and Collier couldn't let him go.

"It would mean some kind of hex," he once confided to Edward Everett.

After two dozen easy ground balls to Nelson, Edward Everett gave him a sign that he was going to start working him a bit harder. Nelson nodded and pounded his glove with his bare hand and got into his stance: hands on his knees, weight forward. Edward Everett hit a hard three-hopper to Nelson's left and it ticked off his glove. He set again and Edward Everett sent another one-hop line drive to his left, and again it glanced off his glove. It was going to be a long night, Edward Everett thought as he tossed another ball into the air and again hit a hard line drive, this time to Nelson's right. Crossing leg over leg, his feet got tangled and he hit the turf. But Nelson was game: back up, gesturing at Edward Everett, *Hit it again.*

Edward Everett liked Nelson, wished that he could hit with more power, had a stronger arm or more speed—anything that would suggest he could move up the line. But it wasn't to be. While Marc Johansen, MS, MBA, often emailed Edward Everett asking for more data about some of his players, he had never asked about Nelson—a sign that he had decided already that Nelson had no future with the organization. But he asked and asked about Webber. Webber who showed up late to training camp because he wanted to stay longer in Jamaica; Webber who went AWOL so he could go to a concert. Webber who wasn't there.

He hit Nelson another dozen ground balls until he began to find the timing, began to anticipate the way the ball would bounce. After he grabbed three in a row without missing, Edward Everett decided it was a good time to stop—when Nelson was feeling confident. It still wouldn't be enough, he knew; ground balls would get past Nelson that wouldn't get past an average second baseman, but he couldn't do anything about it: he was just happy that Clinton had a primarily right-handed hitting lineup, which should cut down on the number of ground balls hit in Nelson's direction.

As he surrendered the field to Clinton for their pre-game warm-ups, telling his hitting and fielding coach, Pete Dominici, to remind Nelson of the other things he'd need to remember as an infielder—when to cover second base if a runner on first attempted to steal, where to position himself for a relay if a ball went to the outfield—he glanced in the direction of the owner's box in the stands. As Collier did before nearly every home game, he was holding court. He was a beefy man near Edward Everett's age but looked considerably younger. He colored his hair and mustache and three months earlier his face had acquired a slightly plastic quality. "Botox," Renee had said. He was with his new wife, a brassy redhead named Ginger who was twenty-seven years younger and whom Collier met when she applied for a job as a secretary at his meatpacking company.

"Can't type," he had said. "But she don't have to."

Tonight, they had brought her two children from her first two marriages—a sour-looking eight-year-old girl who slouched behind her mother, glowering, and a surprisingly bookish eleven-year-old boy who, when he came to the games, rarely looked up from his reading.

Surrounding them were people to whom Collier had given comp tickets, mostly butchers from area groceries, seven or eight of them tonight. Collier's blond intern was carrying an armload of cardboard trays down the aisle, laden with hot dogs wrapped in paper and boxes of popcorn. Trailing her, three of the high school kids carried trays of cups of beer and soda. Although he disliked this pre-game ritual, Edward Everett stopped by the box to say hello. Collier liked him to talk to whatever group he had with him, give them each an autograph as a onetime big league player (whom none of them had ever heard of). "Once pinch-hit for Lou Brock," Collier would always say. "You got to be pretty good to pinch-hit for a Hall of Famer."

Lately, it seemed to Edward Everett that the butchers Collier entertained no longer even knew who Lou Brock was: some were born after Brock had finished his career; as far as they were concerned, he may have played a century ago in the dead-ball era. Nonetheless, Edward Everett sat with them for fifteen minutes and gave them some insight into the game: what to watch for so they could feel a little smarter when they anticipated a hit-and-run or a pitchout—all so they would buy even more Collier Fine Meats.

Twenty minutes later, Edward Everett was in his office, drafting and redrafting a starting lineup without Webber in it, first putting Nelson into the third spot, where Webber usually hit, and then moving him down to seven, putting Vila third, then trying something entirely different and writing Nelson into the leadoff spot and moving Martinez to number three. If Rausch were here, it would be simpler, or if Packer hadn't decided to try to save the world. But neither was here, nor was Webber.

"Knock, knock," Dominici said, appearing in the doorway. "We found Webb."

"Where is he?" Edward Everett asked.

Dominici shook his head. "He said he'd only talk to you."

"How the hell can I go talk to him? Game time is, what? Fifteen minutes?"

Dominici shrugged. "I'm just the messenger, boss," he said, taking the lineup card Edward Everett handed to him. "I tried."

Webber was in an apartment a dozen blocks from the ballpark, sitting on a fire escape four stories above an alley across from a furniture warehouse where Edward Everett had worked in two off-seasons after his then father-in-law had gotten him a job there, answering complaint calls in customer service. Going inside, Edward Everett felt foolish. He was in his uniform, his spikes clacking on the concrete as if he were some sort of damn tap dancer. A couple stepping out of the building as he came up the front stoop held the door for him but the man muttered something that sounded like "Trick-or-treat." His girlfriend laughed.

In the foyer, at the bottom of the stairway, he looked with resignation at the flights that rose above him. His knee hurt: damp weather had a tendency to make the joint swell. Nonetheless, he had no choice. By the time he reached the top floor, the pain radiated into his hip, the joint popping with each step.

At apartment 4-B, he knocked on the door. Affixed to the jamb was a mezuzah, worn smooth as if whoever lived there was devout, touching their fingers to it hundreds of times across the threshold. A young woman answered. She was pretty: dark, Middle-Eastern, with long black hair, and a tiny diamond stud through her left nostril; she was wearing a black T-shirt and black jeans. "I don't know what to do with him," she said, and led him to a bedroom. There, it was obvious that someone had just pulled the comforter up over the sheets in a way to cover the bed but without making it neatly—because, beneath it, the pillows were askew and the top sheet hung crookedly, one edge touching the floor. Through the open window he could see Webber, sitting in the far corner of the fire escape landing, gazing across the alley toward the building where Edward Everett once spent his falls and winters. Edward Everett poked his head through the window.

"What's going on, Webb?" he said. The landing was large enough that someone had set up a small sitting area, a wooden chair and table.

"Ah, shit, Skip," Webber said.

"Personal chauffeur to the park." Edward Everett hoisted himself into the window, resting his hip on the sill. "Game's almost starting, Webb."

"I know," Webber said. "Katrina and I just had something we needed—"

"There's nothing we need to talk about," the woman said, leaning into the window beside Edward Everett.

"How can you say that," Webber said. "After—"

"It's been three weeks," she said. "That's not long enough to say 'after' anything."

"What's the problem?" Edward Everett asked. "Maybe I can help." He pulled himself through the window until he was kneeling on the fire escape. Looking down through the iron bars of the platform, he had a brief moment of dizziness as he saw past the landings below—the barbecue grill someone had set up on the third floor, a large planter on the second—all the way to the broken asphalt of the alley. He felt an anger welling up in him. If it were up to him, he'd tell Webber: *Fine. I'll have Henley clean out your locker.* But he couldn't. He wondered if there was some statistical column that Marc Johansen, MS, MBA, didn't know about: alongside on-base percentage there ought to be pain-in-the-ass factor. Webber might break the all-time record, his talent not a fair trade for his disappearances, the times he loafed to first on a ground ball or pouted if he took a pitch he thought was high but an umpire called "strike three."

The woman sighed. "Brett. It's easier if you just leave."

Below, the steel rear door of the furniture warehouse banged open; a man in a white oxford shirt stepped outside and lit a cigarette.

"Easier on who?" Webber said.

"Whom," the woman said softly.

"Whom," Webber said loudly, banging his hand against the ladder of the fire escape so hard it rattled. In the alley, the man looked up.

"Fuck you," Webber shouted down at him.

"This is partly why," the woman said, stepping back from the window.

"Fuck you," the man shouted back. He stalked toward the fire escape, jumping at the bottom of it, trying to grab the ladder that, thankfully, was retracted onto the first-floor landing.

"I'm sorry, Kitty Kat," Webber said.

"Webb, maybe you and your friend could work this out later," Edward Everett said. It had to be well past first pitch. Webber's status as golden boy in the organization notwithstanding, Edward Everett should have stayed at the park, should have just let Webber show up or not show up. Except that would reflect badly on him. The best thing he could do was to nurse Webber through the season until the big club decided to bump him up the ladder. If he played to his ability, that could be as soon as a month from now.

"Two hours ago . . ." Webber said in a pleading voice but the woman didn't respond. "Kitty Kat?" he called.

From deeper in the apartment, Edward Everett heard the click of heels on hardwood and then a door opening and closing and, after a moment, a lock turning.

"Kat?" Webber called again, moving past Edward Everett, giving no sign that he even remembered his manager was there, and stepped through the window. Edward Everett followed him inside and found him at the front door, which was locked with a dead bolt that required a key to open. Webber pounded on the door, bellowing, "Fuck!"

"I think she's gone," Edward Everett said, laying his hand on Webber's shoulder.

"Skip," Webber said, covering his face with his right hand. Edward Everett couldn't tell for sure, but he appeared to be crying.

On the way to the ballpark, after they'd climbed down the fire escape—thirty minutes past first pitch, Edward Everett noted with anger when he looked at the digital clock in his dash—Webber was silent, staring out the passenger window. At a stoplight, the fountain in front of the Rand National Bank was on and three young children with their shoes off were kicking in the water while two women chatted nearby. He glanced at Webber. It struck him that, despite his enormous talent, he was still little more than a boy.

A week earlier, late in a game that P. City was leading by a run, Pittsfield had runners on second and third with nobody out. The hitter sent a line drive up the middle, over second base. Edward Everett resigned himself to two runs scoring but Webber ranged far to his left, diving for the ball. Just before it got to him, it hit the bag and bounced seemingly out of Webber's reach, but he snatched it with his bare hand, belly-flopped onto the ground, leaped to his feet and fired home, where Vila took the throw and slapped a tag on the runner. It was one of the most remarkable plays Edward Everett had seen in forty years of professional ball but, since the high school kid Collier hired to record the games hadn't shown up, there was no highlight video of it. The play was gone, save for in Edward Everett's memory. Long after, he sat at his computer, trying to describe it for

Marc Johansen, MS, MBA, but gave up—partly because he was no kind of writer but also because, unless it fit into a cell on a spreadsheet, Marc Johansen, MS, MBA, would have no interest in it.

As the light changed to green Edward Everett was trying to reconcile the two Webbers: the man who had both the physical ability to make the play and the game sense to know, in a fraction of a second, what to do when he had the ball, with the boy who was still near, in many ways, to the children kicking in the fountain. He was trying to think of something to say that would bring him out of his sorrow and put him back in whatever state he had to be in to make the kind of play he'd made nine days earlier, when Webber let out a bitter laugh.

"My dad had it right. Women is just bitches," he said. "Them that ain't bitches is just cunts."

Chapter Seventeen

When Edward Everett got home after the game, it was nearly midnight but the street in front of his house was lined with cars, a party going on next door at the Duboises'. People were crowded on the deck, talking over one another, laughing; an indecipherable hum of voices. He stood for a moment in his garage before going into the house, wondering if he would be able to make out Renee's voice or her laugh. What was the occasion? he wondered, thinking back through the years when he'd have been invited as her date and then her husband. *It's a Renee-came-to-her-senses-and-left-him bash,* he thought, simultaneously hearing his mother's voice, although she had been dead for years: *Stop the pity party.*

He closed the garage and crossed the yard in the shadows, not wanting anyone to see him. When he reached his deck, he found the bouquet of roses he'd left for Renee leaning against the back door, the card unopened. On the envelope, she had written two words in the angular printing she'd learned in her brief time as an architecture student, the same hand in which she annotated her drawings and elevations: "Please don't." He tucked the flowers under his arm, got out his key and went inside.

There, he discovered that Grizzly was having a seizure. Edward Everett knew it even before he saw the dog; he could hear his claws clicking in a steady rhythm against the tile. Indeed, Grizzly was lying there, quivering, his water dish overturned, his hindquarters wet, his front paws beating the floor, his head shaking side to side. Edward Everett set the roses onto the counter and went to the linen closet to fetch a towel, which he slipped under the dog's head to make him more comfortable. Flipping off the light because the vet to whom he and Renee had taken Grizzly after his first seizure had told them that dark and quiet would help the dog recover more quickly, he sat on the floor beside him, stroking his fur, while the dog's eyes squinted at him in a way that seemed beseeching. "I wish I could stop it, boy," he said as the dog continued to quake.

Sitting on his kitchen floor until the seizure ended, he listened intently to the loud conversation next door, wondering if Renee's voice or laugh would emerge from the general noise. "No, no, no, no," a man said. There was an explosion of laughter, the squeak of someone raising a plastic cooler lid, the *pffft* when they opened the beer.

He had met the Duboises on the day he moved in: Ron and Rhonda and their three children, whose names also began with "R": Ron Junior, Renee and Rose. Ron Junior was still in high school then and Ron and Rhonda had sent him over to help Edward Everett carry in boxes from the U-Haul and then had invited him for Sunday dinner. "You can't have a thing unpacked yet," Rhonda had said when he protested. "It's just ussens and some KFC. Hope you won't be offended by paper plates and plastic sporks."

It was a crowded table: Ron and Rhonda; their three kids; Rose's fiancé, Chuck; Ron Junior's girlfriend, April; Renee's husband, Art. The Duboises were all plump except for Renee, who had earned a college scholarship for track and still jogged four days a week. Everyone talked at once, nearly shouting, everyone reaching across everyone else for the bucket of legs and breasts, for the dish of potatoes and gravy, and he could make out nothing of what they discussed: it was as if they were piecing together conversations they had been having for years, arguing over ridiculous topics:

I found this picture, remember that Halloween . . .
You promised.

Speaking of that, Chuck, I heard that Paula was back in town.

Almost simultaneously, they all sang, *It's too late to turn back now,* exploding into guffaws.

During the off-season, when Edward Everett was home on Sundays, they sometimes asked him back and began inviting him for family parties: for Chuck and Rose's wedding reception; for the send-off when Ron Junior joined the Army; for Ron Junior's wedding, when he and April decided to get married just before he was deployed to Iraq for his first tour. That was the start of his relationship with Renee.

Then, the yard was crowded with out-of-town relatives who had come to wish Ron Junior and April well and Ron Junior "Godspeed." Over and over, tipsy, bleary-eyed uncles, aunts and cousins came up to him, asking, "Who are you, exactly?" Tired of explaining himself—"I'm just the neighbor"—and wanting to be useful, he'd gone into the kitchen and started scrubbing a pot in which Rhonda had burned the chili. At one point, while he was elbow-deep in the blackened water, his hands raw from the Brillo pad, Renee wandered in looking for ice.

"Hello, baseball man," she shouted, obviously drunk. "Got you on KP." She had shed the beige suit jacket she'd worn for the ceremony, and her white blouse was untucked from the skirt.

"I just thought I'd give your folks a head start on cleaning all this up," he said. Out in the yard, April and her father were dancing to some country song, while the other guests stood along the perimeter, every once in a while a camera flash exploding.

"You're a saint," she said. "Saint. Saint. Saint."

"Not really," he said. "More like a lot of sins to make up for."

There was no ice in the freezer and when Renee went to the bedroom where everyone had dropped their coats and came back with her purse, fishing out her car keys, he stopped her. "You can't drive."

"A saint and a safety patrol boy," she said. "I'm fine, really." But he had insisted, telling her he would take her for the ice. He rinsed his hands under the faucet and poured the dark water in the pot down the drain; disappointed at his lack of progress, he filled the pot with dish soap and water to soak, and followed her to her car.

It was a four-year-old red Corvette—a consolation prize for her recent divorce, she said—with a standard transmission. He had driven nothing but automatics for years, and twice before they even got to the end of his street, he killed it, letting off the clutch too quickly. Then lurching onto Carter, shifting from first to second, he ground the gears.

"I've only made three payments on this thing," she said. "Be careful."

On the way back from the Quik Stop, two bags of ice on the floor at Renee's feet, she abruptly struck the dash with her fist while they were stopped at a traffic signal. "Fuck," she said. "Fuck, fuck, fuck." Her sudden violence startled him; his foot slid off the clutch and the Corvette leaped forward and died. The signal changed to green and the driver of the jacked-up Chevy pickup behind them began flashing its high beams, honking. Edward Everett found the button for the window, lowered it and waved the pickup around. As it roared past, a teenaged boy riding in the bed flung a plastic drink cup at them. It spattered against the windshield, ice and soda trailing across the glass. He managed to get the car started and pulled through the intersection, stopping at the curb.

"Are you all right?" he asked.

"His second cousin!" she said, opening her door and stumbling out, falling to her knees on the sidewalk. He thought she was going to start vomiting but she pushed herself up and started walking at a quick pace up the street in the direction of the store.

He turned off the ignition, pulled himself out of the car—men his age with bad knees were not meant for Corvettes—and followed. "Where are you going?"

"Not back there. 'Where's Art?' 'How's Art?' How the fuck should I know how Art's doing? But I know *who* he's doing. His second cousin; that's who he's doing." She let out a shriek and sat down heavily on a bound stack of newspapers on a step outside a newsstand. "Does that sound like we should be on *Jerry Springer*? 'Man Leaves Wife for Cousin.' " She laughed and fell off the stack of newspapers, bumping her head against the door to the newsstand. He bent to help her back up but she swatted his hand away, sitting up against the door, wrapping her arms around her knees. "I was crazy about him. Shouldn't that be enough? No. 'We couldn't help it,' he said. 'You understand.' Understand what? 'Love,' he said. 'Love doesn't recognize . . .' "

"What?" Edward Everett asked.

"Love doesn't recognize . . . Fuck, I don't remember. Something about the two of them at fourteen and innocent love enduring and blah blah blah."

"You should go back," he said, gently. "Ronnie's leaving and you'd regret—"

She gazed up at him. "You must think I'm crazy," she said. "I mean, I don't even know you. You're the man who comes over for chicken on Sundays. Chicken Ed."

"Saint Chicken Ed," he said. "Come on. I'll take you back." When she stood, she leaned into him; he thought it was to keep her balance, but she put her arms around his neck and pressed against him, moving her face upward toward his. "You're just drunk," he said, stepping back from her, and helped her to the car. When they got back to the party, she bounded out, holding the bag of ice aloft, not waiting for him. "The Icewoman Cometh," she announced brightly, and the guests applauded. Edward Everett took her keys inside, left them on the counter, and went home.

Two weeks later, the evening after he returned from a road trip, she knocked on his back door as he sat at the kitchen table, studying his game logs.

"I saw the light on," she said, holding a six-pack of Coors before her. "Price of admission?" After he invited her in, she twisted two cans out of their plastic yokes, set them on the table and, without asking, opened his refrigerator and put the rest of the beer onto the top shelf. "Whoa," she said, swinging the door wider. "Are you on a hunger strike?" The contents of the refrigerator were spare: a twelve-pack of Diet Coke, half a package of American cheese, a quart of half-and-half; in a drawer, two molding oranges.

"I just got back after ten days," he said, closing the door.

"Sorry," she said. "I didn't mean to get off on that kind of foot." She picked up her beer from the table, but then set it back down without opening it and leaned against the counter. "I thought about never bringing this up," she said, not quite meeting his eyes.

"What?"

She gave him a sideways look, one he would eventually come to know well, the look that would tell him that she knew he was holding something back. "*It*," she said. "I wasn't going to bring *it* up, but then you'd be at Sunday dinner sometime and . . ."

"And what?"

"I don't know. And you'd tell everyone. You'd say, 'Gosh, Renee. Remember that time you got so drunk at Ronnie and April's party and you tried to kiss me?'"

"I wouldn't do that," he said.

"I know. Or pretty much *thought* you wouldn't. My therapist—" She sighed. "Christ. I haven't even told my folks I'm seeing a therapist. But here I am, spilling everything."

"You just got divorced," he said. "A lot of people do that after a divorce."

"You mean, a lot of *weak* people do that."

"I didn't say that."

She shrugged. "Defensiveness is another of my foibles. Keep a list." She picked her beer up, opened it and took a sip. "This is probably a mistake, after last time."

"I'll stop you at one," he said.

"Oh, I see your game. You just want to keep more of my beer for yourself. Anyway, my therapist said I needed to confront the demons that most frighten me. Her words."

"See, you confronted what you were afraid of and it turned out to be nothing."

"As it usually does," she said. "What's all this?" She pointed her beer can toward the cards spread out on the table.

"Long answer or short?"

"Another of the symptoms of my neurosis is insomnia, so the longer the better."

"Not even an insomniac wants to hear the long," he said. "Short. It's homework."

But she'd insisted; they had sat at the table and he had started explaining the cards to her. An hour later, after he had let her copy his starting pitcher's statistics from the scorebook onto a card, she pointed to the column that noted his ratio of fly ball outs to ground ball outs. "In a small park, he would get bombed," she said.

"You've done this before," he said.

"Just a quick study."

"I wish Winslow would be as quick a study, then he'd understand why I keep telling him he needs to stop coming inside so much to certain hitters." He began gathering the cards to put them back into the accordion folder.

"Thanks for this," she said. "You were pretty brave, letting a crazy woman into your house in the middle of the night."

"It's fine," he said. "And you're not so crazy."

When she got up to go, he walked her to the door and she had surprised him with a hug. It was quick and asexual at first, like the hug between an uncle and a niece, her hips back and to the side, but then something shifted between them and then, bang, they were kissing, the first time he had kissed a woman in a year at that point, and he was thinking, *She's not drunk this time.* Then thinking, *She's on the rebound and she's your neighbor's daughter.* Then thinking, *Stop thinking.* Then, bang, they were dating; bang, they got married and she moved into his house and he got her a dog that wasn't smart enough to know he was *her* dog and not *his* dog; then, bang, he came home from a road trip to find her moved out.

Next door, at his former in-laws', someone let out a loud belch that echoed, everyone laughing. If it were anyone else, he could ask them to take it inside, but if he went to the Duboises', it would be awkward. The day after he'd come home from the road trip and learned that Renee had moved out, he had seen Rhonda in her yard, rolling the trash can in from the curb, and he'd raised his hand in greeting, a gesture he had done perfunctorily for years, even before she was his mother-in-law. But this time, she had turned her head away as if his gesture embarrassed her. Too, Renee might be there; the notion struck him that she might be with another man. He saw her sitting close to him, her hand on his knee as she once would have had hers on his, taking a sip from the man's beer can as she used to from his.

It was nearly twelve-thirty when the dog finally stopped quaking and laid his head onto his front paws, exhausted from the seizure. Edward Everett knew he ought to get to bed but, as he often was after a game, he was too wired. He sat at the kitchen table and, with Grizzly sleeping at his feet, got out the accordion file containing his game log cards, opened the scorebook and started to make his entries.

The game had been miserable. When he and Webber reached the park, it was the bottom of the third inning and he could tell it was going badly even without seeing the scoreboard: in the dugout, the players slumped against the back wall, stunned. It was eight–two, all but one of Clinton's runs unearned. Collier's box was empty save for a thin high school kid who slouched in an aisle seat, slurping a maxi-sized soda. Edward Everett had no idea how many fans had been there at first pitch but by the time he and Webber arrived, the crowd was thin, wide gaps among the clusters of people. In the top row just beyond the left field foul line, a solitary couple huddled under a stadium blanket, the nearest fans to them fifty yards off.

When he sat next to Dominici on the bench, his coach handed him the scorebook without a comment, tapping the column where he had been tracking errors by making pencil ticks. Six.

"Really?" Edward Everett said. Dominici shook his head; in sadness, not denial. Edward Everett flipped the book over to the side on which Dominici had been scoring Clinton's innings at the plate. To his chagrin, the story was there: E-4, E-4, E-4, E-4, E-4, E-4. Error on the second baseman.

"How is this possible?" he asked.

"They smelled the blood." Dominici shrugged. "They've been punching the ball to right all game."

He glanced down the bench toward Nelson, who sat at the far end, his head bowed. Edward Everett handed the book to Dominici and walked the length of the dugout toward Nelson. As he passed each player, they all looked away as if they were complicit in some collective guilt. He sat next to Nelson, who lowered his head even more. Edward Everett regarded him. Nelson was a kid. His fingernails were uneven and caked with dirt; his uniform pants were mottled with grass stains and there were pinholes in his white sanitary socks.

"I'm sorry, Skip," he said in a quiet voice.

"You're not a second baseman," he said, and added, "Ross." Nelson looked up at him. Edward Everett never used his players' first names: it was "Nelson" or "Nels."

He wanted to tell Nelson that it was Webber who'd failed them, Webber who had all the talent but not much of anything else, as if the human body only had so much capacity for qualities and his talent had pushed everything else out of him: dedication, responsibility. Edward Everett wished he had a player with Webber's talent and Nelson's everything else. If life were a movie or if it compensated people like Nelson for selflessness, he'd have been the star of the game. His line in the box score would read three hits in three at-bats with five runs driven in. But life wasn't a movie. Edward Everett considered sending Nelson out to left field the next inning, letting him play where he felt comfortable. But the kid was so defeated, his six errors would weigh on him in the outfield, would weigh on him at the plate. Instead, he said, "Why don't you call it a night, Nels. Head on home. Tomorrow . . ." He shrugged. But Nelson stayed.

Now, at his kitchen table, Edward Everett shuffled through the game log cards, looking for Nelson's, and began entering the numbers from the game—the half-dozen errors, the two times at bat and the string of zeros all the way across, save for the column for strikeouts, where he wrote a "2." He looked at the other side of the scorebook, running his finger down the notations for each Clinton player's time at the plate, looking for any four–threes, any four–sixes, any six–fours—any notation that would indicate that Nelson had made a single play in the field, a single assist, a single put-out, but there were none. Clinton had hit six ground balls to him and he'd kicked all six.

Meanwhile, Webber had played as if his fight with Katrina had never happened. Edward Everett had considered punishing him, keeping him on the bench, but with Nelson out of the lineup, there was no choice. In three times at bat, he'd had a double and a triple, and in the ninth, although the game was ten–four by then, he'd dashed with his back to the plate into the gap in left center, dived, caught a flare that few players on any level might have been able to reach and then, from his knees, threw a strike to second base for what should have been a double play, the Clinton runner leaving too soon. The umpire, however, had clearly not expected Webber to make the play and was out of position for the call; he ruled the runner safe although the throw beat him by two steps.

While for Webber it was just one more night in what should be his inevitable march toward the major leagues, there was no way to mitigate what happened for Nelson. Not in the world of Marc Johansen, MS, MBA. No way to mitigate the long string of mediocrity on Nelson's game log card for the season. His willingness to embarrass himself at second, suffer the boos of the crowd and the disappointment of his teammates—because Webber decided that fighting with a woman who wasn't interested in him was more important than showing up—didn't add points to his .227 batting average, didn't compensate for the long string of zeros in the columns for doubles, triples, home runs, runs batted in.

He slid Nelson's card back into the expandable file, knowing that soon there would be no card for him there because Marc Johansen, MS, MBA, didn't have patience for human interest stories. Hell, he realized, it wasn't just Marc Johansen, MS, MBA, who didn't care for human interest stories: it was baseball itself.

Chapter Eighteen

O n his sixtieth birthday, the drains backed up in the ballpark. Collier called him at four-thirty in the morning,
waking him from a dream that dissipated almost immediately: something about his father and a navy blue jacket that was too tight.

"It's a mess," Collier said without returning Edward Everett's
groggy hello. "It's a shit hole. Literally."

After the call, Edward Everett got up and realized that the power
had gone out in his house in a storm he had slept through. The face
of his alarm clock was blank and when he clicked the lamp on the
bedside table, nothing happened. He took a shower that began as
lukewarm and became cold before he had rinsed his hair, and shaved
by standing a flashlight upend on the vanity, leaning in close enough
to the mirror that his breath fogged it over. The bulb cast a pale cone
of light toward the ceiling that reflected in the mirror, making his
face seem gray and indistinct. He was sure that he'd left patches of
whiskers on his cheek and neck, but it would have to do.

In the kitchen, he filled the dog's water and food dishes, and went
to let him out into the backyard to do his business but found that a
bough from his oak tree had fallen onto the steps to the yard. He
tried lifting the bough but it was surprisingly heavy. He gave it a
shove but realized that it was not entirely severed from the tree and

that, to move it, he would have to get a saw and cut the flesh that still connected the bough to the trunk. That would have to wait until later.

He took Grizzly to the front yard. As the dog trotted over the lawn searching for a place to do his business, Edward Everett surveyed the damage from the storm. Next door, the Duboises' Bradford pear had snapped and lay at the curb. At Mrs. Greiner's across the street, the limb of a maple lay across her walk and there were branches down in other yards as well. Not a light shone: not the porch light that the Maxwells left on every night because their twenty-year-old son worked the overnight shift at Walmart, not even the streetlight in front of the Duboises' that Ron Senior had once shot out with a BB gun in a fit of love for Rhonda when she had the flu and complained she couldn't sleep because of the light.

Much of the rest of the town was in similar condition. For a long stretch of his drive to the ballpark, it was dark, traffic lights out for blocks. At some intersections, the police had set up temporary stop signs in the middle of the road, and down one street, Algeier, he could see the work lights of a Central Iowa Power Cooperative crew, hear the generator rumbling, watch a workman riding a cherry picker up alongside a utility pole where there was a downed wire.

At the ballpark, he pulled into the lot beside Collier's silver Escalade. The only other vehicle there was the rusted, fifteen-year-old powder blue Plymouth mini-van that Pete Winston, the night watchman, drove. Edward Everett found them in the home clubhouse, standing at the edge of the darkened shower room, the beams of their flashlights bouncing off the walls and the black pool of sewage.

"I can't tell if it's going down," Collier said.

Winston crouched like the catcher he once had been and focused his flashlight on the center of the room, where the drain was.

"This really sucks the sow's teat," Collier said when he saw Edward Everett. The shower room was perhaps three inches deep in black ooze; flecks of paper floated on the surface and the stench was so overpowering that Edward Everett had to cover his nose with his hand to keep from choking. Around the drain, the sewage bubbled slowly.

"I can't afford any more work on this fucking white elephant of a ballpark," Collier said. "Shit, shit, shit."

"That's what it is, all right," Winston said, standing up, wiping his hands on the legs of his jeans. "The visitor clubhouse is the same. I'm sorry."

"It's not your fault, Win," Collier said. The three stood at the edge of the shower room for another moment, staring at the sludge. Edward Everett may have been mistaken but it seemed it had receded while they were there; the line of concrete that was merely coated instead of submerged seemed to be as much as two inches wide now, whereas it had perhaps been an inch when he'd arrived. Still, at the rate it was sliding back down the drain, it could be hours until it was gone. Then someone would have to clean it up.

As if Winston had read his mind, he said, "You know, Claire and I would come in with mops and some bleach and scour the place real good if that'd help."

"I'd give you a hundred dollars," Collier said.

"Shoot, Mr. Collier. I'd feel like I was taking advantage of someone's misfortune if you paid me that much. Make it fifty."

Collier regarded Winston. If Edward Everett hadn't been there he was certain Collier would have taken the offer but, glancing at Edward Everett, he said, "No, we'll keep it the hundred."

Later, after Winston left them, Collier and Edward Everett stood together in the parking lot. Suddenly the hillside above the ballpark became illuminated as, all along it, the lights in a hundred houses came on. Near the highest point of the hill was Collier's home, a massive, five-thousand-square-foot place on an acre lot. The entire western side of the house was a sunroom with a vaulted ceiling. As the lights there went on, the west wall gleaming, he said, "Shit," and pulled his cellphone out of his pants pocket. "Ginger, turn off the damn lights. We're burning a hundred dollars' worth of electricity and it's five-thirty in the fucking morning." He ended the call and put his phone back into his pocket. Edward Everett had no idea whether he had actually spoken to his wife or just left a message, but a moment later the house went dark.

"I don't know how much longer I can do this," Collier said. "You have any idea how much I've lost the last five years?" He patted the roof of his Escalade. "I coulda bought a fleet of these. Bought a fleet and drove them all into the river, and it woulda been the same thing." He let out a small, bitter laugh. "I remember when my dad bought the team and moved it here. I was five or six and he come home and said, 'Your daddy bought you a toy.' Shit. I thought he bought me a box of Lincoln Logs." He shook his head. "We've had some good times here. Remember that stretch when you first come, three league pennants in a row? That parade after the first was something." Edward Everett had not thought of the parade Collier staged as impressive: six "Collier Fine Meats" refrigerated trucks, two floats and a half-dozen convertibles carrying those players who had showed up, waving embarrassedly to the sparse crowd, trailing the Perabo City High marching band for four blocks. Collier draped an arm around Edward Everett's shoulders in a surprisingly familiar gesture. "It's gonna die with us, amigo. We're the last of the . . ."

"Old fools?" Edward Everett said, finishing Collier's sentence.

"Old somethings anyway."

It was only when he was back home, sitting at his kitchen table, drinking coffee and paging through the newspaper, that Edward Everett realized it was his birthday. Turning to the horoscopes, he saw the familiar date: *If your birthday is today* . . . .

In most years, he gave the event little thought. They were in-season, the day little different from any other: the game, and long hours in the office before and after. Today, however, he had nothing to do and the prospect of the empty day stretched before him in a way that made him uncomfortable. "You work to avoid real life," Renee had said a few months earlier. It struck him then: was that when she had decided to go? If he had said, *You're right,* changed his habits, come home at eleven instead of midnight, would she still be there? He wondered if she would relent long enough to acknowledge his birthday; maybe he would find a card from her in the mail. His first wife, years ago, had been friendly after their divorce and sent him cards for a time until she told him that her new husband thought the practice odd. "You understand," she said in a note. "It's not that he suspects anything or is jealous." Whatever her new husband had been, she'd stopped sending cards after that.

When the mail came, there were more than a dozen cards, but nothing from Renee. Most were from former players. One, Jack Clarendon, who was platooning at second base with the big club, getting into the lineup when they faced left-handed pitching, sent him a hundred-dollar card for Best Buy. Winston, God bless him, sent him a five-dollar card for Starbucks. Even Renee's father, Ron, brought by a card with a twenty-dollar gift certificate for Lowe's. When Edward Everett answered the door, Grizzly barking and skittering across the kitchen tile, Ron was uncomfortable, glancing repeatedly toward his own house, as if he were doing something illicit.

"Don't tell Rhonda," he said after declining Edward Everett's invitation to come inside for coffee. Bending to scratch the dog under his chin, he went on, "She's, well, she don't want to do anything that suggests we're taking sides. Between you, me and the lamppost, though, I'm hoping you guys work things out. Renee . . . I ain't telling you something that's a shock. Once she gets an idea, she's like a dog with a bone. But . . ."

"But?" Edward Everett asked, wondering if Renee had confided something, the "but" being the one thing he could do that would cause her to change her mind, come home as she had before.

"I gotta get back," Ron said, ignoring his question. "You're not going to end up spending the day alone, are you?"

"No," Edward Everett said. "I've got plans."

"That's good." Ron turned to go, but hesitated. "You ever need anyone to watch the dog, you know where I am. He's like a granddoggy to us and I'd hate to see him go to one of those kennels." As if he understood what Ron was saying, the dog stood on its hind legs, pawing at Ron's shins. He bent down, gave him a pat and was gone.

Around noon, Biggie Vincent called. When Edward Everett saw the name on his caller ID, he let it go to voice mail. "Happy birthday!" Vincent said, his voice singsong, making Edward Everett wonder if he was celebrating the day off with a few beers. "Since there's no game, amigo, how about you, the missus, Janice and me go to Out-back? Not that I'll pick up the check. You know how much I'm paid. Or not paid." He laughed.

He considered calling Vincent, telling him that Renee had left. Vincent would take him out for the steak, just the two of them. He'd say the right things, condemn Renee or encourage him to court her, depending on what he perceived Edward Everett wanted. But the thought of the effort Vincent would exert made him tired. "It's just you and me, Grizzly," he said to the dog, deleting the message. Grizzly was lying in a corner of the kitchen and, on hearing his name, picked his head up, regarded Edward Everett and then laid his head back down, covering his face with his paws, as if to say: *Pity party? Count me out.*

"Yeah," Edward Everett said, opening the freezer to find something for lunch. "That's what I think, too." He took out a dinner and put it in the microwave. How, he wondered, had he ended up celebrating his sixtieth birthday with an epileptic Pomeranian as his only companion, standing in the kitchen, watching a Lean Cuisine lasagna, a frozen meal Renee had left behind, rotating in a microwave in a house with a leaky basement in a town where he managed a team that played its games in an honest-to-God cesspool?

Chapter Nineteen

Although he had once promised himself he wouldn't stay in the game if it meant celebrating his thirtieth birthday in a minor league town, he did: Holloway, Iowa. He was with the Cubs organization then, playing for their double-A team at Racine—his fifth franchise in less than three years; St. Louis, Cleveland, Oakland, Baltimore, Chicago, the trajectory of his career akin to a pinball bouncing off bumpers and flippers. He sometimes thought—back to hours on a bus and four-in-a-room at Travelodges and Motel 6s, deep in the heart of the heart of America, where, he was convinced, the only people who were there had gotten lost on their way to somewhere else—that the worst thing that had happened to him were the weeks he'd spent with the Cardinals until he got hurt. It was as if he had been tussling in the backseat with the prom queen: she was passionate, she let you touch her here, here, here, but not there, not just yet, before she dashed off to the powder room, just for a sec, just to freshen up, leaving you waiting with a hard-on, wondering, did she ditch you, was she laughing with her friends, the queen's court, about leaving you there, but then thinking that maybe she didn't after all, and you remember your hand in her bra, and maybe she was standing at the sink, dabbing the corner of her mouth to smooth out the line of lip gloss, thinking about you in the car, and so you waited, the promise enough to keep you waiting in the backseat as the moon set.

In the hinterlands of the Cleveland organization after the tryout camp—Erie, Pennsylvania, hitting .293—he was the number four outfielder and should have read the portents then: the prom queen doesn't come back to the car for number four outfielders. The next year, back at Erie—never a good sign, two seasons in the same minor league town, the professional version of your tires caught in the mud, spinning—and then later that season traded to the A's, at Peoria, Illinois, three weeks there, a throw-in as part of a seven-player deal, hitting .413 in forty-six at-bats, but then shipped out again, to the Baltimore organization, playing at Raleigh but then let go when the season ended, the market cold for twenty-nine-year-old singles-hitting outfielders. He should have read the signs *then* but didn't, the last man in America who still had faith he could get back to the major leagues. So he stuck it out, made some calls, landed with a Cubs minor league team, and woke up starting the fourth decade of his life in a little town he couldn't pick out on a map even though he'd been there.

At the ball game at Holloway, the organist played "The Old Gray Mare" when he stepped to the plate for the first time, and a drunken fan in the stands behind home plate shrieked the words of the song at him—a red-faced man maybe twice his age, venting whatever his life's disappointments were on someone he didn't know, as if it would bring him back whatever he had lost. When Edward Everett struck out, swinging wildly over a pitch that broke down and outside, the old man jeered at him: "Yeah, you go sit down now."

After the game, at a Ponderosa, one of his teammates tipped a waitress—a buxom girl with steak sauce and chocolate pudding staining her apron—to bring him a corn muffin with a candle stuck in it, along with a note calling him "Mithoosla," which took him a while to tease out as "Methuselah." Looking down the table as they grinned back at him over their steaks and their baked potatoes slathered with sour cream, he realized how much older he was than they, thirty an impossible number for them to comprehend. A decade earlier, when he was their age and at single-A, still on his way up—*up* the only conceivable trajectory—and his hitting coach marked his thirtieth birthday (in a far more dignified manner than Edward Everett would; his wife and daughter meeting him at the ballpark, the daughter shyly offering up to him a package wrapped in paper she'd colored herself), another player confided, his face solemn, "I'm killin' myself the day before I turn thirty."

In his kitchen nearly a third of a century after that dinner at Ponderosa, taking the lasagna from the microwave and raising the steaming plastic dish as a toast to his sleeping dog, he thought he should have seen the writing on the wall *then*, but hadn't. Thirty-one, in Dorsett, Nebraska, with the Brewers organization the next season, a year and a half older than the pitching coach, his legs starting to go, average sliding: .271. His roommates—nineteen, twenty, twenty-four—chipped in and bought him a cheap cane with a plastic handle shaped like a baseball. On the bus one night, riding along a dark blacktop road in Illinois, they reminisced about television shows he'd never seen—*Hong Kong Phooey* and *Speed Buggy*—because while they'd been slumped on their parents' couches watching cartoons, he was on another bus coursing through the Midwest or trotting out to left in the shadow of an outfield wall. At one point, his roommate Mikey Phillips, sitting beside him, started a chorus of a TV theme song Edward Everett had never heard and most of the team began shouting the lyrics in unison until the bus hit a pothole, blowing a front tire, one a.m. in the middle of nowhere. Most of them disembarked while the driver tried to rouse a tow truck using the CB radio. As Edward Everett's teammates stretched out in the grass along the shoulder, chatting or smoking cigarettes, he wandered up the road, away from them, to where the manager, Adam Johnson, was talking quietly with the pitching coach. ". . . let him go," Johnson was saying and Edward Everett's skin prickled, certain they meant him. "You weren't supposed to hear that," Johnson said. Edward Everett felt a stone drop in his belly. "Don't say anything to Phillips. We need him for the series in Urbana."

"I won't," Edward Everett said, feeling light-headed from relief that he was being spared but, at the same time, guilt from the lie he'd have to live with Phillips.

Back on the bus hours later, as dawn lightened the eastern horizon, Edward Everett asked Phillips, "Ever think about giving all this up?"

Phillips said, "Naw, man. Hell, guys kill to do this."

"Seriously, what would you do if you couldn't do this anymore?"

Phillips gave him a stricken look. "Skip say something? Fuck. It was two games."

"No," Edward Everett said. "Skip didn't say anything. I was just—"

"Just feeling old," a player behind him said. "Gramps is just feeling his age."

"You're right," he said, but thinking: *It's not just two games. Anyone but you can see that hitters are catching up to your fastball; your slider isn't breaking. Anyone can see that in triple-A they'd pound you.* But he said none of it, simply repeated, "Feeling old. Don't let it happen to you."

For the first time since he had signed the contract after the tryout in Cleveland, he felt fear that he had made a mistake, one from which he could not recover: leaving Connie, giving up the job his uncle had given him, a job that would have guaranteed him a comfortable life for however many decades he lived, a life in which he'd eventually be one of the well-dressed men with Cadillacs, trips to Europe, extended winter stays in Arizona.

The next morning, he slipped into a phone booth at the back of the Denny's where the team went for breakfast, poured a handful of quarters into the coin slot, dialed Connie's number, but an old man with some kind of Eastern European accent answered.

"I'm trying to reach Connie Heidrich," he said loudly into the mouthpiece.

The old man said something he couldn't understand and Edward Everett said again, more slowly, "Con. Nie. Hei. Drich."

The old man said something Edward Everett could not understand, maybe in Polish or some other language, and then hung up. He called his mother.

"What's wrong, Ed?" she said, her voice anxious. "Did you get hurt again?"

"No. I'm fine. I just called for the heck of it."

She let out a breath that whistled in the earpiece. "You never just call . . ."

He had wanted to ask her, by the by, just making conversation, did she ever see Connie anymore? But now he couldn't because the question would have a weight he hadn't meant her to perceive—a weight that she'd read as his coming to his senses, realizing she'd been right and he'd been wrong when he walked away from the life he could have had: the job selling for the mill, the pre-fab family with Connie and Billy. When he'd told her he was taking the Indians' offer, six-fifty a month at double-A Erie, her face softened in the same way he imagined it would if he told her he had cancer. "Oh," she said. She was clipping coupons from the Sunday *Wheeling Intelligencer* and she closed the paper, laid down her scissors and ran her hand over the slick coupon insert.

"What did Connie say?"

"I haven't told her yet," he said.

"I see," she said, and he couldn't read the meaning in that. "And your uncle?"

"I'll tell him—"

She calmly picked up her scissors again and began cutting around the border for a coupon for breakfast cereal. "Your father had forty-seven dollars in the bank when he died," she said. "Twenty-some years of working. Forty-seven dollars." She shrugged. "What's that, two dollars a year?"

"It's not—"

She slammed the scissors onto the table with surprising force. He couldn't remember a time when she had responded with overt anger. She was a long-sufferer, someone who won arguments with his father by silences that could go on forever. Once, when his father decided that he'd had enough of the Catholic Church and announced one Sunday that he would no longer accompany her to Mass, she was silent for a week. A week of his father teasing and cajoling; a week of her refusal to speak, punctuated by the sounds she made as she went about her work: the whisk of a wooden spoon on the side of a saucepan; the clink of dishes put away in the cupboard; the chopping of cabbage. After a week, his father was in the driver's seat of their Studebaker at quarter to eight the next Sunday, waiting to drive her and Edward Everett to Mass.

"You kids have no idea. You think a Depression can't happen again."

"A Depression isn't—"

"You go down to Liar's Bench, on Chestnut, and ask those men who sit there all day drinking. 'Oh, no, the mine can't close!' It closed! 'Oh, no, milk prices will never—' "

"I signed a contract," he said.

She nodded, got up, took her scissors to the utility drawer in the kitchen, opened it, set the scissors into it, closed it, and left the room without another word.

On the phone with her from Vandalia, he chatted for a few minutes, listening to her complain about the new pastor, who was using guitars at Sunday Mass instead of the organ; he asked about her sister, about the ladies in the altar society.

"What's this really about?" she said at last, interrupting him.

He hesitated. In the restaurant, Phillips was jumping out of his booth as if he'd been burned, swiping his hands over his pants legs, which were stained with what appeared to be coffee. Across the table from him, a player they all called Ox was laughing. "I was just wondering what had ever happened to Connie—"

"Oh, Ed," his mother said. "You can't go back, honey."

"I wasn't talking about going back. She just crossed my mind."

"She got married. A year ago. To Randy McLaughlin. He's a vet in Somerville. You went to high school with him."

He remembered McLaughlin, a boy who, in Edward Everett's memory, wore braces the entire four years of high school. Could that be possible, or was just one image of McLaughlin frozen in his memory and that became the sum and substance of McLaughlin: the kid with glasses, braces and red hair, writing meticulous lab notes in biology class as he delicately separated the skin over the belly of a frog?

It surprised him to realize that he had thought, all the while he was on his pinball journey of a life, that everyone else would stay put, that Connie would be waiting, as if she were a deposit he'd made in some sort of lifestyle savings account: deposit it, forget about it and go back to make a withdrawal when he was ready.

"That's great," he said, feeling foolish. For calling her. For thinking he could get off the bus in the middle of Illinois, roll the clock back to before the point at which he'd made his decision that, he saw, had ruined his life.

Four days later, however, Edward Everett had three hits in four times at bat, the last a run-scoring double that meant the win. As he came off the field after Urbana went down in order in the bottom of the ninth, a father with a young boy waved him over to the box seats behind the third base dugout. The boy held up a baseball shyly, along with a pen. "You were amazing," the father said as Edward Everett scrawled his name across the ball and handed it back to the boy, who rubbed his thumb over the signature in a reverential way. By the time he got to the clubhouse, Phillips was in their manager's office, his head bowed, while Johnson pushed a Kleenex box across the desk toward him. The rest of the locker room was loud: players snapping towels at one another. Ox, who'd hit a home run, pounded his chest like a triumphant ape, leaping onto a bench. They were jubilant, he knew—because of the victory, yes, but more because they weren't the one in Johnson's office, the one who'd sit there alone after Johnson left so he could compose himself, the one who would wait until they were all gone, on the bus, before he ventured out of the office and began stuffing his equipment into a duffel bag for the last time, the one on his way back to the World none of them wanted to see again.

Chapter Twenty

On the morning after Edward Everett's birthday, Collier woke him again with a phone call. It was a more civil hour: six o'clock. Although the blinds across his bedroom window were closed, he could, nonetheless, tell that outside the day was clear.

"Don't tell me that the drains backed up again," Edward Everett said.

"No. All cleaned up. I just want you to come up to the house for a chat."

He knew whatever Collier wanted to discuss would not be good news. In most years, Collier invited Edward Everett to his house only twice—once with the entire team for a pre-season barbecue the week before their first game, and again when he asked Edward Everett to come to his Christmas party, where most of the other people were Collier's customers. Then, although he was officially a guest, Edward Everett felt more like part of the catering staff circulating drinks and canapés, serving up his stories of major league ball like conversational hors d'oeuvres. It was little different from when he'd told the stories with his uncle—except then they'd put money in his pocket, while at Collier's parties the stories only earned him flat champagne and greasy, bacon-wrapped water chestnuts.

Driving to Collier's home in the hills, Edward Everett passed home after home where the residents were still cleaning up after the storm, taking chain saws to boughs that lay in driveways, sweeping detritus from their front walks. At one house, two boys carried out a rolled-up carpet that had obviously gotten soaked, the smaller boy struggling to keep his grip around it. At another, a woman used a snow shovel to scoop shingles from her lawn.

At the entrance to Collier's drive, Edward Everett pulled up to the wrought-iron gate, rolled down his window and pressed the "call" button on the intercom. Collier's voice responded almost immediately, crackling with static. "Come on up the drive, boy." Almost simultaneously, the electric gate swung open. At the front door, he pressed the bell. It played a chime version of some country song that Ginger liked but which Edward Everett could never remember the name of.

"That," Collier said, raising the coffee mug he held toward the chimes mounted to the wall beside the door, "needs to go. The dishwasher man comes. 'Tender Years.' The electrician comes. 'Tender Years.' Her little girl's friend comes for a sleepover. 'Tender Years.' It's going to have me in the insane asylum."

Collier led him back through the house. It was cleaning day; women in black slacks and white blouses worked throughout the rooms: one vacuumed the living room, while another polished the stainless steel appliances in the kitchen and a third stood on a step stool in the dining room, spraying Windex on the windows.

In the kitchen on the way to the sunroom, Collier asked Edward Everett if he wanted coffee. When he nodded, Collier said to the woman kneeling at the base of the refrigerator, cleaning it, "Honey, will you get Ed here a cup of coffee?" To his embarrassment, Edward Everett realized she was perhaps ten years older than he was. Without a word, she pushed herself to stand with some difficulty, opened the kitchen cupboard, took down a mug stamped with "Collier's Fine Meats" in silver foil and poured out a cup of coffee from the coffeemaker sitting on the counter.

"Cream? Sugar?" she asked. Edward Everett preferred cream but he said, "Black is fine." She nodded, handed the cup to him and then, using the face of the refrigerator to support herself, got back down onto her knees to resume her cleaning, first wiping away the finger-prints she left when she used the fridge to steady herself.

In the sunroom, Collier settled into one of two massive recliners that sat dead center in the room. "I can't stand cleaning day," he said, flipping the lever to lean back the chair. "I feel like the Czechs in 1939, invaded. I don't have any space of my own."

He indicated with a gesture that Edward Everett should take the other chair. Sitting, he had the feeling of being in a stadium skybox at life's fifty-yard line. From here, he could look down the hill, through the yards of Collier's neighbors—their gated streets, their miniature English rose gardens, their patios with five-thousand-dollar stainless steel barbecue grills—down into the yards of the more modest homes, the ranches and split-levels on postage-stamp yards, ending, at the bottom of the hill, in trailer parks and industrial build-ings and finally the Flann River. It was as if the town's topography were a geographic bar chart of wealth: the higher you were, the more you had. While he could not see his own house, he could spot the beginning of his neighborhood—roughly three-quarters of the way down—and, farther still, the ballpark. Near gate three, what seemed from this perspective a miniature beverage truck of some sort sat, the driver wheeling a handcart stacked with cases of beer or soda inside.

"I still remember the first time I sat here when the house was mine," Collier said. "It was, I don't know, seven, seven-thirty, and from here I could look down into the ballpark. It was November and I called the night guard and told him to turn on the lights. At first he didn't believe it was me and wouldn't do it. I said, 'Hell, you'll believe it's me when I kick your butt and fire you.' When the lights came on, it was the most beautiful thing. 'It's my ballpark,' I thought. 'My family name is on that ballpark.' " Collier laughed. "Cost me a boat-load of money just to turn on the lights for an hour, but what the fuck."

Edward Everett knew that Collier had not invited him to the house to reminisce, but he let Collier have his moment, sitting in si-lence, looking down the hill toward the ballpark. It had never, in the time since Edward Everett came to Perabo City, looked charming in the daylight. Up close, the cracks in the walls were evident; in places, great chunks of concrete were missing and, in a few of the hollowed-out spots, pigeons nested, the walls and walkways around them spattered with droppings. Edward Everett had not had many chances to see the park from a distance at night, when it was lit up, but on the occasions he had—when Collier rented it out for district high school football championships or a clown rodeo—it had looked like a small gem, the light towers washing out nearly everything that surrounded it, the warehouses, the buildings of Collier's meatpacking business, the Diamond Trailer Park where home run balls sometimes knocked out windows. Then, it was almost enough to make up for the ugliness that bordered on it. At night, glowing, it made the entire town appear beautiful.

"I gotta let it go, Ed," Collier said, breaking the silence. "I got grandkids that need college." At first Edward Everett misheard the pronoun as "you," not "it," and he couldn't figure out why it was Collier telling him he was fired and not Marc Johansen, MS, MBA, nor what his abilities as a manager had to do with college for Collier's grandchildren; would Iowa State send Collier's grandson a letter that said: *Your ACT scores are good but there's the matter of your grandfather keeping Yates on as manager. It suggests a congenital deficiency in intelligence.* As Collier went on, though, Edward Everett realized that he was talking about the entire team.

"When I was a kid, my daddy brought me into the business by cleaning out the slaughterhouses, scraping up guts and brains, but kids now—Ginger's Kurt won't eat meat, if you can believe it; an eleven-year-old vegetarian. Even the ones that'll eat a steak don't want to know how it got from Flossie mooing in the field to being on their plate, medium-rare." Collier let out a deep sigh. "Any notion how much the team loses in a year?"

Edward Everett hadn't a clue. He rarely paid attention to the attendance, focused as he was on the game. Twenty-five thousand, he thought, but doubled it. "Fifty grand?"

Collier laughed. "Times it by three."

"Maybe . . ." Edward Everett ventured, although he had no idea what should follow the "maybe."

"Unless you're going to tell me about an oil well behind second base, I thought of everything we could do. We got that stupid giant walking foam owl so that the little kiddies would have something. We got the Owlie girls in hot pants shooting T-shirts into the stands for the daddies of the little kiddies. Ginger says kids these days like rock music. What the hell do I know about rock music? We seen what happened with that."

Late last season, Collier had brought in a band that was doing the county fair circuit. For a month before the date they were going to play, he ran ads on three of the local radio stations, bought billboards, but the concert attendance was sparse. The problem, Edward Everett realized later, was that Collier had brought in a band Ginger had liked in grade school, but they hadn't had a hit in twenty years. Most of the people who stayed after the game for the show were women in their late thirties and beyond, who, even though they were mothers or even grandmothers, screamed the lead singer's name shrilly while their kids slunk up the aisles pretending to be orphans.

Edward Everett didn't know what to say. He read *Baseball America*, knew the stories: a single-A team in Piedmont, Virginia, disbanded mid-season, throwing the entire league into chaos; a low-A team in Pocatello, Idaho, offered for sale on eBay. The auction was a joke but the purpose serious: the owner was looking for publicity to sell it. Even in their own league, foul balls sometimes landed in the stands and rattled around while kids raced from eight, nine sections away to retrieve them.

"The drain thing is the last straw," Collier said. "It wasn't just the rains. When the Roto-Rooter guy come out, he found clay on the snake. Clay means cracked pipes. He says, knock wood, if we don't get any more serious rain, we can get through the season with them not backing up again, but they're gonna need to be replaced. You don't want to know what it's gonna cost. It's more than your bosses pay you." He regarded Edward Everett for a moment, then said, "I wanted you to know. I'm not telling anyone. Not even Ginger, who nags, 'Dump the team; dump the team.' We're not pulling a Piedmont. I'm going to look for someone to buy it. Hope someone from the damn town wants it. That's the first choice. Second is someone buys it and moves it to Bumfuck, South Dakota, or somewheres.

Third—" He arched his eyebrow and made a gesture as if scattering scraps of paper to the wind.

"What about obligations to the franchise?" Edward Everett asked.

Collier smoothed his mustache, a gesture Edward Everett had come to know meant he was considering his words. "Your bosses ain't said nothing?"

"No," Edward Everett said, his skin prickling.

Collier sighed. "This year's the last on the contract."

"I wasn't aware of that," Edward Everett said.

"My lawyers tell me a month ago your bosses shut down the talks."

"I had no idea," Edward Everett said.

Collier sipped his coffee and looked away as if he was composing a sentence carefully in his head. From somewhere in the house a vacuum whined and in the kitchen two women laughed. Collier shook his head. "I assumed your bosses would've told you. We've been talking to Cincinnati since they got a single-A contract up as well. They seem interested but..." He shrugged. "I can't believe your boss ain't said nothing."

"Nothing," Edward Everett said.

"Well, in a way, I'm relieved," Collier said. "I thought we were friends and when I thought maybe you were holding out on me, I was hurt."

He was relieved? Edward Everett thought. *I could be out of a job and he's relieved?*

He realized that Collier had stood, a gesture that said the meeting was over. "Give the missus my best," he said.

Walking through the house, Edward Everett tried not to resent Collier pleading financial straits all the while he employed a platoon of women who were at that moment teetering on step stools to wipe dust off the crystal baubles in the dining room chandelier, taking small brushes to the grout in the tiled floor of the entranceway. Besides, he thought, whether Collier sold the team or dissolved it would not affect him in the end, since even if the Owls stayed in Perabo City, he wouldn't have a job there next season, not if the big club moved the single-A team elsewhere and Cincinnati moved in. He wondered what it meant that Marc Johansen, MS, MBA, hadn't told him they'd stopped negotiating with Collier: did he already know Edward Everett was out, a sixty-year-old fossil who still preferred keeping penciled index cards on his players? He would have to get on the phone, go back to the baseball winter meetings and patrol the lobby of the hotel, taking his resume to player development directors alongside men half his age who understood all of the arcane formulae that people like Marc Johansen, MS, MBA, loved so well.

As he reached the front door, Ginger was walking in, laden with shopping bags, the eleven-year-old boy carrying a bag from the Apple Store, the girl carrying a suit bag from Macy's over her shoulder— maybe more in retail sales, Edward Everett calculated, than he earned in a week, the benefit of Collier being born into a family that had the foresight to start a meat company eighty-something years earlier, when Edward Everett's grandfathers were going down into a mine, the benefit of the Collier family realizing generations ago that it was better to be the sort of people for whom other people worked instead of, like Edward Everett's family, people who worked for other people, people like Collier.

"Oh, good," Ginger said when she registered Edward Everett's presence. "There's two bags from Williams-Sonoma in the trunk I couldn't manage. Would you be a dear?"

Chapter Twenty-one

At the game that evening, as Edward Everett brought out his lineup card to present to the umpires and exchange with the manager from Lincoln, the stadium announcer invited everyone present to serenade him with "Happy Birthday." Phantom Frank struggled through a plodding version of the song, beginning by hitting keys that were off by what Edward Everett imagined was a handsbreadth. Although on most nights he wouldn't have paid attention to the size of the crowd, after his meeting with Collier, he couldn't help but notice there were maybe five hundred fans there; perhaps only a third bothered to sing, starting out and then falling silent as they tried to match what Phantom Frank played. After a moment, as if someone had picked up his hands and put them on the right keys, Phantom Frank played something that sounded close to "Happy Birthday" and a few more joined in, but without spirit. As he arrived at the final note, Phantom Frank added an awkward trill and a handful of fans applauded.

"I'll give you one call today as a gift," the plate umpire said, winking. He was in his mid-twenties, his head shaved since, Edward Everett knew, he was going off for his once-a-month Army Reserve training after the series was over. They were all young, Edward Everett realized: the field umpire might be thirty, tops, and the man-

ager from Lincoln couldn't be any older than thirty-five. Two years
ago, he had a pinch-hit double that drove in the tying run in the
ninth inning of the seventh game of the World Series and then
scored when the opposing pitcher tried to pick him off second base
but threw the ball into center field. A picture of him sliding across
the plate, the ball hanging just above his head as he smashed against
the catcher's outstretched left leg, had been on the cover of *Sports
Illustrated.* They were all on their way up, he realized. In five or so
years, the Lincoln manager would be managing at triple-A, mentioned in rumors whenever a major league manager's job appeared in
jeopardy; the umpires, too, would move up the chain, double-A,
triple-A, fill-in when major league umpires took vacation.

Meanwhile, what would become of him after this season ended?
Twenty-something years ago when he stopped playing and took a job
as a hitting coach in the minor leagues, he had seen himself on the
same track, fully expecting that one day he'd be in the dugout in the
major leagues again—if not as a manager, then as a coach. He'd gotten stuck in the station, though, never offered a job above double-A.
Once, he'd taken a job as a bench coach at Valdosta, Georgia, sitting
next to a manager who, a year earlier, had retired after fourteen years
as a second baseman in the major leagues, a legitimate star, someone
whose face showed up in ads for a car battery, symbolizing the prod-
uct's reliability. As a manager, he was like a lot of former players who
had enormous talent. He had little patience with the journeymen,
couldn't find the words to tell a shortstop how to react more quickly
to a ground ball, became flustered when he tried to teach a batter
how to change his stance to take the merest fraction of a second off
the time it took him to swing through the zone.

But the All-Star was personable, funny and famous. Several times
during the season, network TV crews came to Valdosta to cover his
story; the angle was always that he was giving back to the game,
teaching the new generation. He made jokes, repeated the same
story, about a shortstop who had started the season making an error
in each of the first dozen games and how he'd been patient with him
and, within six weeks, he had been called up to triple-A. "That's
gratifying when you can help a kid do that." He left out that the sea-

son had started the day after the shortstop, a twenty-year-old from Venezuela, had learned that his sister had been arrested in their home country, that no one knew where she was, and that two weeks into the season, the State Department, pressured by the owner of the big club, had negotiated her release and, after that happy resolution, his play improved; he left out the story of the day in the clubhouse when he had screamed at the kid in pidgin English because he himself couldn't speak a word of Spanish, "Bad play-o, bad play-o," while the kid sat on the bench, looking at the floor, curling and uncurling his toes; he left out the story of how Edward Everett had taught himself enough Spanish that he could remind the kid of the basic lessons, using a few words and gestures. "Stay down." *"Permanecer abajo."* "Don't pull away from the ball." *"No torear."* Miming the correct way. It was nothing the kid didn't already know but Edward Everett worked with him for an hour every day until he found himself again; his patience, Edward Everett knew, more important than the instruction.

At the end of the season, the All-Star moved up to manage at triple-A Knoxville. Edward Everett expected he'd be promoted with him but the All-Star had a friend from his days in the major leagues and the friend ended up sitting beside the All-Star at Knoxville and, five years later, they were with the big club, manager and coach, and Edward Everett was back at single-A—the world spinning in excess of 800 miles an hour, him still standing still. Or perhaps, now, falling off it altogether.

The game went badly almost from the start. Pete Sandford was on the mound for P. City and he was throwing strikes, his fastball well into the nineties, but it was flat. In games when he was effective, his pitches moved like a trout through water, slippery, seeming to change elevation and direction on their flight to the plate, as if the ball were avoiding some obstacle only it could perceive. Today, they sat there as if they were on a tray of hors d'oeuvres circulating at a party.

The top two hitters for Lincoln went down: the first on a one-bounce shot to Webber at short, who snared it with a sideways flip of his glove and then tossed it on to first; the second hitter sent

Nelson back against the wall in left, where he caught it chest-high. However, with two outs, and Sandford standing on the back of the mound, facing away from the hitter, rubbing up the ball, Edward Everett felt a prickle of anxiety. He hoped it was only the day off causing Sandford trouble and that, as the game progressed and his arm warmed, his pitches would start moving again. But they didn't.

Before the end of the first, Lincoln was up three–nothing, and when he saw Sandford's shoulders sag, his posture saying "surrender," he sent Biggie out to talk to him on the mound. There, Sandford nodded at whatever Vincent was saying but when Vincent got back to the dugout, he said to Edward Everett, "Better get someone up." He called down to the bullpen, thankful that the day off because of the sewer backing up meant that his pitchers out there were rested. Five minutes later, Lincoln was leading five–nothing and Edward Everett was taking a walk to the mound to remove Sandford from the game, his shortest outing all season, two-thirds of an inning. A few of the fans sent out boos and catcalls, the attendance so spare that Edward Everett could make out what individual fans were shouting. One chanted, "Sandy boy, candy boy." Someone else called out, "Go home so Mommy can wipe your nose." Edward Everett had no idea where what the fans shouted came from; often it was nonsense, something that rose, he supposed, from their own childhoods— their father's disappointment in them, bullying from classmates, the rejection by some girl that still burned years later. At the mound, Edward Everett gripped Sandford's biceps. The pitcher was drenched in sweat; he let out a sigh and shook his head as he handed Edward Everett the ball. "You okay?" Edward Everett asked.

"I couldn't find it, Skip," Sandford said apologetically.

"It's one game," he said, holding on to Sandford's arm, not letting him leave the mound just yet, while the fans continued to boo him. "It's happened to Clemens, Gibson and Maddux. You're in elite company." But the joke didn't work. Sandford gave him a pleading look, his eyes cutting toward the dugout, where he wanted to be.

"Okay," Edward Everett said. "One thing: head up when you go." He was always telling his pitchers that when he took them out; it was his idea of dealing with baseball's version of "flop sweat." Don't let the fans know they got to you. Sandford heeded him, trotted off the mound, head up, but when he got fully off the field and into the shadow of the dugout, he flung his glove the width of the bench before storming into the tunnel and into the clubhouse, where, Edward Everett knew, he'd brood, seeing every pitch over and over until Edward Everett sent Biggie in to tell him to shower.

The game got no better from there on; it was as if the bullpen were infected with whatever ailment Sandford had. By the bottom of the seventh, it was twenty-three—four. Clouds had pushed in by then and Edward Everett found himself hoping they would open up in one of the sudden deluges that occurred sometimes in the Midwest, an all-out soaker, players and umpires scurrying for the cover of the dugouts and tunnels, fans racing for their cars, but God wasn't merciful. While rain did begin to fall in the top of the eighth, it was not much more than mist, and they had to play the entire nine innings. By the last out, there were fewer than a hundred fans remaining in the stands. As Josh Singer grounded out, third to first, to end it, a fan sang out, "Gir-rils; gir-rils, gir-rils."

In the clubhouse, the team was quiet: a post-slaughter shock. Sandford had been showered and dressed for perhaps two hours by then but he'd waited for everyone, in his khaki slacks and Hollister pullover. "I'm sorry," he said in a quiet voice, while other players stripped off their sweat- and dirt-stained jerseys and headed off into the shower room. Edward Everett sat in his office, running up the line totals in the scorebook, listening to the hiss of the water, the plop of wet towels when players dropped them to the floor. The conversation was quiet; he couldn't hear words, just the drone of voices sandwiched among long stretches of silence. He had been present for worse scores—not many, but some. At Green Castle, he once lost forty-one—one, the game summary and box score picked up by the Associated Press because it was the most lopsided score in professional ball in sixty—two years. Another time, six years ago, Perabo City had lost thirty—nothing. It was ugly, there was no question about it, but what he'd said to Sandford was true: it was just one game. They just needed to leave it confined to the box on the calendar corresponding to today, not let it bleed over to the next day.

When he heard the last shower shut off, he went out of his office into the locker room. Nearly everyone was silent, looking at him expectantly, save for Webber, who sat hunched in front of his locker, talking quietly into his cellphone, his right hand cupped over his mouth as if that would make it impossible for anyone to hear what he was saying. "I can't help it."

Edward Everett cleared his throat and Webber looked up, annoyed. "Got to go," he said in a sarcastic tone, as if to say to Edward Everett, *I went two-for-four; I turned two double plays. Don't pin this on me.* Webber might not ever understand, Edward Everett thought, the place of individual glory in a team game.

Edward Everett regarded his players. They sat on the benches, blinking back at him slowly, still stunned. It was easy for him to forget how young they were, not a one more than twenty-three; the oldest had been perhaps in junior high when Edward Everett first came to Perabo City; on the day when he and his team suffered the thirty-run drubbing, some of them were still in eighth grade, their voices only then on the verge of changing. They wanted him to absolve them, explain the reason they had to endure the humiliation. *Oh, now I understand,* they wanted to think. He considered telling them about how that team a half-dozen years ago had sat here, stunned, as they were, but had finished the season in first place—but it was only in the movies that teams responded well to a rousing pep talk after a humiliating defeat. He felt a fury welling in him, not at his players but at Marc Johansen, MS, MBA, and everyone with the big club in whose hands all of their futures lay and who had decided not to tell anyone about whatever plans they had for the team. But it wasn't his players' fault and he took in a breath so they wouldn't see his anger—anger they would read as directed at them. Everything that occurred to him was a cliché but, as Hoppel used to say, there was a reason the cliché was the cliché: tomorrow is another day; don't bring it to the ballpark tomorrow. It was true and it would only be when they discovered for themselves the truth of the clichés that they would be able to move on.

"Go on home," he said quietly, and when no one reacted, he said again, "Go home. We'll get them next time."

After they filed out, he stripped off his uniform, tossed it into the bag for the clubhouse kid to wash and went into the shower room. As he held his hand under the spray, waiting for it to warm, he gave the room a sniff, wondering if the heavy rains banging against the ballpark would make the sewers back up again. All he could smell was bleach, wet concrete and a mix of his players' body washes and shampoos. A crack of thunder exploded, loud enough that it might have been just on the other side of the wall. He remembered something about not showering in an electrical storm but thought, giving a small laugh, if lightning struck him, he wouldn't have to worry about finding a job after the season.

Chapter Twenty-two

The next morning, when he logged onto his email, intending to ask Marc Johansen, MS, MBA, about the organization's plans for his team and whether they'd have a job for him next season, there was already a message from him. A single line: "Acq: J Mraz OF. Uncon Rel: R Nelson OF. MJ MS MBA. Sent from my BlackBerry." *Acquired: Jake Mraz, outfielder; unconditional release: Ross Nelson, outfielder.* He considered typing a single letter expressing his acknowledgment: "K," but Marc Johansen, MS, MBA, would see it for the sarcastic response it was and his position with the organization was too tenuous to risk it. Instead, he picked up the phone. Even as it rang in his ear, he knew the call was fruitless. For one thing, he knew he would not ask directly about his own future or the future of the team. For another, he knew he could not persuade Marc Johansen, MS, MBA, to keep Nelson; he just wanted to tell Nelson something when he called him into his office later that afternoon, something beyond the facts of his status with the team.

But Marc Johansen, MS, MBA, was not at his desk. Instead, Renz answered.

"It's a done deal," he said curtly when Edward Everett told him he was calling about Nelson. "It's on the wire."

"I understand that," Edward Everett said. "I just wanted to tell him something he could take with him."

"What are you, his fucking mommy?" Renz said. "Take with him?" In the background, Edward Everett could hear fingers clicking on a keyboard. "Two-eleven; two-fifty-six; three-oh-one," Renz recited—Nelson's batting average, on-base percentage, slugging average: the numbers were beyond abysmal and revealed Nelson as a hitter—impatient, undisciplined, without power. Edward Everett and Dominici had worked and worked with him, trying to rid his swing of a hitch that had him behind anything but an average fastball, trying to change his stance, the position of his head so that he could get a better look at the ball when it came spinning off the pitcher's fingers. In batting practice, he got it; with Dominici standing behind the cage, snapping "Head!" to remind him to stop tucking his chin so much against his shoulder, snapping "Angle!" to remind him to stop dropping his bat head so far, he sprayed line drives all over the field. But once game time came, everything they had worked on vanished and he flailed at pitches, ticking weak grounders back up the middle, swinging at balls that bounced in the dirt.

"Tell him," Renz went on in his high, nasal voice, "that he's the greatest fucking ballplayer since Babe Ruth but we're too fucking stupid to see that." Then he hung up.

It was eight-thirty; Nelson was probably sleeping at that moment, certain in his life, knowing what he would do today and tomorrow and the next day. Edward Everett could not remember how many players he had given the bad news to; over all his years as a manager it might have been seventy or eighty. Most had been angry. Four years ago, a kid whose name he couldn't recall, Jim or Jack something, flipped a chair across Edward Everett's office with so much force that one of the legs chipped a small chunk from the concrete block wall. The gouge was still there, visible when Edward Everett closed the door.

Anger he could tolerate, even though he was just the messenger boy, a Western Union–gram of disappointment; as long as they did not become violent, he could let them vent. After they ran out of steam, he told them he had been there, on their side of the desk. He told them about the form letter the Cardinals sent him, and sometimes added an embellishment: that they had misspelled his name. The worst were the kids who fell silent. Edward Everett could not tell what they were thinking. One of the first players he gave the bad news to—a kid whose name he would never forget who played for him in Cumberland, Florida: Tripp Burroway; William T. Burroway, the third, the son and grandson of heart surgeons—killed himself an hour and a half after he left Edward Everett's office. When Edward Everett told him: "I'm sorry. It's not my decision," Burroway sat in silence, blinking slowly, the color washing out of his face, before he nodded, stood up, sat back down again as if he had lost his balance, then left the ballpark without even passing by his locker. When the three players he shared an apartment with got home after the game, they found him dead from an overdose of Halcion. Edward Everett had no idea Burroway was medicated, that he suffered from serious anxiety. He was intense: in the dugout, when he wasn't on the field, he would sit jiggling his legs up and down furiously, so hard that it sometimes made the entire bench vibrate. But Edward Everett thought it was just competitive fire. When he called Burroway's family a week later to offer condolences, his mother hung up on him as soon as he told her who he was. He would forever be, for the Burroway family, the man who killed their son.

At ten, the rain started again, so hard Edward Everett could hear it hissing against the ballpark as he sat in his windowless office. He went down the tunnel toward the field and even before he reached the dugout, could see it might be the heaviest rain of the year so far; it blew in waves into the dugout, spraying water back up the tunnel toward him. Puddles stood deep in the outfield grass and streams of water ran down the creases in the bright yellow tarp stretched across the infield.

As he stood there, a brilliant fork of lightning flashed beyond the far edge of the right field wall and the nearly simultaneous boom of thunder shook the stadium so hard he felt the vibration in his chest.

The fluorescent tubes illuminating the tunnel flickered, went out, came back on and then went out again. An odd silence fell on the ballpark—a silence of the systems shutting off: no more buzzing of the fluorescent tubes, no more drone and rattle of the air-conditioning— just the incessant roar of the rain beating against the roof of the dugout and rattling against the tarp.

He knew the ballpark from his years of nearly living in it but still he could not remember being there in pitch darkness. He stepped carefully back along the tunnel, inching over until he felt the rough concrete of the wall, and then crept slowly toward the clubhouse, keeping his right hand in contact with the wall, trying to remember if there were any obstacles—a stack of Coke cases or baseball bats that he might fall over. In the clubhouse, making his way in the total blackness toward his office, he barked his shin on one of the benches. He sat down heavily, waiting until the throbbing subsided, letting his eyes adjust to the dark. After a moment, he could begin to make out vague silhouettes: the lockers, the refrigerator against one wall for water and soda, the cubbyholes of athletic tape, gauze and analgesic cream, the barrel of cracked bats. He stood up, his right shin still smarting, and went back to his office. There, he sat in the darkness, considering what to do. *It is pointless to stay,* he thought. He closed his laptop, gathered his game log cards and shoved them into his accordion file. At the door to the parking lot he stood for a moment, his laptop and folder tucked under his arm. The rain whipsawed the lot. Hail the size of gum balls bounced crazily across the pavement. Everywhere, water had taken over: pouring off the flat roofs of the warehouses across the street, pulsing against the storm drains along the periphery of the parking lot, pelting the roof of his car.

It was perhaps fifty yards to his car and he had no umbrella but he knew he could not stand there forever and so he sprinted across the lot, splashing through ankle-deep puddles, wishing he had paid for a remote key entry, as he had to fumble with the lock when he reached his car. Once inside, he started the engine and turned the defroster on full force. He was soaked, his jersey plastered to his back, water dripping from his face and hair pooling in his lap. He wiped his palm across the glass and as he waited for the windshield to clear enough that he could see, he thought about where to go. What he wanted to do was go home, take a hot shower, change out of his wet uniform. But first, he decided, he would go give Nelson the bad news. Better, he thought, to tell him sooner rather than wait for the next time he would be at the ballpark.

Nelson rented a small house trailer in River View Gardens, roughly a mile from the ballpark. The wooden sign hanging on a post just at the entrance bore a painting of a log cabin sitting beside a river with a trout jumping out of the water. As did many real estate signs, it lied, because River View Gardens consisted of a tight circle of eight narrow trailers and nothing resembling a garden. Three of the trailers were vacant and at one, two windows were broken, rain beating inside. The trailer that Nelson rented for himself and his family— although he was barely twenty, he had two children, three and six months—was missing part of the plastic skirting designed to hide the cinder blocks on which the trailer rested. Beneath it, a child's wagon with one wheel missing tilted in the shadows and, when Edward Everett pulled up, a cat sat up in the wagon long enough to make note of him, gave a stretch and hunkered back down.

Walking to the stack of cinder blocks that functioned as the trailer's front steps, Edward Everett sloshed through puddles, his bad knee sending jolts into his hip. He wondered if he would ever be dry again; the legs of his pants were caked with mud. At the trailer, he rapped lightly on the door, the cheap aluminum shaking.

"Ah, jeez," Nelson said when he opened the door and saw Edward Everett.

"Come in," Nelson's wife said from behind her husband. "Ross. It's pouring."

Edward Everett hesitated, wondering if he should, indeed, go in. It was clear that Nelson already knew why he was there; a manager did not drop by for a social call. He could just turn around, get in his car, go home, take a hot shower.

"Come in," Nelson's wife repeated, and Edward Everett mounted the steps. "I'm Cindy," she said. She was a round-faced girl, perhaps not even twenty, in shorts and a man's T-shirt that fell almost to her knees, her long dark hair pulled back with an elastic band.

"I'll ruin your carpet," he said and, indeed, he was dripping all over the small braided rug set just inside the trailer.

"I'll put something down on the sofa," Cindy said, and she disappeared around a corner and was back almost instantly with a beach towel that, when she unfolded it to lay on the sofa, bore a large screen print of a baseball sitting in the pocket of a mitt, and the words "Baseball is life. All the rest is just details." She handed him a second towel and said, "You can dry off." Edward Everett toweled off his hair, face and arms and Cindy took the towel back from him, disappearing around the corner again. He didn't want to sit but his knee ached so much that he plopped down onto the towel Cindy had spread over the couch for him, sinking because the springs were bad.

"Skip—" Nelson said, sitting in a recliner chair across from him, the chair tilting to the left, creaking under his weight.

"I'm sorry," Edward Everett said but before he could go on, Cindy was back, carrying the six-month-old and bringing the three-year-old into the room by the hand. The older one, a boy, was blond and shy, curling himself around behind his mother's legs, poking a finger into his mouth, peeking out at Edward Everett. The infant wore a one-piece sleeper and, although her hair was wispy, there was a plastic pink bow clipped to it—perhaps to signify she was a girl.

"This is Sarah," Cindy said, kissing the infant on the top of her head, "and Jacob," giving the boy's hand a gentle tug so that he emerged for a moment from behind his mother.

"They're very cute," he said, not wanting to know this about Nelson, not wanting to think of him in this way, someone's daddy, someone other than a name on his roster he was deleting.

"I just thought you'd like to meet them," she said. "They're the apples of Ross' eye." She regarded him for a moment in a way he knew carried meaning and then took the children back down the short hall and Edward Everett heard a door click shut.

"Skip . . ." Nelson said. "I know I haven't hit like I could. My little girl, she has colic and I don't get the sleep I—"

"It's not my call," Edward Everett said, knowing he was about to say something he shouldn't—that he was going to give Nelson hope he shouldn't have. "You're a helluva team player. If it was up to me . . ." He gave a shrug. "I'll make a couple calls. See if we can't find another organization." He hated himself for the lie as soon as it was out of his mouth. What was wrong with him? he wondered. The years had made him efficient in delivering this kind of news. Maybe it was a mistake coming out here, to Nelson's turf, where Nelson's wife could make him feel guilty by bringing out their children as if that would change things: *You're hitting barely two hundred but you have two kids so here's a ticket to the major leagues.* Edward Everett couldn't tell who made him angrier: Renz for reducing everything to a string of numbers or Nelson and his wife for reducing everything to the human factor, the yin and the yang of baseball.

He couldn't tell but it seemed Nelson was tearing up and then he was weeping like the boy he still was—a boy-man with a wife who slept beside him and children who shared a room across the narrow passageway that served for a hall in this cramped trailer—hunched over, his face buried in his hands, and then Cindy was back beside him, sitting precariously on the left arm of the recliner, the chair cracking under the weight. She leaned into Nelson, plopping the infant onto his lap, while Jacob stood to the other side of him, patting his father on the knee. "Don't be 'set, Daddy; don't be 'set."

"Maybe you should go," Cindy said. "You've done whatever you came to do."

"I'm sorry," he said. "I shouldn't have come. It's just that we won't have a game."

"We don't care a damn about the game," Cindy said in a measured tone, stroking her husband's hair.

What Edward Everett had wanted to say was that he wanted to spare Nelson coming all the way down to the park in the downpour, that he thought he was doing him a favor by coming out here, but there was no point in his saying it.

At the door, he stopped and studied the family huddled together in the face of what they most likely saw as a worse storm than the one battering their trailer, Nelson planting kisses on his daughter's head as if she were the one who needed comforting.

Before he turned the knob of the door to go back out into the deluge, he stopped and decided to do Nelson one last act of kindness, although he might never see it that way—not even in sixty years, if he lived that long. The chances were, he would see it as one more act of cruelty. But no matter: a generous act was still a generous act even if the person receiving it could not recognize it.

"I lied," Edward Everett said. "You should do something else with your life. Sell straw," he said, echoing Hoppel's last comment to him more than thirty years earlier—my God, a third of a century in the past, he thought—a remark he had heard as sarcasm but which, he realized, was the kindest thing anyone might have said to him. "Sell straw," he said again, and let himself back out where the rain continued to pound, while behind him, Nelson, whether he knew it or not, was on his way to a better life. Before he closed the door, he glanced once more at the family. Nelson certainly had far more than he ever had.

Chapter Twenty-three

For a dozen years, Julie sent him photographs of the boy, which was the only way he had of thinking about him— "the boy"—since there was never a note, nothing about what his name was. Edward, after him? A name from her father, uncle, a pop star crush: Bobby, Davey, Paul? So he remained "the boy." The boy in someone's arms, wearing a white christening gown with a blue cross embroidered at the neck, squeezing his eyes closed against the sun, one plump fist raised as if someone had startled him from a sleep he very much did not want to leave. The boy, still an infant, in a yellow sleeper, wearing a red-and-green felt elf cap topped with a small bell, held up by someone before a Christmas tree, torn wrapping paper scattered in the background. The boy in a high chair, his face, slightly blurred, averted from the camera, as if something had distracted his attention just at the moment the shutter clicked. The boy asleep in a dim room on a wide bed covered by coats. The boy, naked except for a diaper, squatting in the arc of a lawn sprinkler. The boy at five or six, holding a lunch box, his hair slicked back, wearing a beige windbreaker, slouching on the porch of a house. The boy at seven, in a white jacket and black slacks, on the step of an altar in a church. The boy in a suit at a table in a white-linen restaurant, raising a glass aloft as if in a toast. The boy on the banks of a river, green swim trunks exposing skinny legs and a thin torso, reaching back to throw a stone into a lake. The boy at a kitchen table, schoolbooks before him, chewing on the eraser of a pencil, looking intently at a worksheet. The boy, seated on a bicycle, his back to the camera, head turned toward it, his right foot on a pedal, his left on the ground, as if he was about to push off, ride away.

That was the last picture he received. Until then, they came at the rate of two or three a year after the first, the Polaroid of the infant in the hospital nursery, all addressed to him in care of whatever minor league team he was with: Erie, Peoria, Raleigh, Topeka, Little Rock, Cedar Rapids, Medicine Hat, Carbondale, Sioux City, Providence, Omaha, Cumberland. Each came like the first, folded into a blank sheet of paper, in an envelope with no return address. Most carried a Chicago postmark but two were from Bloomington, Indiana, and one from St. Louis.

For a long while he looked for them, Julie and the boy without a name. In ballparks in Decatur, Springfield, Iowa City, Rockford, Peoria, he would study the crowd, looking for young women cradling infants. In Peoria, he was certain he'd found them, sitting five rows behind the visitors' dugout, a redheaded woman in a denim jumper alone with a baby. He spotted them in the third inning as he trotted in from left field, the woman balancing the infant on her lap, holding on to its hands as it stood on her legs, bouncing up and down in an excited fashion. As he crossed the first base line, she seemed to wave. He felt a lurch in his chest and raised his hand to wave back but she seemed not to notice and was, instead, looking beyond him. When he turned around, he saw the Peoria shortstop waving back at her: *his* wife, *his* child.

Another time, in Duluth, as he sat on the bus, leaving town after a Sunday afternoon game, they stopped at a traffic signal beside a Dairy Queen. Through the plate-glass window, he was certain he saw her in one of the booths, spooning ice cream into the mouth of a child in a high chair. As the bus idled there, the woman turned to the window and squinted out into the day as the light changed and the bus pulled away. When they arrived at their next town, Oshkosh, Wisconsin, he called directory assistance for Duluth, asked for listings under her last name but there were none.

He developed a ritual: whenever they arrived in a new town, he would take the white pages from his room, carry it to a phone booth and call everyone sharing Julie's last name, thinking: *I may not find her, but certainly a cousin, an aunt, an uncle.* He tried to remember if she had siblings. Her name was not common and, as it was in Duluth, often there were no listings, but occasionally there were. Once, in Racine, he thought he'd found her. It was during a bad stretch for him, a handful of hits in he-didn't-want-to-think-how-many at-bats. Two days before, his manager—Mike Norman, then—had called him into his office for what he thought was going to be yet another death sentence in yet another organization but it wasn't; he was in a professional coma, on life support: Norman was sitting him down for a few games—he'd been pressing, was too conscious of everything when he was at the plate; had his hands always been an inch from the knob of the bat or was it three-quarters? No matter where he put his feet, his stance felt off balance. It all distracted him, slowing his swing a few-hundredths of a second; even on curves that didn't break and which he should have driven hard, he was popping meekly to the second baseman.

He had begun to think that his looking for a woman and a baby he'd never find would mean the end to his career; he vowed to give it up. She knew where he was; she kept sending him the photographs. If she wanted to see him again, she could. But, in the room, the phone book was already sitting on the desk and he flipped it open and found a listing there: "Aylesworth," initial "J," and thought, all right, once more, and called it. A woman answered. There was considerable noise where she was, music and voices, as if a party was going on, and the thought struck him that he could not remember when, exactly, his son had been born, and so, maybe in some grand coincidence, he had called on his birthday, when Julie and her family were celebrating.

"I'm looking for Julie Aylesworth," he said.

"This is her," she said, and his stomach tightened.

"This is Ed—" he began, and she interrupted him.

"Ed? We've been waiting for you."

"Ed!" several voices in the background exclaimed. "Finally!"

"Are you coming?" the woman asked.

"I don't know where you are," he said, his heart racing. He saw himself calling a cab, giving the driver Julie's address, being dropped at the curb, the door opening, a swarm of people, his son standing there in a paper birthday hat.

"Oh, God," the woman said. "Are you drunk?" Then she said to someone where she was, "He's so drunk, he doesn't remember his way."

"No," he said. "I'm not drunk. I—" But where the woman was, a doorbell chimed and the woman said, "Ed! How can you be here and on the phone?"

"I think there's a mistake," Edward Everett said. "I guess I was looking for another Julie."

"Who's Julie?" the woman said. "This is Judy. Ju-dee."

"I'm sorry," he said, but she had hung up.

At one point, he realized that the boy would no longer be a boy but a young man. This was when he was in Montana, a bad year, a year out of baseball after the Angels organization fired him the January following his one season managing their low-A team at Missoula, too late for him to find work with another franchise. He was seeing a woman who was a photographer for the *Missoulian,* Melissa Hungate, the widow of a firefighter who had gotten trapped in a paper mill fire, and when Edward Everett lost his job, he took it as a sign that he should settle down and they went to Las Vegas over a weekend and married. "Second time's a charm," she exclaimed optimistically when he suggested it. He took a job delivering the newspaper, up at two-thirty in the morning, hurling papers out of the window of a four-wheel-drive Jeep in the dark before dawn. After his route, he and Melissa met for coffee and eggs in a diner called "Le Café" and once while he sat waiting for her, watching the snow fall outside the window, thinking it was most likely time to get out the tire chains, a kid came in—eighteen, maybe nineteen—wearing insulated coveralls and an orange hunter's vest. He sat at the counter and something about him caught Edward Everett's attention: the way he slung his left leg over the stool as he sat, akin to the way Edward Everett imagined one mounted a horse; he remembered his own father had done that when he used to take Edward Everett to Tucker's for pie after football practices when Edward Everett was a boy. He watched, a prickle raising the hair on his arms, as the kid set a stainless steel thermos onto the counter, unscrewed the cap and slid it across toward the teenaged waitress so she could fill it with coffee. When she returned it to him, the kid leaned toward her. The notion came to Edward Everett: *This is my son,* and he realized he was holding his breath, thinking, *What do I say?* The door to the outside opened, the bell above it jingling, and a middle-aged man, wearing identical insulated coveralls and an orange hunter's vest, paused at the threshold to stomp the snow off his boots. "The deer ain't waiting, son," he said in a jovial manner, and the kid and waitress exchanged a brief kiss and then he was gone.

Then, after four months of being married, Melissa came to him to say it had been a mistake and besides she had discovered she was in love with her late husband's brother. "His spirit is in there," she had said wistfully when she left, and Edward Everett went back to baseball, managing in independent ball in Limon, Colorado, the lowest rung on the ladder, but back in baseball, nonetheless, and again he thought he'd found the boy: an outfielder from Illinois who was fast, fast, fast, the only thing keeping him out of organized ball a lack of discipline at the plate, but it was a lack of discipline that came from a fire that reminded Edward Everett of his own that year in Springfield before the Cardinals called him up. For half the season, Edward Everett worked with him so closely that the other players called him "teacher's pet," sitting beside him on the bench and explaining the nuances of the game: when to play shallow and when to play deep; the counts and situations when a pitcher was more likely to throw a breaking ball and the times when Edward Everett could nearly guarantee he'd see a fastball; how to determine what sort of pitch was coming in by the direction the seams spun.

It helped—the Giants picked him up in early July, assigning him to their single-A team in Tucson—but then his parents came to Colorado to help move him to Arizona and Edward Everett saw that the player was the spitting image of the man he introduced to Edward

Everett as his father, had the same way of ducking his head when he made a joke and waited for a laugh. The father was effusive when he met Edward Everett, shaking his hand enthusiastically. "I can't say enough about what you did for my boy," he said, his voice nearly identical to his son's, slightly high-pitched. "We'll remember you for this."

What were the chances the boy in the Polaroids would end up in professional ball anyway? Fifty-million-to-one? Yet, for years, he often felt the same prickle he'd felt in the café in Missoula—a shortstop at Quincy, an opposing pitcher when he was managing at Rockford, another outfielder when he was in Lansing. None were his son, of course, and then he was in Perabo City, moving through his fifties while the baby, toddler, boy in the Polaroid snapshots would be moving on through his twenties into his thirties—too old to be playing ball at the level Edward Everett managed—and he stopped looking for him.

Chapter Twenty-four

Nelson turned out to be a problem. Two days after Edward Everett told him the organization had released him, when the team met at the ballpark to board the bus for a road swing that would begin with three games against Quad Cities, Nelson was on it, in a window seat, scrunched as far against the wall as he could be. When Edward Everett climbed the steps and saw him, Nelson gave him a quick glance and then looked away in a manner that reminded Edward Everett of the childish game If I Can't See You, You Can't See Me. Letting out a deep sigh, he dropped his briefcase onto the seat just behind the driver and made his way back, plopping into the seat in front of Nelson.

"I'm not getting off," Nelson said in a low, flat voice.

"Ross," Edward Everett said, "you can't do this." Nelson only shook his head. He did not look well; he was wan and there were dark circles under his eyes. He had a tic Edward Everett had never noticed before, scratching a fingernail rapidly against the lobe of his right ear and then flicking the underside of the lobe over and over. His eyes blinked rapidly as if he had just come into a harsh light.

"No," Nelson said, turning his attention to outside the window. Edward Everett regarded him, weighing his options: Did he order Nelson off the bus? Should he call the police, have them escort him away? He had never seen anything like this in the forty years he had been in the game. Players just went away: one day there, the next gone, their lockers emptied or a new player's uniform hanging there.

"You should—" he began but Nelson took an iPod out of his pocket, plugged the earbuds in, turned it on, the volume loud enough that Edward Everett could hear the music nearly as plainly as if he were plugged in as well. Did it make any difference, really? he wondered. He got out of the seat and made his way back to the front of the bus.

"What the fuck you doing?" Dominici said in a low voice that was still loud enough that Nelson—and everyone else—could no doubt hear.

"You go tell him to get off," Edward Everett said.

Dominici got up and strode back to Nelson, grabbed his arm, trying to yank him to stand, but Nelson wrenched free. "Get off," Dominici said through clenched teeth. When Nelson shook his head, Dominici balled his right hand into a fist and raised it but then let it drop and returned to his seat near the front of the bus, behind Edward Everett. "You're going to lose control of the team, letting him pull this shit," he said.

As the bus driver swung the doors closed and shifted into gear, Vincent moved from his own seat and slid beside Edward Everett. "This ain't that kid all over again, Skip. That doctor's son, what's-his-name."

"Tripp Burroway," Edward Everett said.

"Burroway; yeah. How many kids you cut loose? You only run into one of them in a lifetime. If at all."

"He'll get tired and just go away," Edward Everett said.

Nelson did not, in fact, go away. He dressed for the game in Quad Cities, appropriating a locker near the back of the clubhouse, setting up the small framed photograph of his wife and children on the shelf, just as he had all season; set up, as well, the tiny plastic baseball player his son had gotten for him out of a gum ball machine and a small polished stone he'd once told Edward Everett his wife had found on a parking lot on their honeymoon to Branson, Missouri—all of his good luck charms that had brought him nothing of the sort. During the team meeting Edward Everett held before the game, Nelson stood in a corner, listening intently and then, along with everyone else, trotted down the tunnel, laid his bats into one of the cubbyholes in the dugout, turning them all so that his initials and uniform number written in indelible marker on the end of the knobs faced right-side up, grabbed his glove and went out to shag flies with the other outfielders. When he tried to take batting practice, however, stepping into the cage when Webber was slow to take his turn, Webber yanked him away from the plate. "Get the fuck out of here." They stood in a staring contest until Edward Everett approached them. Even before he said anything, Nelson ducked his head and slunk away.

At game time, he sat at the end of the bench, popping sunflower seeds into his mouth, chewing them, spitting out the husks. When the team began a rally, he leaped to his feet, shouting, exhorting. When a run crossed the plate, he dashed out of the dugout and embraced the runner in a bear hug, lifting him off the ground.

For most of the trip, Edward Everett wondered if his kindness in letting Nelson stay with them and pretend he was still a professional ballplayer had earned them all some sort of blessing. The weather turned in their favor as the gloom and rains that had colored nearly the entire spring and summer stayed behind them; their days and nights were warm, the skies clear and the trip was filled with marvels, some part of a game, some not. During the seventh-inning stretch on their second day in the Quad Cities, a stunt hang-glider sailed into the ballpark from over the right-field bleachers, landing on the infield, stutter-stepping as he touched down near second base, and when he stopped, his silk kite rippling, everyone could see the words printed on it: "Missy, will you marry me?" In Peoria the first night, the team brought out six-year-old triplets to sing "The Star-Spangled Banner," and as their flat and uncertain "*braaaaaaave*" finished the anthem, a golf cart bounced onto the field ferrying their father, a corporal on leave from Iraq, surprising his daughters, who'd had no idea he was coming home. Even some of Edward Everett's players teared up on the bench when the girls rushed to the cart, shrieking, "Daddy," in better unison than they'd had when they sang.

On the field, Perabo City played inspired ball, taking two of three in Quad Cities and all three in Peoria, two of the wins small gems by Sandford, who seemed to have pushed past his five-inning limit, going seven innings in his first game and the full nine in the second, a neat, two-hit shutout. Webber, too, seemed a changed person; for the first time since he'd joined the team, he wasn't surly; even more than his ten hits and four walks in twenty-six trips to the plate, what surprised Edward Everett was that in the eighth inning of the last game in Peoria, with the score two–two, a runner on second and none out, Webber shortened his swing and punched a slow ground ball to the right side of the infield. He was out, but the runner moved to third and scored what turned out to be the winning run on a fly ball by Tanner, hitting next. When Edward Everett looked at Webber's game logs, he realized it might have been the only time all season Webb deliberately offered himself for the good of the team.

In Urbana, however, their good fortune vanished. When they got to town, the rain caught up with them again, a vicious storm that froze traffic, their bus creeping along the highway at ten miles an hour and stopping entirely for twenty minutes because of an accident, their exit less than a hundred yards ahead of them. When they got to their motel, things got worse: their reservation was wrong. Consulting the computer when they tried to check in, the clerk—a strawberry blond girl who might have been eighteen—said, "I don't have you here until next month." Dominici, irritable because he had a corn on his right foot that had started bleeding from being squeezed into baseball spikes, snapped, "So, we're just figments of your imagination?" He swept his hand in a gesture meant to call attention to the thirty wet men clustered in the small lobby, but accidentally knocked a glass dish of mints off the counter, shattering it on the floor.

In the end, the motel manager found them six rooms, pushing folding cots in between the double beds. Edward Everett hadn't shared a room in years—a single was one of his few perks as manager—but ended up bunking with Dominici, Vincent, Sandford and Webber. It was a miserable night. With the two folding cots made up for sleep, the already small room was cramped; the only way he could get to the bathroom was to sit on one of the cots, swing his legs around to the other side, take two steps to the second cot, sit on it, swing his legs around to the other side. Beyond that, Webber and Sandford clearly despised each other. Webber was loud, turning on ESPN even at midnight so he could watch the baseball report. When Sandford went into the bathroom before bed, Webber snapped at him, "Leave hot water. Not like in QC." Sandford did not respond in an overt way but the manner in which his eyes flicked toward Edward Everett told him that if he weren't there, it might have escalated into a physical response.

Then, when the lights went out, the room became almost unbearable: Dominici was flatulent and every time he farted, Webber let out an obvious groan. Vincent, who fell asleep within moments of the room becoming dark, snored, as did Sandford and Webber once they fell asleep. It seemed the only one who could not sleep was Edward Everett. He lay on the cot, one of the metal braces digging into his shoulder blades through the thin mattress, listening to the cacophony mixed with the traffic outside.

Nelson seemed to have gotten worse. In the clubhouse, as he dressed before the game the next day, he muttered to himself, words that Edward Everett could not understand, and when he took his clothes off, he did so in anger, snapping his shirttail when he whipped it off, flicking it against Sandford. Someone else might have hit him back but Sandford just cocked his head to one side, curious, while Nelson hung his shirt on a hook in the locker he had taken for himself.

During the game, P. City seemed transformed into a baseball version of the Keystone Kops, kicking easy ground balls, dropping pop flies. In the third inning, the Urbana hitter sent a grounder between first and second. Moose Shriver, his first baseman, snared it, sprawling on the wet ground, but when he came up to throw to the pitcher, who should have been covering the base, Petey Mosley was still standing on the mound, gazing at the play. "You're not a fucking spectator," Webber yelled. In the ninth, down four–nothing, P. City briefly woke up. With two outs, Webber, Mraz and Vila hit consecutive singles, Webber scoring. That was all they had, however. Batting next, Shriver swung at a pitch that bounced in front of the plate and trickled a ball that the catcher pounced on and threw to first for the final out.

The next day it rained, the game washed out, the team cooped up in the motel. Fortunately, the wedding party that had booked so many of the rooms had checked out. Because the desk had made the mistake with their reservations, Edward Everett convinced the manager to let the team have enough rooms so that the players could be two to a room instead of four, meaning a bed each. Maybe it would change their luck back to good, he thought as he handed out the key cards; at least maybe the team would get some rest.

In his own room, he stripped down to his boxers and T-shirt and got into the bed, tried to sleep but couldn't. His room faced the parking lot and on the edge of it was a truck stop, diesel engines rumbling. He got up, resigned to exhaustion, and sat at the desk with his laptop so he could upload the stats from the night before, but found that if the room had wireless Internet, it wasn't working. There was, however, an Ethernet jack in the wall at the base of the desk and so he started pulling open drawers, looking for a cable. He didn't find one, but in one drawer he found a Gideon's Bible, into which someone with a crude sense of humor had folded a flyer promoting a place that called itself an "adult supercenter," featuring half a dozen badly photocopied pictures of naked women. He returned the Bible to the drawer after crumpling the flyer and putting it into the trash and then reconsidered: picturing a maid finding it there, thinking, *Dirty old man*, he tore the flyer into small pieces and folded them into a Kleenex before discarding it.

In another drawer, he found a telephone book. Although it had been years since he'd done so, he opened it to the "A's," looking for an "Aylesworth." To his surprise, he found one: "Aylesworth, Colin, MD." It could be a cousin, he thought; had Julie a brother? It struck him that he still pictured her as the young girl who had exhausted herself pushing his wheelchair through Montreal, but she would be past fifty by now. Then it struck him: the boy might have her last name, and "Aylesworth, Colin, MD" could be the boy in the photographs she'd stopped sending him well more than twenty years ago. He opened his cellphone and punched in the number but then closed it in the middle of the first ring. What would he even say if someone answered? *Was your mother...? Are you...?* Maybe, it struck him, Julie had never told the boy anything about him. *Your father died. Your father was lost at sea.* Maybe she had married while the boy was an infant, too young to remember otherwise, and he'd gone through his life thinking someone else entirely was his father, calling the insurance broker or the druggist or the dentist or the chemistry teacher "Daddy."

He put the phone book back in the drawer, returned his laptop to its case and left the room, walking through the rain to the lobby to log onto the Internet there.

Later that afternoon when he tried again to sleep, it came to him grudgingly and when he woke—what, forty-five minutes later?—there was a commotion outside. Loud voices. Banging. When he opened his door, he could see a semicircle of his players knotted on the parking lot in the rain, enraged by something, shouting. Two or three of them pushed forward and then he could see a fight going on, players trying to pull bodies apart.

"Hey," he shouted, jogging barefoot across the wet lot, the gravel prickling his feet, but the fight continued as if no one had heard him. He shoved into the scrum. Someone thrust him backwards and he pushed into it again, aware that Dominici and Vincent were there with him, shoving men backwards. An elbow caught Edward Everett in his cheek, stunning him. Dominici was yelling, "Stop it! Stop it!" Finally, they got to the bottom, two players grappling with each other on the ground. Webber and Nelson, Webber sitting on Nelson's belly, Nelson grasping Webber's wrists, straining under him.

"You cocksucker," Webber was shrieking, flailing, trying to get his arms free of Nelson's grasp. Together, Dominici and Vila finally succeeded in pulling Webber away, Vila by locking his elbows in

Webber's, Dominici shoving against his chest until he tumbled backwards. There was a crack and then Webber stopped struggling,

"What the hell happened?" Edward Everett said.

The players looked everywhere but at him. Nelson was up on his knees, breathing hard, spitting something out of his mouth: saliva mixed with blood.

"What happened?" Edward Everett said to Webber, who was still on the ground, moaning now, holding his right shoulder with his left hand, rolling side to side.

"It was—" Sandford began, but Martinez interrupted him with a syllable: "San!"

"What happened, Sandy?" Edward Everett asked.

Sandford gave Martinez a look. Martinez shook his head, tight-lipped.

"Oh, shit," Sandford said. "Webber's an asshole." He turned to Edward Everett. "Webber just jumped Nelson, saying something crazy."

"Nelson don't belong anymore," Martinez said through clenched teeth. Nelson was on his feet now, rubbing his jaw. His left eye was swollen shut and his top lip was fat, curled into an exaggerated sneer. Martinez made a lunge for him, but Sandford restrained him. Nelson danced back. "You better fucking get out of here," Martinez said, trying to wrest himself free of Sandford's grasp. Nelson glanced briefly at Edward Everett.

"What did Webber say?" Edward Everett asked him. Nelson shook his head and limped across the parking lot toward the service station next door, rubbing his left ear.

"Skip," Vincent said. He was crouched beside Webber, his hand on Webber's shoulder. "I think he's hurt. I mean bad." When Edward Everett knelt beside Webber on the wet gravel, he could see he was pale and shivering. He gently tried to roll him from his side onto his back but Webber gave out a yell and stayed curled on his side.

"Well, fuck," he said, standing. "Somebody call 911."

They had to wait for four hours in the emergency room. It was Saturday night: "crazy night," the girl at the reception desk called it when they registered. The place swarmed with patients and their friends and families: people who came in bloodied, children racked with coughs; EMTs rushing people on gurneys through the automatic doors. A gas station clerk stabbed in a robbery. An older man dying from cancer. As Edward Everett and Webber sat waiting for someone to call his name, Webber rocked in his chair, cradling his right arm, saying over and over, "Jesus, Jesus, Jesus, Jesus."

When a nurse came to take Webber back to an examining room, Edward Everett followed them, lying, saying he was Webber's father. Where she left them was not a room, exactly—merely a bed, a chair and a small table, separated from the other rooms by a drape. On the other side of it, the dying man moaned incoherently. Edward Everett could hear soft voices: a nurse explaining that she had given him something to ease the pain, the staff was doing its best to get him into a room upstairs. Edward Everett sat beside Webber and when he began weeping, Edward Everett laid his hand on his hurt shoulder. Webber reached up abruptly and grabbed his hand; at first he thought it was a response to pain but Webber was squeezing tightly, as if he was afraid Edward Everett would leave him there, alone.

By the time the doctor came to examine Webber, the dying man had been moved elsewhere and his place was taken by a small child who had pushed a piece of candy up his nose. "Don't be mad, Mommy," the child said. The doctor who came to see Webber was a willowy Indian woman who may have been less than thirty but was, despite her age, crisply efficient. "It would be better if you left us," she said, already peeling back the sleeve of Webber's hospital gown and touching his shoulder tenderly.

When Webber winced even at her delicate touch, Edward Everett started to protest but Webber snapped, "Fuck, go, go, go."

He wandered down the hall to another waiting room farther from the admissions desk. It was quieter, only one other person there, a woman knitting. A television mounted to the ceiling played a ball game with the volume muted, the Cubs and the Cardinals, the top of the fifteenth, a one–one tie, and he sat down to watch. The Cubs' half inning ended and the camera showed a long shot of the view from behind home plate in the new St. Louis ballpark, the one where he had played knocked down years ago by a wrecking ball. Beyond the center field wall, the city skyline rose and, at the center, the Saarinen Arch glinted. The camera panned the crowd: tens of thousands of people in red and blue, animated, raising index fingers, waving. It was all so prosperous, Major League Baseball was. He realized where he sat was roughly halfway between the two cities, but it might as well have been on another continent.

When the doctor came out to tell him that Webber was asking for him, she told him that Webber's shoulder was broken. "A proximal humerus fracture," she called it. Her accent made it sound like something beautiful.

"What does that mean?" he asked.

"With surgery . . ." She shrugged.

"He's a ballplayer," he said. "A good one." One to whom someone once gave a two-million-dollar signing bonus, he thought, and who should, if he stopped letting his immaturity get in the way of his talent, make more than fifty times as much in his career.

"He can live a normal life," she said. "But baseball . . ." She shook her head.

"He can't . . ." He didn't finish the sentence. *Be through*, he was going to say. He didn't like Webber. He took his talent for granted, was a jerk to his teammates, shrugged whenever Edward Everett gave him advice, as if to say, *You have no idea what it's like to be able to play the game as I can.* Edward Everett felt suddenly angry—at Webber, at Nelson, at the doctor. She was from a country where they didn't play baseball. There, it was cricket: what could she know about baseball? She flinched and he realized that she could see the anger crossing his face.

"He's so young," he said. "He could heal, couldn't he?" A page came over the intercom for Dr. Abadeen.

"I'm sorry," she said, pointing in the direction of the speaker in the ceiling, and she turned, hurrying down the corridor.

On the television, one of the Cardinals players was digging around third, sweeping wide, dashing down the line toward home plate, colliding with the catcher, who took a throw from the cutoff man, the ball jarring free, bounding away, the Cardinals pouring out of the dugout to greet the runner who brought home the win.

Edward Everett turned away and went back toward Webber, trying to figure out how to tell him that he wouldn't ever be one of those players on the television. Not for their club. Nor for Pittsburgh nor St. Louis nor Boston. Nor anyone. He was twenty and his life as he expected it to be was over.

Chapter Twenty-five

When Edward Everett got home on Sunday night after a miserable doubleheader—two losses, eight–one and, in a second game to make up for the rainout on the day before, four–zip—he had two voice mail messages. He expected one to be from Marc Johansen, MS, MBA, demanding more information about Webber's injury. Almost immediately after the taxi had brought him back to the motel from the hospital, he'd taken his laptop to the lobby to email a report about Webber's injury and prognosis to Johansen. It took him more than half an hour to compose since he wanted to be accurate, but also he kept changing it, first reporting Nelson's part in it, then deleting him from the account because he had no idea how Marc Johansen, MS, MBA, would react to his allowing Nelson to stay with the team after the organization had released him. Finally, he'd said only, "injured off-field in physical altercation with person not a team member." It was after all the truth. Since then, he'd obsessively checked his cellphone, expecting he'd find a missed call from Mark Johansen, MS, MBA, but the big club was ominously silent.

As for Nelson, he had vanished. When the bus left the lot at the Urbana ballpark after the final game, Edward Everett scanned the faces on board: no Nelson. As the bus sat at the exit from the parking lot, waiting for traffic to clear before making its turn, he expected to see Nelson running toward them, but he didn't show up, leaving him God knew where. Perhaps, Edward Everett thought, Webber—pitiful Webber, still in the hospital, his mind doped with Percodan—had knocked into Nelson the sense he needed, as if one of the punches had shaken loose the last bit of—what, insanity? eccentricity?—whatever had made Nelson keep showing up to a team where he did not belong anymore.

The first message on his voice mail at home was from Collier. "Gimme a call," he said. It was almost eleven when he heard the message; Collier was probably still up—he suffered from insomnia; in the past, he had called Edward Everett even later than this for no particular reason except that, Edward Everett could tell, his house was too quiet and there was nothing on television. Collier would not want to hear about Webber, one of only a few players who drew fans to a game—what fans there were.

The second message was a hang up, just the sound of what seemed like a woman's voice exclaiming a syllable he couldn't discern and then a receiver clattering twice before the dial tone came on. When he checked his caller ID, it read, "Blocked." He replayed the message several times, raising the volume, wondering if it was Renee's voice, wondering if he could understand something of what she had been trying to say. "Ha" was all he could make out, or "Ah." It may have been a frustrated exhalation, or the start of a sardonic laugh, but it also could have been the beginning of a word: "Hon," maybe, he thought. Nonetheless, he clicked "save" and, after seeing that the kitchen light was on at the Duboises' house, went next door to get the dog.

On the team's way out of Urbana, Edward Everett had asked the bus driver to stop at a Czech bakery they passed. Once, Renee had joined him on a road trip there and, exploring the town while Edward Everett was at the ballpark, had discovered the bakery. She took him there for coffee and kolache, Renee trying out the little Czech she knew, greeting the tiny, white-haired woman behind the glassed counter of bread and sweets, *"Dobry den."* The woman had brightened and begun speaking rapidly before Renee blushed and said, apologetically, that "hello" was the extent of what she remembered from the lessons her maternal grandmother had given her when she was a small girl. Nonetheless, the baker had not accepted any payment for the pastries they ordered and had also made them take a box of them for the road. "Grandma used to make these at Easter," Renee said on their drive back to Perabo City, opening the white box, filling the car with the scent of flour, sugar and raspberry.

On this trip, he'd bought a box of the kolache, and now he took them over to the Duboises' house. He crossed through the two yards, up the back steps to the deck off the kitchen, since he didn't want to ring the front doorbell. Rhonda often had the six a.m. shift at Lowe's, meaning she had to leave at five to get there on time. When he peered through the window beside the door, he could see that Ron sat at the table, a sheaf of papers spread across it. Edward Everett tapped on the glass and Ron gave a start, staring out at him, coming cautiously to the back door, squinting as if that would help him see into the darkness.

"It's me," Edward Everett said.

Ron opened the back door cautiously. "You about gave me another heart attack."

"I brought these," Edward Everett said, holding out the box of pastries to Ron. "They're from this bakery in Urbana that Renee once found and I thought—"

Ron's face softened. "Ah, jeez," he said, taking the box, but reluctantly, in a manner that Edward Everett imagined resembled someone accepting the cremains of a loved one. "Renee . . ." he said, his eyes not meeting Edward Everett's.

"What?" Edward Everett asked.

"You know I like you, Ed," Ron said, hefting the box as if he were weighing it. "But this is just not a good idea."

"Is someone there, honey?" Rhonda called from another room. When she came into the kitchen and saw Edward Everett, however, she stopped at the doorway, her posture stiffening. "Oh," she said.

"It's a thank-you for watching Grizzly," Edward Everett said, nodding toward the box. "I know he's an imposition."

"Did you tell him?" Rhonda asked her husband.

"Tell me what?" Edward Everett said to her.

"Ron, you said you were going to." When Ron didn't respond immediately, she said, "I'll get the dog."

Ron held out the box of kolache and Edward Everett took it from him. "I don't think it'd be good for us to watch Grizzly anymore," he said. "It's not personal. It's just that—"

Then Rhonda was back, carrying the dog. She set him on the floor, her eyes not meeting Edward Everett's. "I'm sorry," she said, her voice all but inaudible, and left the room.

"Renee just asked us not to do anything that might . . ." Ron said, shrugging.

"Might?" Edward Everett asked.

"Encourage you," Ron said quietly. "I really hate this."

"I don't even know what the problem was," Edward Everett said.

Ron regarded him in a manner that Edward Everett took to mean he was considering giving him information someone—Renee?—had asked him not to.

"Ron," Rhonda called from another room. "It's pretty late."

Ron shook his head sadly. "I wish things were different. But they're not. That's all."

After he and Grizzly were outside, on the deck, Grizzly dashing ahead of him for their own yard, Edward Everett watched his neighbor through the window. Ron sat down heavily at the table, idly flipping the edges of the papers lying there for a moment. He seemed old and tired and Edward Everett knew that his visit had made him that way. They had been friends but now they weren't: the Sunday chicken dinners, Ron's awkward, drunken embrace at his and Renee's wedding, Ron chuckling as he called him "my new son"—none of it mattered, and now, after a decade, they were just people connected by an accident of adjacent addresses, another part of his life closed off to him.

The next morning, he called Collier, who said, "Hike on up to the estate."

Collier's house was once again swarming with workpeople, this time a carpet cleaning service—three men in olive green coveralls unloading a machine from a van, wheeling it through the front door.

Edward Everett stood in the open doorway. "Hello?" he called into the house. "We're in here," Collier replied. When Edward Everett stepped into the foyer, he found Collier and Ginger in the living room, sitting with a woman in a tailored suit, a large book of drapery samples open on Ginger's lap.

"My hero," Collier said, jovially. "You saved me from hours of looking at fabric."

"Coll," Ginger said in a tone that was half-scolding.

"Honey, you know the deal. Your taste, my checkbook." He got up from the sofa, gave Ginger a quick kiss on the top of her head and came out to greet Edward Everett.

"Nick of time." He slung his arm around Edward Everett's shoulder and guided him past the dining room, where the carpet cleaners were plugging in their machine and switching it on, the cleaner lurching as the worker lost control of it for a moment, then hissing as he began steaming the carpet. He and Collier headed out to the sunroom.

"I won't dillydally," Collier said even before they had settled into the recliners that looked out on the town. Below—far below—pockets of people were sandbagging, along the edge of the parking lot for the elementary school, near one of the Baptist churches. Until that moment, Edward Everett hadn't realized that the town was flooded: was it possible he had been so caught up in his own turmoil that he'd missed the news? At the high school football field, just the tips of the goalposts rose above the water, a soccer goal bobbing in it. Beyond that, an entire neighborhood was submerged, water lapping against front doors and bay windows, a police johnboat puttering among the houses.

"It's a good-news, bad-news thing," Collier said. "What do you want first?"

Edward Everett saw no point in delaying. "Bad news, I guess."

Collier laughed. "Attaboy. Get to the problem first. Bad: the ballpark is for shit. Turns out the asshole who snaked the drains called the health department. I won't go into details but it's some big fucking list of reasons the ballpark is the A-number-one killer in P. City. Drains, asbestos. All kinds of crap. When they got into it, they kept digging. It's cheaper to knock it down than fix it up. Short answer: no more games at Francis P. Collier Field."

"We've got another thirty—"

"Yeah, I know. Home games. I got Mavis working on that. We got a contractual obligation to finish out the season, and as I said, we're not going to pull a Piedmont."

Mavis has to work fast, Edward Everett thought.

As if Collier knew what he was thinking, he said, "Got a lead on a place. It's . . . well, a sweet country spot, and it's regulation. We talked to the league. Beyond that . . ." He shrugged.

Edward Everett imagined a meadow somewhere, baselines marked by an umpire pacing off distances, paper plates tacked down in place of the bags.

"Two," Collier said, holding up his index finger and thumb. "The good: found a buyer. Contacted me almost right away, soon as the broker got the news out."

There are brokers for sports teams? Edward Everett thought.

"Three," Collier said, holding up his thumb, index and middle fingers. "Bad is, he wants to move the team to Corn Row, Indiana."

"Corn Row?"

"That's not what it's called but it's some town he comes from. It's a sad day for P. City; baseball's been here since Ike was president."

"Who is this guy?" Edward Everett asked, thinking simultaneously, *Get the house ready for the market; find an agent in Whatever Town, Indiana.* Then the idea struck him: *I have no idea whether I'll be with the club next year.*

"He does something in TV. I haven't met him; just on the phone and a couple emails. Lawyers doing most of the talking. But . . ." Collier hesitated.

"What?" Edward Everett asked.

"What are your bosses saying?"

"About . . . ?"

Collier regarded him a moment; had they called him about Webber's accident?

"What have you heard?" Edward Everett asked, his neck prickling.

"We're changing affiliation," Collier said. "That's good for me, since I couldn't've sold her without an affiliation. Cincinnati." He shrugged. "You sure your outfit never said anything to you about what they're doing to replace P. City in the organization?"

Edward Everett shook his head; he had the sensation of growing physically smaller. Why wouldn't Marc Johansen, MS, MBA, have said anything about this? Maybe that was why he hadn't contacted him about Webber's injury: it didn't matter; Edward Everett was obviously persona non grata with the big club. He saw himself getting his mail a few months down the road, maybe the day after Christmas again, another thin envelope: *Your services are no longer required.*

"Those fucking bastards," Collier said. "How many years you been with them?"

"I don't know," Edward Everett said. He couldn't think clearly: how long had he been with the organization? Before Perabo City, he'd been with another single-A team for a year, in Lexington. Eleven years and out, a man with no savings to speak of; a man with no 401(k), no IRA, an old man but still someone too young to collect Social Security.

"You all right?" Collier was saying.

He stared out of the bank of windows, the glass so clear it might not even have been there. Three years ago, the organization had wanted him to move to Danville, double-A, be a hitting coach, but that was when Ron had had his heart attack, and Renee hadn't wanted to leave her father, and the organization had agreed to let him stay for another year. Then another. Then another. And now, end of the line.

Down on the water, the police drew the boat alongside a house where a woman leaned out of a window. She was large, her bulk filling the window, and when the officers helped her into the boat, it settled significantly in the water before it puttered off toward dry land, the woman clearly leaving behind everything she had.

Get over yourself, he heard his mother saying. *There are people with worse problems. Yes,* he thought. A little water in the basement was as bad as the storms had made it for him. Still, he felt his chest tightening and realized he was shaking. He saw himself the next year as one of the pathetic old men he'd known when he was a kid in the game: a codger who kept his house only by renting rooms to players, someone willing to clip money off the rent if they listened to his stories: *There was this time in Montreal . . .*

"I know this leaves you in something of a lurch," Collier said. "I don't know if it will do any good, but I put in a word with this guy." He shrugged.

"That's great," Edward Everett said. Nothing would come from it; the Reds would have their own people. He thought: he would have to sell the house, hope there was enough equity in it to let him live until he could find work. But his house was in no condition to sell. He hadn't painted anything since Renee and he gave it a polish before she moved in. The leak in the basement. The kitchen looked like something from 1975.

"We been friends a long time," Collier said, his voice soft. "Ain't many people in this town I can talk to, you know, mano to mano. The folks here . . ." He swept his arm to the side. "Doctors, lawyers. They got education. All I got come from the College of Bust Your Ass Till You Get Blisters." He reached into his pants pocket, jiggling his body in the recliner, the braces creaking, and came out with a folded piece of paper. A check. Collier opened it, read the amount as if he had no idea what was written on its face, folded it but continued to hold it. "I know I ain't obligated, you know?"

"I know," Edward Everett said.

"It's just a small token, you know. Appreciation and blah blah blah. But you're gonna have expenses." He held it out to Edward Everett, who reached for it, but Collier pulled it back slightly. "You can't breathe a word of this. Not a word to nobody. Especially not the wife. God, especially not her." He laughed.

"I won't."

Collier extended the check once more and Edward Everett took it, thinking: three thousand, five thousand, enough to reface the cabinets, enough to hire the college kid painters who tack their flyers to the bulletin board at the supermarket. He started to slip it into his shirt pocket but Collier said, "Go ahead," winking. Edward Everett unfolded it. Three hundred dollars. He was not certain whether to laugh. How could Collier be enough of a businessman to run a meat-packing business and have no idea how small an amount three hundred dollars was, even to someone like Edward Everett? "Now, I'm sure you gotta scoot," Collier said. "And I gotta get on Mavis's buttocks to nail down that place for you guys to play out the string here."

Edward Everett stood to leave but Collier grabbed hold of his sleeve, keeping him back. "You know I wouldn't of sold if I had a choice," he said. "If the town fuckers would of anted up for a new ballpark . . . but that's as likely as Mrs. Collier saying her days at Macy's are over."

"I know," Edward Everett said. In the living room, Ginger and the woman in the tailored suit were still looking at fabric swatches, three large books already on the floor.

"Now, this one costs a little more, but I think you'll see what I mean," the design consultant said. Ginger ran her hand over the material with her eyes closed. "Yes, yes," she said. "I see what you mean." She opened her eyes. "Coll?" she said.

"Jesus, woman," Collier said, "you're gonna break me."

Edward Everett let himself out.

Chapter Twenty-six

L ater that afternoon, Edward Everett was on his way out to meet Collier, Vincent and Dominici to look at the field Mavis had found, when Nelson's wife showed up at his house. If his printer hadn't jammed in the middle of running out the MapQuest directions Collier had emailed, Edward Everett would have missed her visit altogether.

When he opened the door to find her on the porch, along with a policeman, he didn't immediately recognize her. Grizzly began yapping from the kitchen, rattling the baby gate that corralled him, and Edward Everett stepped onto the porch, shutting the door. He assumed they were collecting for a charity, some organization that supported widows of policemen. "Sorry about the dog," he said. "He's small but he's feisty about his territory."

Neither the woman nor the police officer laughed at his joke and then he realized who she was; he tried to remember her name but it didn't come to him. She was a different woman from the one who had invited him into her trailer during the storm, who had given him a towel to dry his hair and had asked him to sit as if he were any other guest and not someone there to ruin her husband's life, and then had tried to use her children as a feeble argument against the club's irreversible decision. Now she was pale, dark circles swelling under her eyes, her hair pulled back in an untidy ponytail, a dried blot of what he assumed was baby spit-up on the shoulder of her Sugarland T-shirt.

"What happened?" Edward Everett asked, seeing Nelson's dead body turning up in an alley in Urbana; seeing him in prison, arrested after trying to rob a liquor store.

"Maybe it'd be better if we came in, sir," the policeman said, laying his hand gently against the small of Nelson's wife's back. He was a poster boy for law enforcement, tall, his torso that of a weight lifter, his blond hair in a buzz cut.

Inside, Edward Everett left them in the living room to go to the kitchen to give Grizzly a snack to quiet his barking. When he came out, Nelson's wife and the policeman were sitting side by side on the couch, the policeman's arm around her; he was speaking quietly to her but she was shaking her head.

"I'm Cindy's brother," the policeman said. He stood, extending his hand to shake Edward Everett's. "Earl. I'm not here in any official way. This isn't even my jurisdiction."

"The police here aren't interested in helping," Nelson's wife said.

"They can only do so much," Earl said in a tone that suggested it wasn't the first time he'd explained that to her.

"But they're not doing anything." She pounded her fist against one of her knees so hard it made Edward Everett wince as if he was the one she had struck. Earl sat and took her hand, gave it a squeeze and then set it on the couch between them.

"What's going on?" Edward Everett asked in a tone he hoped sounded consoling.

"Ross has gone missing," Earl said, "and we're trying to talk to anyone who might have some information."

"We haven't seen him in more than a week," Nelson's wife said. "I tried to file a missing persons but—" She laughed bitterly, making a dismissive wave of her hand.

"Cin, I've explained—" Earl started to say but she interrupted him angrily.

"They wouldn't even listen to me," she said, fiercely. " 'He's an adult, ma'am,' " she said, clearly imitating someone, her voice deep and flat. " 'He has the right to come and go.' He wouldn't just come and go. He has children."

"Unless he's a danger to himself or others, the police won't take a report," Earl said to Edward Everett. "It's not TV," he said to his sister.

Edward Everett's cellphone rang. He knew it would be Collier or one of his coaches, asking where he was. "I'm sorry," he said. "I don't mean to be rude but I had an appointment and—this will just take me a minute."

Nelson's wife let out a single, bitter laugh, shaking her head, Edward Everett another in the list of people indifferent to her missing husband. Earl patted her knee. "He needs to take this call," he said. He nodded to Edward Everett. "Go ahead."

Edward Everett flipped open his phone, stepping over the baby gate and into the kitchen. "Skip, where the hell are you?" Vincent said even before he could say hello.

"Something came up I needed to take care of," he said in a quiet voice and then added, his hand cupped over the mouthpiece, "About Nelson."

"Oh, fuck," Vincent said. "Hello? Clueless Boy? You're not wanted." Edward Everett flinched, although it was not possible that Nelson's wife or her brother could have overheard the remark.

"It's complicated," he said.

"Better you than me," Vincent said, laughing. "Skip, you gotta see this place. You know St. Aloysius, that high school that closed, shit, who knows how long ago?"

"I've never been there," Edward Everett said, glancing around the corner toward Nelson's wife and her brother. They were involved in an earnest conversation but in voices too low for him to understand, Nelson's wife shaking her head vigorously.

"Well, let's say it's *Night of the Living Dead* meets Fenway Park meets . . . hell, I don't know. Whoever built it must've been from Boston, because there's a miniature Green Monster in left. Or used to be, since it's all but falling down. The grass is three foot high."

From where Vincent was, Edward Everett could hear a voice exclaim "Fuck."

Vincent laughed, then shouted to someone, "You lame city boy!"

"What's going on?" Edward Everett asked, wanting to finish the conversation so he could get back to Nelson's wife and her brother, tell them what he knew. Or didn't know. Get them out of the house.

"Dominici just found a snake in the outfield," Vincent said.

"Biggie, I'm sorry, but I really——"

"Yeah," Vincent said. "I'll let you go. But wait till you see this place."

"All right," Edward Everett said impatiently.

"See ya," Vincent said. "Say hi to crazy Nellie for all of us."

In the living room, Nelson's wife and her brother had finished their conversation and were sitting in an obviously uncomfortable silence; she had moved apart from him and had her head turned away.

"I'm sorry," Edward Everett said, sitting in the overstuffed chair near the couch. "There was something with the team I had to take care of. Things are . . . well, in a mess."

"I'm sorry if our family problems have inconvenienced you and your team, Mr. Yates," Nelson's wife said in a carefully measured tone.

"Cindy," her brother said, laying a hand on her shoulder, but she shook it off. "My sister has been through a lot," Earl said to Edward Everett. "You'll have to forgive her."

"I understand," Edward Everett said.

"You understand," Cindy said in a sarcastic tone. "How nice of you."

"This isn't going to get us anywhere," Earl said.

"I didn't want to come here," Cindy said. "He——" She stabbed the air, pointing at Edward Everett, but whatever her accusation was, she stopped short of saying it.

"It wasn't my choice," he said. "I was just the one who had to give him the news."

"Cindy, maybe we should go."

"No," Cindy said, standing and taking a step toward Edward Everett. "You have no idea how he felt about you, do you? How you let him down?"

"Nelson—Ross was . . ." Edward Everett started to say, shrinking back into the chair, wondering if she was going to hit him; he had no idea if he could bring himself to defend himself against a woman who attacked him. *Never hit a girl*, his mother used to say. *Even if she hits me?* he asked. *Never*, she said.

" 'Skip says I have to work on this and that,' " Cindy said. " 'Skip says I have to keep my hands back.' 'Skip says I pull my head out.' Skip says, Skip says." She let out a snort. "Do you know how many times I woke up in the middle of the night and I'd find him in the bathroom, going through his swing slow motion in front of the mirror? 'Skip's right,' he would say if he saw me watching him."

Earl stood up and tugged on Cindy's arm. "Cindy," he said in a quiet voice. "This isn't why we came." She let him guide her back to the couch.

"When was the last time you saw Ross?" Earl asked, patting his sister's hand.

"In Urbana," Edward Everett said. "At the hotel, when he—" But he stopped; he didn't see any point in bringing up the fight he'd had with Webber.

"What was he doing in Urbana?" Earl asked.

Edward Everett flicked his eyes between them, considering his response. "He followed the team there," he said cautiously.

"Oh, God," Cindy said, shaking her head. "Ross, Ross, Ross."

"And when was that?" Earl asked.

"This was Saturday," Edward Everett said. Could it have been only the day before yesterday? It seemed much longer ago.

Cindy bent her face to her knees, starting to weep, her brother rubbing her back.

"Do you have any idea where he might have gone?" Earl asked.

Edward Everett shook his head. There was Webber on the ground, his shoulder broken, on the verge of finding out he would never play ball again, and there was Nelson slinking off across the lot, limping through the raised rock bed that served as a divider between the motel lot and the gas station. Edward Everett saw him twisting to avoid the yucca plants in the bed, and then . . . ? He had no idea. He had turned around to look at Webber, to tell someone to call 911. Had he thought to look again for Nelson? He couldn't remember. "No," he said. "I have no idea."

"Was he close to anyone on the team?" Earl asked.

Wouldn't Cindy know that? he wondered. She gave no sign that she had an answer and Edward Everett tried to think: had he ever seen Nelson friendly with anyone? There was Nelson in the locker room, surrounded by the other players, but in the image that came to him, Nelson was on the periphery, listening but seldom talking, laughing at a joke someone told but never telling one himself, just going about the business of being a ballplayer, waiting for someone to tell him what to do. *Get into the cage and take some cuts, Nels. Go shag some flies, Nels.* And he took batting practice, chased fly balls, went out to the field when Edward Everett put him into the lineup, sat down when Edward Everett didn't. Other players got angry if Edward Everett took them out, if he didn't start them. Vila once knocked over a five-gallon plastic cooler of Gatorade when Edward Everett sent a right-handed batter to pinch-hit for him in a close game. Webber flung his glove against the dugout wall when Edward Everett pulled him from a game to discipline him. Webber and Vila had fire; until he went crazy, Nelson just nodded and sat down, tossed a handful of sunflower seeds into his mouth and watched the game, spitting out the husks, clapping if someone drove in a run or made a diving catch. "I don't think he was close to anyone," he said.

Earl nodded, glanced at Cindy, then back at Edward Everett. "Did you ever have a chance to see Ross play in high school?" he asked, the interview—what interview there was—clearly over, Edward Everett no help to them.

"No," Edward Everett said. "I don't do that. There are scouts."

"He was something, you know?" Earl said. "He was All-Conference his last year. He was the best of the best. Once—"

But Cindy interrupted him. "Earl, I don't think Mr. Yates needs us to rehash Ross's past glories."

"Sorry," Earl said. "But we all thought he was the real deal back then. I got a kick out of being able to say that my sister was marrying Ross Nelson." He paused. "But I guess everyone who gets this far was the real deal somewhere, right?"

"True," Edward Everett said, resisting the impulse to look at his watch. He needed to get to the park, wherever the hell it was, to get ready for the game. "Is there anything else I can tell you? I liked Nelson. Ross, I mean. He was—"

"I wish you wouldn't," Cindy said, standing. "I really don't want to listen to you say nice things about him."

Earl stood as well and took his wallet out of his hip pocket. Edward Everett wondered if he was going to pay him for his time but Earl took out a business card. *Officer Earl Heidenry, Lakeport Police Department*, with a phone number and an email address. "If you see him or hear from him," he said, giving the card to Edward Everett.

"Sure," he said, standing.

At the door, Cindy turned back. "I love Ross," she said. "He's . . . well, I love him. But I don't know what I'm going to do."

"How do you mean?" Edward Everett asked.

"Do you have any children?" she asked.

"No," he said. It was a lie he had told so often that it usually came easily but this time he wasn't able to meet her eyes.

"Well, then you won't understand," she said. "But if you have kids, you do what they need. No matter what that costs. I hope Ross—" She stopped, let out a breath. "But if he doesn't, I have to make sure my kids are okay. If you see him, tell him I said so."

"I don't think I'll see him," he said. "But if I do, I will."

After Nelson's wife and her brother left, Edward Everett went to retrieve the map and directions from his printer tray. Although he realized he needed to get to the new park soon, he was nonetheless curious if Marc Johansen, MS, MBA, had finally responded to his report on Webber, and he opened his email program, simultaneously wanting and not wanting a response. When his email loaded, his cursor sat at the last one; it was from Marc Johansen, MS, MBA. "Organizational Changes," the subject line said. Edward Everett sat down at the table, watching the cursor blink. As he hesitated before opening the email, he remembered someone he once knew, Mitch Weil, his team trainer when he managed at Lexington. Every week, Weil bought a lottery ticket and waited until long after the drawing to check the numbers. "I've had an unlucky life," he once confided to Edward Everett, "but as long as I don't check the ticket, it's a winner and my luck has changed." As long as he didn't open the message, Edward Everett thought, he still had his job.

When he did click it, however, he found that it didn't concern him, not directly, at any rate. "As you know, when I joined the organization, I said we wouldn't make any changes until I was certain I was confident in our direction," the email read. "My office has spent a long while evaluating our structure. Today, as the first move among others to come, I am announcing that, at the end of the season, Hale Claussen will be leaving his position as manager of our club at Gary and joining our scouting department's Mountain States region as a special consultant. We appreciate his years of service and look forward to his contributions in this essential aspect of our operation. I will keep you apprised as we continue our review. Marc Johansen, MS, MBA."

"Special consultant for the scouting department's Mountain States region" was a euphemism, Edward Everett knew: as manager at triple-A Gary, Claussen had been a hairsbreadth from the big show; now he'd spend his days driving long distances between small towns in Montana, Wyoming and Idaho, looking for talent no one else had spotted, all without a salary, merely the promise that if he found someone no one else had, the team would pay him a bonus. If Claussen took the job, Edward Everett knew he was likely to earn little, since "undiscovered talent" was a myth nowadays, when everyone with modest ability, a cellphone camera and an Internet connection was posting videos on YouTube of themselves hitting home runs or striking people out. It was just a way for Marc Johansen, MS, MBA, to avoid saying *We fired him; so long and good luck*.

When he clicked "delete" to erase the message, Edward Everett realized that he had been holding his breath. He was safe, for now, but the first casualty had fallen. There would be others, Marc Johansen, MS, MBA, promised.

He collected the map and directions and went out to see what sort of field Collier had found, to learn how much farther he had fallen in the cosmology of the game.

Chapter Twenty-seven

Despite the MapQuest directions and Collier's email that
had said all Edward Everett needed to do was look for
the county fairgrounds and take the first left past them, it took him
an hour to find the field; he drove back and forth along the blacktop
road near the fairgrounds three or four times until he finally saw the
stone sign for the school, "St. Aloysius," and a statue of the patron
saint, all but concealed by a thick stand of goldenrod. When he got
there, he saw that Vincent had been right about the place. Although
Collier had promised "a sweet country spot," it was the worst field he
had seen in more than forty years of professional ball. It sat behind
the abandoned high school, down a crumbling set of forty or so concrete steps from the school's parking lot. When the school was in
operation, the ballpark, no doubt, was a fine place for high school
baseball. As Vincent had said, the builders had modeled it after Fenway Park; a miniature Green Monster rose ten or twelve feet high at
the edge of left field. By now, however, much of the green paint had
flaked away and some of the boards from the face of the wall were
missing, revealing rotting cross braces. If there ever had been a fence
in center field or right, none stood any longer. The grass in the
outfield was several feet high, and when Edward Everett arrived, a
bushwhacker rumbled across it, not so much mowing the grass as

harvesting it, leaving thick cuttings in its wake. On the pitching mound, a high school boy was pushing a steel turf roller to smooth it, while near first base, another worked away at a mound of stones, hefting them into the back of a pickup parked there.

Beyond the poor condition of the field, there were also no dugouts—only two long, weathered wooden benches running beside the first and third base lines, separated from the field by rusting chain-link fencing. Behind the bench on the home team side, a ramshackle concession stand sat against a stone retaining wall holding back the hill that rose behind it.

"There is an upside," Vincent said from the top of the steps. When Edward Everett turned around, Vincent pointed to the hill beyond right field and the edge of the fairgrounds visible above the rise. "We get a honey of a seat for the fireworks show the last weekend of August. Come on and I'll show you the clubhouse. Or I should say 'clubhouse.' " He wiggled his fingers, drawing quotation marks in the air.

The "clubhouse" was what had once been the boys' locker room. "The visitors get the girls'," Vincent said, smirking, opening the door, showing Edward Everett what was little more than a dank concrete cave with two facing lines of steel lockers; ductwork and copper plumbing crisscrossed the ceiling. Martinez and Mraz were already there, the first of his players to arrive, neither in uniform, their equipment bags unopened on the floor.

"This is a big fucking joke," Martinez said when Edward Everett came in.

"My high school was eighty times better than this POS," Mraz said, kicking at a locker, which popped open, a sheaf of papers spilling across the cement floor. "What fucking dipshit organization did I get traded to?"

"This is home," Edward Everett said, trying to conceal his rage at Collier. Whatever his feelings toward him, it would not help his players if he fed their disgust. "Pitching rubber is still sixty feet six inches from home; bases are still ninety feet apart." At least he hoped that was true. He realized he had no office here. In the back, in a small alcove just before the shower room, sat a small desk stacked with cardboard boxes, soccer goal netting and metal basketball hoops. He began collecting the junk from the desktop and putting it into one of the cartons.

"What if we refuse to play?" Mraz said.

"Then we forfeit," Edward Everett said.

"Shit," Mraz said, kicking at another locker, popping another door open, this one filled with football pads, which clattered out.

"It's not the best, but it's what we have for the rest of the year," Edward Everett said, putting the last armload of junk from the desk into the cardboard box. He sat at the desk, unsnapping the elastic binding from around the accordion folder with his scorebooks and game logs.

"Maybe we could call Webber," Mraz said. "He's got a couple mill. Maybe he could buy us a new park."

"He's probably sitting on his ass on a beach," Martinez said, "drinking mai tais and hitting on supermodels."

"He's the only one of us who got any brains," Mraz said.

"Who is?" Tanner said, coming in with Sandford. He groaned. "What the fuck?"

"Webber is," Mraz said.

"He's the only one of us who ain't going to play again," Sandford said.

"Jesus, Sand, bring everyone down," Mraz said.

By game time, the crowd was pathetic. In fact, Edward Everett thought, to call it a crowd was inaccurate. He did not know whether Collier—who did not show up—put a sign at the ballpark or how the pitifully small number of people had found their way to St. Aloysius, but there were fewer than a hundred scattered throughout the bleachers. Edward Everett was curious whether Nelson would appear and realized he was worried both that Nelson would show up and that he would not. Whenever anyone ventured down the steps, he glanced at them, wondering if it was Nelson; it never was.

Just before first pitch, as Edward Everett exchanged his lineup card with the umpires and the Quad Cities manager, the plate umpire poked a chaw of tobacco between his cheek and gum and asked, "What crime did ya'll commit to end up here?"

"Must've been a major felony," Edward Everett said, grimacing, not wanting them to think this was his doing—he didn't flood the ballpark, he didn't choose this place.

The Quad Cities manager spat into the dirt at Edward Everett's feet. "It's fucked-up." He was maybe thirty, still in playing shape. "I don't know if this field is regulation."

"Relax, Pete," the field umpire said. "We measured it; we talked to the league. It may look like shit but it's by the book." He scanned the diamond. "Barely."

One day, years ago, Edward Everett had calculated how many professional games he'd been part of. At the time, he was sitting in a bar, five or six beers deep into a reunion with Danny Matthias, his one-time roommate at double-A. Matthias by then was ten years out of baseball after hanging on for eight seasons in the majors as a second- and third-string catcher and sometime first baseman; he was "into real estate," he said, but that meant he had invested in apartment complexes and then moved into commercial space, owning more buildings than he could count. As a player, he'd been squat, but by the time he and Edward Everett met for drinks when Matthias came to Lansing, where Edward Everett was that season, he had let himself go to fat, and he reclined more than sat in the chair across the table from Edward Everett. "You know what," he said at one point, his eyes little more than slits because of the alcohol, "I miss it." He asked Edward Everett how many games he'd seen from the inside and Edward Everett had asked their waitress for a pen and then made calculations on an unfolded napkin. The figure came to four thousand six hundred and something. Both he and Matthias sat back in awe of the staggering number, the more than ten thousand hours those games would have consumed. "Wow!" Matthias exclaimed. "You are one lucky son of a bitch."

Edward Everett had never repeated the exercise but as he sat on the sagging bench behind first base at the decaying high school field, the thought struck him that he had most likely climbed near to six thousand games by now, maybe fifteen thousand hours of watching men pitch a roughly three-inch-diameter ball, spinning, dipping, tailing, to other men, who were trying to hit the hell out of it. When he was younger, the thought struck him often, "Someone is paying me to be here, playing ball," and regularly something occurred that took his breath away: a teammate digging his spikes into a padded outfield wall, willing to sacrifice everything to catch what otherwise would have been a home run; a teammate getting the sweet spot of the bat on a ninety-five-mile-an-hour fastball and launching it into the upper deck.

By now, the capacity for the game to surprise him had diminished. But on that ordinary Monday night in late June in a dying town in the middle of Iowa, with roughly ten dozen people on hand, Sandford surprised Edward Everett, as if the pitcher had decided that he was going to remind them all that it wasn't the park or the ambience or the size of the crowd that mattered, but what happened between the foul lines—specifically, what happened in the narrow, sixty-and-a-half-foot corridor that ran between the mound and home plate. For two and a half hours, it was enough that Edward Everett forgot that his career was tenuous, that his wife had left him, that one of his crazy former players had gone missing.

From Sandford's first pitch, Edward Everett could tell that he was on. It was a fastball with movement on it, slicing the barest edge of the outside of the plate. The umpire missed it, called it "ball one," but Edward Everett didn't complain: there was no point in grousing about one pitch. The umpire did not miss the next, another snake-in-the-water fastball, this one on the inside edge, knee-high: strike one. The third pitch—a curve with a wicked, twelve-o'clock-to-six break—the hitter topped back to Sandford, who tossed it to Turner at first for the out. Four pitches later, the inning was over: another ground ball, this one to Rausch at second, and a foul pop fly to the third baseman.

Perabo City scored in their half of the first, three runs, two of them coming on a fly ball by Mraz that the Quad Cities right fielder misjudged and then, when he realized he could not catch it, waited back on it for the hop, which never came. Instead, the ball settled into the thick mown grass, cradled gently as an egg. He plucked it out of the straw and threw home, but too late to catch Tanner, sliding across ahead of the tag. The dust rose in a cloud, drifting across the left field bench and bleachers.

When the inning ended, the Quad Cities manager complained to the umpire about the condition of the outfield, but there was nothing in the rules that said the mown grass had to be raked away.

In the second, Sandford struck out the first hitter on three pitches, the third strike on a curve that seemed to start out head-high and then broke down over the plate as if the ball had just remembered it was subject to gravity. The next two hitters went down on one pitch each, a pop foul that Vila caught and a gentle liner to Rojas at short.

That was when Edward Everett realized that Sandford was doing something special that night; on the mound he seemed oblivious to everything except the ball and where Vila wanted him to throw it. The third, fourth and fifth innings echoed the first two, Sandford pitching what seemed effortlessly, the Quad Cities hitters compliant—four more strikeouts, nothing hard hit.

Edward Everett began watching the sixth inning standing behind the fencing in front of the Perabo City bench, his fingers laced through the links, and then, without realizing it, he drifted down the line until he was behind the backstop, from over the umpire's left shoulder watching Sandford work. Sandford seemed in a trance, not in a game at all, but present in the nano-second of each individual moment flowing into the nano-second of the next: his eyes registering Vila's signals, Sandford's windup and pitch, his movement fluid, his face blank and inscrutable. It was only when the plate umpire turned and saw Edward Everett, yelling, "Hey, get the fuck out from behind there," that he realized where he was and went back to sit on the bench. By the top of the ninth, with Perabo City up by five—nothing, Quad Cities still had not had a base runner—no hits, no walks, no Perabo City errors. In five thousand however-many-hundred games that Edward Everett had seen from the field, from the bench, from the coach's box at first base or third, he had never seen a perfect game, twenty-seven men up, twenty-seven men down. He wondered if Sandford realized what he was doing, but on the mound, as he threw his last warm-up pitch and then stepped aside so Vila could throw the ball to second base to start the pre-inning around-the-horn, his face still seemed blank, a man without a conscious mind. The first hitter for Quad Cities took strike one, and then as Sandford released the second pitch, the hitter shortened up, tried to punch a bunt trickling toward third base. A few fans in the bleachers booed; Sandford stumbled slightly going after the ball, recovered, took it up in his bare hand and threw to first, nailing the runner by two steps. One out. Edward Everett glanced at the crowd—no, it wasn't a crowd, a few score of die-hard baseball fans who had come out for the game and not the radio-controlled car races between innings, nor the Owl mascot, whom Collier had also not sent, nor the college girls in hot pants and belly shirts (also not there). As Sandford stood on the backside of the mound, rubbing the baseball between his two large palms, they were all intent, leaning forward. One held his iPhone in front of his face, shooting video; another had a camera. The Perabo City players not on the field were all standing behind the fence separating them from the field, their fingers laced through the chain links, still and expectant.

The second hitter went to two balls and two strikes—had Sandford even allowed as many as two balls to any hitter that night until then? Edward Everett would have to check Vincent's pitching chart but he couldn't remember anyone—and then hit a hard line drive to center field. Edward Everett groaned but Mraz had picked it up as soon as the ball came off the bat and dashed into deep center, catching the ball over his left shoulder like the tight end he'd been in high school would have caught a pass.

Then it was over. The third hitter swung at the first pitch and popped it up to the infield. Rausch came in, windmilling his arms to call off the other fielders, yelling, "I got it. I got it. It's mine." He squeezed his glove around the ball an instant too soon, clearly wanting badly the perfect game, for Sandford and for all of them. The ball bounced out of his glove and banged against his chest. For a moment it seemed as if it would fall, the hitter reaching base on an error, the perfect game not perfect after all, but he hugged it against himself, clapping his glove over his heart like someone about to pledge allegiance, and Edward Everett thought, *There it is, the final out,* but then Rausch didn't have control over it after all, and it slipped out of his glove, bounced off his knee and hit the dirt, trickling away. Rausch stood there, stunned, while the Quad Cities runner kept going, hitting the bag at first and making his turn toward second.

"Pick it up, pick it up," someone was shouting, but still Rausch stared at the ball, until finally Rojas knocked him aside, scooped it up and flung it toward second base, where, miraculously, Mraz was standing, come in all the way from center field for some reason (Because he was dashing in to celebrate the perfect game? Because he had the baseball sense to realize that no one was covering the base?), and he took the throw, and put down the tag, getting the runner on the ankle as he slid into the base. The field umpire hesitated and then threw up his right thumb, *out*, the game over and won, Sandford's twelfth against three losses, no longer a perfect game, but a no-hitter. A no-hitter was a marvelous thing, but a perfect game—that would have been a miracle, and there was no miracle tonight. ˙

In the locker room, his team was sour. They showered and changed in silence as if they had suffered a heartbreaking loss, not won the game. Rausch sat in front of his locker, his head hanging, as his team-mates avoided him—not, Edward Everett knew, out of anger, but because they weren't certain how to console him. Finally, Sandford sat beside him, draped one of his long arms around Rausch's shoulders and spoke quietly to him, Rausch shaking his head slowly, but when Sandford got up, Rausch stood, finally, and went to take his shower, then changed and left hurriedly. As for Sandford, he stayed under the water a long while, although it was cold by then and the shower room stank of mildew, until everyone else save Edward Everett was gone.

Edward Everett waited until Sandford had finished changing and then said, "You were incredible tonight."

"I really, really wanted it, you know, there at the end," Sandford said, zipping his equipment bag. "I told Rauschy it was okay but I lied. I'm trying real hard not to let it matter but I just keep seeing the ball drop out of his glove."

"You're an amazing pitcher," Edward Everett said. "But here's the thing, you can only control what you can control." He shuffled through the game log cards until he found Sandford's and pointed at the line for the game. Eighty-nine pitches, sixty-four of them for strikes, a good balance of fastballs, curves and changeups, seven strikeouts, only five fly balls to the outfield. "You cannot do any better than this," he said. "It's a team game, but all you need to focus on is what you do."

Sandford nodded but Edward Everett could tell he wasn't convinced. He was only twenty-one, just a few months past being able to buy beer legally, and again Edward Everett thought, *He's still a boy.* "You'll pitch a long time and eventually you'll figure out that when one game is over, it's over, and all that matters is, what did you learn out there that will make you a better pitcher the next time you take the mound?"

Sandford nodded again but Edward Everett knew he was only trying to end the conversation, be able to go home, and so he said, "Have a good night."

When Sandford left, Edward Everett was alone in the locker room. From the shower room, water dripped and something *ping*ed in the pipes. It really was a terrible place, he thought, the concrete pockmarked, graffiti scrawled on some of the lockers, no place for a professional baseball team. Someone with Sandford's gift deserved better; Collier's easy answer for their home for the rest of the season—a solution that Edward Everett knew rose out of his desire to spend as little of his money as possible on the team, just so his silly wife could buy more drapes, more dresses from Macy's—it was an insult to all of them but especially to someone as rare as Sandford.

He looked again at Sandford's game log card, the row of numbers that Marc Johansen, MS, MBA, believed in so fiercely. As he studied it, he could see Sandford on the mound, the man who for more than two hours lived and breathed in an alternate universe from everyone else there, who could only watch him from the outside and get a glimpse of a world that transcended the rusted fence, the cracked home plate—but only a glimpse. Yet when Marc Johansen, MS, MBA, looked at the numbers after Edward Everett uploaded them, they'd be merely elements in an equation, digits on a screen.

His cellphone startled him, Elton John's "Your Song," his ring tone for Renee.

"The most amazing thing happened," he started to say, but she interrupted him.

"I know you're probably not fond of me right now," she said, "but I need to ask you for a favor."

"Sure," he said, thinking she was going to say, *Will you water my plants? My car is going in the shop tomorrow, can you pick me up and give me a ride to work?* Thinking, here was the chink in her resistance, the pastries maybe having done the trick, although they sat, the box still full, on his kitchen counter.

But she said, "Please leave my parents alone."

"I don't—" he began.

"Whatever you think of me, my parents are upset enough already—my dad especially. Please don't try to use them to make me change my mind."

"I wasn't doing that," he said.

She sighed. "Those pastries?"

"I was just doing something nice for your folks," he said.

"Please," she said. "We may not be together now but we were together long enough that I know a little about how your mind works."

"The last time—"

"I was stupid the last time. Stupid and weak." She sighed. "I wanted to keep this simple, as much for you as for me," she said. "I'm seeing my lawyer tomorrow. I really should have done it sooner. It wasn't fair to you for me to draw things out for as long as I did."

He wasn't aware she had drawn things out. How long ago had she left? Wasn't she gone for just as long between last Thanksgiving and Christmas?

She went on, "You don't even have to hire your own lawyer if you don't want; I'm not asking for anything from you."

"Can we meet and talk about this?" he said. "I really have no idea why—"

"There's no point," she said, then added, her voice quieter, "I've moved on."

"What do you mean, you've 'moved on'?"

From where she was he thought he heard another voice but it was indistinct; it could have been interference. "No, I don't need you to do that," Renee said quietly.

"You don't need me to do what?" he asked.

Renee sighed. "Ed, some relationships are like a car on a lake." It sounded like another sentence she would have taken from a book. "There's nothing wrong with being a car and nothing wrong with being a lake but the two aren't meant to be together. That's all."

"A car and a lake?" he asked. Which one was he? Then he understood the meaning of her remark that she had "moved on." He laughed.

"What's so funny?" she said, her voice tight.

"You've *moved on*," he said. "There's someone else."

Renee did not respond. She had hung up. He looked at the phone for a minute as the illuminated screen eventually went black, thinking about calling her back, but packed up his scorebook and game log cards and went home to what seemed even more like an empty house. Two days later, as she had promised, a courier delivered the divorce papers.

Chapter Twenty-eight

O nce, between the first time she left him and the second, Renee came home from work and told him a story: she was setting up a PowerPoint display to show a redesign of the bank's logo to a focus group and while she was plugging the projector into her laptop, one of the women there was telling everyone about her mother, who was in the hospital after a stroke, on a respirator, expected to die. Among them was a new assistant manager, a freshly minted MBA from Marquette, and when the woman finished her story, he had shaken his head and said, "What is she? Sixty? She's had a good life. Let her go." Edward Everett and Renee laughed about the story. "You've had a good life," she would say when he complained about feeling stiff on waking in the morning, when, before the season started, he sometimes said that he was ready for bed as early as nine p.m., when he asked her to repeat something she had said.

For the days that remained of the home stand after he received the divorce papers, the joke came back to him often but it was no longer funny. Until now, sixty was another generation, not his. Even when he had turned sixty, it hadn't seemed anything more than a number he would write on a form that asked "age." *Sixty* was his mother when he lived with her after his injury in Montreal, his mother counting out blood pressure and cholesterol pills at the break-fast table. *Sixty* was his uncle dying of a heart attack four years after Edward Everett stopped working with him, too many steaks and cig-arettes.

But now, with his wife gone and as he waited for the "Organiza-tional Changes" email with his name in it, he felt the full brunt of sixty: *sixty* and no idea of how he'd arrived there so quickly; *sixty* and no notion of where he would be next year. *You've had a good life. You've had a good life.*

At the ballpark—*not quite a ballpark*—he went through the mo-tions, twenty years of managing making it like riding a bike, still saying the right things, making the right moves, knowing when to pull a pitcher, when to pinch-hit, when to shift the fielders in a situ-ation where a hitter would be more likely to hit the other way, effec-tive enough that they went on a winning streak, the home stand nine wins and two losses.

Then, after the games, he cleared out quickly, often even before all of his players had gone home. Two nights after Sandford's gem of a game, alone in the damp locker room, the dripping showerheads leaking water even more rapidly, the pipes developing a whine, it struck him that his father had hung himself in such a place, bitter over the fateful "no" he had said to the man who became one of the greatest football coaches in college history. What had sent him over the edge? he wondered. Did suicide sit in the body like a cancer gene, waiting, inevitable? Was it festering in him?

But at home, things were no better. He began over and over the steps he knew he needed to take. He studied the financial form at-tached to the divorce agreement—assets, debts, property—but every time he set out to make progress on it, it seemed daunting. How much *was* his car worth? How much *could* he sell his house for? As for his bank statements, they were all a jumble, stacked in a drawer, still in their envelopes and in no particular order: May 2007 on top of January 2003 on top of March 2006. How had he let it get to such a state? He put the financial disclosure aside, still blank, and went down to his basement, regarding the boxes that filled so much of the space there, so many things he had no need to hold on to, thinking he should haul them to the curb, take them to the Goodwill, but it all seemed so overwhelming and so he went back upstairs, closing the door on the chaos.

Renee haunted the house—the bedroom, yes, where he lay awake at night, seeing her with whoever represented her "moving on," a man younger than he was, faceless, propping himself above Renee on his elbows, driving into her, Renee's face fixed in a way he remembered too well, her eyes squeezed shut, her lips parted slightly, on the very edge of coming. They were in the living room, on the sofa, on the floor. In the kitchen, as he shook dog food out of the bag into Grizzly's bowl, they were with him at the table, Renee leaning across toward her faceless "moving on," a foot nudging his foot. (*I have an idea*, the two stumbling toward the bedroom.) He wondered if the man had been there when he'd been on the road, and stripped the bed, looking for proof, knowing at the same time it was ludicrous, the ghost of stains mottling the mattress pad offering him evidence of nothing. .

To avoid seeing them, the hours away from the ballpark became a wasteland of television and junk food; he wallowed in nostalgia (But then, wasn't that the purpose of nostalgia, the wallowing?), watching especially game shows from the late 1960s and the 1970s, the time he had come to think of as his prime, Edward Everett, the invincible athletic stud: *Let's Make a Deal, The Match Game, The Newlywed Game*, studying the contestants in their thirty-year-old fashions and hairstyles, the men in broad-lapeled jackets and wide ties, the women jumping up and down in polyester slacks and blouses, beehive hairdos and perfect perms. He wondered if they sometimes stumbled upon their younger selves when they, too, sleepless, were flipping channels, and sat thinking, *How did I become who I am now?* How many of the contestants were still alive, how many of the couples laughing about their ignorance of each other were still together, still preferred the morning when they made whoopee, still called each other "babycakes"?

In the early morning hours, when the game shows disappeared and the infomercials moved in, magic vitamins and foolproof investment schemes, he went through his boxes of game log cards, counting his players who had left the game long ago, smarter men than he, players who saw their years in the minor leagues as an interesting diversion on their way to practicing law or opening a pharmacy or becoming, as one of them had, a professional fishing guide in Montana. He found Christmas cards they'd sent with small notes letting him know how far they had moved away from the game he could never seem to let go: "Here's me and the missus at the lake." "Here's the kids with Santa." More recently, the cards from some of them contained snapshots of grandchildren, fat-cheeked infants with oversized baseball caps sitting cockeyed on their heads. He realized they had seen the open door to the world outside the locker room as an invitation and not banishment; baseball was just an interesting visa stamp in the passport of their lives, while he had gotten stuck at the border, unable to cross.

One day, going through boxes, he found the snapshots that Julie had sent him.

He spread them across the kitchen table, arranging them chronologically by the dates on the postmarks: two dozen images of the boy lined up, looking back at him, the father he had never met: the father, it struck Edward Everett, he may never have known he had. He wondered if the boy had ever thought to look for him; maybe he had trailed him up until Lexington, where Edward Everett lived before Perabo City, and then had given up one address short, just missing the connection.

One by one, Edward Everett picked up the photographs, looking closely into the face. The boy's eyes were brown, he realized—his color, not Julie's—but the child's face more closely resembled hers, was round where his was more angular, and yet the chin was his, not Julie's: while hers came to a slight point—he had once called her his little elf—the boy's chin was square. How odd, he thought, to have pieces of himself out there, somewhere, eyes, chin, hair. He tried to envision what the boy would look like by now, the grown man he would have turned into, thirty-two, thirty-three, maybe a father himself. *I promise you, son, I won't abandon you the way my own father did.*

Sitting in the kitchen, trying not to acknowledge the ghost of Renee and her new man who tugged at his consciousness (*I have an idea,* hand extended, stumbling toward the bedroom), he realized that the photographs revealed nearly nothing about the life the boy was living. It occurred to him that Julie must have chosen the photographs in the same spirit that caused her to refuse to give him a return address or to write a note giving him news of herself or the boy. There was never another person in any of the photographs, only fragments of them: the forearm and shoulder of whoever held the boy outside the church at his baptism; a disembodied upraised beefy hand of a man holding a glass aloft, joining the boy in the toast he was making; the edge of a white dress worn by the girl standing beside him on the altar at his First Communion; the shadow of whoever snapped the last photograph, the boy on his bike, the shadow spilling across the sidewalk, submerging the bike's rear tire.

What anger she must have carried, he thought. He couldn't even recall the name of the woman in Montreal: Hester, Heather, something; did he ever know her last name? He couldn't even conjure her face, what color her hair was. He saw his hand on her hip, remembered that her dress had been some slick and shiny material: silk? He remembered her stockinged feet, high heels in her hand, an orchid behind her ear, her slapping her fiancé. Nothing beyond that. She was upset and he comforted her; it was a response out of kindness, wasn't it? It was a blip in his life; she had vanished into the vast country of the past.

He collected the photos, returned them to the envelope and then lost them again; the next night, home before midnight following a seven–three win, a complete game by Sandford, he wondered if he had perhaps missed something in them that might give him a clue about where they had been taken. But he couldn't find them.

Searching for them, however, led him to wonder if he had done enough to try to find Julie and the boy. He remembered the phone number he had punched into his cellphone on the day Webber broke his shoulder and scrolled through the call log looking for it. On the third ring, a woman answered and he gripped the phone more tightly.

"Is this the home of Colin Aylesworth?" he said. "I'm looking for—"

"I'm sorry," the woman said. "He's deceased."

His son was dead. He sucked in his breath, his forehead suddenly clammy.

"I know this is awkward," Edward Everett said. "But what was . . . how old was he?"

"He was eighty-three," the woman said. "I was his . . ." She was going to say *daughter,* he knew, and it would turn out to be Julie, after all these years. *Ed?* she would say, her voice full of forgiveness. But the woman went on. ". . . wife. Are you a former patient of his?"

"Yes," Edward Everett lied.

"It's been touching how many have called to say what a wonderful doctor he was," she said. "He was always so good with the children who came to see him."

"Are you at all related to a Julie Aylesworth?" he asked.

"He had a sister, Julie, but she passed a long while ago, when they were just children themselves," the woman said.

"No other?" he asked.

"I'm sorry?" she said. "I don't know what his sister has to do—"

"I meant, I'm sorry for your loss. Your husband was a wonderful doctor."

"Did your scars heal?" she asked.

"Scars?"

"Most of the children—the burns—but he worked so hard to make sure that their faces, at least . . . so they could lead normal lives. Did yours heal well?"

"Yes," he said. "Your husband did good work. He saved my life."

He went through boxes in his basement, hauled mildewed books and clothing to the curb and took to the Goodwill what the water in his basement hadn't ruined, wondering: *When did I acquire this and why did I hold on to it?*—golf clubs, tennis rackets, copies of *Street & Smith's Baseball Yearbook* from the 1960s to the 1980s. He was in one of them, he realized, and found the issue for the 1977 season that contained the statistics for anyone who had appeared in a major league game the year before. The pages were gray and brittle, flecks of paper drifting to his living room rug, settling onto the folds in his shirt, the tips of his shoes. He found himself in the back, at the final entry of an appendix, "Players with fewer than ten official at-bats," his last name and first initial, a single game and a string of zeros, save for the columns for batting average and slugging percentage, which read simply "—," the equation a mathematical impossibility, zero-indivisible-by-zero. Still, that single impotent line was evidence he had been there.

He pulled out the issue and boxed the others and took them to the Goodwill, along with two boxes of his father's clothing his mother had sent him twenty-five years earlier, when she finally got around to clearing out his father's possessions. "You might be able to wear some of these," she had written in a brief note, scrawled on a sheet of green paper she'd torn from a stenographer's notebook. When they arrived, he was living in Sioux City, his second season coaching, and he had come home after midnight to find the boxes in the hall of his apartment building, blocking his door. He'd opened them, the inside of the box musty, and stared at the wrinkled, hastily folded shirts and slacks. He had no idea what his mother might have been thinking: what would he want with the clothes of a dead man? He considered throwing them away but felt a twinge of guilt: these clothes had once been something his father would have run his hands across as he flipped through the shirts, trying to decide what to put on his body that day. So he had hauled them around for nearly half his life. But, by now, certainly whatever obligation he had to them as remnants of his father had expired; they were just pieces of stitched cotton and rayon.

Out making his runs to charity, he noticed that so many of the landmarks of his life had disappeared. The jeweler's where he found Renee's ring was shut, the name and hours of operation painted on the glass front door nearly chipped away: how long had it been closed? The office of the physical therapist where he'd gone after surgery on what had been his good knee had vanished—the operation necessary because too many years of favoring his injured one wore the other out as well. Now the building was missing, just a dark gap between a bowling alley and a nail-and-tanning salon. When had that happened? Gone, too, was the diner where he'd met the first woman he dated when he moved to Perabo City—Sheila? Shirley? She'd been a waitress, they'd flirted, he left her extravagant tips—five dollars for a four-dollar meal—and they'd seen each other for two months.

It was not just the ball club that was leaving town: the town was leaving town.

One night, as he watched a bearded man and his skinny wife win a new refrigerator on *The Newlywed Game,* he could hear another party next door at the Duboises'. He moved through the kitchen and out onto his deck, easing the door closed, wincing at the sharp click of the latch, and stood in the shadow, listening. On the deck next door, all he could make out were silhouettes of perhaps a dozen people, voices overlapping voices, until he heard Rhonda exclaim, "Oh, Neh Neh," her nickname for Renee that she resurrected when she'd been drinking. He stepped farther out onto his deck, squinting into the night as if it would make the dark forms somehow distinct. Renee's laugh came back to him, followed by a male voice: "If I'd known this, I'd never—" Never what? *Never have taken you from your husband.*

He went back inside. Grizzly lay sleeping in his corner of the kitchen and he raised his head, briefly and indifferently, and then pawed at his bedding for a moment before going back to sleep. In the living room, *The Newlywed Game* had given way to *The Dating Game,* and as the host introduced the three bachelors sitting smugly on their high stools—all wide lapels, permed hair and toothy smiles—and the bachelorette began asking them questions peppered with double entendres, Edward Everett got the itch to call women he'd known, and the next day he did. Certainly one was stuck in her own bit of stasis while everyone else rushed on into their private futures; certainly one would exclaim, *Oh. I was just thinking of you.* Anita answered the phone, breathless after dashing inside from unloading groceries from the car, she said, thinking it was her daughter calling to be picked up from dance class, and then was confused when

Edward Everett told her who he was. Magda, whom he'd met on her second day in the country after she'd emigrated from Poland, didn't answer but her answering machine had two voices on it: "Hi, this is Roger. And Maaaagdaaaa! We're probably out walking our Weimaraners. Leave a message." Some had just disappeared: Sharon's number was disconnected; Liz's belonged to a body shop.

One was happy to hear from him, Audrey, a new-accounts clerk he'd met when he took one of his Spanish-speaking players to the bank to help him open an account. "Ed," she said in a delighted voice when he told her who he was. "We must be on the same wavelength." She had a confession, she said. "I called you once but didn't have the nerve to leave a message. And now here you are. It's kismet." But soon, she was crying, going on about her most recent boyfriend, whom she'd learned too late was married with a baby on the way; going on about a fight she'd had with a co-worker who, she was convinced, had dinged her car in the parking lot but denied it. He remembered why he'd stopped seeing her and as soon as he could graciously do so, got off the phone, agreeing vaguely when she suggested he drive over to see her after the season ended.

On another night—after a one–nothing win, another gem for Sandford, the win coming when Mraz ended it with a ninth-inning home run arcing over the decaying green wall in left—he called directory assistance in Osterville and asked for the number for McLaughlin, Randall, and called it without hesitating because if he hesitated he would come to his senses. Even as the phone rang, he thought, *Hang up.* As it rang a second time, he thought: *Hang up.* In the middle of the third ring, Connie answered in a cheery voice and he was caught off guard.

"Hi," he croaked out.

"Can I help you?" she asked from six hundred fifteen miles away.

"Con?" he said.

"Who is this?" she asked, and when he told her, she exclaimed, "Oh, my gosh. Ed. My Lord, it's been . . . well, a lot of water under, as they say."

"Yes," he said. "Too long."

"Your name came up last year, at the reunion. Forty years since high school, if you can believe that. People started asking about people who weren't there."

He wondered if she was still married to McLaughlin, how he could ask. He saw them starting out slowly, phone calls every couple of weeks. When the season was over and he was at the end of baseball, he could drive over to see her. They could have dinner; maybe the Victorian tearoom where they'd had their first, awful date thirty years earlier was still open. They'd see how things went. The thought struck him: was she jowly, double-chinned, her white hair thinning? He was no prize, though: not obese, but slow, achy in the morning, his knee forever in pain.

"How's Billy?" he asked, her son's name pushing into his memory: the frail boy yelling "Stop" when they wanted to put the giant stuffed bear into the trunk.

She laughed. "He's William now. Not Billy. His son, William Junior, got married last year and they're expecting a baby. I keep saying, 'I'm too young to be a great-grandmother.' What about you? I'll bet you're married and have a whole passel of kids."

"No," he said. "I was. Married, I mean." He shrugged, although she couldn't possibly see that over the phone.

"I'm so sorry," she said, a touch of what seemed genuine concern in her voice. He waited for her to tell him about herself, about marrying McLaughlin and divorcing him—a rebound relationship after he had gone off to Erie.

"Randy and I . . ." *Got divorced,* he waited for her to say, but she went on. "I guess you don't know. I married Randy McLaughlin. It's been thirty years." She laughed. "I can hear you thinking, *him?* But he's a dear, a good daddy to Billy. William, I mean. We should all get together sometime if you're over this way."

Edward Everett wanted the call to end after he learned that she and Randy McLaughlin were still together, but he couldn't graciously hang up until the conversation came to some kind of ending. Finally, she said, "Oh, Randy just drove up. He would love to say hey."

"I'd like to," he lied, "but I have a conference call in fifteen minutes and I have to go over some game logs beforehand."

"Conference call? This late at night?"

"The director of PD is . . . Well, he wants what he wants when he wants it."

"I know the type. Now that you have my number, don't be a stranger. And I've got yours off caller ID. William gave us this fancy phone package for Christmas. It's all beyond me. Call waiting. Wireless Internet." From the background of where she was, he heard a male voice calling, "Hello? Hon?"

"I need to get going here, Connie."

"Sure, stay in touch."

He started to hang up but not before, from her end, he heard her say, "You won't believe . . ."

He sat in the darkness, folding the scrap of paper with her number in half, then in quarters, then eighths, until it was so small he couldn't make any more folds in it. He pushed himself out of the chair and used the foot lever to spring open the trash can and dropped the scrap on top of the coffee filter from earlier in the day and went to bed.

Two days later, on the weekend before the All-Star break, Marc Johansen, MS, MBA, emailed to say he wanted to meet. "I'm in St. Louis for family business," he wrote. "Am overnighting a plane ticket for Sunday. Meet Monday. Directions attached." Short, efficient. Edward Everett wondered if Claussen's email from Mark Johansen, MS, MBA, just before the organization had fired him had been as curt.

Chapter Twenty-nine

It had been years since he'd flown and it was only when his stomach gave its slight drop as the plane lifted from the tarmac in Cedar Rapids that he remembered how much he hated it, the anxious moments as the jets roared to give the plane its lift, the precarious bounce of the wing outside his window seat, making him question the integrity of bolts and welds; the mechanical grinding and bump as the wheels retracted; his ears filling, giving him the illusion that sound was traveling from another room—the muted hum of conversation, the scratch of paper from the woman beside him turning the pages of a pulp mystery novel, the nervous clicking of a ballpoint pen button by a woman across the aisle.

Before they finished their climb, rain began pelting the window beside him, the drops slithering like silver slugs across the scratched and clouded plastic. He pulled down the plastic shade and closed his eyes, his pulse thrumming in his jaw. A baby behind him wailed and the woman beside him closed her book.

"I really hate flying," she said. She was near his age, gray-haired, wearing a peach silk blouse tucked neatly into a charcoal pencil skirt, small, heart-shaped diamond studs in her earlobes, her manicured nails polished pale pink. "Yet, here I am again."

"I haven't done it in almost fifteen years," Edward Everett said.

The woman gave a small, hoarse laugh, her breath clearly that of a smoker, peppermint not fully masking the tobacco odor. "Dummy me; I'm up here a dozen times a year for business. My doctor usually gives me a scrip for Ativan but it makes me feel so stupid sleepy. I didn't take it this time, since I'm going to see my daughter and grand-daughter, and she's old enough that she'd notice if I seemed drunk." She made her voice small and high-pitched. "Mommy, why is Gamma falling down?"

When the plane leveled off, she gave him a polite half-smile and went back to her book. He opened the shade beside him and saw that the sky was blue, the rain clouds beneath them, illuminated periodically by a pulsing pale light. Around him, everyone seemed to be relaxing, only forty more minutes in the air ahead of them. Across the aisle, the woman with the pen was writing what appeared to be thank-you notes onto cards so highly calendered they glinted under the ceiling light. She was, he realized, most likely a recent bride, her all-but-useless right hand curled in on itself, a clear symptom of cerebral palsy, nonetheless happy as any woman he had ever seen, glancing appreciatively toward her new husband.

As if she understood his thinking, the woman beside him said in a quiet tone, "They seem happy. I give them five years."

"Five?" he asked.

"But then, I'm eternally romantic," she replied, a laugh rattling in her throat. She opened a small silver clutch that had been pressed between her hip and the side of her seat but then snapped it shut and held it on her lap. "You'd think after all of my time in the air I'd remember I can't smoke." She opened her purse again and canted it toward him so that he could see she was fingering a cigarette she'd loosened from a pack of Tareytons. "Sad, isn't it?" She set down her purse and returned to her book. Edward Everett leaned his head back, closed his eyes and tried to sleep.

He gave up after several minutes when he heard the flight attendant beginning to push the refreshment cart up the aisle, popping open cans of Coke and Sprite, pouring coffee into plastic cups, unscrewing caps from one-ounce bottles of booze. When the cart was beside them, the woman who shared his row sat up.

"Rum and Coke," she said, plucking up her purse again and snapping it open, fishing out a ten-dollar bill.

"Anything for you, sir?" the attendant asked, already fixing the woman her drink.

"I hope you won't make me drink alone," the woman said.

"Okay," he said. "Bud Light?"

He leaned forward to take out his wallet but the woman laid her hand on his arm. "The least I can do is buy."

"You don't have to," he said, pulling his wallet from his hip pocket.

"I'm paying for two," the woman said to the attendant, who glanced in Edward Everett's direction for his approval. He gave her a small shrug and put his wallet away.

When they had their drinks, the woman clicked her plastic cup against his. "To long life." She took a sip. "I shouldn't have said what I did about that couple. I'm sure they'll be insufferably adoring even when they're a hundred."

"That's a long while to be insufferably adoring," he said.

"All right, then, ninety-five."

They sat in silence, sipping their drinks, until the woman gave him a slight smile, a gesture he took to mean she was releasing him from further social obligation. She went back to her book and he regretted not having one himself. He plucked the in-flight catalog from the pocket of the seat in front of him and read it idly: good-looking men and women wearing polo shirts with the airline's logo stitched above a pocket; a dozen golf balls resting in a polished wood box; carved wooden ducks—so many things no one needed. He closed it, returned it to the pocket just as the plane gave a shudder and the woman let out a gasp, some of her drink splashing out of the cup, spotting her blouse. "Damn," she said, opening her purse and taking out a wadded tissue, blotting at the stains darkening the silk. "That's not going away."

"Would some water help?" he asked, raising a hand to signal the flight attendant.

"Not on silk," she said, continuing to dab at her blouse. She unlatched her seatbelt and turned sideways toward him. "How bad is it?" One obvious teardrop-shaped spot, perhaps half an inch long, was surrounded by an irregular pattern of tiny dots.

"It's not that terrible," he lied. She sat back in her seat again and closed her eyes. "Fuck," she said through a clenched jaw, then drained her drink and raised her hand, shaking her glass, an ice cube spiraling out and bouncing onto the aisle. "Stewardess?" she called. "A second rum and Coke." She took in a deep breath, then let it out slowly. "I'm sorry," she said, touching two manicured fingers to his forearm. "It's only a blouse."

The flight attendant delivered the drink. "This one is on me," Edward Everett said, taking out his wallet, pulling out a five-dollar bill and offering it to the flight attendant before the woman could open her purse. Rather than protest, she gave him a smile of acknowledgment and took the drink. "Even without taking a sip, I know this second one will be a royal mistake." The plane gave another shudder. "This is the first time I've gone to visit my daughter and her little girl since—" She shook her head. "Never mind. You don't want to hear my sad story."

"I don't have anywhere else I need to be," he said.

"You're sweet, but it's really all right."

They sat in silence, the woman clearly caught in a reverie, as every so often she shook her head and let out a short hiss with her tongue against her teeth.

"You know," she said at last. "I'm a good person. When my mother lost her mind—that's a terrible way to put it but it's the truth—who took care of her? Lord, not my father." She tapped a finger against her sternum. "Me. When my husband. My *ex*-husband decided, after finishing law school, not to take the bar because he was no longer passionate about the law, did I ask him if he was crazy or did I take a second job so he could become a luthier? A *luthier*. Right again. When my daughter—never mind, but if your answer was that I was there for her when her father wouldn't speak to her, well, right again." She shook her head. "Then when I find my backbone and tell my husband—who made all of eleven hundred dollars last year selling two guitars—that I was leaving, does anything go right? Correct. I have to sell the house we bought because of money I earned so I can pay him for his half. *His* half." She paused. "I should've had the Ativan," she said. "No muss, no fuss, no stain on a hundred-dollar blouse." She giggled. "If I pronounce it 'bluss' instead, it rhymes. No muss, no fuss, no stain on a hundred-dollar bluss. It could be a book by Dr. Seuss I read to Avril." She took a swallow of her drink. "Tell me, who names their daughter 'Avril'?"

"I'm guessing your daughter did."

"Actually, the idea was her partner's. Her *female* partner." She gave him a sideways look. "I'm open-minded. When her father wouldn't talk to her after she came out, I supported her. Hell, sisterhood, rah, and all that, but this is not what I— I really need to be quiet." She gave his shoulder a good-natured nudge. "Altitude plus alcohol equals . . . I don't know, 'A' something. Ambivalence. Airheadedness. I don't know, give me an 'A' word that works here."

The alcohol from the beer had made his mind fuzzy and so all of the words that occurred to him made no sense: "aardvark," "ambition," "Aaron." Still, he offered, " 'Aerial'?"

She gave out a laugh. "I'm definitely aerial." She held out her right hand. "Meg."

"Ed," he said, and they shook.

"Well, Edward, what takes you to St. Louis?"

He considered telling her the truth but he had no grasp on what the truth was. *I've been summoned,* he thought before settling on an answer more vague. "Business."

"Oh, that's too bad," she said. "Business seems . . . well, business. Oh, I think we're starting to descend." She leaned across him to peer out. He could both feel and smell her breath, now a more complicated warm mix of tobacco, mint and rum. He realized that one of the buttons of her blouse had come undone and he could see the swell of her small breasts above a red lace bra. When he shifted his eyes, he saw that she was watching him. Instead of being incensed, however, she gave a quick wink, sat up, snapped open her purse, removed a tube of lipstick and began making herself up. It was clear they were, indeed, moving to lower altitudes; wisps of the cloud bank they'd been above drifted across the wing, at first seeming like smoke dispersing, and then the cabin darkened slightly as they moved more fully into the clouds. From beneath them, he could hear the *thunk* of the landing gear doors, followed by a mechanical hum.

"I think I've monopolized our time together, Edward," she said. "Telling you all about my troubles and asking you nothing about yourself. What business are you in?"

"Flour," he said impulsively.

She arched an eyebrow. "You're a florist?"

"No," he said. "I sell flour to, you know, groceries and—"

The mechanical hum resumed, quieted, and then resumed again, changing in pitch.

"My grandfather was a wheat farmer in Kansas," she said. "Maybe some of your flour comes from there. Wouldn't it be funny if you were selling something that grew on the land where I used to play?"

The plane banked as it began moving through to the underside of the clouds. He could see a broad expanse of countryside but they were too high for him to distinguish landmarks in the irregular checkerboard of browns and greens. The mechanical hum began again; it became clear to him that something was wrong as the hum resumed, ceased, resumed and ceased again. The flight attendant who had served their drinks hurried past, moving toward the front of the plane.

"Who do you work for?" she asked.

Half-distracted, he gave her the name of the mill he and his uncle had sold for.

"I don't know them."

He had no idea whether they were still in business. "You most likely wouldn't, unless—it's commercial. Bakeries, private labels," he said, dredging the phrase "private label" out of that past with his uncle. Again, the mechanical hum began, and this time it was persistent, a grinding sound with a pitch that rose and fell.

"Private label," she said, waggling her head from side to side. "La di—" And then she furrowed her brow, studying his face. "What's wrong?"

"It's—" he began but then the pilot's voice came over the intercom, his words not quite audible above the thrum of the engine and the continued mechanical grinding beneath Edward Everett's feet. All he could make out was the phrase "hydraulic system" and the words "approach" and "gear." The flight attendant was moving unsteadily up the aisle, pausing at each row, bracing herself on seat backs, bending to say something to passengers as she stopped. When she got to their row, her voice was even but Edward Everett could nonetheless sense tension, as her eyes would not meet either his or Meg's. "Everything's going to be fine," she said. "There's a glitch in the hydraulics that the crew are working to resolve."

"What does that mean?" Meg asked. "The hydraulics."

The flight attendant hesitated. "The crew has everything under control," she said, then moved on to the row behind them.

" 'Hydraulics' equals shit soup," a man across the aisle and a row back said.

Meg let out a bitter laugh. "Of course." She shook her head. "Thank you, God."

The plane arced and he could once more see the countryside beneath them, the long blue snake of a river. The "fasten seatbelt" sign lit up with a *ding* and the captain's voice came over the intercom again, clear this time, his tone making Edward Everett wonder if in pilot school they learned how to deliver bad news in a reassuring way.

"Good afternoon, ladies and gentlemen," the captain said, his voice pleasant. "We've got a small situation with our landing gear. We're going to divert to Scott Air Force Base on the Illinois side. We apologize for any inconvenience."

"Why Scott?" a woman asked from a few rows in front of Edward Everett.

"If we crash, they don't want us in a high-traffic airport," a man said.

They began descending again, the engines changing pitch as they slowed. Edward Everett leaned his head back against the cushion, closing his eyes, aware of his pulse thrumming in his ears so furiously he wondered if he was having a heart attack. Around him, passengers sobbed. Several talked on cellphones. "I love you," someone said. "Tell the kids—" another said. Edward Everett fingered the cellphone in his pocket but thought, *Who would I call?* How pathetic it was to be in a plane about to crash and have no one in his life that he could call.

Meg gripped his forearm suddenly, her long nails cutting into his skin, and he found himself laying his left hand over her right, giving it a squeeze as he began thinking of all the divergent roads in his life that had brought him here, to a plane that was most likely going to crash, holding on to the hand of a woman who hadn't been part of his life until an hour earlier when they nodded pleasantly to each other as she sat down: if, if, if. If he had pursued football as his father wanted, he would be in an office in a high school, playing around with next year's depth chart, his worst problem that the All-Conference running back who had graduated in June would be hard to replace. If he hadn't gotten injured in Montreal, if he had let that fly ball go and not gotten hung up in the fence, he would be fat and retired someplace warm—a tanned hacker on the golf course, lining up a putt on eighteen, taking a phone call from his agent: *A baseball card show in Tucson would work fine next month.* But even if he had made the decision to chase that fly ball in Montreal but hadn't gone to Cleveland for the tryout, if he had been content selling flour with his uncle, content marrying Connie, raising her son, he would have a wife and son who would sit with him at a banquet when—long after he had taken over his uncle's territory, long after he had his own house beside a pond—someone would call his name from the dais and he would rise to applause and make his way forward to receive the sort of honor that successful men gave to other successful men.

He realized that Meg was saying something: ". . . was sorry."

"What?" he asked. His ears were even more closed up now, her voice even more distant than it had been before.

"I wish I could tell her I was sorry," she said.

"Who?" he asked.

"Patience," she said.

"What?" He wondered if she had suddenly gone mad: patience, for what? Was there a moment coming at which it would be better for her to answer his question?

"My daughter, Patience," she said. "Oh, God, I was so terrible to her."

"I'm sure you weren't," he said.

"You don't know," she said. She took an iPhone from her purse but sat holding it in her lap. She laughed. "And I can't even call her to tell her. What kind of person in the twenty-first century doesn't have a phone?" She shook her phone at him in an accusing way, as if he was responsible for something—for whatever she'd done to her daughter. For her not being able to tell her daughter she was sorry. For the plane's mechanical problems.

"What could you have possibly done?" he asked.

"I thought I wanted a little girl," she said, almost so quietly he had a hard time hearing her over the drone of the engines and with his ears as clogged as they were. "Momma's little girl. But when I had her, I had no idea what to do with her. Change her diapers. Clean up her poop. Her father was no help. 'She's your child,' he said. 'You wanted her.' Hiding in the basement, making fucking guitars. I took it out on her. Oh, I wish I could tell her it wasn't her fault. 'Am I bad, Mommy?' she'd ask. What can a four-year-old do that could be bad? But I . . . there were times she would cry in her crib and I would sit in the living room and turn the volume up on whatever I was watching. *Falcon Crest, Dallas,* with the volume up while she wailed." She closed her eyes and he wondered if she was going to cry but she didn't. "That's what I'd tell her. That I was sorry—for that and for so much more."

Through the window now, he could see the landscape changing, becoming more residential. Tracts of homes, a shopping mall, an industrial court.

"What do you regret?" She laid her hand gently on his, giving him a small pat.

He turned his head toward her. Just because she had told him what she regretted didn't mean he had to tell her. They were strangers. The plane shook, at first twice, then three times, and then started quaking violently. The flight attendant coming back up the aisle swayed from side to side from the force of it, not so much walking as pulling herself up the aisle, as if she was struggling against a wind.

"I had a boy," he said, glancing at Meg and then turning away. "I had a boy but I never got to see him. His mother left before he was born and I never met him."

"Never," she said. She curled her hand into his, lacing her fingers through his.

"No," he said. The photos came to him. The baby fending off bright sunlight at its baptism. The boy raising a glass. And then the boy in the image lowered the glass and glanced up at him, smiling, and Edward Everett realized he had never thought of the boy as animate before.

"I've never told anyone about him," he said. "Not my wives. No one." *On Connie's porch after the first picture came: "What's wrong?" "Nothing. I just love you."*

"Oh, my," Meg said. "How awful to carry that with you all this time."

He realized he was crying and squeezed his eyes to stop the tears. "I wish—" he said, then cleared his throat to steady his voice. "I wish I could have known him a little."

"You poor, poor dear." Meg patted his face. "She was terrible to do that to you. Kidnapping. Did you ever try to find them?"

"I did," he said. "I looked—"

"Maybe he tried to find you," Meg said. "Maybe he's looking this moment. That's something to live for."

The captain's voice came over the loudspeaker. "I'm asking the flight crew to belt themselves in," he said.

Through the window, Edward Everett could make out something that looked like a factory and then the edge of downtown St. Louis, the distinctive Arch glinting dully against the gray sky. The loudspeaker began crackling, the captain's voice mixed with cracks and pops. ". . . crash position . . ." and then the loudspeaker went silent. Throughout the cabin, passengers bent their faces toward their knees, locking their hands behind their necks, and Edward Everett imitated them.

The engines slowed yet again. Edward Everett could feel the pull of gravity, and pressure built in his ears. Everything seemed far away: the sounds of the engine, the crying of a baby, a woman. It seemed as if he was hearing it all through water. Then came the roar of the engines reversing. He lifted his head momentarily to glance out the window. They were coming in fast, past a parking lot filled with military jeeps, past a mass of airmen running in pale blue shorts and T-shirts. It seemed they should be on the ground by then; he braced himself, thinking, *Oh, my God, I am heartily sorry for having offended you,* but at the same time thinking of how that was cheating in a way, something he wasn't certain he believed in but hedging his bets, in the event Sister Annunciata was right, an Act of Contrition could pull him out of a free fall toward hell at the last moment. The landscape continued to flash past, rows of clapboard military housing, a field with jets lined up as if at some sort of aeronautical parade rest, watching them speed past. From somewhere ahead of them, he caught sight of flashing blue and red lights. They were barely above the ground, all but skimming it; part of him willed them to touch down, to get whatever was going to happen over, while part of him willed them to stay up.

"Oh, my God," Meg said, and she pushed at his head, shoving it back toward his knees, his legs pressing against his torso making it difficult to breathe. The engines were nearly deafening, and then he felt them hit the ground with an impact that jarred him in his seat, the plane bouncing, the front end rising and falling, rising and falling, shaking him wildly. His head banged against his knee hard enough that he thought he might have fractured his cheekbone. He thought, incongruously and wryly: *Renee will end up a widow and not a divorcee after all,* would inherit everything he had, and then the plane seemed to be careening, the fuselage screeching as they rode the ground, a long *eeeeeeeeeeeeee* rising above the drone of the engines, a sound he felt in his fingertips, in his groin. All around him, passengers were screaming: was he? No. His mouth was open, but no sound was coming out. A drink cart from the front of the plane broke free of what had tethered it and bounced along the aisle, banging into seats, bottles and cans spilling out, some breaking, filling the cabin with a strong scent of alcohol and sugar. Overhead compartments popped open, carry-on bags falling all around them. The plane seemed on the verge of tumbling, fishtailing side to side.

He turned his head against his thighs to look up and out through the window. Something outside whipping madly at the fuselage:

smoke, he realized, pouring up around the wing. For some reason, he had thought the impact would be the worst, tear him apart; he had not considered the possibility of fire and he sucked in his breath, closing his eyes, waiting for the fuel to ignite. His body jerked front to back, side to side, his head shaking so violently he wondered that he didn't fall unconscious. When they hit a hard bump, his jaw clamped abruptly and a small hard fragment of something came loose in his mouth, most likely a piece of a tooth, pricking the under-side of his tongue, making him taste blood. Then, suddenly, it seemed they were slowing. They were slowing, no longer careening, but skid-ding, smoke obscuring his view outside the window, until they came to rest, finally, with a savage bump that made the belt strain against his midsection so hard that it drove the wind out of him, and he thought, *It's cutting through me,* but then they were still. They were still and, he realized, quiet, as the engines were off. There was only the distant crying of his fellow passengers, and the gentle creaking of the plane settling—as if, after terrorizing them, it had decided to lull them to sleep.

Chapter Thirty

Later, safe in his suite in the airport Hilton, twisting the cap off a mini-bar bottle of Jim Beam and slumping, drained and dumb, into an upholstered wing chair in the room, while plane after plane thundered over him, the aftermath of the crash came to him in pieces like a collection of photographs someone had once organized to illustrate a sequence but then dropped, scattering them, confusing the order:

From outside the plane, he could hear sirens approaching but the smoke outside made it impossible to see how near the vehicles were. Inside, the crew was up and moving, forcing open heavy doors, unfurling a gray inflatable slide.

"Please," the flight attendant who had served their drinks implored, "orderly, orderly." But passengers ignored her, shoving one another. A plump man wearing a Cardinals cap knocked into the attendant and she tumbled against a small girl. A teenaged boy with a faint blond mustache dusting his upper lip clambered over seat backs, kicking the newlywed husband in the head.

Outside the plane, emergency crews were spraying white foam. It slid across the wing in a wave, some of it blowing in through the emergency exit in the row behind Edward Everett and he felt it wet and sticky on his face, burning his tongue, gagging him.

He was little more than part of a herd, following dumbly the hand signals and exhortations of airmen in uniform directing them across the field, away from the wrecked plane, the tight knot of a hundred or so fellow human beings stumbling across uneven ground, kicking up grasshoppers that stung his hands when they flung themselves up to avoid being trampled. Meg held on to him, unsteady in her impractical heels.

Beside him on the plane, Meg was sobbing. The newly married woman unclasped her seatbelt and stood but it was evident from her vacant gaze that she had no notion she was standing. When she sat back down, she miscalculated, landing partly on the armrest, and slumped into the aisle, her legs splayed in front of her until her husband stood, losing his balance briefly, and then righting himself to take her limp left hand, her good hand, and tug on it gently until she showed him a sign of recognition and he helped her up.

The right leg and crotch of his jeans were damp. At first he worried that he had peed himself, but when he dabbed at the stain tentatively with two fingers of his right hand and held them up to his nose, he realized it was beer.

Beside him in the frenzy of passengers surging for the exits, Meg laid her hand in the crook of his elbow, giving him a squeeze that he understood as *Don't leave me.*

Meg was taking his hand and tugging it, insistent, pulling him toward an exit, where he lost his balance and slid headfirst down the chute, clawing at it to keep from falling onto the newly married woman, who was below him, but banging into her shoulder, the fire suppression foam covering their clothing, soaking their hair, until he tumbled at last onto the ground, his face buried momentarily in the foam, and he shoved at the bodies falling into him, thinking: *how odd to survive the crash only to drown.*

On the bus, he gazed back at the plane. Its underside was scorched, the fuselage sitting in a lake of foam that was beginning to melt. The emergency vehicles turning around made broad arcs in the high grass, clouds of grasshoppers appearing and vanishing, appearing and vanishing, as the vehicles bounced across the field to the roadway. He thought: *My laptop! My luggage!* But the bus was pulling away, joining the line of other buses, its engine rough, the foul scent of diesel fuel filling his nostrils.

He spit something hard and sharp out of his mouth into his cupped hand, a fragment of a tooth, one edge tinged with black, the decay that had made it vulnerable. He considered dropping it onto the floor but it seemed somehow valuable and so he slipped it into the change pocket in his jeans.

Disembarking at the curb outside the St. Louis airport, they moved as a herd, docile now, unlike their frantic push to get out of the plane, down the steps of the bus into the hot and humid St. Louis late morning. He stepped onto a splotch of bubble gum, which stuck to the sole of his right shoe, and every time he took a step his foot made a sucking *schmack*. Inside the air-conditioned dimness, the terminal seemed frenetic, a pace that confused all of them. They stood there, blinking, as a soldier in camouflage fatigues set down his pack and embraced a gray-haired man.

On the bus—or was it the plane?—Meg handed him a folded piece of paper. He opened it but his mind couldn't make sense of it: letters and numbers in an unsteady hand, as if someone either very old or very young had written it, and he stared at it until she took it back, folded it again, and slipped it into the pocket of his shirt, saying, "Where are you staying?" But he couldn't remember if he answered her.

In the hotel room, he finished the whiskey, drinking directly from the bottle, replaced the cap and returned it to the mini-bar and then realized what he was doing, removed it and laid it delicately into the lined wastebasket beneath the desk. He went into the bedroom. It was then that it struck him he had no change of clothes, no tooth-brush, no razor. He sat on the edge of the bed and lay back, thinking he would get up in a moment, at least wash his face and hands, but he closed his eyes. He had the sensation of his body spinning. Then it occurred to him that he could not go to his meeting with Marc Johansen, MS, MBA, in clothing reeking of sweat and beer. He sat up, took off his clothes, pulled the complimentary robe off the hanger in the closet, put it on and went down to the laundry on the ground floor. When his clothes were finished, he went back to his room, and lay down without pulling back the blankets. From across the room, his cellphone rang and he thought he should answer it but closed his eyes and didn't remember it ceasing to ring as he fell asleep.

The directions Marc Johansen, MS, MBA, gave him took him thirty miles from the Hilton, past affluent residential developments and a shopping plaza with stores designed after Swiss chalets, past exit after exit of Denny's and McDonald's and Ruby Tuesdays and Lowe's. He realized he was out of sync with the pace of heavy traffic in a large city and, as the stream of cars and trucks rushed past, he kept his rented sub-compact in the right lane, often caught behind lum-bering trucks hauling heavy construction equipment.

After a time, he came to a state route that led him to a series of county roads that rose and fell along the edge of the Ozark Moun-tains, past modest tract houses and trailer parks, and then farther still, past limestone rock faces and wooded areas, until he reached a narrow private road marked with an etched wooden sign reading "Gossage Farms" and turned onto it, creeping uphill between trees so dense their branches scraped the roof of his car. When he crested the hill, the landscape opened onto a lush pasture on both sides of the road, bounded by wire fencing. Spread across it, forty or fifty horses grazed while, a hundred yards off, two figures cantered along a ridge.

Finally, he came to a metal gate at the end of a drive leading to a barn and, beyond that, a broad stone house with a wraparound porch. The gate was closed and he pulled over and got out, struck immediately by the overwhelming stench of manure and damp hay. As he was about to lift the fence latch, a voice called out, "Jesus, don't," and a man he hadn't noticed trotted toward him. He was short but fit, wearing a black Stetson that shadowed his face. His rubber boots and the cuffs of his jeans were caked with what at first seemed graying mud but when he reached the gate, Edward Everett could smell that it was manure. The man lifted the cover on a metal box mounted to a fence post, flicked a switch and a humming Edward Everett hadn't previously heard ceased.

"We don't need any lawsuits," the man said, unlatching the gate. "You can leave your car there so it doesn't get filthy." Once Edward Everett was through the gate, the man shut it and turned the current back on, the fence sparking briefly as an insect flew against it. "Be careful where you step." The man pointed to a dollop of manure less than a foot from where Edward Everett stood, black and green flies swirling above it.

"I'm looking for—" Edward Everett said, trying to watch his feet among the manure piles and yet keep pace with the man who was taking careless strides along the gravel drive, clearly unconcerned when he stepped into one of the piles.

"Me," the man said, and Edward Everett realized it was Marc Johansen, MS, MBA.

"I didn't recognize you," he said. "I'm sorry."

"I have no idea why," Johansen said, his tone suggesting he might be joking but Edward Everett wasn't sure. "This is one of my mother's places and every year I come out and pretend to be a rancher for a week."

He led Edward Everett to the porch, stopping at the bottom of the steps leading to it to slip off his boots. "Come on in," he said. "Give me a chance to clean up and then we can get down to business."

Inside, Johansen left him in a massive great room with a granite floor and a two-story-high exposed-beam ceiling. Along one wall, four large windows looked out onto another pasture, which ran unimpeded for as far as he could see. Dotting it, rolled bales of hay browned in the sun. The room was furnished with several dark leather couches as well as cherrywood coffee tables bearing carefully arranged arrays of thick, glossy magazines fanned out. He sat gingerly on one of the couches, waiting. A rush of water poured through the plumbing as if someone had flushed a toilet, soon followed by a steady hiss.

After a few moments, he felt uncomfortable sitting idly and so picked up one of the magazines and realized that every one of them was an identical issue of *Architectural Digest*. He flipped through it. "Italian Marble Renaissance," read one headline for an article on bathroom floors. "Peak Performance," read another about slate and tile roofs. As he started to close it he saw that the spine was broken and when he laid it flat, it opened naturally to the beginning of a spread about the very house he was in, a full-page photograph of the room in which he sat, sunlight slanting in through the windows. On page after page, the spread showed stone floors, granite counters, bathrooms with sunken tubs, cherrywood cabinets that reflected recessed ceiling lights.

He turned to the opening page: "As a girl, Sylvia Johansen cherished her family's annual visits to the Missouri horse farm of her grandfather, Michael Gossage," it began. " 'When my husband died, I asked myself where I wanted to spend the next thirty years of my life and I realized that was it,' Mrs. Johansen said. Her family had sold the original property in 1973 and so she spent fourteen million for a rolling five-hundred-acre expanse in nearby Franklin County and another nine million re-creating her grandfather's house. Using the family's extensive collection of historical photographs, she turned to architect—"

He closed the magazine and returned it to the table. The house was silent, Johansen clearly finished with his shower, and Edward Everett wondered if they were the only people in it. *This must be what real wealth sounds like*, he thought, *this almost utter silence, as if the house were reverential of the very money that had built it. Twenty-three million dollars*, he thought. Did that include the furnishings? How much did the couch he was sitting on cost? Could a couch cost as much as five thousand dollars? The last one he'd bought came from a closeout sale at a bankrupt furniture store, the one he and Renee had bought last Christmas when she announced abruptly that she was tired of the used furniture they owned and he had taken her to the store as a way of placating her. It had cost what had seemed to him the improbable sum of nine hundred dollars and he had cringed when he signed the credit card receipt that, with tax and delivery, called for just north of a thousand dollars. For a short while, it had made her happy and she had scoured the ads from the Sunday *Des Moines Register* for other bargains, but then one day she noticed that Grizzly's claws had begun snagging the fabric when he jumped on the couch to sit with them while they watched television and that had been the end of her happiness over it. Less than a year after he'd bought it, the fabric was water-stained and the cushion where he sat sagged. A thousand dollars, more than he had ever spent for a single piece of furniture in his life, but compared with the substantial piece he was on, it seemed made of balsa wood and cheap cotton.

Then it struck him: *The furnishings in this room cost more than I earn in a year.* He felt a sick weight in his chest. What could someone possibly do to afford such a place? *It's one of my mother's places,* Johansen had said. Edward Everett had thought of Collier as wealthy, with his splendid home in the hills of Perabo City and his eleventh-floor condo two blocks from a beach in Destin, Florida, but Johansen and his mother made Collier appear middle-class—made Edward Everett seem two inches from welfare. Perhaps over all the years of his getting up every day and going to a ballpark somewhere in a small town, he had earned a million; with the jobs he had in some winters, maybe as much as a million and a half. What was that? Five percent of the cost of this house?

"I'm sorry to have kept you waiting," Johansen said, coming into the room. He was barefoot, his hair damp, his feet slapping on the stone as he walked across it. He had changed into black jeans and a beige polo shirt with the big club's logo over the left breast, a cartoon snarling cougar. He sat on the couch perpendicular to the one where Edward Everett sat, glancing at the row of *Architectural Digest* magazines on the table. "I had hoped she would have put those away by now. There's something gauche about it. Oh well, I didn't bring you here to talk about my mother's choice in magazines. Look—" He tapped a palm against his forehead. "Slow down, Marc; manners. How was your flight?"

Edward Everett considered telling him the truth but said, "It was fine." He suddenly felt even more self-conscious in Johansen's presence, here in the same pair of jeans and shirt he'd worn on the flight while Johansen felt comfortable enough to slouch on a how-many-thousand-dollar sofa and rest his feet on the coffee table.

"I hate like hell all the flying I have to do," Johansen went on. "Last year, I logged ninety-six thousand miles. It's a hassle and a half. All the security crap. I guess there's a reason for it, post nine-eleven, but I'm thinking anything under four hundred miles, I'm driving." He let out a breath. "Look, I've never been good at chitchat. I work on it because my wife tells me I ought to. 'They're not just employees, they're people,' she says. And so, fine. Cross that off the list." He made a motion in the air as if he was drawing a check mark. "I hope you'll forgive me if I get down to things. I have to get to Dallas for a breakfast meeting tomorrow. Things are . . . well, you'll understand in a minute."

He paused, evidently giving Edward Everett an opening to say something, but he wasn't sure what the moment demanded, and so Johansen went on. "When I came on board I promised the brass I wouldn't make any significant changes until I had reasonable confidence that I understood how things were. I think I'm there now."

He paused again and, because the moment clearly demanded some sort of response from him, Edward Everett said, "I know there have been problems."

"So, you've seen them, too?" Johansen said.

"I know that Webber's getting hurt hasn't helped things," Edward Everett said. "Maybe I could have—"

"Webber?" Johansen said.

"The shortstop," he said. "The one whose shoulder . . ."

Johansen furrowed his brow. Could it be that he had no idea, without being in front of his almighty spreadsheets, who Webber was?

"I filed a report," Edward Everett said. "He's having surgery this week but he'll probably never—"

"Oh, wait," Johansen said. "I remember. Kid we picked up from Baltimore. What about him?"

"You mentioned problems and so I thought that was one I could explain."

Johansen snorted. "This is about larger issues. We certainly aren't going to kill one of our franchises over one hurt player."

Edward Everett felt a flutter in his chest. "So, Perabo City is killed."

"That's a good part of the reason I brought you down here," Johansen said. "We decided to shut it down sometime back. I thought you knew."

"No," Edward Everett said. So there it was, he thought. *Killed*, Johansen had said. He thought he had been prepared for this moment but it was like when his mother died. He'd been expecting it for more than a year but when a nurse called him from the hospital, it had still come as a shock—the finality nothing could prepare you for.

"We needed to rebalance our portfolio, to use some of the lingo from my former life," Johansen said. "I know that the routine is to say, 'It was a hard decision,' but it really wasn't. The fact of the matter is that the owner, what's-his-name, the meat guy . . ."

"Collier," Edward Everett offered.

"Collier. Right. A piece of work. He ran a shoddy, cut-rate franchise. I mean, who operates an entire baseball operation out of a meat company? Then he tried to play hardball with the wrong people. So when we had to get rid of one of our single-A teams it didn't take long to decide where the hammer should come down."

"What did he do?" Edward Everett asked, thinking that it was so much like Collier to make a mistake and leave others to pay the price.

"He'd probably sue me for saying I didn't like his shirt and so I'll just say he played his hand as if he were sitting on four aces when all he had was seven-high."

So it was over, Edward Everett thought; there was no softening it. Marc Johansen, MS, MBA, had made him get on a plane that had nearly killed him and come here to sit in a house that cost more than what he would make in twenty lifetimes for this. *You can't fire people long-distance*, he could hear Johansen's wife saying. His being here was just another exercise in her making her husband into a better human being.

"Tell me," Johansen said, "does he pull that shit with the Lincoln Logs story all the time?"

"What?" Edward Everett said, his tone perhaps sharper than he intended.

"You know. 'My daddy told me he got me something and I thought it was Lincoln Logs' and all that crap."

"Oh," Edward Everett said. "Yes."

So, Edward Everett thought, *I'm nothing more than collateral damage.* He wondered how much longer he needed to stay. He pictured himself on the drive back to the airport hotel, defeated, someone who belonged in the slow lane, a frightened old man confused in traffic. What would he do now? He saw himself as Johansen surely must: gray, balding, fleshy, not much different from the lost old men that Edward Everett saw in supermarkets, lame men slumped in motorized shopping carts, straining to reach the canned soup on the higher shelves.

"So, look——" Johansen began. The door from the wraparound porch opened and Johansen stopped speaking. A woman was saying, ". . . have Dr. Tao look at his fetlock."

"I hope it's all right," said another woman. "It's so soon after you had to put down Falcon. I shouldn't have taken that jump."

"You've done it a hundred times," said the first woman. "I'm sure——" The women stopped at the entrance to the room. In the dimness, they seemed to be twins, both slight, not much over five feet tall, their hair done in identical shoulder-length braids. "I'm sorry," the first woman said. "I didn't realize anyone was here."

Johansen stood and Edward Everett did as well. "Mother, Joni," Johansen said as the two women came into the room, their boots clacking on the stone floor.

"I'm Syl Johansen," the first woman said, and as they came nearer, Edward Everett could tell they were not, in fact, twins. While the first woman was clearly older than he was, perhaps in her midseventies, the younger woman was no more than thirty. Syl extended her hand to shake Edward Everett's, her grip much stronger than he would have expected from someone so tiny.

"I'm Ed Yates," he said dully, not wanting to but nonetheless thinking of the money she had.

Syl cocked her head to one side. "Like the Irish poet or the American novelist?"

"I'm sorry?" Edward Everett said. "I don't—"

"Ed manages for us up in Iowa," Johansen said.

"Oh," Syl said, giving the younger woman a look that clearly suggested the answer Johansen had given had immediately moved Edward Everett from one category, "men who were interesting," to another, "men for whom she had no use."

"Mother thinks of you as something like a two-legged polo pony," Johansen said.

"I do not," Sylvia said.

"Your words, Mother," Johansen said, adding a wink, as if Edward Everett were now part of a conspiracy he didn't fully understand. "As far as Mother is concerned, I live in two worlds. There's my old world, working for my grandfather's company, and there's my new world, where I deal with two-legged polo ponies. Ed, sorry to say, you're part of the second."

"Stop it," Sylvia said. "Mr. Yates, I don't know what my son is—"

"Last month," Johansen said, "at the Bridle Boutique—that's B-R-I-D-L-E, as in horses, it's a fund-raiser for abused equines—those things always have such clever—"

"I'm sorry," Edward Everett interrupted, no longer masking his anger over being caught in a game between Johansen and his mother just when Johansen was about to tell him he was finished. "I'm sorry, but I think I'm just going to go."

"I don't understand—" Johansen said.

"I didn't fly all the way here to lose my job and be made the butt of a joke."

"Lose your job?" Johansen said.

"Marc, did you fly this man all the way—" Joni said.

"Good Lord, Ed," Johansen said, laying a hand on Edward Everett's shoulder. "I wouldn't have flown you here to tell you I was letting you go."

"He's too much of a coward for that," Sylvia said.

"Syl, you promised," Joni said. "Mr. Yates, I apologize for my mother-in-law's rudeness, interrupting your business with my husband."

"Business?" Sylvia snapped. "The company his grandfather started is *business*. *This* is a hobby."

Her daughter-in-law took her arm firmly. "Enough," she said, sharply, pulling Sylvia with her out of the room.

"Joan, this is . . ." Sylvia began to say, but whatever *this* was, Edward Everett did not hear because they were soon beyond earshot.

"Please," Johansen said, his voice soft, perhaps even penitent. "Sit down and hear me out. I wasn't going to fire you. I was going to ask you if you wanted a job."

By the time he left Johansen, it was dark, nearly nine p.m. As he crept down the long, narrow, steep road that led from the horse farm, he slid one of the CDs Johansen had given him into the car's stereo. After a moment, a woman's voice came from the speaker: "It's a pleasure to meet you. *Es un gusto conocerie.*"

He repeated the phrase. He could hear the Midwestern awkwardness in his pronunciation and he said it once again before the woman's voice went on: "The pleasure is mine. *El gusto es mio.*"

"*El gusto es mio,*" he repeated.

He was going to Costa Rica and he had Renz to thank. Renz, whose voice dripped with sarcasm when he complained about delinquent spreadsheets, when he spoke to him about pitiful Ross Nelson. He'd hated Renz and now he had to thank him for his new job.

"What do you know about any of the proprietary metrics we've been using?" Johansen had asked after the two sat down again.

"A little," Edward Everett had said tentatively, thinking surely Johansen was not offering him a job centered on the arcane statistics he and Renz loved so much.

"There won't be a test," Johansen said, his voice still soft, no doubt to compensate for his mother's shocking behavior. "The main point is that we've been taking a look at some of the Poe scores across the organization."

"Poe?"

"I'm sorry. P-O-E. Performance Over Expectation. It's a value we derive by combining several—" Johansen laughed. "Short story: Renz—did you know he sleeps maybe three hours a night? He's going to have my job before the year's out . . . That would make my mother happy, at least. At any rate, Renz started playing around with . . . well, the tools we use when we prepare for the draft. We think they can predict, with some accuracy, how a player will perform at various levels in the organization based on . . . well, never mind what it's based on. At any rate, he thought that if we back-doored it, took a look at what the numbers might have predicted about players who already had a track record, we could tweak it so it would have even more accuracy as a predictor. Renz started to notice that some players were outliers—"

Edward Everett opened his mouth to ask what an "outlier" was but Johansen caught himself, smacking his forehead. "Look, I am who I am and so forgive the jargon, because the method is not important. What's important is that Renz asked: what conclusions can we draw about the outliers—you know, the players who perform better than the numbers would have predicted—and one of the factors he looked at was coaching. I mean, it's simple. *I* should have thought of that but I didn't. Renz did. The already-too-long story made short is that he took a look at data for players that've run through your teams going back twenty years and found a not inconsequential—oh, hell. When we started correlating aggregate POE scores to coaching, your numbers were damn good. This year, for example, Martinez—we really thought he was nothing more than an organization player, maybe he'd get, best case, three years, but surely not much above A ball. But now he could turn out to be something. And there was that kid you had in Missoula, independent ball, who stuck it out for four seasons with the Giants. How many guys in indie ball ever get to the big leagues? One in a thousand? A handful of outliers—you can ascribe that to acceptable error, but yours were not statistically insignificant."

Not statistically insignificant. In the world of Marc Johansen, MS, MBA, that amounted to something approaching praise, Edward Everett guessed.

On the CD, the woman was saying, "Can you direct me to... *Puede usted decirme cómo llegar a.*" He laughed. He'd fretted about hanging on in Perabo City, as if managing a broken-down single-A team was something to fight to hang on to. He'd let his vision narrow. Baseball was dead in Perabo City, but it wasn't dead to him.

Costa Rica. He had no idea where it was, exactly. Somewhere south, somewhere they spoke a language he knew only well enough to communicate in a rudimentary way with his Latin players. "Untapped territory," Johansen had called it. "Think of Nicaragua, Venezuela, the Dominican Republic as tapped-out mines. Everyone and his brother has scouted every bush, every rock." Costa Rica was another story and Costa Rica was where he was headed. "We're going to find the best athletes and you'll help turn as many of them into ballplayers as you can," Johansen said.

They would pay him half again as much as he earned for this season. "We'll make it a three-year contract," Johansen had said. "We know you don't want to leave everything without a guarantee." *Leave what?* Edward Everett thought. If he stuck out the full three years, they would give him another year's salary in deferred compensation to reward him for staying. It was nowhere near twenty-three million dollars but it was something most people didn't have: a guarantee he wouldn't be destitute for the rest of his life.

When he got back to the hotel, it was past ten. Parking the car, he thought of himself as he'd been the day before: someone certain he was going to lose his job, someone certain, for how many minutes, that he was going to die in a crash with a hundred strangers. That was a different self. That self was grateful for what amounted to table scraps from the banquet of life, as his father had once said apropos of his own settling. The self shifting the car into "park" and setting the emergency brake as a massive American Airlines jet swooped over him had a guarantee of more than a quarter million dollars over the next thirty-six months, all for leaving a town that no longer had any hold on him and moving to a country he couldn't even pick out on a map.

Hell, he thought, the self he had been when he left this very lot earlier in the day was a different man. That man had been stunned, that man had despised Marc Johansen, MS, MBA, for the decision Edward Everett was certain would mean deprivation for the rest of his days. That self never would have seen Marc Johansen, MS, MBA, as a living, breathing human being with a mother he'd made unhappy—a mother who made the same pronouncement about her son's desire to be part of baseball that Edward Everett's had three decades ago when he had told her that he had signed the minor league contract with the Cleveland organization. *We're brothers of a sort*, he thought with a laugh. *He's the rich brother, sure, but brothers.*

Just before Edward Everett had left, Johansen walked him out to his car. After he shut off the current to the fence, as Edward Everett was about to open his car door, Johansen had said, his voice kind, "You know, what happened to you was the shit."

"How do you mean?"

"That injury. Montreal," Johansen said. "I Googled you. What a day you were having, and then, bang, all over." Even in the darkness as they stood on either side of the gate, Edward Everett could see Johansen shake his head sadly. "I don't know how you didn't give up. Someone else, they'd've thrown in the towel. Succumbed to bitterness."

Touched, Edward Everett said, "It never occurred to me." Of course, it had—but in this new version of his life, he hadn't fallen into bitterness over his bad luck.

"It's probably no consolation," Johansen said, "but at least you got there. You know? For a minute and a half. I . . . A lot of guys say that it was the curveball that kept them out of baseball, but for me it was everything. Hit the curve? Hell, I couldn't hit a fastball. Or a change. Or a ball someone laid out there on a plate and said, 'Take your best cut.' " They shook hands and Johansen said, "You must really love the game."

"I guess I do," Edward Everett said.

Walking from his car toward the bright foyer of the hotel, he thought, *What a difference a day makes.* There was a song like that, it struck him, and he pushed open the door to the air-conditioned lobby humming the tune. He hummed it as he jabbed the button for the elevator and was humming it still when, just as the doors slid open and he waited for two children in swimsuits to exit, a woman coming up behind him spoke his name.

"I kept telling myself I was going to leave in fifteen minutes," she said when he turned around. Meg. The woman from the flight. "For an hour and a half, I kept saying, 'Fifteen minutes, fifteen minutes,' but every time fifteen minutes passed, I thought about going back to my daughter's and how messed up they were—all of their New Age blady-blah about how this had to happen and there was a reason I survived. But then I thought about how I at least have a messed-up daughter who I can visit and a granddaughter who doesn't deserve her silly name. But you had this boy that you never—and I felt so sorry for you." She shrugged. "Maybe it's my own New Age blady-blah but something told me I should come here." She laid a hand gently on his arm. "Is it okay to go upstairs?"

"Yes," he said.

In the morning when he woke, she was gone. She left a note on a hotel postcard. "Forgive my presumption." And then a phone number with an area code the same as his. Just before he checked out, when he was pulling back the covers to make certain he wasn't leaving anything behind—despite the fact that he had no luggage, it was a force of habit after hundreds of nights in hotels—he found a pink sock she evidently hadn't been able to find whenever she'd left, an anklet with the fabric worn thin at the heel. He folded it neatly and put it into the pocket of his jeans.

The flight, as he felt fate owed him, was uneventful. There was no rain and nearly no turbulence. When the plane began its descent, they passed over a river he thought must be the Flann, the one that ran along the edge of Perabo City. Fields around it were in flood still; the tops of trees poked out from the water, as did the roofs of houses and barns. The water seemed placid, unthreatening to anything at all. It ebbed and flowed gently against the sides of buildings and their reflections rippled against the actual structures. Under the full sun, the water gleamed and he thought that it was actually beautiful. What would that be in Spanish? he wondered. *"Agua"* was "water" and *"hermoso"* was "beautiful" but how would he say it in a sentence? *El agua es hermoso. That isn't right,* he thought, *but close enough.* *"Agua es hermoso,"* he said aloud. *"Agua es hermoso."*

Chapter Thirty-one

He decided his team would win the pennant. In the great scheme of life, in the universe of a hundred billion galaxies, who won and who lost a single-A championship in the middle of America mattered perhaps not at all. But it was one small thing he could try to give Johansen, something to move the organization higher in the *Baseball America* rankings; something to give his players. When the season was over, as many as half of them would get the same sort of thin envelope the Cardinals had sent him a dozen years before any of them was born: *We hereby grant... unconditional release*—victims of the organization "rebalancing its portfolio," as Johansen had put it to him in his mother's million-dollar great room, the organization investing in talent in another country rather than the talent it already had. It wouldn't matter a whit if, at the end of it all, it was Perabo City players rushing out of a dugout on a ball field the last Sunday in August, fists raised in triumph, but it would be one moment that his players could have for when they were sixty and had been out of ball themselves for decades, working behind the counter at an auto parts store or at a desk in the lobby of a bank, and be able to say, *Oh, man, I remember this one year*, the twenty-year-old young men they'd been reawakening for a moment inside their sixty-year-old selves.

As they moved past the All-Star break and into August, whatever new arrangement the stars had shifted themselves into seemed enough to change all their fortunes. In the series after he came back from St. Louis, they lost the first of three games against Oshkosh but then took the other two, the last game eleven–ten on a walk-off, bases-loaded double by Martinez with two outs in the ninth. Quincy moved in and Perabo City took two of three, and then all three against Urbana, a tidy seven–two record for the home stand. It was a streak that nearly no one noticed. The attendance was almost nonexistent; for the two Sunday afternoon contests in the home stand, the crowd might have reached 150, but no other crowd came close to that. Although Sandford did not match the brilliance of his first game in their god-awful park, he pitched eight innings in his next appearance and in the one after earned a complete game, although he was spent when he heaved the final pitch, a breaking ball that came in fat and flat above the strike zone. A more mature hitter would have let it go or would have had the discipline to wait on it and drive it a long way, but the Urbana hitter was green, a second baseman maybe five foot seven, and his eyes grew large at the pitch sitting there, saying, *Hit me.* He stood on his toes to reach it, swinging hard, thinking home run, but getting under it weakly, a pop out to second. "You're doing a good job bringing Sandford along," Marc Johansen, MS, MBA, commented after Edward Everett uploaded the statistics from the game.

Twice during the home stand, he saw Meg, the first time after a Sunday afternoon game when he drove to meet her in Cedar Falls, where she lived in what had been a carriage house behind a three-story Victorian brick home, much of her life still in boxes she had shoved into the attic crawl space. "After two years, you'd think I'd have fully moved in," she said when she had him poke his head into the crawl space to look at the stacks of cartons. "I worry the whole ceiling will come in on top of me sometime." She showed him the house she'd had to sell after her divorce, a tidy ranch that the new owners were letting fall down already, and drove him past where her ex-husband was living, an apartment above an accountant's office, one of his windows broken out, replaced by a sheet of cardboard. For dinner, she cooked a miserable lasagna, the casserole runny, the noodles stiff as cardboard. "I should warn you, I am not domestic in the least," she said, and then added, blushing, "Not that I'm expecting you to have to know that about me. No promises, no obligations."

The second time he saw her was late on a Wednesday, after she called him while he was driving home from the ballpark (*not quite a ballpark*).

"What are you doing?" she asked. When he told her, she went on, "How'd you like to keep going another fifty miles or so? Halfway between us? There's a Holiday Inn."

When he got there, after going home briefly to let Grizzly out, she confessed that she had already been there when she called.

"How did you know I would drive up here?" he asked.

She slipped her hand beneath his belt and said in a low voice, "You're male, aren't you?"

Later, while she read the room service menu—she wanted something with beef and grease—she looked at him and said, "I know I'm too old to think this but sometimes all we really need in our lives to be happy is someone who wants to fuck us bad enough that they will drive a hundred miles on the spur of the moment." She laughed. "The real test will be when you have to drive here all the way from Costa Rica." She raised the menu again but then lowered it and asked, winking, "So, tell me, Mr. Flour Salesman, what kind of bread goes best with Angus beef and Swiss cheese?"

He flushed, remembering the conversation when he'd admitted the truth about who he was, the first time he called after he got back from St. Louis, worrying the lie would be a deal-breaker. Instead, she'd laughed. "That's far more interesting," she said. "Before, all we could have talked about was wheat. Now I can have you describe all the naked athletes you've seen in the locker room."

In the Holiday Inn, she gave him a quick peck, reaching for the phone to order the food. "I love reminding you of that because you're so darn cute when you get embarrassed."

The next day when he got home, he looked for the divorce agreement and financial disclosure and filled them out, surprised at how much easier it was than he had expected it to be, and took it to the bank so he could sign it in front of a notary. "I'm so sorry," she said. She was a stout older woman with three chins and a floral print dress that spread across her ample girth like a slipcover would an over-stuffed chair. "I shouldn't comment," she said. "I know that—just sign, stamp and off with you. But I see so many sad things—some good, yes, but a lot of sad, and I can't help myself sometimes." When she slid the document across the desk toward him, she patted his hand in a maternal way. "Things will get better. I know that maybe you can't see that right now but they will."

He considered telling her that he was already all right but only said, "Thank you," and then slipped the document back into its envelope and took it to the Duboises'. When Rhonda answered his knock, he handed it to her. "This is for Renee," he said, and left so that she wouldn't think it was something he needed to talk about. Which it wasn't.

The team kept winning after they went on the road—their longest trip of the season, seventeen days in Illinois and up into Wisconsin. It was fortunate that they were leaving town when they did, since the rains came back to Perabo City the day they departed, a hard storm that began as large, spare drops plopping against the windows of the bus as it pulled out of the lot and then buffeted the bus as it picked up speed on Highway 17. It followed them nearly all the way to Peoria, the sun appearing only half an hour before they pulled into the lot at the Bradley Inn near the university where the minor league team played its games.

After weeks of dressing in the dark and mildew-stinking locker room at the shuttered high school, the visitors' clubhouse at Bradley was something to behold: recently painted, brightly lit, carpeted, the lockers wide and with wooden doors that the maintenance staff had recently refinished, the wood gleaming.

"Shit," said Vila. "Did we die on the way here and end up in heaven?"

Glen Perkins lay on the carpet in the middle of the room and swept his arms and legs over it as if he were making a snow angel, sighing, "Ahhhh." When he stood, there was indeed the faint outline of a winged, robed figure in the carpet pile.

"I have a good feeling about the game today," Rausch said, pointing to the image. For the entire three days they were in Peoria, they trod around it so that, by the time they left—a three-game sweep, including another complete-game shutout by Sandford, number fifteen for him—the faint image was still there. After they had all showered following that last game, Mraz stepped onto the edge of the image.

"What are you doin', man?" Vila shouted, yanking him away.

"Just didn't want the mojo left for the next team," Mraz said.

"Man," Vila said, "you call down the sacred, you don't send it back. You better light a candle or something when we get to Rockford or we don't know what'll happen."

"I ain't Catholic," Mraz said.

"It don't matter," Vila said.

Then, as the bus cruised into Rockford, and they passed a Catholic church—Our Redeemer—Mraz yelled out, "Bussy. Bussy. You gotta stop."

The bus driver caught Edward Everett's eye in the rearview mirror and he gave him a nod. The driver pulled to the curb and Mraz hopped off. The first door he tried at the church was locked but the second was open. He was back out in five minutes. "I lit two, man," he said. "Just to be on the safe side."

In Rockford, they dropped the first game, four–three. If Edward Everett were more superstitious, he would have said that Mraz should have lit five candles. Even the numbers Edward Everett entered into his game log revealed that: five times at bat for Mraz, no hits, no runs, no RBIs, three strikeouts, two errors. Twice, Mraz had come to bat with a runner on third and fewer than two outs, and twice he struck out, the second time watching a flat fastball cross the middle of the plate. "I froze," he said when he slumped back to the dugout. "I was thinking, 'Swing,' but I couldn't." Sitting beside him, Tanner made a show of moving away from him on the bench. But the team was loose: everyone laughed and the next day Mraz batted in the seventh with runners on second and third, the team down three–one, and laced a triple in the alley, two runs scoring to tie the game, and then came in with what proved to be the winning run on a passed ball, setting up a rubber game the next day, which the team won eight–four, Sandford starting and good enough to get through seven, his sixteenth win against three losses.

Marc Johansen, MS, MBA, was pleased: "Effective management of Sandford," he wrote in an email. "Likelihood he reach 20 W? Sent from my BlackBerry." *20 W.* Twenty wins; the notion had never occurred to Edward Everett. How many years had it been since a pitcher had won twenty in a minor league season? Twenty-five? Sitting on the bus on their way north to Oshkosh the next day, he got out his accordion folder, flipped through the cards until he found Sandford's and counted how many more starts he would have: six. If he pitched as he had been, he could end up with twenty wins, but it would take a lot of luck—a lot of angels on a lot of locker room carpeting. And for what? The truth was, who could even name the last pitcher to win twenty in a minor league uniform? The truth was, what happened in the minor leagues stayed in the minor leagues. Still, Sandford was Johansen's property and Edward Everett thought it a small gift he could give him. "Okay," he replied.

By the end of the trip, Sandford had two more, seventeen and eighteen—but they were far from pretty. His game log still looked good: number seventeen, seven innings, ninety pitches, three runs, five hits, three walks, four strikeouts. Number eighteen, six and a third, eighty-seven pitches, four runs, seven hits, four walks, two strikeouts. But the raw statistics concealed cracks that bore watching: the number of his walks was creeping up, and in number eighteen Madison had hit him hard late in the game; he was saved largely because the ballpark had a large center field, four hundred twenty-eight feet to the wall, and Mraz caught two flies deep, one just at the edge of the warning track, the other with his back pressed to the wall. In any other park, they would have been gone, and Sandford's line would look far worse—eight runs instead of four.

He was worrying, Edward Everett knew. *You're not happy unless you're anxious,* Renee had joked to him once when they hadn't been married long, when his flaws were still part of his charm. It was true:

by all other measures, the team was successful. They came back from the trip in second place, two games out of first—not bad for a club without a home, he thought wryly. And other things were going well. Martinez had started listening to him about plate discipline and he was walking more; the chart recording the locations of Tanner's hits showed that he had stopped trying to pull everything to left, was collecting hits to right and center; Singer, on the other hand, had started to pull the ball more, take advantage of his size and power. He had no business being a slap hitter.

Maybe, Edward Everett thought, he was a good enough coach that more of his players would survive the post-season purge than he had expected before the road trip. Riding the bus back to Perabo City, he went through his game log cards, scrutinizing the numbers on them as Johansen would, asking who would survive, who would not? The first time he sorted them, he decided that eleven would make the cut, thirteen would not. The second time, it was a dozen on each side of the ledger. He hoped he was wrong; he hoped that more of them would end up being outliers.

Then Nelson came back.

Chapter Thirty-two

When he got to the high school for the first home game after the long road trip, Edward Everett found that someone had put duct tape over the latch bolt, preventing it from locking. "Hello?" he called, stepping tentatively into the locker room. From the darkness, he heard something clatter, someone say "Shit," and then bare feet slapping on cement. He wondered if he should get out, call the police. But he flicked on the light switch next to the door. "Hello," he said again, walking cautiously across the locker room. In the equipment cage, a silhouette of a man pressed into the back corner, wedged between the wall and a stack of boxes.

"Nelson?" Edward Everett said when he recognized him.

"I'm sorry, Skip," Nelson said, still hiding in the corner.

"Come on out, Nels," he said gently.

Nelson hesitated, then stepped out of the corner, blinking in the light. He looked terrible—pale and unshaven, wearing boxers and a ripped Houston Astros T-shirt.

"Jesus. You look like crap," Edward Everett said, not meaning to.

"I don't know what to do," Nelson said, working a finger into a hole in his shirt.

"The first thing is to take a shower." Edward Everett went back to where he had dropped his equipment bag, took out the towel he had meant for his own shower after the game and brought it to Nelson, who regarded it suspiciously. "It's a towel," Edward Everett said. "You use it to dry yourself after a shower."

While Nelson showered, Edward Everett sat at the small desk in the corner of the locker room and began transferring the data from his game log cards into the spreadsheet. After Nelson finished, Edward Everett became conscious of him sitting on a bench behind him, watching him type the figures into the Excel sheets and make notes about what he wanted to highlight in his email to Johansen in his attempt to improve more of his players' chances at surviving the cuts the team was planning, if it wasn't too late.

"Is that what done me in?" Nelson said, his voice small.

"I don't know what you mean," Edward Everett said.

"The numbers," Nelson said.

"It's complicated," Edward Everett said.

"Complicated," Nelson said. "That's the kind of shit someone says when they don't want to tell you the truth. Like when Cindy said she was going to stay with her folks. 'Why are you going?' I asked her. 'It's complicated,' she said."

"Nelson," Edward Everett said, turning to face him, weighing whether to tell him Cindy and her brother had come to see him. Nelson didn't look much better than he did before he showered; the only noticeable difference was that his hair was wet and he had pulled on a pair of jeans. "Why aren't you home?"

Nelson laughed. "I don't have a home. Got to have a job to have a home."

"Well, what about . . ." He hesitated, not wanting to do something as intimate as saying Cindy's name. ". . . your wife and kids. I think they miss you."

"Jesus fucking Christ!" Nelson bellowed. "Haven't you been listening? She's gone back to her folks."

"I only meant that you could go there, too," Edward Everett said, quietly hoping his tone would defuse Nelson's anger.

"Right," Nelson said. "Go knock on her daddy's door. 'Here is little loser boy.' "

"Ross," he said.

"I don't know what to do besides this," Nelson said, patting the bench he sat on.

"But you're not really doing *this*."

Nelson was silent, clearly thinking. "All I've ever done is baseball," he said finally. "Cindy says I took my shot and . . . Christ almighty, Skip. 'I took my shot'—like it's a fucking carnival game and either you win the doll or you don't."

"Look at yourself," Edward Everett said. "You're sleeping in a locker room in a closed-down school, and when's the last time you ate anything?"

"I eat," Nelson said defensively.

"What? What do you eat?"

"Food. What the fuck do you think I eat?"

Edward Everett knew he would regret doing it but he reached into his hip pocket and brought out his wallet, fingering first a ten and then the ten and a twenty. Nelson might be crazy but he had to eat. "Here," he said, holding out the thirty dollars to him.

The outside door to the locker room squealed open. Because whoever came in was backlit by the sun and the locker room was dim, all Edward Everett could make out was a silhouette. "Oh, fuck, Nelson," the figure said—Tanner. Nelson looked at the money that Edward Everett held out, perhaps weighing his empty belly against his need for pride. He swiped at the bills, grabbing the twenty but dropping the ten, and dashed out of the locker room, shoving Tanner aside as he went through the door.

"Shit, Skip," Tanner said, coming in, rubbing his shoulder where it had banged against the steel doorjamb. "You should call the cops or something."

"Tanner . . ." *That's you maybe in a month*, he wanted to say but didn't. What was the point? They all thought they were invincible; that it would go on forever and ever, amen. "Just cut Nelson some slack, all right?" He picked up the bill Nelson had dropped.

"He belongs in a psycho ward. Someone said they saw him going through a dumpster last week."

"Who needs a psycho ward?" Martinez said, coming into the locker room.

"Oh, shit," Tanner said. "We was just talking about you."

"Fuck you, Tanner," Martinez said.

And then Nelson was gone and Edward Everett did not see him again until the last day of the season.

For half a day on the last Sunday of the home stand, they were tied for first when they won their third in a row from Peoria, one they almost lost save for what was most likely a gift from the field umpire, the final out coming with the bases loaded when the Peoria hitter lined a shot up the middle that Rausch snagged, diving, hitting the turf hard enough to knock the wind out of himself, the umpire throwing up his right thumb, signaling the out and the end of the game. The Peoria manager burst off the bench and onto the field, protesting that Rausch had trapped the ball, not caught it. "You weren't in position to see for sure that he did," he shouted.

"You got no proof he didn't," the umpire said in a slow drawl, taking a stick of Big Red gum out of his pants pocket, unwrapping it, folding it into his mouth, where he already had half a dozen pieces, and then strolled off the field. The Peoria manager kicked at the dirt but said no more; Perabo City had come back from a long way down in the standings, two weeks to play and all even.

Chapter Thirty-three

They came into the final weekend of the season still tied with Quad Cities for first place, just as Quad Cities was coming to town for a three-game series. The math was simple, Edward Everett knew: to win, Perabo City needed to take two of the three games. On Friday before the first game, Renz emailed the list of players Johansen would release after the season and the list of players he would assign to other teams in the organization. It stunned Edward Everett. They were releasing seventeen players and keeping but seven: Sandford, Martinez, Vila, Mraz, Rausch, Singer and Rojas. Thinking that his own secure place with the club might be enough that he could convince Johansen to change his mind on two or three players, he called his office. At the very least, he thought, he should be able to convince him to consider saving his pitcher Riggins, who had started poorly but had allowed only one earned run in his last eleven games out of the bullpen. It was not Johansen who answered the phone, however, but Renz, and the conversation echoed the one they'd had when he'd called on Nelson's behalf.

"The projection for him doesn't make it work," Renz said after Edward Everett made his case.

"What about—" he started to say, wanting to remind Renz of the conversation he'd had with Johansen, about the club wanting to blend numbers with other, more human judgment. Certainly, Johansen had conveyed that to Renz.

"The numbers are the numbers."

"But——" he said.

"Oh, we might have added one more of your players to the list of 'keepers,' " Renz said, and then went on before Edward Everett could ask who it was. "But that someone fractured his knee on your watch." Before Edward Everett could correct him, telling him it was Webber's shoulder, not his knee, Renz hung up.

He went to the ballpark knowing he would share none of the news with anyone—not the lucky seven, not the unlucky seventeen. The organization had given him a future and he owed them some loyalty for that—but it didn't extend to his breaking the hearts of nearly three-fourths of his players sooner than he had to.

It was the weekend of the county fair. From the ball field at St. Aloysius, Edward Everett could see the fairgrounds that overlooked the school, a slash of the western edge—four booths and the top arch of the Ferris wheel. Because of the poor economy and the flooding, the radio told him, the fair organizers expected attendance to hit its lowest point in recent memory. "We considered canceling it," a woman said. "But so many people have put so much time into this." "Besides," said a second woman, "at times like these, people need some sort of diversion."

As the team went through batting practice two hours before first pitch, the organizers' prediction seemed accurate. At the visible edge of the fairgrounds, minutes passed between fairgoers appearing at any of the booths. At one point, the Ferris wheel seemed not to move for ten minutes, the purple and yellow neon lights tracing its circumference blinking off and on. Compared to his team's attendance for the opening game of the series, however, the fair was successful. As he stood at home plate, handing over his lineup card to the umpires and the Quad Cities manager, he could count thirty people in the bleachers behind the Perabo City bench; there were no more than that in the bleachers along the third base line. Collier had given up any pretense of caring: he did not even pay anyone to open the concession stand, and while the umpire reminded the Quad Cities manager of the ground rules, Edward Everett caught sight of a heavy, balding man in a nylon Perabo City Owls windbreaker—a remnant from when the team had fans who wore clothing with their logo—leading a three-year-old boy up to what should have been the concession window, knocking on the plywood covering it, the boy saying, "Want ice cream." They left the ball field, the boy crying all the way up the long flight of steps to the parking lot, a major dent in the attendance even before anyone had thrown a pitch.

Early in the game, it became clear that the man had probably done a shrewd thing in leaving, as it was a sloppy contest. A cool drizzle fell intermittently throughout—never hard enough for the umpires to stop the game, although the field was wet. In the top of the fourth, Perabo City made three errors, two by Vern Stuckey after there were two outs. The first, he slipped on the wet grass in right field, his feet flying up in the air like a silent comedian stepping on a banana peel, the ball popping out of his glove, letting a runner on third score. The second, he fielded a base hit cleanly and snapped the ball toward second to try to catch a runner who had rounded the base too far, but his throw sailed over the head of Rausch covering the base, the Quad Cities runner banging into him trying to get back to the bag, knocking him down. For a moment, Rausch lay there, Edward Everett sending Dominici out to see if he was hurt, but he'd just had the wind knocked out of him, and Dominici helped him up. The perhaps five dozen people in the bleachers gave him polite applause. By the sixth inning, Perabo City was down eleven–three. On the mound, his starter, Matt Pearson, paused before nearly every pitch, looking pointedly at Edward Everett, as if to ask: *When is it enough?* Finally, with only one out and the bases loaded, Edward Everett called time-out and went to the mound to talk to him.

"I'm sorry, Skip," Pearson said, handing him the baseball. "I just can't work the kinks out today." Edward Everett took his left arm by the wrist, popping the baseball back into the pocket of his glove. "I'm sorry, Pearson. I didn't come out to get you."

"Jesus Christ, Skip," he said through clenched teeth. "I'm getting demolished."

"I know, and I'm sorry, but I need the pen for tomorrow and Sunday."

"You're saying this one is lost and I'm the sacrificial lamb?"

"I need you to give me whatever you can."

"Christ, my numbers."

Edward Everett regarded him. *You're on the wrong list,* he thought. *Your numbers don't matter.* "Look," he said, not meeting Pearson's eyes, "shut 'em down; the more innings with no more damage, the better your numbers."

"Fuck you, Skip." Pearson walked away, rubbing the baseball between his hands.

As it turned out, he might have done better to remove the pitcher when Pearson had wanted to leave the game. Perabo City scored four in the seventh and seven in the eighth and if he had replaced Pearson with someone who might have shut down Quad Cities, Perabo City might well have won; but he left Pearson out there and, perhaps through some perverse obstinacy, the pitcher allowed half a dozen more runs to score, glaring at Edward Everett each time someone got a hit or he walked a batter: *Take that, you bastard.* Finally, Edward Everett relented, sending someone else in for the ninth, Pearson stomping angrily up the steps to the locker room, no longer interested in any show of restraint, screaming, "Fuck, fuck, fuck, fuck," the entire way up, the final score seventeen–fifteen, Quad Cities in first by one with two to play.

The second game went better. Perhaps because his team had gotten such a large lead in the first game and Perabo City had picked away at it, the Quad Cities manager had not been as restrained in his use of the bullpen as had Edward Everett, and he'd used seven pitchers in all to lock down the win. As a result, when his starting pitcher got into trouble in the second game, it was his turn to leave him out there, resting his other pitchers for the final game—the one that would decide the league. Perabo City scored three in the second, two in the fourth, five in the sixth, and led twelve–one by the bottom of the eighth inning when the featured act for the weekend at the fair took the stage up the hill from the game: a Motown group that'd had a few top-40 hits in the 1960s. Their songs—some familiar, most not—floated down the hill, the volume increasing and decreasing with the direction and speed of the wind. On the Perabo City bench, with the lead they had, the team was loose. When the band played its most famous hit—one Edward Everett remembered from his junior prom, a slow number during which the disc jockey had lowered the lights and Edward Everett and his date held tightly to each other, turning in the slowest of circles while above them the fluorescent stars tacked to the gymnasium ceiling twinkled—Vila stood up on the bench.

"My grandma used to play this to get me to go to sleep when I was at her house while my mom was at work," he said. He started swaying on the bench, singing the lyrics, trying to mimic the movements Edward Everett remembered the group going through when they performed on *American Bandstand.* Four or five other players got up, watching his moves, trying to imitate him, shouting out the lyrics when they knew them, getting them wrong when they didn't. When the song finished, just as Vila had to leave the bench to warm up in the on-deck circle, the few fans in the ballpark applauded.

On his way home, Edward Everett was restless. *It has come down to the last game of the year,* he thought; *of course it has.* The final game for the pennant and for Sandford's shot at twenty wins. In all his years, he had seen few other pitchers he would rather have starting a game that mattered as this one did. He realized he had fooled himself when he'd said that winning the pennant would mean little to him and for a brief moment pictured his team pouring onto the field after the last out, hefting him to their shoulders, although he realized at the same time that it was something that would happen in the movies, a movie about a main character who was someone like him. In life, he knew, his players thought of themselves as the main characters. They were all driving home with their own visions of the team picking them up and carrying them off the field.

He called Meg and she answered the phone after the first ring.

"I was hoping you'd call," she said.

He told her about the game and the one tomorrow for all the marbles.

"Not bad for a little old flour salesman," she said.

Although he knew it was crazy, he suggested they meet at the Holiday Inn. He wouldn't get there until almost midnight and would have to leave the next morning by five to get back home to prepare for the game, and yet he didn't want to be alone.

"What makes you think I can just pick up like that, at this hour?" she asked, and then, as disappointment was settling on him, said quickly, "Just kidding. I didn't think I'd get to see you until after the season, when you'd exploit me to help you pack to move.".

This time, even stopping at home to care for Grizzly, he was at the hotel first and had to wait for her, worrying that she had changed her mind. He sat on the edge of the bed, half watching the MLB Network, video of the best plays of the day, men doing extraordinary things on the field: a first baseman for St. Louis leaping onto a rolled-up tarp to backhand a pop foul; a Tampa Bay shortstop diving into left field to snag a deep ground ball and then throwing to second while still on his back. If Webber hadn't gotten hurt, that might have been him in a few years. Not long before Webber's accident, Edward Everett remembered, he was convinced that it would be Webber who survived the season and that he would be out—but the story is not over until the story is over; he was still in the game and Webber was back home in Ohio, going through physical therapy to build up the muscles in his damaged shoulder, but only so he could live a normal life in the World. It would not be enough for him to ever play again.

When Meg got there, she tapped nervously on the door, quietly, as if she were afraid someone in the hall might hear. When he opened the door, she was wearing a London Fog raincoat, which surprised him, since it was dry and 90 degrees, but in the room, the door shut, she dropped it to show him that she was already naked under it.

"I always wanted to do that," she said, hugging him, helping him pull off his shirt. "It was something on my bucket list. So there you have it, check off something else."

After sex, he was usually sleepy, but tonight he was alert, nervous, and she fell asleep while he lay there, thinking, first inning, second inning, third inning, going through the Quad Cities roster in his mind, thinking, *If they bring in Wong, I'll pinch-hit Perkins; if they bring in Didier with Rausch up, I'll tell Rausch to look for the slider.*

At one point, Meg woke and saw him sleepless. "I think it's sweet you care so much about this for them," she said, shifting so that her head lay on his shoulder. He kissed her hair and realized she didn't smell of tobacco.

"I quit a week ago," she said as if she knew what he was thinking. "Now, don't run scared, because I'm not expecting anything from you. I'm going to miss you when you go to Costa Rica but maybe you'll come back, and then, who knows? That's something to live for, in my book." She opened her eyes, looked at him briefly, and then shut them again. "And at my age. Who woulda thunk it."

Chapter Thirty-four

On Sunday morning, Edward Everett left the hotel at four, slipping out quietly and not showering because he hadn't wanted to wake Meg, who didn't stir when he got up. It was still dark when he got home and as he opened his back door, the thought came to him that it was likely most of his players' last day in baseball. Nineteen years old, twenty, twenty-one, certain for most of their lives that, beginning in late winter, they would be on a diamond somewhere under the sun in some southern state, jogging, working out the kinks, throwing, hitting. He thought about his first professional camp, short-season rookie ball, Johnson City, Tennessee, late June 1967. He was thin as a rail then, waist thirty-one, inseam thirty-four. He saw himself stepping out of the dim tunnel from the clubhouse on his first day, his nose twitching from the mold that grew on the dark, cool concrete, the ballpark already alive with the sounds of the game that never failed to make his heart beat faster, his teammates running and shouting and tossing baseballs. All of his teammates from then were long out of the game now, some when they were as young as Edward Everett's players, who were going to get their own dismissals any day. Only three from his cohorts made it as far as the big leagues, and none lasted more than four seasons. A pitcher. What was his name, the relative long-timer? George? Ken? Joe? *God, so long ago,* he thought.

By the time he showered, finished eating cereal, having first one and then a second cup of coffee, and read the slender Sunday paper, it was only seven-fifteen. If he still had an office at the ballpark, he would have gone to it—there were many mornings when he woke early and restless and had gotten to his office while the sun was beginning to crest above the stands along the third base line. But he did not want to go to St. Aloysius and sit alone in the poorly lit, reeking locker room.

He wished he had waked Meg and asked her to come with him. He could go back to bed with her, clean and fresh-smelling, and then thought: *That part of my life should be over.* To be sixty and randy was absurd, but he was. He calculated the distance from the hotel to his house, thinking about waking Meg in the room—where she, no doubt, still slept—asking her to drive down. By the time she arrived, however, it would be past nine. Besides, he thought: did she have clothing to wear? She must have, but he imagined her driving back to her house, naked, truckers who saw her giving a long blast of their diesel horns, *Man, you wouldn't believe what I saw!*

The notion of going to Mass occurred to him. He'd been once in the last year, the past Christmas Eve, not long after Renee had come back from the first time she left, when he was doing everything he could to keep her from leaving again. She had said, "You know what I miss? Mass." Then, going up the steps to St. Monica's in a light snow, she had seized his elbow just before he opened the door. "Are we going to be struck by lightning? What do we have between us, two divorces and who knows what else terrible?" But the choir inside began singing "Adeste Fidelis," and she had closed her eyes in a kind of bliss he hadn't seen in a while, and they'd gone in. Back then, the church had been decorated for the holiday, but the last Sunday of the baseball season was just a Sunday in Ordinary Time—there would not be the pomp of Christmas, the crèche adorned by lights, the tree near the altar with porcelain angels hung on it, the excited children frantic for the next day, when they would come down in the morning

and find their own presents under the tree their parents had decorated.

He went to Mass. The congregation was sparse, but still, he noted,
it was far more than what would show up for the last game ever in
Perabo City: maybe 150 people scattered in the pews. Throughout
the service, he was distracted. It did not help that there was something wrong with the priest's radio microphone and for long periods
of the service, sitting on the aisle in the last pew, he could not hear
anything but the buzz and pop of the audio system and the priest's
mumbled prayers. During the homily, long stretches went by without him being able to hear anything, just an occasional phrase: "today,
Jesus," "the lesson of the leper," "our neighbors suffering from
flood." Nonetheless, he tried to focus on the prayers, tried to follow in
his own halting, half-remembering way the hymns that the small
guitar choir strummed through—but other business kept pushing
into his head: What was he going to do the next day or two weeks
from now? What did he need to do to sell his house? The market was
bad and he should have called an agent the day after he came back
from meeting with Johansen. He thought about his bullpen: who
would follow Sandford if the starting pitcher faltered; *if* they could
get a lead by the fifth inning and *if* Sandford could last that long and
if they held on to win the game, it would be Sandford's twentieth, the
magic number that Johansen had asked for.

He thought: I should buy champagne for if we win, at least a case
so that my players can follow the rituals they'd seen on the networks
when the major league teams won championships and the players
sprayed one another with bubbly. Then he thought: half the team
was underage; he'd have to buy sparkling grape juice—look the other
way if any of them who were not twenty-one took a sip of alcohol.

At Communion, at first he decided not to go: he was not in any
state of grace, had not been to confession for decades. Remarriage
after divorce was a mortal sin. As the two women and one man who
occupied his pew stood to move to the front of the church, he stepped
into the aisle to let them pass but when the first woman indicated he
should precede her, he decided to go. When he got to the front, he

was surprised to see that Renee was the extraordinary minister hold-ing the chalice of wine. She was in a beige linen suit with an organdy blouse, one of the collar points turned up slightly. As Edward Everett reached her, she swiped the white linen cloth across the rim of the ceramic cup and held it to him. "The Blood of Christ," she said. It was only then that she recognized him, and she nearly dropped the chalice as he gave it back to her. When he stepped away, she glanced at him as if she wanted to say something more but did not. "The Blood of Christ," she said to the woman behind him, stammering slightly.

At the end of the Mass, he looked for her, not sure of what he would say but feeling he ought to say something. *I'm leaving town.* Something.

When he found her, she was talking to a man who towered over her, someone who was nearly six foot six and who looked familiar. As he approached them, Renee kept glancing between the man and Ed-ward Everett. He stopped at what he thought was an appropriate distance to wait for her but she laid her hand on the man's elbow, turning him slightly to face Edward Everett. Then Edward Everett knew where he had seen him: her former husband. Art. The one who had left her for his cousin.

"Art," Renee said. "You remember Ed." Art colored slightly but extended his hand to shake Edward Everett's. His palm was massive, engulfing Edward Everett's. "Can I talk to Ed for a minute?" Renee asked. Art eyed Edward Everett in a way that suggested he suspected he might assault Renee but nodded and stepped away. Renee gave him a nod, meaning, *a little farther,* and after hesitating, he left them there, walking to the vestibule, glancing over his shoulder several times.

"So," Renee said. "You finally tracked me down."

He realized that she assumed the only reason he had been at Mass was to see her. "No," he said. "I just decided to come to church."

"Just decided," Renee said. "Right." She shook her head sadly. "I thought, since you signed the divorce, you had let go. You really need to, Ed. I'm not coming back." She held up her left hand, a slender gold band glinting from the fourth finger. "Art and I remarried."

"I thought—what happened to his cousin?"

"We've all made mistakes," she said. "It's not common but some-times life lets you use a delete key." She shrugged. "This was one of those times."

"That was . . ." *Fast,* he was going to say; how long had it been since he signed the divorce papers?

"You know what? As far as Mother Church is concerned, we were always married—Art and I. No divorce in the Church."

"What about us?" he said.

She shrugged. "In here," she gestured to take in the church, "we never happened. So maybe it's best if you think of it that way. I'm really not coming back. It's not like before."

He shook his head. "I wasn't trying . . ." he began but then just said, "I was just coming up to say good-bye."

"What?"

"I'm leaving," he said. "I have a new job. In another country."

"Another county?"

"Country. With an 'r.' "

She furrowed her brow and cocked her head to one side—what he had come to know as her sign that she was dubious.

"And I forgive you," he said on impulse.

"You forgive me?" she said. "That suggests—"

He didn't want to argue and so he interrupted her. "I've got to go." He left her there, although she snapped, "Wait," her voice echo-ing in the church. "Wait!"

Outside, small knots of families chatted amiably. Standing on the top step leading to the street, the priest shook his hand. "Thank you for coming. Have a blessed day."

It was a benediction, he thought, walking to his car, feeling peace-ful. Whether it was the Mass or his conversation with Renee that had allowed him to put a period at the end of their relationship, he wasn't sure—it was not absolute absolution but perhaps the promise of one, and as he got into his car, he did feel blessed.

As he put on his jersey for the game, he found that some of the threads affixing the initial "P" in the town's name had broken, the top arc of the letter flopped over. Leaving the jersey unbuttoned, he went to the kitchen to fish through the junk drawer to look for a needle and thread. Before he got there, however, his doorbell rang.

When he opened the door, Nelson was on his front porch, more disheveled than he'd been the last time Edward Everett had seen him, running away from St. Aloysius. Blades of grass clung to his four or five days of beard and there was a redbud leaf stuck behind his right ear, the leaf skeletonized by an insect. He wondered if Nelson had been sleeping outdoors. His face looked as if he had been in a fight: scratches across his left cheek, his eyes swollen. His clothing was torn: his nylon gym shorts; the sweatshirt that seemed stretched out longer on the right than on the left; his canvas skater shoes.

"Jesus, Nelson," he said, not meaning to. "You look bad."

"How did you expect I'd look?" he said, glancing over his shoulder as a car passed.

"Come on in," Edward Everett said, not wanting him to but not wanting him on his porch, either. Taking the step up from the porch into the house, Nelson staggered, clutching Edward Everett's arm to steady himself, nearly pulling him down. That close, he thought he smelled beer on Nelson's breath, on his clothing.

"I brung you this," Nelson said, pulling a crumpled twenty-dollar bill from his sweatshirt pocket and thrusting it toward Edward Everett.

"I just thought you could use something," Edward Everett said, not taking the money. "You need to eat," he said. "When's the last time you ate?"

"I don't know," he said. He tugged at the fuzz on his chin, hard enough that it seemed it should hurt. "Yesterday, maybe. Fuck, what day is it? What does it matter?"

"It's Sunday."

"Sunday," Nelson said in a way that suggested the word was one he was trying out for the first time. "Sun. Day."

"You should use that," Edward Everett said, nodding at the bill in Nelson's hand.

"I'm no charity case," he said. "Besides, a twenty ain't going to fix much, Skip." He held out the bill but when Edward Everett didn't take it, he let it flutter to the floor.

"Look, Nels—Ross, sit down. I'll get you something to eat. I have to get going."

"Ball game?" Nelson said. "Season's still going on?"

"Last game," Edward Everett said. "We're—" *Tied with Quad Cities,* he was going to say but caught himself. If he were Nelson, he wouldn't want to know anything about that. He finished his sentence, "—wrapping things up."

"The guys miss me, Skip?" Nelson said. "I know how it is. It's like I was never there. I seen it when I was one of the guys that stuck. The hole closes up behind you. *Shoomp.* Like a fucking vacuum."

"No, Nelson—Ross."

"Don't lie to me, Skip. It's like a fucking vacuum."

"I'm going to get you some food," he said. "If you just eat—"

"It's feed a cold, starve a fever," Nelson said. "This ain't a cold, Skip."

"Look, I'll get you something," he said; he went out to the kitchen and opened the refrigerator. He had no idea what Nelson would want. "What are you in the mood for?" he called, as if he were entertaining an ordinary guest, a friend who had just dropped by for a visit.

Nelson didn't respond. Edward Everett took a loaf of bread and three wrapped slices of cheese out of the refrigerator. He could at least make him a sandwich; something was better than nothing.

From the living room, he could hear Grizzly growling in a low, menacing way and he went to check on him. Nelson was standing on the couch, rocking side to side on the cushions to keep his balance. It reminded Edward Everett of a child bouncing on a bed. Grizzly was crouched low, his hindquarters up, his teeth bared.

"Get him the fuck away from me," Nelson said, slapping at his sweatshirt pocket. When he brought his hand back up, he was holding a gun.

Edward Everett dropped the bread and cheese. "What the fuck, Nelson?"

Grizzly lunged toward the couch, trying to leap onto it, but fell short. Startled, Nelson tumbled over the back of it, slamming against a box of the game log cards Edward Everett had brought up from the basement weeks earlier, the box tearing open, cards skittering across the floor. Again Grizzly leaped for the couch, and made it that time, barking furiously, Nelson scrambling to his feet, slipping on the loose cards, pointing the gun in the direction of the dog, his hand shaking. Edward Everett eyed the front door and then the kitchen behind him: which was the easier way out? If he ran, would Nelson shoot him?

"Ross," he said in a voice he hoped was calming, but he could hear a tremor in it.

"Do something about the fucking dog," Nelson shouted, still pointing the gun toward Grizzly, who was barking and leaping toward him. "I hate dogs."

"Let me get him." Edward Everett took a tentative step toward the couch. "Just getting the dog," he said, holding up his hand at an angle: a foolish gesture, he realized, as if that would shield him if Nelson pulled the trigger. He snatched at Grizzly's collar but the dog twisted, snapping at him, biting the base of his right thumb, drawing blood and getting away. The second time he reached for the dog's collar, he managed to snag it, picking him up, Grizzly flailing the air with his paws, his teeth flashing. He held him at arm's length, barely keeping his fingers laced through the collar, managed to open the door to the closet near the front door, hurled the dog in and slammed the door. On the other side, Grizzly flung himself against the door, the hangers on which Edward Everett had hung his coats clanging.

Nelson was pale, leaning over, his free hand braced on the back of the couch, breathing shallowly, while Grizzly barked wildly. Maybe Nelson would hyperventilate, pass out, Edward Everett thought, but he sucked in a breath, let it out and straightened.

"Fuck, Skip. I'm fucking going to shoot that fucking dog."

"Grizzly," Edward Everett bellowed, so loudly that Nelson startled. The dog did stop barking but then another noise began in the closet: the dog's nails clicking against the hardwood floor, every once in a while something knocking against the wall. It was his head, Edward Everett knew, Grizzly in the throes of a seizure.

"Ross," he said. "Let's just put the gun away. We can talk. Long as you want."

"Skip," Nelson said, leaning against the back of the sofa, the gun resting on a cushion. "I'm fucked."

"No you're not," he said, keeping his eye on the gun.

With his free hand, Nelson fumbled in his sweatshirt pocket and came out with a folded wad of paper: something with a pale blue cover sheet. A legal document. Nelson tried unfolding it with one hand but became frustrated and thrust it at Edward Everett, who took it, his own hand shaking so much the paper rattled. Unfolding it, he saw it was an order of protection, prohibiting Nelson from coming within fifty yards of the petitioner, Cynthia Nelson, as well as Jacob Nelson and Sarah Nelson, minor children.

"I don't know what this means, Skip," Nelson said. He was crying and he reached up to wipe his eyes with the wrist of his hand that held the gun. What kind of weapon was it? Edward Everett wondered. Not a revolver; a gun that loaded with a clip in the handle. He knew nothing about guns except what he had seen in movies and on television, but he thought: *Guns like that have a safety.* He squinted at it, trying to find it, but had no idea where it would be or what it would look like on or off.

"Oh, fuck, Skip," Nelson said, pointing the gun in Edward Everett's direction. "Don't even think of trying to get this away from me."

"I wasn't," Edward Everett said. His head was suddenly light. He wanted to sit down and, without thinking of how Nelson would respond, he staggered back until his knees felt one of the upholstered chairs he had in his living room, and he sat.

"Order of protection," Nelson said. He moved unsteadily around the couch until he was on the other side and sank into it, sitting, dangling the gun between his knees. "I would never hurt Cindy or . . . My God. My kids. Why would she say something like that?"

Because you're crazy, Edward Everett thought. *Because you're in my house with a gun.* He said nothing, pretending to study the document. He could comprehend nothing on the page now, not even individual letters; they were squiggles, circles and slashes.

"Fuck, Skip. I really screwed things up," Nelson said.

"I don't know, Nelson," he said, talking quietly. "What did you do?"

"I went to her dad's house. He said, 'She doesn't want to see you.' 'Like hell,' I said. 'She doesn't want to see you. You need to leave.' Then he fucking closed the door."

"What did you do then?"

"I didn't fucking leave, that's what I did. I stayed on their fucking porch and he called the cops. They came and took me away and next day, order of protection." He moved abruptly toward Edward Everett, making him flinch, snatched the document out of his hand and ripped it into two pieces, then ripped it again, until it was too thick for him to tear easily and he flung the pieces around the room. "I wish I'd had the gun then. I'd've fucking shot him, right there on his fucking porch."

"I don't think you would do that, Ross," Edward Everett said. "I don't think you're the kind of person who could shoot someone."

"You think so?" Nelson said. He raised the gun and eyed along the barrel, squinting. "If he was here, I would so pull the fucking trigger."

"We can fix this, Ross," Edward Everett said.

"I'd say we're pretty far past the fixing stage."

Was he going to shoot them both or just himself? Edward Everett wondered. Maybe someone would come by. Meg. *Surprise! I missed you, honey.* Or maybe Vincent, who wanted to pay more of the money he owed for his girlfriend's root canal. *I'm a good person,* Edward Everett thought. *The kind of person who lends a thousand dollars to someone and doesn't pester him to pay it back.* He thought, *It's entirely possible that Vincent will choose this moment to come by.* When he knocked, Nelson would say, *Don't.*

If I don't answer, he'll know something is wrong.

Okay, but no funny business, Nelson would say.

At the door, Edward Everett would find a word that Vincent would understand but Nelson wouldn't. Vincent would leave and call the police. But, Edward Everett realized, that was only something that happened in movies so that someone could save the day at the last instant.

"Let's talk about how to fix this," Edward Everett said.

"Just shut up for a minute, Skip. I have a headache." He rubbed his temples.

It must be past ten o'clock, Edward Everett thought. Meg would not be on her way here but at her house, having a cup of coffee, no idea of what was happening to him. Vincent and Dominici would be at St. Aloysius, the rest of the team coming in, the players jittery with the idea of winning a professional title, none knowing the decision that the organization had made already; you stay, you go. The ones going didn't know yet that the game wasn't interested in them anymore, that they had only filled a role, shadows in the background for players like Sandford, and like Webber should have become. They all hated Nelson, he thought, but they were more like him than they realized.

The game had told Edward Everett the same thing thirty years ago, had tried to throw him out, but he'd come back and come back and come back and was on the edge of reward for his tenacity. *I don't deserve this,* he thought. *I deserve Costa Rica and the four years' pay for three years' work and the cheap real estate that could make it a good place to retire.*

"Skip," Nelson said, his voice quiet, almost a little boy's voice—the boy that Nelson would have been when Edward Everett first came to Perabo City. Back then, Nelson had been, what? Ten, a child with a soprano voice that was still several years from changing, a boy nursing an inkling that, yes, maybe, yes, he could do something with a baseball other boys couldn't. But not enough. Most of them could never do enough.

"Skip," Nelson said again. "I can't lose my family." He was playing with a small switch on the gun, flicking it one way and then the other: the safety, Edward Everett realized. One way, the other, one way, the other, clicking it, clicking it. Which was on and which was off?

"I know how you feel," he said, his eyes on the switch Nelson was flicking.

"Yeah, Skip?" One way, the other, one way, the other.

"I had a boy. Like your boy," he said, not certain what he would say next.

"I didn't know, Skip." One way, the other. One way, the other.

"But his mother—she took him away." He shook his head. "Before I had a chance to meet him." In the closet, Grizzly was quieter, his seizure nearly over. Soon, he would fully come out of it, start barking and lunging at the door. It would set Nelson off again. How long until then? One minute? Five? "See, I know what you're going through."

"What do you mean, Skip?" One way. The other.

Edward Everett told him about Julie, about Montreal and getting hurt, about asking her to marry him, about the woman, Estelle. He remembered her name when he hadn't in a long time. Herron. Two "r's," not like the bird. About Julie finding him with Estelle and leaving him there, his not knowing about the boy until he got the first photograph and then the next and the next. "I spent years looking for that boy," he said, telling him about the towns and the phone calls, but telling it so quickly, he had no idea if his story made sense. He paused, listening for signs of Grizzly's waking, wondering if that was the moment it would all come crashing down, the dog fully aware and barking, Nelson hysterical again. He had stopped flicking the lever, Edward Everett realized. Was it on or off?

"So, you see," he said. "I've been where you are."

Nelson sat up, the gun still dangling between his knees. "You're nothing like me."

"What?" Edward Everett said.

"I never cheated on my family," Nelson said.

Edward Everett was confused. This was not what he intended. They were brothers, of a sort. "We're brothers, of a sort," he said.

"You did a terrible thing," Nelson said. "We're not brothers."

"No, wait," Edward Everett said, frantic, the story he thought would lull Nelson only making things worse. "We worked things out."

"You worked things out?" Nelson asked, leaning forward, cocking his head.

"I found him," Edward Everett said cautiously, having the sense of being a man creeping across a frozen pond, the ice groaning and popping with each step, no going back, the only choice to keep on toward the far bank. "Just this summer. It was the craziest thing. I looked up his name in the phone book and called and it was him."

Hi, this is a billion-to-one shot, but is your mother named Julie?
Dad? Oh, my God! Dad! Wait until I tell Mom.

"I found him," Edward Everett said. "I screwed up, I admit it, worse than anything, worse than you, but I found him and worked things out."

"That's a helluva tale," Nelson said, but in a way that Edward Everett couldn't read: did he believe him or did he not believe him?

"We've become close," Edward Everett said, closing his eyes, straining to conjure what occurred next in the story he was telling. "Everything's fine. He became a pediatrician. He saved so many lives. Maybe he helped your kids." The images came to him as clearly as the photographs of the boy-stranger he had carried around for so long: himself and the boy-stranger-now-man-son drinking beer, watching a ball game, Edward Everett saying, *Look where the second baseman is playing. Here's what's going to happen.* His son saying, *You really know a lot about this.* A picnic they went on, Edward Everett and the boy-now-man. As he told the story, the park where they picnicked grew around him, becoming as vivid as if he had been there: near their table, a rusted barbecue grill caked with ash that drifted over them in a breeze, specks settling onto their sandwiches. The heat of the sun warming his back. Then a new boy appeared. The boy-now-man's own son. Edward Everett's grandson. *His name is Edward. I had no idea that was your name when he was born but it came to me the first time I held him.* "You're Edward." *It must have been in the stars.* Mustard spotting his chin, the boy smiled up at Edward Everett, the man from whom he'd gotten his name.

Nelson tilted his head to the side in a manner that suggested he was weighing the story that Edward Everett had told. It was, he knew, a fantastic story.

"In fact, he's on his way here now," Edward Everett said. He saw a red Prius moving between sunlight and shadow as it passed beneath the trees lining the street. No, not a Prius. That was Renee's car in her new circumstances. The car approaching was a Maverick, like the one he drove when he sold flour. "I was just waiting to take him to the game. Him and his son. My grandson. He's never been before but he's going today. His first game."

In the closet, the dog was stirring. Edward Everett could hear the hangers clanging as Grizzly got to his feet, rustling the coats.

He saw the Maverick slowing outside, the driver—someone who had been there countless times by then and so knew all of the neighbors, and they knew him—rolling down his window, waving at Mrs. Greiner, who was digging in her flower bed, waving at Ron Dubois next door, setting up a ladder to paint his fascia board. They knew his grandson, too, the boy waving from the passenger seat. *I'm going to see my grandpa!*

Your grandpa is such a lucky man!

Edward Everett stood up and moved toward the door. "I think I hear him coming up the steps." Nelson leaned forward and they both looked toward the door, listening for footsteps on the stone stairs.

It could happen, Edward Everett thought. *It could happen. My son is going to knock on the door. He's going to knock on the door right now.*

I'm so glad to see you, he would say when he opened the door. *I'm so happy you're finally here.*

Epilogue

In November, Nelson's widow sent back the cashier's check he had given her. He was in the breakfast nook in his house in Heredia when his housekeeper, Lucia, brought the mail she had picked up from the post office the afternoon before, several weeks-old copies of *The Sporting News*, a calendar for the next year Meg had made using photographs of Grizzly—Grizzly sleeping on her canopied bed; Grizzly sunning himself on her porch; Grizzly on his hind legs, begging for a snack—a handful of bills and a plain white envelope with no return address that the Perabo City post office had forwarded to him in Costa Rica. Even before he opened it, he knew what it would contain, since it was the third time Cindy Nelson had returned the check. The other times she'd done so with no note, but this time there was one, two words, unsigned: "Please stop."

He had tried to give the check to her the first time at Nelson's wake, leaving an envelope in the wicker basket on the table with the guest book outside the parlor where Nelson's body lay in a closed casket; three thousand dollars. On the memo line he'd had the bank teller type, "For your children." Three days later, when he came home from the hardware store with Meg—back from buying closet organizers, wire racks for his kitchen cupboards, mulch for his neglected flower beds, all to "stage his house" for sale, Meg said—the envelope lay on his back deck.

"Oh, a fan letter," Meg said, stepping over it, carrying in a bag.

"Not quite," Edward Everett said, bending to pick it up.

After he told her what it was, Meg said, "I can't believe you would do that for her, after what her husband put you through."

I don't see it that way, Edward Everett thought, but he only shook his head and mailed the check the next day to Nelson's widow again, in care of her brother at the Lakeport Police Department. Four days later, it came back again, this time in the mail, with no return address. When he sent it a third time—a week before he got on a plane for Costa Rica—and it didn't come back, he thought maybe she had finally accepted it, forgiven him, seen it as a chance to do a small thing for her son and daughter who had lost their father. But then, almost two months after that, it found him again.

When no one came to the door—when the son Edward Everett had never met didn't pull to the curb in a 1973 Maverick; didn't, on his way up the front walk, wave to Ron Dubois touching up the paint on the fascia board under his gutters; didn't knock on the door in the distinctive manner Edward Everett might have recognized had his son ever been there—Nelson stood up from the couch. Edward Everett shut his eyes in a way he would always think of as cowardly, and waited for the gunshot, wondering, would he hear it first? What he did hear was the front door creaking open and then clicking shut, gently, as if whoever closed it wanted to be certain he did not damage the door or the frame. As he sat, quaking, thinking, *It's over*, telling himself to call someone, from outside came what sounded like a single, quick hammer blow driving a nail, and then someone shouted, "Oh, my God." He pushed himself out of the chair but his legs were so weak he fell back again. By the time he managed to get outside, Ron Dubois was sprinting from his yard into Edward Everett's faster than he would have thought someone sixty pounds overweight could move, yanking his paint-spattered T-shirt over his head. "For God's sake, Ed, call 911," he shouted.

Then Ron was kneeling on the lawn and laying his shirt delicately over Nelson's face, blood pooling on the grass. When Ron glanced up, he said, "Don't look."

Although Meg told him he shouldn't, he went to the wake. The lot was so full he had to park on the street, and at first he thought it was for Nelson, that some of his former teammates had come, but it wasn't. A man who had operated an Italian restaurant for thirty-seven years had also died and his wake was in a large double parlor, the room shoulder to shoulder with people talking in muted tones, every once in a while someone laughing. Nelson was in an anteroom near the back, and when Edward Everett arrived, there were only four people there, Nelson's wife and her brother, and an older man and woman he imagined were Nelson's parents. He stopped to sign the guest book and lay his envelope in the basket, where there was only one other card. As he stepped into the parlor, Nelson's widow looked toward the doorway with expectation but then her eyes narrowed and she said something quietly to her brother. Everyone there turned in his direction as Earl approached him. "You really shouldn't be here," he said to Edward Everett, cupping a hand beneath his elbow to guide him back out.

To think that any of the team would come was absurd, he realized later. Nelson had been right; the team closed up like a vacuum after you left, especially if you were a lunatic who couldn't let go when the game told you to. They had all scattered by then anyway, left town disappointed when they lost the final, Quad Cities the one celebrating the meaningless championship in the middle of the infield in that sorry, sorry ballpark.

Of course they wouldn't come to the wake, because they all hated Nelson, although most would soon learn they were more kin to him than they might have thought—maybe not enough kin to shoot themselves but enough that the release note they received would gnaw at them for a long time. Some would call Edward Everett as he had called Hoppel. "What if," some would ask. "What if I learned to switch-hit?" "What if I worked on my slider?" *What if, what if?* He told them, "No; you're a different person now." When they pushed further, he said gently, "Be grateful for the life you have rather than regret the one you don't."

In the breakfast nook in his small house in Heredia, he took the check he had tried to give to Nelson's widow and put it on the refrigerator with a magnet, alongside the photo that Meg had sent him, one that she had Photoshopped, the one of his son about to ride off on his bicycle. She had added him to the image and unless he studied it closely he really did seem to be there, as if he were the person his son was looking toward for approval: *You'll be fine; I'll be here when you ride back.* He would keep sending the check to Nelson's widow until she stopped returning it. Since it was a cashier's check, he would have no way of knowing whether she cashed it or just tore it up. Either way, he had given her the money.

At eight o'clock, he called a car to pick him up to take him to the ballpark, and when he reached it, there were already forty boys there, some as young as thirteen, none older than eighteen, all serious and eager, playing catch before any of the coaches had to tell them to do so. Some of their fathers were there as well, sitting in the shade of the roof over the grandstand, and when Edward Everett walked onto the field, the ten boys the club had assigned to him for the day gathered around him, their fathers leaning forward in the stands, clasping their hands on the seat backs in front of them, all of them waiting for Edward Everett to tell them something that would change their lives forever.

Acknowledgments

I owe more than I can express to Amanda Urban for her advocacy and Jennifer Smith for her smart editorial guidance, and to Ken Cook and Margot Livesey, who read drafts of this novel and whose insightful criticism helped shape it. This book would not exist without the generosity of all of them. Thanks also to those who encouraged me, especially Debra Carpenter, Tony DiMartino, John Eschen, Eileen Solomon, Kirk Swearingen, and my parents and brothers and sisters. Thank you, as well, to Webster University for time to work on this during parts of two sabbaticals. Much of my understanding of a life in baseball came from interviews I did for a number of articles I wrote about ballplayers whose major league careers lasted less than a full season, and I am grateful to the editors who assigned those articles, especially David Levine and Steve Zesch, and to the many players I interviewed for them, especially Rich Beck, Doug Clarey, Chip Coulter, Jeff Doyle, Ed Phillips, Herman (Ham) Schultehenrich, Bill Southworth and Robert Slaybaugh, whose tragic injury in a spring training game kept him from ever appearing in the major leagues. I also owe a debt to every writing teacher who has graced my life, especially, in chronological order, Thomas Hoobler, Carl Smith, Shannon Ravenel, Jean Thompson and Richard Russo.

ABOUT THE AUTHOR

JOSEPH M. SCHUSTER lives near St. Louis, Missouri, and teaches at Webster University. His short fiction has appeared in *The Kenyon Review*, *The Iowa Review*, and *The Missouri Review*, among other journals. He is married and the father of five children.

ABOUT THE TYPE

The book was set in Walbaum, a typeface designed in 1810 by German punch cutter J. E. Walbaum. Walbaum's type is more French than German in appearance. Like Bodoni, it is a classical typeface, yet its openness and slight irregularities give it a human, romantic quality.